⫻ IMPOSTOR ⫻

Despite himself, Thomas cannot resist putting her to the test, reminiscing aloud about his childhood in the castle, purposely getting details wrong. "And in winter when I'd come back from rolling in the snow, you'd wrap me in a great bearskin and make me drink hyssop tea while you sang about the ice queen."

Intrigued by the shatter-glass blue of his eyes and the calm strength in his voice, she simply nods.

"There was no bearskin," he accuses, his eyes narrowing slyly. He says in a half-mocking accusation: "How can you be my grandmother! Only an impostor would not remember these things!"

She put a hand to her brow and her eyes flutters. "That was a robe of stitched marten pelts, Thomas," she manages. "And it was comfrey you drank while I teased you with silly stories about Jack Frost. Don't make much of my lapses. It merely distracts me to see you grown into such a striking man."

"I'm sorry, Grandmere—" Thomas casts his hands up, abashed. "Forgive me. Your youthfulness, and your beauty disarm me."

Also by A.A. Attanasio

Wyvern
Hunting the Ghost Dancer

Published by
HarperPaperbacks

Kingdom
of the Grail ❀ ❀ ❀

A.A. Attanasio

HarperPaperbacks
A Division of HarperCollinsPublishers

This is a work of fiction. The characters, incidents, and dialogues are products of the author's imagination and are not to be construed as real. Any resemblance to actual events or persons, living or dead, is entirely coincidental.

HarperPaperbacks   *A Division of* HarperCollins*Publishers*
          10 East 53rd Street, New York, N.Y. 10022

A hardcover edition of this book was published in 1992 by HarperCollins*Publishers*.

Cover illustration by Karen Barnes/Stansbury, Ronsaville, Wood, Inc.

First HarperPaperbacks printing: October 1992

Printed in the United States of America

HarperPaperbacks and colophon are trademarks of HarperCollins*Publishers*

❖ 10 9 8 7 6 5 4 3 2 1

For Sheryl Dare—who found the Grail in the story
and the story in my heart

◆⟨≈⟩◆

Love is an inborn suffering.

—Le Chapelin's *The Book of True Love* (ca. AD. 1190)

CONTENTS

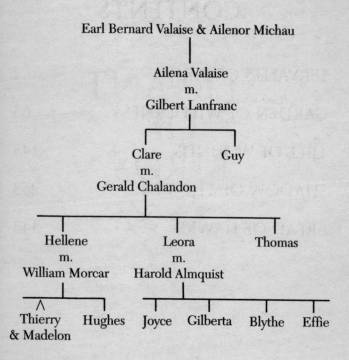

Earl Bernard Valaise & Ailenor Michau
|
Ailena Valaise
m.
Gilbert Lanfranc
|
Clare   Guy
m.
Gerald Chalandon
|
Hellene   Leora   Thomas
m.   m.
William Morcar   Harold Almquist

Thierry & Madelon   Hughes   Joyce   Gilberta   Blythe   Effie

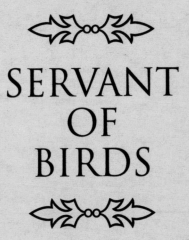

SERVANT OF BIRDS

*The Grail is the chalice from
which Christ drank at the
Last Supper.*

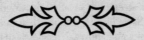

A child screams and screams. Among the reeds, a crone jerks upright from where she is bent over, her heart suddenly big in the small cage of her chest. Dusk has drawn the curtains of the marsh, and the old woman's round eyes stare hard but see no child in the cane brakes or in the long grass, only mist creeping among the slender trees. Her heart grows bigger, expecting a ghost.

The child's shrill pain comes again. The crone's gaze follows it to the top of the bog bank, where a ringed moon peers among the sheaves gathered at the roadside. Slowly, she makes out the dark shape of a rabbit caught in a snare of osier twine. One of the men lurches black against the twilight and stoops to retrieve his catch.

The old woman's swollen heart shrivels to a sigh. She shakes her gray head and stretches a kink from her back, her legs rooted in marsh mud. Beyond the sheaves of June's hay crop, destined as fodder for the seigneur's stables, the hills gleam scarlet in the last light of the longest day. Bonfires must be blazing at the castle for the midsummer's dance, she thinks, even though the big celebration is yet two days away. The feast of the nativity of John the

Baptist will want an abundance of frogs' legs and snails for the castle revelers. But before bending back to her harvest, she glimpses a distant movement.

Shadows flicker along the high road of the gleaming hills. "Who would be riding the steep trails so late?" she wonders aloud. "And galloping so fast, as if Satan himself troubles their heels. They must know these wends well enough to hurry so recklessly in the falling light."

The bent shadow of another peasant beside the crone grunts, does not stir to look up. "Guy's siege," the shadow mumbles, lifting a fat frog out of the black water and dropping it deftly into a lidded basket. "Something's amiss or aright. We'll hear of it on the morrow."

After securing her basket of frogs from an alder branch where the dogs and pigs could not reach it, and having laid a nettle crown atop it so no cats could bat it loose, the crone pauses outside her hovel to watch the summer stars kindling above the black hills. The village, which lies east beyond a stand of alder and ancient elms, has already sounded the loud horn for *cover fires*.

Into wads of spongy watercress, she ties with bine the snails to be delivered to the castle the next morning and drops them into the basket with the frogs. This night she will sleep only after having laid the bundle against the door, to keep the nightmare from passing under its lintel. Spirits will not abide waterplants, she knows. This is a particular caution she must take on full moon nights, though every night is dangerous: burrowed as it is out of a dungheap, her hovel attracts the most evil of wraiths.

Deep in the night, a throb of thunder startles the crone awake. Sitting up on her straw pallet, she sees her door thrown open and moonlight standing on her threshold. With one hand she grabs the crucifix hooked to the wall and with the other the cudgel in the straw at her side.

A ponderous shadow rises to fill the portal. The villagers have come to take her life then; it has not been enough to mire her in this dungheap these past ten years. They have come finally to slit her throat as well. The old woman raises the cudgel high. "Come at me, rogue, and I'll open your skull to the moonlight!"

"Be still, woman," a man's voice gruffs. "I am Erec Rhiwlas, chieftain Howel's son. I've not come to harm you."

Lowering her club, the crone peers at the silhouette in the doorway, at the bristly outline of a beard and the bulky hide of a mantle. It is not the custom of the Invaders to wear beards, nor would any but the most noble have a mantle of fur. "Howel's Erec?" she whispers skeptically. "Erec the Bold, who raided Guy's cattle from their sheds all this past winter?"

"The same," the heavy voice answers, "though a mite taller now, with this new bump atop my head. You've a treacherous mat at your threshold."

"My snails," the old woman grunts, catching her breath. Working for the Invaders might well be a crime to a chieftain's son. Though surely he already knows she works for them. Why else would she be living in the village dungheap?

"Snails are they? They slid underfoot like eels. Show some Welsh charity, old mother, and invite the son of Howel into your dungpile."

With the help of her cudgel, the crone pulls herself up from her pallet. The crude crucifix made from two sticks tied together with hemp trembles in her hand, and she lays it down with the cudgel on a rickety bench. She straightens the rumples from her rag shift, then picks up the watercress wad, feels the hardshelled snails intact within, and beckons the large man to enter. "Come in then. I will start a fire and prepare you some acorn flummery."

Erec bends to enter the tiny hovel, and the fecal stink of the enclosure hurts his sinuses. By the moonlight gushing through the open door, he makes out the sad shapes of the tottery bench, a hobbled stool, the straw pallet, and a squat fireplace, really just three stones leaning together before a hole in the dungwall for a flue. "Come, old mother. I think it best we talk outside, under the stars."

"So you are Dwn of Margam." Erec studies the crone, and her round, black eyes blink. He knows she cannot believe that he is before her—a chieftain's son venturing so close to an Invader's keep with no other men. But he is not alone. A clansman stands guard out of sight among the black trees. There is grave danger for a fighting man on such a cloudless, moony night in the enemy's croft, yet he is patient and does not cower. This woman of the fields has never seen the fierce likes of a Welsh warrior before, and he lets her examine him closely in the brash moonlight.

Indeed, he has the undeniable marks of nobility about him—the full brindled beard, battle-bent nose, regal brow, and deep-set eyes of a Cambrian Warrior—not the refined bearing or imperious features of the clean-shaven Norman gentry, yet nonetheless the agile poise of a chief, rough-hewn yet proud. Slick beaverskin covers his broad shoulders; red leather, maroon in the silver light, straps his waist and lower legs; and a short sword hangs at his hip, its hilt of buck's horn polished dark with grasping.

"Dwn of Margam—" She speaks softly. "I am she, though I've not seen Margam since I was a child."

"Why did you leave?"

She blinks again, wondering why a chieftain's son would care. The wicker coop nearby quivers with hens troubled by these voices in the night. Farther off, among the trees, the warrior's pearl-gray horse shimmers like a patch of fog. Its glorious presence alone is enough to convince her of Erec's identity.

"My father was a *taeog*, a bondsman, and I was the youngest of his many children. He sold me when I was seven to an earl, Bernard Valaise." Dwn regards him anxiously and adds with what fierce conviction she can muster: "If you've come to take my life for aiding the Invaders, I'll not resist you. I am too old. Death would be a gift."

"I'm not here for vengeance," Erec says softly. "Your father sold you to the Invaders. That was punishment enough."

"Then forgive me for asking—why *are* you here? Why bother an old woman who lives in a dungheap?"

"Once you lived in the castle. What did you do there?"

"I was a maid," she answers, aware to mute the pride in her voice. "For many years, I was the handmaid to the earl's daughter."

"And what became of that earl's daughter?"

"That is a long and wearisome story," the crone protests.

"Then shorten it and tell it sprightly, and afterward I'll tell you my business."

She squints at him shrewdly in the moonlight, wondering what he really wants, then brushes straw from the kirtle she has thrown over her rag shift. "Very well then. Ailena was her name. She lived her first nine years across the Channel, in the Périgord, where her mother held large estates in common with her brothers. It was when Ailena's mother died that Bernard Valaise, titled but landless, brought his daughter here to make his fortune."

"By claiming Welsh land," Erec interrupts bitterly. "To the Invaders, we are barbarians and our land wilderness only too happy to be tamed by their grain." He stares hard at the breeze harping among the branches. "Well, go on. Bernard claimed our land, built his castle, and bought you to be his daughter's handmaid. Why? Why a Welsh girl?"

"Bernard wanted these hills to be their home," Dwn replies. "He insisted his daughter speak the language of the people she ruled."

"And you taught her our tongue and our ways."

Dwn nods meekly, her small dark eyes clouding with the memory of it. "Yes. We were companions from childhood. I . . . served her forty-nine years." She straightens her back.

"Then Archbishop Baldwin came here preaching the Crusade, and your mistress set out for the Holy Land to win peace for her soul in the afterlife. Is that not right?"

"Ten years ago that was. But she did not set out. She was put out. By her son, Guy Lanfranc."

"Exiled by her own son?" Erec snorts in contemptuous amazement at the callousness of the Normans.

Dwn cocks her head. "But tell me, why should Erec the Bold suddenly care to know this tired story?"

"Ah, old mother, for truth's sake my father Howel would know; he has sent me to you to learn all I can of Ailena Valaise."

"Christ bless us, why? Ailena was old when she left, her bones bent and barbed. Surely she has found her way to her soul's eternal repose by now."

"It would appear not, Dwn of Margam." A smile opens the warrior's full beard. "My father's scouts have just brought word from Brecon. The baroness has returned from the Holy Land. Only yesterday, she crossed the Usk at Trefarg, and she camps this night on its northern bank. Our scouts believe she will arrive at her castle by midday."

Pale in the moonlight, the old woman's face drains of all expression. For several minutes, she stares at Erec with her dark, round eyes, suspecting cruelty, looking for contempt in the broad, whiskered face. *He is laughing at me—and then he will kill me, for I have betrayed my own people. I have served the Invaders my whole life, and now I must pay with my life.*

But the Welshman stares back with benevolent intensity, almost with amusement at her shock. When he speaks again, his voice has a soothing cadence: "Old woman, do not think we intend harm. The baroness, when she ruled this domain, was generous to our people. It was she gave free passage to the tribes when we moved our herds through these river meadows. She traded her castle's crafts for our cattle. She even sent gifts each year to the chieftains. But her son—" Erec's expression hardens, his eyes narrow to slits of disdain. "In her absence, Guy Lanfranc has not only denied us passage, he has built a fortalice near the river to extend his domain, and from there he has attacked our camps. Whole settlements have been burned, the people scattered into the forests to live like animals. And many who did not flee fast enough were killed, cut down by sword and arrow. Families who would not leave their cattle have been slaughtered— women and children." His face contorts with poisonous hatred, and he must draw a deep breath before he can speak calmly again. "Howel seeks to know if the return of the baroness will temper her wicked son. I am come to find out."

Dwn lies on her straw pallet too excited to sleep. Her eyes flex in the darkness, seeing back through time to the bone-warped old woman who had been carried howling from her castle ten years ago. "Do not weep for me, Dwn," Ailena had said the last time they spoke, even as Guy's knights strapped her into the litter that would carry her from the castle. "I am already on my way back."

Tears spurted hotter in Dwn's eyes to see that ruined face promising to return. The handmaid had been certain that within the year her mistress's skull would be a beetle's palace.

Her rage has kept her alive, Dwn is sure, staring into the darkness and seeing the baroness's face, wrinkled, pale as a wedge of fungus on the arthritic tree of her body. *Her rage is carrying her home to die.*

Dwn's heart beats against her ribs to think of the fury that has sustained the baroness all these years. Ailena Valaise had not always been a twisted old harridan, Dwn recalls, but she had been full of rage from the first. Even as a young girl, when Dwn, who had learned langue d'oc on the Norman estate where her father served, first met Ailena, the dark-haired, dimple-chinned girl was surly. Ailena had resented leaving the sunny, cultivated dales of the Périgord for the mountainous wilderness of Wales. The only joy she expressed in those first years of her long unhappiness was the laughter that jangled from her whenever she released the small birds the earl trapped for his falcons. They were red-legged crows peculiar to Wales, and watching them spurt from their opened cages, Ailena's delight made her beautiful. "Welsh crows should not be pressed to feed Norman hawks," she said once, and the Welsh workers that the earl kept on his estate repeated it often enough to earn the dour Norman girl the Welsh nickname Servant of Birds.

Dwn closes her eyes. These memories—keen as incisions— score her heart, and she soothes herself by thinking, *Whoever is coming back, whatever angry hag will appear tomorrow, she will not be the Servant of Birds.*

That old friend died piece by piece years before her vicious son threw her out. The damp seeped into her bones and swelled her joints, the cold hardened her marrow, and the black wind that shivers the stars snuffed the last warmth from her heart long ago. *Whoever is coming back will not be she,* Dwn admits, and curls around the darkness that is left to her.

Waking slowly, Dwn sees first light slanting through the laths that shutter her round windows. *Is it a dream?* she asks and sits up so that the threads of gray light touch her haggard face and ignite the amber of her eyes. The laths across the round windholes in the thick wall of dung keep the cats out at night. Each morning, when she opens the shutters, a cat or two comes in to eat the small mice and voles that have crept under the door during the night. But this morning, she shoes the eager cat away, more eager herself to stick her grizzled head out the small hole and look for the gray horse.

She blinks stupidly. The horse is gone, but there is a man squatting by the creek, drinking water from his hand, a large, ruddy man with a brown beard streaked orange above his lips and from the corners of his mouth. His hair is bowl-cut in the country style, but he wears no beaverskin mantle, nor the red leather leggings, and certainly no sword. Instead, he is dressed in a coarse blouse of dirt-colored cloth with a hemp belt. His trousers, too, are of cheap cloth, baggy and tucked loosely into crude and heavy leathern boots. Had the moonlight addled her last night and made this common villein appear as a warrior-prince?

"Where is your fine horse?" Dwn calls out from the windhole.

Erec presses a finger to his lips and gestures toward the alders. There, budging through the morning mist, are the scrawny village pigs, six evil-eyed swine rooting along the creek bed for grubs. "The swineherd will not be far afield." Erec crosses the creek in one stride, scattering the wild cats from their coverts in the mint grass. Up close in the light, his countenance is harsher, more belli-cose, the pale track of a lethal scar glinting across the bridge of his bent nose. Greenish-hazel eyes lock steadily onto the old woman's and hold her fast. "Think me no longer Howel's son. For now I am simply Erec, some distant cousin of yours from the hills, a tanner come to trade his hides."

Over his shoulder, on the grassy tuft beside the hennery where they had sat last night, Dwn sees a bundle of animal skins. "Where is your fine steed? And your sword and mantle?"

"They've strolled back into the hills with my guard." Erec winks cunningly. "Gather your frogs and your snails, old mother. We've no time to squander if we wish to see for ourselves the return of your baroness."

Among the billowy drapery of ivy-hung alder and elm, on the way to the village, Erec says, "Tell me about Ailena Valaise. I was but a lad when she left for the Holy Land. All the grief in my life began then, for that was when Guy Lanfranc began his murderous raids, when his warmaster Roger Billancourt began killing our cattle rather than driving them to the castle. He could slaughter more than he could drive, and that was as good as killing the people, for it starved us."

"Roger Billancourt—" Dwn makes a vile face. "He is a godless, evil man. He was warmaster to Guy's father, too. It was his idea to take our castle by cunning when Ailena was a girl in mourning—fifteen she was when the earl Bernard died of quinsy—fifteen when Gilbert Lanfranc married her by the sword—"

The mention of a sword makes Erec stare about reflexively at the lush undergrowth, looking for others among the golden sunshafts of the alder copse. But they are alone, wading through purple loosestrife and luxuriant tangled locks of willowherb and comfrey. "She must have learned cruelty well from Gilbert and Roger for her son to hate her so and put her out in her old age."

"Bah!" Dwn's disgust startles a willow-wren from the dark selvedge of the creek, and it blurs past and disappears twittering in the radiant canopy. "Ailena was gruff but never cruel. Her son hates her because he thinks she killed his father. But Gilbert killed himself with his drinking. He was always besotted. Made him churlish. He beat Ailena without remorse, even when she was with child. She lost all her babies to his blows before they were born—all but the two, Guy and his sister Clare—one to torment each of the parents. Clare hated her father for beating Ailena, but the young Guy loved the brute and played with him constantly. Gilbert had the boy on horseback when he was three, hawking by four. They were a famous pair in the castle and countryside, riding everywhere together. Guy was six when his Da was thrown from his horse, right in the main courtyard, while shouting with his wife. Guy forever believed Ailena spooked the horse on purpose and killed Gilbert."

They pause under a silver birch beside a weir in the creek that has lifted the flow of the stream to shining shoulders of green water. "Were you there?"

"Yes. I saw it all. It was one of their typical rows. He was drunk and shouting about her favorite game, the court of love she held in the *palais* with her daughter Clare and the maids. Ailena stamped her foot with frustration. The horse reared, and Gilbert, in a drunken daze, flew off, smote his head on the pavement right in front of Guy, and never rose again."

Erec nods, finally grasping the black reasoning of Guy's murderous soul. "And from then Ailena ruled without a master—but with a viper for a son?"

"Thirty years she kept that viper in her nest without it biting her," Dwn says, and leads the way through a natural orchard of wild cherry, crabapple, and sloe. "There was ample time then for the troubadours, mimes, prestidigitators, and the courts of love. Plenty of time to indulge all her whims, for she never blundered into marriage again."

"Courts of love?"

Dwn places a hand over her mouth and cackles. "An impish game Ailena learned in the Périgord. The women reign over the court of love and make rules for the men. And the women's rules can be quite exacting."

Erec has long felt a secret fascination with Norman women, whom he has seen only from a distance. With their long hair and slender throats, those haughty, tall creatures are very different from the sturdy, shorn women of the hills. He wants to enquire further about them, to learn their passions and weaknesses from this maid who served them. But through the sun's rays slanting among the trees, the thatched roofs of the village come into view, and Erec silences himself, bows his head under the burden of his hides, and becomes a simple tanner from the hills.

Looming majestically above the morning mists, the Castle Lanfranc rises from the river Llan. The swift and deep stream plunging out of the hills bounds the fortress on three sides, like a noose. For Erec, who has seen the bewildering jumble of turrets, walls, bartizans, and battlements from afar, the massive brown castle had always seemed a toy. Now, at the toll bridge—where he is close enough to gaze upon the stark masonry patched with moss and ivy and thick tufts of weed—the vast bulwarks rear up sheer as cliffs, defiant and formidable. High above all the palisades, garrets, and towers soars the donjon, the great central tower, upon which summit baron Guy Lanfranc's black and green banner idly trails. A glimpse of the Lanfranc Griffin—the eagle-headed lion with its talons splayed to strike—drops Erec's gaze back to earth.

The tollkeeper nods sleepily at Dwn. He is older than even she is and remembers when she lived in the castle, remembers when she would come thundering across the bridge on her red palfrey beside the baroness and her black charger. He glances only briefly at her sturdy companion hunched under his roll of hides, and no explanation is needed. The other villeins, herding their geese to the feast of the nativity of St. John the Baptist and hauling their sheaves of spring hay for the seigneur's stables, are too busy and tired to enquire after another lout come down from the hills to sell his skins.

Over the bridge, the road passes before the enormous garden to the right, which fades in the dispersing fog to the orchards and the hunting forest. To the left is the parade ground, expansive fields dotted with a few cattle sheds and a shanty for the herdsman. The road banks, crosses the exercise grounds, and reaches the barbican, the first outwork of the fortress, a palisade of keenly pointed staves and piles too high to clamber over.

The porter has already thrown open the heavy wooden gate of the barbican, and the villeins enter freely. All are familiar faces, and the porter hardly seems to notice them from where he sits on a high stool with his legs propped up on the crossbar of the open gate. With a lazy gesture, he stops Erec. Dwn quickly—too quickly for Erec—steps forward and delivers their agreed-upon story. The porter's rheumy eyes study the Welshman and his hides. They are elk and otter hides, clearly valuable, and the porter admits them.

Inside the barbican, the road crosses another open field, the lists, where a sergeant and a squire are working with a frisky stallion. To either side of the lists the ground falls away in steep, rocky slopes down to the broken banks of the Llan. Directly ahead is a moat fronting colossal masonry walls. Several varlets are wading up to their hips in the algal-green water, catching frogs for the cookhouse.

The drawbridge is down, the iron gate of the portcullis hoisted, and the villeins are piled up against the enormous oaken gates. The gates are strapped with metal and have not been unbarred, but a small door in one of the gates, barely large enough for a horse, admits the townspeople two abreast. Before Dwn and Erec pass through, the crone casts a furtive glance at a keyhole window in the turret beside the portcullis. The chief porter watches from there, and she is hoping that he will take no special notice of her country cousin.

Dwn's hope shrivels as they cross the threshold into the bailey and a sergeant steps from the turret door and calls them aside. He speaks langue d'oc, and Erec, though he does not understand the words, knows what he is asking. He lowers his bundle in front of him so that, if he must, he can heave it at the stout man and shove his way out through the door to take his chances against the archers overlooking the lists.

The sergeant, in a chain-mail vest and cowl, is gruff and keeps one hand on the hilt of his sword. He does not like the look of this Welshman, for he is bigger than most, and though he wears rude clothing there is something arrogant about him. He stands too erect, and his stance is broad and slightly askew, like a man trained to fight with a sword.

"Speak you French?" the sergeant asks in elementary Welsh and slaps Erec's sides, feeling for weapons.

Erec shakes his head, motions to his hides and points to the hills. The sergeant draws his sword and hacks off the hemp rope around the bundle. The skins flop open. Assured that no weapons are hidden among the hides, the sergeant taps Erec's boots with the flat of the blade, sounding for knives, and runs the sword up the outside and inside of the tanner's legs. With curt indifference, the Norman then motions him to pick up his skins and enter.

Dwn knows her way through the back wynds of the bailey and is able to show Erec, away from the throngs of villeins and merchants in the courtyard, the thatched-roof stable with its long row of stalls, where more than three dozen horses are champing their morning fodder. Ricks of hay and heaps of muck jam the spaces between the stables and the animal pens, and dogs, pigs, and hens forage freely there.

Alongside the stables are ramshackle but commodious wooden structures—the barracks for the men-at-arms whom Guy has hired to aid him in his siege of a neighboring baron's castle. Erec hurries from there gladly, not wanting to rub shoulders with the very men the Invaders' king has oftentimes used to murder good Welshmen.

Dwn leads him past a noisy carpenter shop and the ringing forge of a smithy, where a master armorer is manufacturing crossbow bolts and spearheads. They pass shops of cobblers, chandlers, spinners, tinkers, glaziers, and tailors. From the alleys between the workshops and the long storehouses, they glimpse sheds alive with shrill screams. These are the baron's hawk mews, where the chief falconer is dangling rags of meat.

Past cows being milked and braying donkeys overladen with roof tiles and firewood, Dwn and Erec shoulder their way among red-capped guildsmen and their bareheaded apprentices. No one else seems aware that the baroness is returning, for all are going about their business as on any other day. A small crowd with sacks over their shoulders has gathered before a round building with a tall chimney; this is the seigneur's great oven, where all the villagers bring their flour to be baked into bread.

Dwn stops Erec there so that they can observe the adjacent chapel, an incongruous building of elegant blackstone pinnacles and sculptured saints. Behind it is another moat and a massive wall with towers protecting the inner ward. The drawbridge is down, the portcullis raised, and Erec gazes in open fascination at the vast inner courtyard and the *palais*, an L-shaped stone building with high-wrought pinnacles, large, pointed windows, and sloping roof of red tiles. Rearing above the *palais*, at the far extreme of the castle, he sees the great keep, the round citadel that dwarfs all the other towers. At its top is a gibbet for hanging enemies and a flagstaff upon which flies the black Griffin against a green field.

The gate tower trumpet blares. The people milling at the front of the bailey clear out of the way as squires dash from the barracks and the stables. The gates are heaved open; five bareheaded horsemen in full armor boom over the drawbridge, surge into the bailey, and dismount.

Erec immediately recognizes the baron, Guy Lanfranc, though he has never seen him from this close distance. Neither tall nor powerfully built, Lanfranc's jowly face—with its single deep crease across his forehead, and dense black eyebrows joined above a pug nose—nevertheless radiates a brute command. His thick jet hair is long and pulled back severely, tied off military-style in a topknot. And his complexion, dark as oiled walnut, gleams with tension as he shouts orders to the squires who remove his armor so he can mount a fresh horse for the ride to the *palais*.

Erec also identifies Guy's warmaster and eyes him well as he strides past in his dented and scarred armor on his way to the smithy. Roger Billancourt wears his gray hair cropped close to his square skull, erased at the temples by a lifetime of wearing a helmet. His weatherbeaten face, marred with ancient scars that break his stubbly beard into patches, glowers at all who met his steely gaze.

Dwn whispers and points with her face to a burly knight at the baron's side, "The one with the Breton mustache is William Morcar."

Morcar's face is graven, like an outcrop of the castle's masonry, with a bushy yellow mustache that droops past the boot-tip of his jaw.

The old handmaid's stare fixes on an angular knight with the soft face of a clerk. "The tall one with the bald head is Harold Almquist."

Erec's gaze slips off the rangy Almquist, whose shiny pate gleams with sweat above a cuff of frizzy orange hair. He has not the look of a warrior to the Welshman. But the man behind him does—a long-shouldered archer, his bow slung across his arm. He looks feline, his cheeks beardless and hollow, no eyebrows above his green, wide-apart stare. His hair, cut short at the back of his neck, is so fair it shines white as chalk in the sunlight.

"That is Denis Hezetre, the baron's childhood friend. He and Guy adventured together in Ireland when they came to manhood and could no longer abide the baroness's rule. He looks far younger than his years and is admired among the ladies, though he has never taken a wife nor favors any lady."

"Perhaps he prefers to be mounted."

"I think not. While in Ireland, Guy saved his life but took a dire wound in the groin and lost his little worm. As Guy deprived himself of woman's love to rescue his friend, so Denis swore then to shun such love himself. He has lived as celibate as a monk since."

Erec and Dwn sit on the stone molding of the chapel with the sun in their eyes. This benefits the crone, whose damp bones are warmed and who has earned three silver pennies from the sale of Erec's hides. Once the sun found them so did the guildsmen. Already the bootmaker and the clothier have sent their apprentices to look over the skins, and Erec is pleased to turn over the money they have paid him to the old woman. She sits with her hands open in her lap, her riven face upturned, eyes closed, basking in the hot rays.

An excited trumpet blast brings Erec to his feet. The trumpeter extends the alarm to a flourish, announcing the approach of a dignitary. Dwn clutches at Erec's arm and pulls herself upright. "It is she! She has come back!"

The people in the bailey, who clearly are not expecting anyone of stature now that their seigneur is in the castle, stop in the midst of their endeavors and share baffled looks and murmurs. "Guy has kept the secret well," Erec remarks, taking Dwn's hand and leading her toward the front gate.

"Perhaps he does not know?"

"He knows. Else why would he have returned from the heat of his siege? The message was borne to him late yesterday on the high road."

Ah yes, Dwn remembers: the riders galloping on the steep hill trails at nightfall yesterday. "Ailena is wise to have kept her return secret. Treachery is not beneath her son. Yet I cannot reason her return. She will have no strength to match her son's wrath."

"Unless, old mother, she's come back to face him with the most immutable strength of all."

Dwn stops, her face contracting as the sudden and harsh truth of these words blows coldly through her. "Surely, you have guessed right, Bold Erec. Ailena has returned as a corpse."

Guy Lanfranc charges out of the gate of the inner ward astride a brown destrier, his face locked in a grim scowl. He does not believe that Mother would dare return even as a corpse. He suspects this is one of his enemies' deceptions, and he will have none of it. The flag signal he had his men send from atop the donjon commanded the bailey porter to drop the outer portcullis. He will not be fooled by a Trojan horse.

At the front gate, Guy's knights catch up with him. Roger Billancourt, his gray head covered with a chain-mail cowl, dismounts and receives the gatekeeper's report. "The party is small," he repeats for the others. "Three sumpter mules and an oxcart that flies the Swan."

"What trickery is this?" Guy mutters.

Roger advances to the gate and peers through a looking-hole. "They have two strange beasts with them. And two mounted knights. But the oxcart is too small for more than a half dozen men."

"Lift the portcullis," Guy calls impatiently. "Swing wide the gate. I'll quail no more before my mother's ghost. Let's be done with this. Our siege waits on us."

As soon as the gate opens, Guy lurches ahead and bends forward so as not to strike his head on the rising portcullis. Across the drawbridge, he pulls up short, his upper body surging back and forth with the impatient movements of his horse as he tries to comprehend the spectacle approaching him.

There, on the road before him, waits a hide-covered carriage drawn by two oxen, its banner emblazoned with a Swan, black-masked head serenely bowed. At the reins sits a dwarf in motley garb, and on his hunched shoulder squats a black monkey dressed as a squire. Beside the dwarf, a Jew in a burgundy tunic mumbles prayers, his bushy beard and long gray temple locks bobbing as he sways back and forth.

To one side of the carriage, two Bactrian camels richly caparisoned, with scarlet reins and silver tassels, regard the startled crowd at the gate with nonchalant hauteur. Atop one perches a tall blond-bearded knight in a turban and billowy robes. Across his lap, a crooked saber lies, hilt and baldric inlaid with gold. A Mamluk dagger glints at his hip, and from the saddle bow dangles a quiver of four-foot-long javelins. Around his neck, a thick golden band catches sunlight.

On the other side of the oxcart, a sleek, wispy-legged white stallion carries a bareheaded knight garbed entirely in black but for a scarlet formée cross over his heart. Behind him three heavily-laden mules nibble the grass at the roadside.

"Ho! Castle Valaise!" the dwarf calls out in langue d'oc thickly accented with Italian inflections. "Your mistress is returned!"

"Fie!" Guy shouts back. "This is Castle Lanfranc. No mistress rules here."

The knights cross the drawbridge and assemble beside Guy, gawking and murmuring among themselves before this strange menagerie. From behind them, the villeins filling the gateway buzz with excitement at the sight of the baroness's banner and the strange creatures. And across the river, the villagers have gathered to gape.

"I am Guy Lanfranc, earl of Epynt, baron of this castle. State your business."

The dwarf stands up, the monkey clambering atop his head, and gestures to the banner of the Swan. "*This* is our business. Do you not recognize the ensign of this domain's right ruler? Make way for the baroness Ailena Valaise!" The dwarf snaps the reins, and the oxen plod forward.

"Halt!" Guy bellows. "Stand fast and be recognized!"

The oxcart whines to a stop.

At the gateway, sergeants gruffly shove aside villeins to make way for an ample dame in a fur-edged pelisson of the finest Flanders cloth, escorted by a long-skulled man with sallow skin and foppish bearing: Gerald Chalandon and his wife Clare advance hurriedly through the crowd.

"*Merde!*" Guy growls under his breath when he sees his sister and her husband. "Keep them back, Harold. This smells foul."

Gangly, bald-pated Harold Almquist dismounts and runs to stop the anxious couple. Clare is already calling, "Mother? Mother—show yourself."

Guy signals Roger Billancourt and William Morcar forward. "Search the carriage."

Immediately the camel-mounted knight moves to block their advance, says something in a foreign tongue. The black knight trots to his side and speaks out in elegant French with a southern lilt, "Noble lord, brave knights, dear lady, and good people of Epynt—herein, forsooth, is the baroness Ailena Valaise. She has journeyed from far Jerusalem under our guardianship. I am Gianni Rieti from the Canons Regular of the Holy Sepulcher. To my right is Falan Askersund, a Swedish cavalier, who has served in the Holy Land, but who lost his faith in the Church and gave his soul to Mahomet and the Saracen god. He is the baroness's thrall, a gift of a Muslim caliph. And we are her knights, sworn to protect her well-being and honor by both your king, his high majesty Richard Coeur de Lion, and by his esteemed Holiness, our Holy Father in Rome, Pope Celestine the Third. Through us, they send their greetings and extend their rightful will."

"His tongue is more slippery than a snail's ass," Denis Hezetre whispers to Guy.

"Reveal the baroness, that she may be recognized," Guy demands.

The black knight reaches into a saddlebag and, with a pronounced flourish, produces two vellum packets. "Herewith are documents from King Richard and from our Holy Father, both affixed with official seals. I trust you will find them accurate and binding."

Gianni Rieti prances forward on his steed, light as a flame, and gracefully hands the vellums to Roger Billancourt.

When Guy receives the documents, he glances at them only briefly. They appear authentic, and he passes them gruffly to Denis. "These are mere vellum. They could be forgeries," he sneers. "Show us the baroness or turn about and be gone."

"I cannot comply," Rieti says with sincere regret. "For the baroness to reveal herself outside her own castle would be too great an indignity for us to permit. She will show herself only within the gates."

"That's horseshit," Guy barks. "If the old bitch is in there have her come forward and show herself. I've no time for your games."

The Italian knight rears back with indignation. "Your disrespect for your mother offends me and dishonors the teachings of our faith."

"Trickery!" Roger Billancourt cries, hand on his sword. "Don't let them in the castle," he tells Guy. "Kill them out here."

Gianni Rieti smiles serenely at the irate warrior, gesticulating vaguely at the sky. "Your king and our Holy Father will be sore displeased if you slay their emissaries." He turns his handsome smile on Guy. "Without doubt, dear sir, you will lose your barony—and probably your head."

"Let Mother enter!" Clare shouts from where Harold and Gerald have stopped her at the drawbridge. Her thick face contorts with impacted resentment at her brother, and she flies forward toward the carriage until restrained by Harold.

"What harm?" Denis whispers to Guy. "They are too few to threaten us, no matter how many they pack in that carriage."

Guy gnashes his teeth, reels about, and returns to the castle.

Denis and William lead the baroness's oxcart across the drawbridge, the camels alongside. Roger follows, his hand still on his sword.

Clare beseeches Gerald and Harold to let her approach the carriage, but they firmly guide her back into the bailey. There, her servitors surround her to buffer her from the excited throng. "It *is* Mother," she breathes hotly, with conviction. "This is her way. She never gave an inch to Guy."

Erec and Dwn press closer to the clearing Guy has enforced by stamping his horse in a wide circle. The Welshman's massive shoulders wedge through the curious crowd. At the front rank, he leads the old woman forward to stand before him so that her view is unobstructed.

Gasps of awe spark across the courtyard as the camels stride into the bailey, the turbaned rider staring impassively ahead. The oxcart, creaky and travel-worn, is commonplace and hardly a worthy conveyance for nobility; indeed, it is the dwarf driver and his black monkey, which now stands on his shoulder saluting the assembled crowd, that elicit the most excited murmurings. Head bowed, body waving back and forth, the old Jew mutters prayers. The mules clop forward and behind them rides the Italian knight, regal and dashing on his white charger. With his curly, blue-black hair and his precisely trimmed mustache and beard, he is the image of the foreign cavalier, and when he smiles at the crowd he draws spontaneous cheers.

"People of Valaise!" Gianni Rieti calls out, his dark eyes glittering with joy. "I bring you wondrous news! Your mistress is returned—but not as she left. A miracle has been wrought. Both the Muslim knight Falan Askersund"—he gestures at the turbaned rider—"and myself beheld this miracle with our own eyes, as did many others, and we have come this long way from the Holy Land with the baroness by the grace of God and with the approval of our Holy Father to bear witness to the glory of our Savior. Good people, blessed by faith and fear of the Lord, behold your baroness, Ailena Valaise!"

The dwarf pulls a rope, and the hide coverings of the carriage fall away, revealing a young woman sitting on a tapestried bench. Under dark, wavy hair spilling past her shoulders in shadowy gleams of auburn, she regards the gathering with the weight of moonlight in her face. Her large, ebony eyes are circles of clarity, looking for recognition from her people. She holds her head high on a long, frail neck, displaying proud cheekbones, a long, patrician nose, and a confident mouth with small underlip and swollen overbite.

At the sight of her, Dwn's memory jerks backward through the years so swiftly that a sensation of falling bewilders her legs and sends her toppling into Erec's arms.

"Deceiver!" Guy bawls.

Amazed shouts mingle with angry groans. Maître Pornic, the local abbot, a starved-faced man in silver tonsure and a mantle of coarse black serge, squirms through the crowd to stand beside Guy. "This is blasphemy! Have this shameless liar removed at once!"

The young woman in the carriage stands and holds her left hand high. "I am Ailena Valaise," she says in a voice surprisingly husky for so slender a woman. "I wear my father's signet ring, as I wore it on Saint Fandulf's day, nigh ten years ago, when I left this castle to join the Crusade."

The crowd presses forward. Rushing in front of them to push them back, Guy stops before the young woman. "Do you think we are fools?" he shouts at her, spit flying.

Deftly, the camel bearing Falan Askersund skitters backward and separates Guy from the carriage. Guy's horse, alarmed by the scent and sight of the camel, bucks nervously to the side.

"A miracle has been wrought!" Gianni Rieti shouts and points to the vellum documents still in Denis Hezetre's hands. "Our Holy Father has himself authenticated this miracle. We have his seal. Please, gentle knight, to read his proclamation aloud."

Denis, himself stunned at the resemblance of this woman to his childhood memory of the old baroness, opens the papal document and reads it to the crowd:

"'Celestine the pope, to all the faithful: we bestow the blessing of our Lord and Savior Jesus Christ upon you and bid your obedience to this instrument of the Church, written in our own hand. In witness to the truth of our Savior's miraculous interdiction and by apostolic authority we recognize Ailena Valaise as the glorified recipient of God's grace through the manifestation of the Sacred Chalice, from which she has drunk and been restored to her youth, wholesome and sanctified and worthy of restoration to her title as baroness of Epynt, where by our will she shall resume her rightful place as the King of England's legate, with all commensurate powers and duties returned to her.

"'Given at the Lateran, on the feast of Saint Anne, in the seventh year of our pontificate.'"

Denis sits tall in the saddle and raises the open document so all can see the purple script and the gold imprint. "In truth, this bears the pope's seal," he says with awe and holds it before Maître Pornic, whose eyes bulge like a startled mare's.

Cries of astonishment and shouts for salvation pierce the crowd. Many cross themselves and fall to their knees.

The baroness urgently signs for them to rise. "I am not to be worshiped," she declares loudly, but her voice is lost in the mounting frenzy of amazement. Denis draws his sword and points the hilt toward her, signifying his allegiance. Several sergeants in the crowd do likewise. The other knights look to Guy, who glowers blackly at the young woman before him.

Erec lifts Dwn above the press of the awestruck crowd and shakes her gently until her senses return. She puts her arms about his thick neck and gazes over the heads of the throng at the young woman in the carriage.

"Is she indeed the baroness?" Erec asks loudly enough to be heard above the excitement.

"I did think so," Dwn replies hesitantly, "but my eyes are old. I must get closer—to be assured."

Sergeants thrust through the crush with long quarter-staves, making way for Clare, Gerald, and Harold. But Erec shifts the old woman so that she sits on his shoulder, and he barges through the horde to follow in their wake. A sergeant blocks his way with a cross-staff, and Erec shouts in his mightiest voice, "Seigneur Gerald!"

Gerald and Clare turn. Clare's face is greased with tears, her red eyes wild. But sallow-skinned Gerald looks sullenly sober. At the sight of the old handmaid, he brightens suddenly, his eyes sparkling craftily, and he taps the shoulder of the sergeant and beckons them forward.

"Is she your mistress?" Gerald asks the crone.

Dwn feels strangely radiant with heat. At any instant, she thinks to herself, light will ray from her eyes, ears, mouth. Vainly, she strives to contain her wonder, strives to stare at this young woman and not see the likeness. But the likeness grows more vivid the closer she gets. A drafty fear bites into her as she realizes that in moments they will come face to face. Carried by the strong Welshman, she feels she has fallen from this world into eternity, escaping somehow the finality and greatness of death.

Gerald turns a stern look upon her. "Not a word to her now, until she speaks to you first. If she is your mistress, she will recognize you."

Ahead, Clare has already reached the oxcart, and the sergeants are helping her up. The crowd is falling silent, to hear the miracle-blessed baroness greet her daughter. The baroness takes Clare's hands, and Clare, her heavy face quivering, totters, nearly swoons.

"God bless you, dear child," the baroness speaks, her pale face suddenly hot as flame. "My dear, dear child, Clare. Let me hold you to my heart. Come to your mother. Don't be afraid. Our Lord has touched me with His grace."

With a thick sob, Clare seizes the young woman, and the two nearly topple from the oxcart but for the alertness of the camel-rider, who reaches over and steadies them.

Gerald separates the two women. Clare sits down heavily on the bench in the carriage bed, her shoulders heaving with sobs, her watery eyes fixed on the young baroness. At Gerald's sign, the crone is hoisted up into the oxcart. Again, he nails the old woman with a harsh stare, and Dwn stands there, shivering in icy wafts of dread and awe.

The young woman gazes down at the shriveled woman, kindly as the madonna. She takes the crone's quavering hands in her own warm grasp, and before she even speaks, there is no longer any doubt in Dwn's soul. The full cut of her dark eyebrows, the pollen-fair down along the line of her jaw, the faint dimple in her chin—she observes these well-remembered traits with a widening stare and a new fear, that all her groping prayers have been heard in God's silence.

"Dwn, do you recognize me?" the young baroness asks in Welsh laced with the accent of her native tongue. "It is surely I, the Servant of Birds."

Dwn's hands pull away from the grasp of her lost friend as from a fire, and she covers her gaping mouth. A cry ekes out and then tears of bewilderment. The baroness enfolds the old woman in her embrace and strokes her gray head. "You have left your hair uncut. But that is all that remains unchanged. You have suffered in my absence. My dear Dwn. Where are your fine clothes? And why do you stink of the sty?"

"No matter, my dearest Ailena," Dwn breathes into the baroness's shoulder. "No matter at all now that you are come home."

Guy cries out: "This is trickery!"

Ailena glares at him and separates herself from her ancient friend. "No trickery, Guy—but the Good Lord's wondrous will. I fully expect you to doubt, my son, you who never had even a mustard seed of faith."

Roger Billancourt angles his steed through the suddenly boisterous assembly until he is alongside Guy. "For Godsake, do not challenge her out here. Get her away from the rabble."

"I see you whispering your mischief, Roger Billancourt," the baroness calls out loudly. "It was your idea—was it not?—to be rid of me by casting me out penniless to the pilgrimage. How clever. And Guy, the poor fool, cannot resist heeding you." She cocks her head haughtily. "Assembled brethren, I come to tell you, I fulfilled my pilgrimage, and the Savior answered my prayers, as my son could well see if he were not blinded by malice. Now it is his turn to journey to the Holy Land and beg our Lord's forgiveness."

The crowd hushes at this challenge. Ailena holds her gaze of locked defiance with Roger for a long, angry moment before she looks into the crowd. Surrounded by guardsmen are the family members who have rushed from the *palais*. Watching her with cold amazement are two women in elegant robes, one ginger-haired, the other freckled, with tresses of fox-red. Ailena smiles and nods. "Hellene and Leora"—she names Clare's daughters—"do you recognize me? You've never seen me without my wrinkles."

Ailena looks with surprise at the offspring surrounding the women. "I recognize William's son Thierry," she says, regarding a brawny lad with the haughty bearing of an heir and the thrust jaw of a bully. "You were a mere child when I left. You must be fifteen now. And your twin—where is Madelon?"

A slender young woman with golden elflocks and a pixie face steps out from behind her mother Hellene. She curtsies. "Welcome home, Arrière-grandmère."

Ailena smiles generously at her, then points to a husky, snub-nosed boy. "And you, of course, are their younger brother Hugues. You were a baby of two summers when I saw you last. Now look at you. You've the girth of your father." She casts a bemused look to William Morcar, who sits astride his steed, scrutinizing her and stroking his yellow mustache.

"And are all these yours and Harold's, Leora?" Ailena asks the fox-haired woman and gestures to the gaggle of well-dressed but restless girls flocking about her. "They're too young for me to know any of them."

Leora beams proudly. "The eldest was born the year after you left, Grandmère." She taps each of their heads, "Joyce, Gilberta, Blythe, and Effie."

Ailena sighs. "It has been so long." She scans the crowd and frowns. "And my one grandson?" She turns to Clare. "Where is your boy Thomas?"

"He is at the abbey," Clare answers through her joyful tears. "He is studying the holy books, preparing for priesthood."

"There is much that has changed," she says and looks to Guy, whose face is clamped in a frown. "Much that is new." She faces toward the inner ward. "Denis," she beseeches the one knight who has offered her his sword, and he straightens in the saddle at the mention of his name. "Lead me to the *palais*, where I will wipe the dust of Jerusalem from my boots."

As Denis obediently begins to clear a path toward the inner ward and the camels take the lead, the baroness bids Dwn sit beside Clare. Then she faces about to the man behind her. "Gerald, do not stand at my back gawking like a turniphead. Your wife needs your comfort in the distress of her joy. Have you forgotten everything you once professed of chivalry?"

Gerald closes his mouth and bows his head. Chastened, he sits meekly beside Clare. Ailena braces herself by grasping the carriage's roof-pole, and as the dwarf snaps the reins and the oxen lurch forward to the muttered cadence of the Jew's prayers, the baroness smiles benignly at the bailey crowd, and waves.

Erec watches the oxcart trundle off, not taking his eyes from the baroness until she disappears beyond the chapel. Her absence leaves a humming stillness around him like a pause in the wind. And though the crowd is jabbering excitedly around him, their voices are distant echoes. He saw and heard the baroness himself! He witnessed her speaking to the old woman, and he heard her, in his tongue, call herself by her secret name, the Servant of Birds.

The crush of people jostle him, but the blows pass through him as though he has become a wraith. He drifts toward the outer gate, looking inward, studying his fresh memory of the young baroness, seeing again her quiet black eyes, her nose long as a Roman statue's in the ancient baths at Caermathon, and the swollen upper lip that, even as she smiled, made her seem as though she were about to cry.

Jolted by the crowd, he makes his way out of the castle, marveling to himself, *She speaks our tongue.* The sound of her sandy voice continues in his mind, lightening his step, as though, like the mythic Owen, he walks with flowers sprouting under each of his footfalls.

"She is the Devil! The Devil incarnate!" Maître Pornic shouts, and his denouncement rings sharply along the carved wood-and-stonework of the *palais*.

Clare rouses from the heavy wooden chair where she has collapsed in her shock. Her face is dark with fury. "Dare you slander my mother?" she bellows back, her voice crashing among the rafters.

Gerald lays a calming hand on her arm, clucks soothingly. "We are all stunned."

"It is a miracle," Denis Hezetre avers from the corner where he is leaning, staring vacantly. "We have witnessed a miracle."

Guy Lanfranc, who sits at the head of a massive wooden table, passes a hawklike stare among the other knights sitting before him. Roger Billancourt reflects his ire, but the others are indeed stupefied. Both Harold Almquist and William Morcar look numbly at their folded hands on the tabletop, not knowing what to think or feel.

"There are the documents," Gerald offers weakly.

"Forgeries!" Roger snaps.

"I think not," Denis says and steps to the table, unfolding the vellums. "This is an authentic charter." He leans over the table, where he has spread the documents, and reads aloud:

"'Richard, king of the English, to all his faithful men: greetings. We order and command you, as you have faith in us and as you love yourselves and all that is yours, to grant Ailena Valaise, daughter of Earl Bernard, widow of Gilbert Lanfranc, free passage through my kingdom to her domain of Epynt in the frontier of Wales, where she is recognized by us as chief authority and legate.

"'Myself as witness, in the Levant, on the fifth day of June.'

"The seal matches with other documents we have received from the king. Of course, you must realize, if we defy this charter, we defy the king."

Guy pounds the tabletop with his fist. "Impossible! I am the lord of this manor and domain!"

Clare sneers at him. "Throw a fit, dear brother. That will surely impress the king. Do you think Richard has forgotten that you supported his defiant brother John's rebellion while he was in the Holy Land?"

Guy rises half out of his seat, his brows darkening. "I have agreed to pay the king's men their penalty for my alliance with John."

"John *Lackland*, you fool," Clare scoffs. "He has no authority and no domain but what he tried to steal from his brother. Now you are forced to sack Branden Neufmarché's domain to pay the penalty. I daresay, Mother will not approve of that, brother."

"She is not Mother."

"The king and the pope say she is," Clare persists vehemently.

Maître Pornic raps a knuckle against the table, commanding silence. "We must not make too much of these documents. Celestine the Third gave up his soul to heaven in January. Our new Holy Father, Innocent the Third, will surely retract this authorization. After all, Celestine was in his nineties when he drew up this vellum. I will write our new Holy Father at once about this matter." He faces the glum baron. "I insist, Guy, that you leave this inquisition to me. This woman claims a miracle has been performed. She jeopardizes her soul by such an outlandish pretext."

Clare's eyes narrowly regard the abbot. "Do you, a scion of the Church, doubt that God can work miracles? Do you dare proscribe God's will?"

Maître Pornic presses his bony fingers together and lowers his face reverently, his severe, liver-dark lips drawn tight. "I would never doubt God's power to work wonders. But Satan is full of deceptions. We must not prejudge appearances."

"Well and good," Clare declares with finality. "Until proven otherwise, we will assume that the Holy Father's document is valid and that my mother has returned from the Holy Land, 'restored to her youth, wholesome and sanctified' as this papal writ declares."

A servitor appears in the arched doorway and announces that the baroness requests the presence of the entire household in the main hall. Clare, glaring triumphantly at her brother, leaves with Gerald at once; the other knights linger, looking to Guy.

Guy rises slowly, jaw pulsing. "Let us not keep *Mother* waiting."

Dwn's fingers look like tubers against the fine material of her chemise. Despite the hot water bath she has just taken, dirt still laces the fine crevices of her gnarly hands. Twice, the water from the long wooden bathtub needed to be emptied and refilled, and still she is not wholly clean. But the caustic lye of the soap and the ample quantities of lilac petals have nearly removed the stink of dung.

In the mirror, Dwn watches as Clare's maids bring her a pelisson, a lightweight cloak of blue silk edged thinly with white fur. The baroness is visible across the room, just stepping from her bath. No longer visible are the moles and small scars that Dwn remembers on her mistress's nakedness; a different constellation of freckles and beauty marks patterns her body, a consequence, the baroness has explained to her daughter's queries, of the miracle that has renewed her youth.

A brushed cotton robe is lifted over Dwn's head and falls lambently across flesh that has grown accustomed to coarse fibers. She runs her hands over the smooth material, and her fingertips are astonished. The maids help her don an azure bliaut—a sheer, ankle-length tunic—taking care to adjust the long, trailing sleeves and the belt of woven silk cords so that the fit is comfortable and aesthetic. Over this, the airy, fur-trimmed pelisson is draped.

Dwn, while another maid combs and plaits her hair, watches her mistress standing naked before her own full-length mirror. Trembling, awestruck maids dab her dry. She glows blue as milk, or winter, her womb taut as a girl's, her breasts round as small rabbits, pink nipples not yet stained by pregnancy. Visible under a curled mat of fine hair, which is almost a mist of dark smoke, is the wild plum of her sex. She is just barely a woman, and one can still see the child in her spindly elbow bones and narrow thighs.

Dwn's insides quaver with eagerness to question her old friend, to hear at once how God came to her. But she observes the dreaminess in her mistress's mien, the way she stares at everything with a distracted stare, and she restrains herself.

"Servant of Birds," Dwn says in Welsh, hoping to draw her out, "you are beautiful. The Lord has made you beautiful again."

Ailena smiles at her in the mirror, retorting through a giggle, "And you have become wise as the chestnut."

Dwn smiles, remembering this exchange from when they were girls and an old Welsh gardener taught them how to accept his compliments on their fresh beauty. "Tell the old they are wise as chestnuts, and they'll find no fault with you, for the chestnut knows how to survive the drought, and its shell opens like an eye in autumn when the land wears its most florid beauty."

"Talk in French so I can understand you," Clare complains giddily, feeling as though she is awake inside a dream. She herself carries the garments that her mother will wear, and she lays them carefully on a dressing rack beside the mirror. "When I was a girl, you two were always chattering in Welsh so Father would not understand you."

"That only fanned his rages," the baroness recalls. "He forbade Welsh in the castle and even in the village—but we defied him."

"And you took the blows for that defiance," Dwn reminds her.

"All so long ago." Clare presents her mother with a chemise

from her daughter Leora's wardrobe and stands in awe before the young woman. "Tell me everything, Mother. Dwn and I want to hear about the miracle."

Ailena fingers the fine fabric of the chemise, says in a quiet voice, "Later. I will tell you all that has changed me later." She looks at her daughter and handmaiden in the mirror, her gaze abruptly crisp. "But now I want to hear about you—about all that has happened since I've been away."

Clare fixes on Ailena's keen gaze. Color drains suddenly from her face as the miraculous import of what has happened occurs again to her: here is the body that birthed her, its clay reshaped by God's own hand to a shape slender as the lily. Her legs give out, and, crashing to the ground, she presses her face to her mother's knees and weeps like a child.

"There are no troubadours anymore," Clare sobs bitterly. "No music anymore. Not since you've left. Guy scoffs at *chansons*. He likes only acrobats."

"And war," Dwn adds. "He favors war."

"Oh, Mother, there has been so much killing. Every spring he raids the Welsh tribes and comes back—" Her tears choke her, and she gasps for breath to speak. "He comes back with their ears!"

Ailena's gaze goes soft again, and her eyes lid sleepily. Dwn signs for the maids to bring a stool, and she drapes the chemise over the baroness as she sits.

Clare, oblivious to her mother's abstraction, continues: "And now he attacks his own kind. He has hired mercenaries from Hereford to besiege Branden Neufmarché's castle. All because he's in debt to the king for siding with Count John. And the soldiers are such brutes. They bully our guildsmen, debauch their daughters, and ransack our village. In the Welsh quarter, the villeins are almost all gone, fled back to the hills."

The young baroness puts a hand to her face, and when it comes away she is clear-eyed and alert. "All shall be well," she promises, stroking her daughter's head. "All manner of things shall be well."

Dwn steps over to plait her mistress's hair and marvel at the filaments of red-gold among the dark tresses, highlights she has not seen in decades.

"Have you the banner with my device upon it?" Ailena asks.

"Guy destroyed all he could lay hands on," Clare answers. "But I have one I have preserved in my chest."

"Have it brought to me. We will bring down the Griffin and raise the Swan."

Clare bites a knuckle. "The donjon is guarded by Guy's sergeants. They protect the flagstaff with their lives."

"Then they will lose their lives," the baroness says sweetly.

The shutters of the main hall have been thrown open to admit the strong summer light. Hastily, the finest sendel silk tapestries have been hung from the walls and the paved floor strewn with fresh rushes and flowers, roses and mint, which crackle softly and fragrantly under the feet of the assembly. Among the sun's bright rectangles, the household has gathered—the baroness's family taking the upholstered settles, the servants behind them on wooden benches. Guy and Roger refuse to sit; they stand, legs apart and arms crossed truculently, by the base of the dais at the head of the chamber.

On the dais, the Griffin-embroidered cushions have been removed from the large oak-carved chair of state, and red squabs have been installed. There, dressed opulently in white silk and ermine, the long braids of her hair intertwined with ribbons and crested with a floral chaplet of gold, sits Ailena Valaise, flanked on either side by her knights, Dwn, and the elderly Jew. The dwarf and his monkey wait in an alcove at the back of the hall, where only the sergeants from the barracks can see them.

"I've not sat here in ten years," the baroness begins in a voice rich enough to fill the chamber. "Many of the youngest of you have never seen me. Others have changed little." She looks pointedly at Guy and Roger. "Family, I've gathered you here that you may confront me before we sit at table. I know my presence and appearance are shocking to you, all the more so"—she nods at her son—"for those who never expected to see me again.

"After our meal together, I will relate to you in detail the truly wondrous events that have transpired since I last occupied this chair.

For now, suffice it that I introduce myself again to you and declare the intent of my return as our Savior has so instructed me to do."

Maître Pornic, seated in the front rank, rises, his fast-withered body bent from a lifetime of kneeling prayer. "Lady, are we to understand that you have spoken with the Son of God?"

"Indeed, our Lord Jesus has deigned to speak with me," Ailena declares in a steady voice. "And he has instructed me to return here and to rule this estate as a true Christian domain—a realm that He himself would recognize were He to walk the earth again."

Maître Pornic blows a gust of disbelief through his dark lips and sits down, shaking his silver head and covering his face with his gaunt hands.

"As it is apparent that the good abbot disbelieves," Ailena continues, "I herewith appoint the canon Gianni Rieti as our parish priest." Gianni rises, attired in a white surplice with a crimson cross above his heart and a tapering sword with a pearl-gilded hilt at his side. His half-military, half-monastic appearance inspires mutterings from the back benches; the servants have never before seen a warrior-priest.

"Canon Rieti is a true father in Christ," Ailena assures the mumbling crowd.

"Then why does he not wear the tonsure?" Maître Pornic demands.

"By your leave," Gianni asks the baroness and bows at her nod. "I am an ordained member of the Canons Regular of the Holy Sepulcher," he informs the assembly. "We are sworn to fight the Saracens until Jerusalem is restored to Christian rule. That our Lord Jesus himself abhorred violence, we are keenly aware. Yet we have chosen to live and die by the sword for the greater glory of the Church. To distinguish our brotherhood's martial efforts on behalf of our faith from the wholly religious and scholarly pursuits of other Christian orders, we abjure tonsure and have been so excepted by our Holy Father the Pope."

Gianni sits, and Ailena motions for Falan Askersund to rise. The Swede, dressed as a Muslim, with white turbaned head, baggy brown trousers, and green leather shoes with upturned toes, steps forward and eyes the crowd coolly. His sleeveless white blouse exposes long-muscled arms burned almost black by the Palestinian sun, so that the fair hair on his skin glints like gold. His face too, is dark as a Moor's, and his close-cropped blond beard shines ash-white.

"Falan Askersund speaks neither French nor Welsh," Ailena explains. "But there is no need for us to speak with him. He is in constant prayer with his god who, he believes, is the one god, Allah, and . . ."

"He has deserted his faith for the heathens!" Maître Pornic interrupts.

"Yes, he has," Ailena admits. "Now he is a devout Muslim. Yet he is also my thrall. See there the gold band about his throat, which is the bond-ring of his servitude? On it, the Arabic script says that he is my property, a gift from a caliph who learned of the miracle wrought on me by our Savior."

"The heathens have no faith in our Savior," Maître Pornic protests. "Why would a Saracen gift you with a bondsman?"

"Their holy book, the Qur'an, identifies Jesus as a prophet of God," Ailena answers patiently. "That God would work a miracle through one of his prophets is obviously more believable to the heathens than to you, Maître."

"This is a mockery!" Guy shouts. Maître Pornic frowns at him, but he goes on, "This woman is not my mother. I will not tolerate any more of this hoax."

Angry mutterings sweep through the hall, and Maître Pornic rises and approaches Roger Billancourt. "Silence him," he commands. "This is a religious question. If it is handled brusquely, blood will spill."

Roger takes his baron's arm, leans close to whisper. "Will you make a martyr of her and yourself a Judas? She must be discredited before we attack her. Calm yourself. Let the abbot have at her."

"If your Muslim knight is a thrall," Maître Pornic asks, pointing to the scimitar at Falan's side, "why is it he is armed?"

"Even a holy man such as yourself will admit, this is a treacherous world," Ailena answers. "The caliph has commanded Falan to protect me, and for that, alone, I keep him."

"His sword is too thin to do more than fend dogs," Roger snorts, and the sergeants at the back of the hall echo his derision.

Quickly, Ailena mutters a guttural command in Arabic and points to her neck. The curved saber glazes the air like a stroke of lightning, hissing to the side of the baroness's throat. In a flash, the weapon is again in its sheath. Ailena reaches up and plucks a lock of hair and curl of ribbon that the blade has cleanly cut. She knots the ribbon about the lock and tosses it to Guy. "A memento of your mother, son. And by this be warned: no Christian sword could cut so accurately."

The baroness motions Falan to his seat and beckons the Jew forward. "If there are no more interruptions, we may continue. Family, this is David Tibbon, a Jew I have engaged to teach me the language that our Lord and Savior spoke while he dwelled among us. It is my intention to live as near to the manner and custom of our Lord as possible. And I invite all in my family who would study with this erudite and devout biblical scholar to join me."

Guy guffaws loudly. "My mother was never a religious woman. She knitted during Mass and ate flesh to her fill on Fridays and throughout the Lenten season. She fornicated adulterously with Drew Neufmarché and voiced nothing but loathing for priests, whom she considered parasites. Albeit she did all this out of sight and earshot of good Maître Pornic. But to us, who suffered her presence, it was no secret—from the time God strangled the life of her father on his own vomit, she lived faithlessly. Why do you expect us to believe that God would work a miracle for her?"

"Surely, Guy," the baroness smiles indulgently at him, "it is the faithless who are most in need of miracles. All that you say of me is true, but only of my past. My soul has been renewed with my flesh. As Jesus forgave the harlot at the well, so has he forgiven me and bade me to go forth and sin no more."

"Mother," Clare interjects, "call on our Savior now to give us a sign so that the disbelievers will know that you are in God's favor."

"Dear Clare, that is not in my power. I am not a saint. I have no miraculous powers. God has restored my youth but conferred no supernatural strength on me. I am a wholly natural woman, and I will not permit myself to be worshiped or regarded as a holy woman."

"If you are indeed the Baroness Valaise, as you so claim," Roger challenges, "then you will remember the destrier that your husband rode when he first came to this castle with me at his side."

Ailena's stare hardens. "So now I am to be tested." She nods ruefully. "That is to be expected from one who has always believed the Church exists for children, the infirm, and the dying. Well, Roger Billancourt, it is your memory the years have impaired. Gilbert did not ride a destrier when he first came to my father's castle. He did not own such a fine horse. He was rich in courage and ferocity but not in goods, neither material nor spiritual. Until he married me and acquired my father's hard-won wealth, he rode a mere palfrey, a brown mare with a narrow breast and a broad face. Her name was Delai, for she was not swift."

The older servitors and sergeants who knew Gilbert Lanfranc chatter knowingly and nod, and Roger turns away with a troubled frown.

The assembly silences as Maître Pornic stands again. "How can you assure us that you have been returned to your youth by our Good Lord and not by Satan?"

"Would Satan bring a writ from the Pope and a priest from the Holy Land?"

Thierry Morcar, prodded by his father William, hails his great-grandmother. "Arrière-grandmère—"

Ailena acknowledges the square-faced youth whose small eyes gaze at her coldly. "Your harsh stare troubles me, Thierry. But I am not surprised you would doubt me, since you were too young to know me well. Have you come to knighthood yet?"

"I have, Arrière-grandmère," he answers proudly. "My father granted me adubbement in the spring. I am well trained by my father and this castle's knights in the manner of combat. And from them I have learned many feints, many tricks by which men are deceived into giving up their lives. That has weakened my faith in things seen let alone things unseen." He looks at his father for confidence, and the mustached knight nods for him to continue. "Forgive me, then, Arrière-grandmère, for putting a question to you to bolster my faith. Name the priest who baptized me."

"That was long ago, Thierry."

"My Arrière-grandmère would remember."

"Yes, she would, and, indeed, she should—" Ailena's face grows even paler, and her eyes look startled. "That was a time of much suffering. We only live in fire. You and your twin sister Madelon were born in the winter of eighty-three, when the blizzards kept our Maître Pornic shut away in his abbey. We would have waited for the thaw to baptize the two of you, but a scourge of cholera plagued the village and threatened the castle. We lived indeed in a time of fire. We only live in fire. But we knew it then. Your dear mother, Hellene, burned with it even as you were born. An old priest from Brecon blew in with the storm, and he baptized you both that your souls would be purged of Adam's sin in the event the cholera took you. It did not, but, God rest his soul, it took him later that winter. His name was Father Aimery."

Ailena stands, and the assembly rises with her. "We only live in fire, consumed by it or purified. Either way, we burn. Our blood burns. We feel the heat in our flesh. It is our lifelong purification, this fire that is God's love, this intolerable fire that consumes us. This is the death of fire, which is the life of fire."

David Tibbon has come up behind the baroness. He lays a knobby hand on her arm, and she looks at him, surprised.

"This inquisition is tiresome," she says. "Let us reconvene at table." She smiles down at Guy and Roger. "You can sharpen your questions while we dull our appetites."

In the dining hall, the dwarf approaches the Jew. While the baroness and the other nobles refresh themselves in their rooms before the meal, the dwarf has been parading around the long and narrow tables, watching the attendants spread out the enormous tablecloths and double the napkins. The monkey has several times darted under the billowing sheets before they could be laid, causing the attendants to leap back and scream.

"Ta-Toh!" the dwarf shouts, and the monkey flies back to his shoulder, wearing a napkin like a mantle.

"Tonight, at last, we will eat well," the dwarf tells the Jew.

David Tibbon, in russet cloak and dark green tunic, sits on a bench beside the entrance, where he has situated himself since the baroness's brief address in the main hall. The entrance, an arched doorway facing south into the court garden, streams with sunlight, bird song, and floral fragrances, and David has read the leather-bound book in his lap and napped here while the servitors prepare a chamber for him in the *palais*. Particularly in the sunlight, he looks noticeably like a patriarch of the Bible, with coriaceous skin and intensely somber eyes. His long gray beard is forked, the dangling locks at his temples loosely braided, and upon his head he wears a small cap of black velvet. "I will not eat well, Ummu," he answers the dwarf in slow, thoughtful langue d'oc, "until I have found a place to eat where there is only one God."

Ummu leans his elbow on David's knee and rests his bulbous head on his hand to gaze up at the sculptures of saints in the stonework between the tapered windows. "Idolators," the dwarf concurs. "Yet they think not. No contradiction to them that there is one God with three parts. They've a mind for contradictions that baffles their enemies. Don't let it disturb your appetite, son of Abraham. For that, there'll be plenty of steaming pork dishes wafting under your nose!"

The dwarf barks a laugh that startles his monkey, and the two prance across the dining hall to trouble the steward, who is now laying out the drinking vessels, the knives, and the spoons.

David shakes his old head remorsefully and turns his stare on the garden. His eyes hurt from reading, and he is glad to stretch his sight among bouncing butterflies and amber streaks of bees. Under a rose arbor, silhouetted against the broad, golden rays of the afternoon sun, several children are watching him. He wags his beard at them playfully and they scatter, except for one, who approaches with trepidation. She is the youngest, a tow-haired child with gray, wondering eyes, dressed in a little robe of taffeta and fur.

"Are you a Jew?" she asks.

"Yes. I am David Tibbon. And who are you?"

"Blythe Almquist. I'm a Christian. Why did you kill Jesus?"

David puts his hand on the young child's head and smiles sadly. "I did not kill Jesus."

"Yes you did. The Jews killed Jesus. Maître Pornic has told us so."

"That is not true, child. Jesus was a Jew. Why would we kill one of our own? It was the Romans who killed Jesus."

"Jesus was a Jew?"

"Yes, of course."

"But Maître Pornic tells us that Jesus is the son of God."

"Then the son of God is a Jew."

The nurse, looking flustered, enters from the garden and, seeing Blythe standing under David's arm, anxiously pulls the girl away. "Come, Blythe, we must dress for dinner."

"But I'm talking with David Tibbon. He's a Jew—and he says Jesus is also a Jew!"

The nurse gives David a black look and hurries the child away. David pinches the tired flesh between his eyes and turns his attention to the dwarf, who has armed his monkey with a spoon and is dueling with it atop one of the tables. The steward drives them off. He is setting little dishes filled with salt at the center of the tables. David stares at the white mounds and remembers the years when the only salt he knew was in his eyes.

Guy and Roger are huddled with their sergeants at the gate of the inner ward when one of the men startles and points up at the donjon. Atop the great keep, the Griffin banner is descending.

"God's eyes!" Guy shouts. He leaps atop the nearest steed and rides at full gallop across the court.

By the time he reaches the donjon, the white Swan on the blue field is flying. He drops from his horse and seizes the sergeant at the entrance of the donjon. "Why are you alive?" he yells at the quaking man and throws him against the stone wall.

"I moved to draw my weapon, lord," the sergeant yammers, "but the Muslim, the Swedish Muslim, cut my baldric clean off before my hand could reach the hilt!" He shows his liege the severed leather strap.

"And the others?" Guy asks furiously.

"The others were moved by reason," a foreign-spiced voice says from the dark of the entrance. Gianni Rieti emerges. "I am the pope's emissary. I have the power to damn souls. How reasonable of your men that none wished to die by a Muslim sword in a state of fallen grace."

Since Ailena's departure for the Holy Land, Clare has occupied the baroness's spacious bedroom, but now she insists on returning it to her mother. Among the canvas-wrapped satchels of Ailena's baggage, the young children frolic, fresh from playing in the garden, their long tresses bright with the blossoms they wear like chaplets.

Ailena sits in a window chair, mantled in sunlight, admiring the females of her family. The youngest, three-year-old Effie, playing with her hair ribbons, lies content in her great-grandmother's lap. Daughter Clare is happily overseeing the servitors unwrapping the baggage, granddaughters Hellene and Leora and great-granddaughter Madelon perch on the edge of the platform where the great canopied bed is being aired, curtains drawn, sheets stripped. Dwn watches from a stool beside Ailena, feeling drunk in the heady bouquet of lilac and the silky caress of her fine garments.

"Be still, girls," Ailena urges. "I have gifts from the Holy Land for everyone. But you must receive them like young ladies."

The playing comes to an abrupt halt, and the girls array themselves before the baroness in order of age. "Joyce, Gilberta, Blythe, and Effie," Ailena repeats the names she has learned, touching each affectionately on the chin. "You are the youngest, born after I departed this castle, so your gifts are first." At her side, propped on a bench draped with the canvas that had covered it, is a casket inlaid with black, silver, and rainbow-hued abalone. From it, she removes four small, precisely carved beasts: a dromedary, crocodile, elephant, and lion. "These strange and remarkable creatures, which do exist—I have seen them all—were carved by Saracens out of ivory, the tusk of the behemoth."

The girls, young Effie included, finger the magical figurines with reverent amazement.

"Madelon, in my absence you have become a beautiful woman," Ailena says, beckoning her forward and presenting her with a kirtle of silver fabric as shimmery as moonlight. "Damascene silk, the finest in all of Byzantium."

While Madelon stands enraptured before the mirror with the elegant gown held against her narrow body, Ailena distributes the other gifts: perfumes—oil of myrcia and bergamot—for Hellene and Leora; vials of jasmine water and balm of Gilead for Dwn and the most valued servants; incense cakes of calambac and lignaloes for the chapel and the abbey; intricately tooled cinctures of blue leather for the boys, Thierry and Hugues; Arabian bridle tassels in bold colors for the knights; a curved Mamluk dagger with a pearl handle and gem-studded sheath she will give to Guy; and, for Clare, a gold necklace.

The women cluster together, admiring their gifts, and Ailena sits back, pleased by their giddy wonder. A movement outside the window catches her eye, and she turns her head to see Guy galloping full-out across the courtyard. A sardonic smile touches her lips.

Guy has rallied his knights in a back room of the barracks. Sprawled upon the crude settles of the empty room Roger, William, and Harold, looking nervous and morose, wait for him to begin. Denis is the last to enter, summoned by a page from archery practice behind the stables. His right hand is still strapped in leather. After nodding to the others, he straddles a bench facing Guy, who stands with his back to the room, staring out a square window. The baron's gaze is locked on the donjon, where the Swan ensign of his mother flies.

If all these years I've been wrong about God being an invention of people's despair, he thinks, *if Creation is as perverse as the Church fathers say and this young thing is truly Mother restored by a miracle, then God is no better than the Devil, for she slew Father as sure as Clytemnestra slew Agamemnon. I will not submit to her!* His clenched fists ache with determination. *I will send her back to the Devil! And if she is an impostor—as she must be, for where is God when martyrs are slain and pilgrims perish?—if she is an impostor sent by Mother to unseat me, then I will acquaint her with the Devil!*

When he turns to face his knights, the single, deep crease across his brow is black.

"The Griffin is struck," he says, and his voice is oddly soft and woebegone. "The bitch has been here only hours, and already our banner is struck."

"We should have slaughtered them in the lists, as I said," Roger's voice growls, his scarred gray head shaking with remorse. "We should never have let them in."

"But they are in," Guy snaps, "and they've made our castle their own. Our holy man, Maître Pornic, is already displaced by that oily-tongued canon. The servitors bustle in the *palais* preparing rooms for a Muslim and a Jew! And even the cookhouse is afluster, hurrying ahead our Saint John's feast to honor the bitch."

"Your mother is no dog," Denis speaks up timorously.

"Indeed, *is* she my mother?"

"We've all watched her closely," Denis counters. "She bears all the striking traits. Even her gait and voice are as we remember. And she's answered all the queries put to her. But, most telling of all, she has acted with the asseveration and privilege that were always her custom. Only your mother would dare strike the Griffin." Denis looks anxiously at the others. "Does anyone here say otherwise? Has anyone here detected in her any feature other than the very semblance of the baroness?"

"The baroness left here aged and crippled," Roger says. "I aver, this is not the same woman."

"Your faithlessness blinds you," Denis retorts.

"She speaks like a mad woman," Roger says. "You heard her in the great hall, ranting about fire. She is a mad woman who thinks she is the baroness."

"Who would not rant if a miracle had been worked upon him?" Denis asks. "She has been made new by her faith. We must answer her in kind."

"Faith!" Guy cries. "Am I to lose all that is mine for . . . for a mere word? Faith! Men—my faith has ever been in my sword. By that we have won lands my mother was too docile to claim. Will we now lose all we have fought for because of faith? This woman is an impostor. I have faith in that."

"What say you, William . . . Harold?" Denis asks. "You have heard her speak. You have watched her move. Is she not the baroness?"

Harold runs a hand over his bald and freckled cope and nods. "This is truly the most marvelous change I have ever witnessed. God's hand alone could do this. It is a miracle. How else could it be?"

William shrugs and makes provisional noises.

"Speak, William," Denis insists. "Do you recognize her?"

"I am not accustomed to miracles," William answers hesitantly. "I have seen no miracles before nor have I ever expected to."

"Is she the baroness?" Denis presses.

William tugs at his great mustache. "I must think on it, Denis. She is among us too short a time."

"What of Neufmarché?" Roger demands. "Our miners have nearly sundered his curtain wall. The men we have hired from Hereford are waiting upon our return to complete this siege. We must go back at once."

"Yes," Guy asserts. "Neufmarché is ready to be shucked like an oyster. We will take his castle for our own, and the Griffin will fly again within the day."

"William," Roger asks, "are you with us?"

William nods and looks to Harold.

"It is right and just that we finish what we have begun," Harold replies.

Denis meets the expectant gazes of the other knights, then faces Guy with a hard stare. "Guy, our obedience belongs to your mother now. We must present the siege to her."

Guy's mouth gapes in a silent, incredulous laugh. "Denis, Mother was Neufmarché-père's bed-warmer. She'll not bless our sacking his son's castle."

"Then we'll pay off the Hereford men and send them back."

"Pay them off?" Roger erupts. "With what? Shall we sack our own castle?"

"The baroness should be apprised."

"Oh, I'm sure she is being well apprised by sister Clare," Guy says glumly and sits down on the bench beside Denis. His harsh countenance softens. "We have faced off many a foe and brazened many a harrowing time together, you and I. Don't turn from me now, Denis."

Denis engages Guy's imploring stare with stricken sincerity. "I will never turn from you, Guy. Not even death will turn me aside—so long as you do not turn from what is right."

"Is it the king you fear? That did not take you from my side when we joined Count John's men. We harried the squires of Gloucester as comrades."

"Yes, I have defied the king with you. But—" Denis looks away. "It is not in me to defy God."

Guy grimaces. "God is on high. Need I remind you, He did not stoop to spare your family when the scarlet death left you an orphan. Yet my father took you in, found you a good gentry family and spared you a villein's fate. God cares little enough for the pilgrims who die by the score on their way to the Holy Land. Yet are we to believe God has worked a miracle for my mother, who never breathed a heartfelt prayer her adult life?"

"Shall I deny my own eyes? God, for whatever divine reason, has worked a miracle."

Guy passes a befuddled look to Roger, who glares back with annoyance. "I will expose this impostor," Guy swears and seizes Denis by the shoulders. "I must. For I will not lose you, Denis."

A trumpet clarion summons the household to the welcoming feast. Clare and Gerald act as hosts and first lead Maître Pornic to the lavatory before the entrance, a table set with water basins and jugs. Deeply offended that he has been replaced as the castle's chief ecclesiastic by an unknown canon, Maître Pornic had intended to return to his abbey that night, but Clare prevailed on him to stay. And now, with true Christian humility, he makes ready to wash his hands for supper though he wears a bitter expression.

Two well-groomed varlets bow to the priest: one holds a jug over a small basin and dexterously pours water over the holy man's fingers. Immediately, the second varlet wipes them dry with a towel. After the cleric's hands are cleaned, Ailena and Dwn have their hands washed and then are led to the seats of honor under the canopy at the high table.

The guests follow and are seated at the tables: Canon Rieti, Falan, Guy, and Roger, the knights and their families, and the castle's wealthiest merchants and guildsmen. Then, the castle's chief servitors and sergeants are admitted and seated at the boards that have been set on sawhorses at the back of the hall. The dwarf and the Jew are situated in a distant corner. After everyone is placed, Canon Rieti says grace, whereupon the great dishes are carried in.

A haunch of stag is brought out first, and while Gerald is carving and the young girls of the nobility are serving one plate to be shared by two, Ailena leans over to Clare. "I wish David Tibbon to be seated here at the high table."

"Mother—the man's a Jew! Leora says he's been filling Blythe's ears with nonsense—Jesus being a Jew and such!"

Ailena's stare is level and cold. "Bring David to the high table."

Clare's mouth hangs open. "Mother, no one will share a plate with him."

"David will share my plate."

Clare does not hide her hurt as she beckons a servitor and whispers the baroness's command. She had intended to share her mother's plate but now displaces the old woman Dwn's place with Gerald.

Canon Rieti recognizes the problem, and he signals for his dwarf to join him. They will share a plate, and Dwn may take the Canon's place with Falan Askersund. As the Jew and the dwarf ascend to the high table, a hush falls over the hall and scandalized murmurs buzz among the diners. But then the boar's head glazed in herb sauce is brought in, followed by a stuffed swan replete with outspread wings and shyly bowed neck, and the assembly's interest is diverted.

Unobtrusively, Guy signals one of his squires, who leaps up from the boards and disappears into the garden. A moment later, he returns with a sleepy old boarhound. At Guy's nod, the squire guides the tired dog to the high table.

"Is that Halegrin my favorite?" Ailena asks at the sight of the dog. Swiftly, she seizes a choice piece of stag and throws it to the hound. "You are still in this world?" She pets the animal as it gnaws at the meat. "Like faithful Argos come to greet travel-worn Odysseus."

Clare lifts her nose at her brother's attempt to discredit Ailena with the aged dog. Denis, too, catches Guy's attention and shakes his head ruefully.

Legs of pork are carried in, and Ailena signs for the servitors to leave them on the lower tables. "I will not eat the flesh our Savior himself eschewed," she declares loudly.

Maître Pornic's frown deepens. "The Fathers of the Church made clear long ago that we are not to confuse our Lord's earthly lineage through his blessed Mary to King David with his heavenly mission, which comes from his Father. The Church recognizes the Messiah, the culmination of Jewish tradition. Thus we are not constrained to obey Jewish law, only heavenly law, which the Church alone is fit to discern."

"Oh, please, Maître Pornic," Clare sighs. "Let us not debate Church matters at this feast. Let us celebrate, instead, my mother's safe and miraculous return."

"This was to be a feast for Saint John the Baptist," Maître Pornic acidly reminds his hostess.

"But that is yet two days away," Clare counters. "The cooks troubled themselves greatly to have this meal ready for us now, to honor my mother's homecoming."

Ailena lays a soft hand on her daughter's arm. "I have come from the Holy Land. Spiritual concerns are much on my mind and in my heart. But Clare is right. There will be time later for discussing our souls. Let us fortify our bodies first."

The cooks and servitors, awed by the miraculous transformation of the baroness, have outdone themselves, and the procession from the cookhouse seems endless: braised beef, roasted rabbit and teal, woodcock and snipe in onion gravy, mutton in saffron, pork pies, frogs' legs with sorrel and rosemary, snails with fried filberts, venison pasties, hot custards, aspics of crane and heron, fruit jellies, and, out of the baroness's baggage from Jerusalem, figs and dates, all washed down with hippocras—spiced wine—and serat—buttermilk boiled up with onions and garlic.

As dogs fight over scraps under the tables and jongleurs at the boards break from their meals to juggle hot roast apples, there is much laughter and, among the younger people, flirting and horseplay. William and Harold feast lustily with their families, and Denis leads the boisterous sergeants in toasting the baroness with each new course. Even Maître Pornic, infused with good will after his second cup of hippocras, laughs at greasy-faced Ummu, whose monkey Ta-Toh leaps among the tables bringing back choice tidbits and sometimes even the knives from the plates of other diners to feed his master. Everyone is merry, save Guy and Roger. They pick at their food sullenly, awaiting the return of the messenger they have dispatched to the siege.

The cooks themselves enter with the final grand dish, a huge pastry shaped as a swan with a gilt beak and honey-glass feathers which have been whitened with flour and prinked out as if alive and swimming. The assembly applauds the cooks, who present the knife to the baroness. Amid expectant whispers, Ailena rises and slashes open the pastry. Dozens of ortolans flutter out and dart about the great hall, but the exits are blocked by the castle's grinning falconers, who unhood their hawks. In a confusion of feathers and shrill cries, the hawks kill the small birds in the air above the tables, to the delighted shouts of the assembly.

During the scrambling to retrieve the hawks, a page dashes into the hall. He rushes to Guy and Roger and whispers the news they have been waiting to hear: tonight the excavation under the wall at Castle Neufmarché is complete. The wooden posts supporting the mine already have been soaked with tallow and, at Guy's command, will be set alight, ready to devour the posts and collapse the castle's defense.

Instantly, Guy and his warmaster rise to depart and sign for their knights and sergeants to meet them in the garden. But Ailena motions to Falan and Gianni at the far end of the table, and the two knights block the stairs of the dais.

"Make way!" Guy demands, but Falan stands poised and impassive, his swart hand on the hilt of his saber.

"Where are you off so soon?" the baroness enquires sweetly. "After pastries and sugar plums we shall retire to the garden. It is a beautiful summer night. Under the stars, you will hear my story. It is wondrous, and you mustn't miss it."

"We are called away," Guy says flatly, facing the baroness with an arrogant grimace.

"To Neufmarché's castle?" Ailena shakes her head. "Clare has told me about your siege. But there's no need to attend to it now. I am calling it off."

"What?" Roger Billancourt erupts so loudly even the shrieking revelers are hushed. "You dare not! You have no authority."

"I dare, indeed. By the authority granted me from the king and the pope and my own birthright. This is my father's castle and mine. No war shall be waged from these walls without my command. The siege at Neufmarché is lifted. I have already dispatched messengers. The war machines will be withdrawn."

Guy fixes her with a murderous glare, upper lip curling with a hint of fang, before he wheels about and shoulders past Falan. Signing to let him pass, Ailena watches calmly as he and Roger stride through the hall. They pause before Denis, William, and

Harold; but the knights will not move, and only Denis meets their hot eyes before they march out of the hall.

"To my mother—the baroness Ailena Valaise!" Clare blurts out suddenly, raising her goblet.

Accordingly, goblets are hoisted, and cheers resound from the great hall and echo through the *palais*.

Small frogs sing from the moat, and fireflies pulse among the trellises and arbors of the inner court's *jardin*. The entire household have assembled in the spacious garden, but for the porters, the tower watch, and Guy and Roger, who have ridden off into the night. Maître Pornic, Clare, and Gerald share the seat of honor on a cushioned marble bench beneath the long fingers of a willow. The younger children are gathered on a quilt laid over the roots. Hugues sits in the groin of the tree. Thierry and Madelon share a smaller stone bench carved as a mushroom. The others sit on the ground or on chairs they have carried from the hall. Everyone is arranged in a great circle around the central rose arbor of the garden, where the baroness is seated in a tall-backed chair with an oil lamp dangling from a tall trivet beside her.

"As you know, I left here on Saint Fandulf's day in the year of our Lord eleven hundred and eighty-eight, the fifth day after Saint Michael's, the Sunday before my fifty-eighth autumn in this world. I could not walk more than a dozen paces without falling, my bones were that bent, my muscles that enfeebled. My bearers, pilgrims all, merchants and monks from Saint David's, plodded through the late summer's dust and heat, bearing me to Newport, from whence we sailed to Normandie.

"I left a bitter woman, having been turned out of the castle my father had built—turned out by my son. I wish Guy had elected to hear my tale this night, for I would tell him, he was right to set me penniless on my way. I was a harsh old woman, soured by the abuse of my husband Gilbert many years before and never recovered. The journey taught me pain of the flesh to match the hurt in my soul. It was a most gruesome pilgrimage—but I was made whole by that suffering.

"Tonight I will not relate all the difficulties I endured on that long journey south—the brigands, the storms, the wretched people in the dark forests who live as animals and eat human flesh. All these, by God's grace alone, I escaped with my life though only rarely unscathed. Many horrors I beheld. Many good souls perished before my eyes. There are stories enough from those first years of my travels for many another night. But this night, I will tell you the most wondrous story of all, my encounter with Prester John in his strange kingdom east of the lands of Babel and Teman. There, where Paradise once touched earth, I came, shriven of my sins through much agony and many trials, and was received into a domain whose marvels today I would doubt myself had I not been entirely changed by them.

"But my words are only smoky mirrors, foxed by dreams, mine and yours. What I tell you now comes from the edges of the earth, where the mirrors are broken and where reason is the poor cousin of truth. My story will put the pieces back together again. But, I have learned, they fit best in silence."

"Out of Smirna, on our way to Samo along the goat steps of craggy mountains, my bearers, three monks from an abbey in Hólar of Iceland, with whom I could speak only with the little Latin I know, became lost in a raging storm. We took shelter in a mountain cave. There we were set upon by some gypsy rovers, who worship the moon and would have sacrificed us to their goddess. My bearers carried me deeper into the cave, and we strove to hide in the darkness. But the gypsies burned nettle shrubs at the mouth of the cavern, trying to drive us out and onto the sharp points of their long knives.

"Choking on the vile fumes, we retreated deeper into the cave, choosing to die by suffocation rather than be mutilated alive. But, to our amazed relief, the cavern did not conclude in a rocky talus but penetrated ever deeper. My bearers had in their baggage oil lanterns by which they were accustomed to read the Holy Scriptures at night. By the wan glow of those lamps, we discerned that our cave was but a portal to a great complex of caverns. One vaulted chamber opened into another.

"Sometimes the ground narrowed to footpaths no wider than a

man's palm, falling away on either side to black, plumbless chasms. There, I was forced to walk on my own, for no bearers could keep their balance with my weight on their shoulders. Rocks kicked over the side plunged soundlessly, hitting no bottom in that lightless abyss. Pungent and sulfurous fumes assailed our sinuses, and the monks feared that we were trespassing in Satan's lair.

"For many days we wandered thus, sometimes over slender bridges, other times across vast subterranean fields and through forests of stone columns that supported the earth above us. We drank the water trickling in rivulets down the rock walls, and we ate lichen and mushrooms tiny as beads of sand that grew in great profusion among the crevices.

"Hour by hour, the monks prayed for salvation, and eventually their prayers were answered: a star appeared in the distance and gradually grew brighter as we approached. The star became a sun. We approached with our hands covering our eyes, staring through the bones of our fingers until we reached the mouth of a cave. Blinded by the luminosity of daylight, we crouched at the end of our dark journey a long time before we could see again.

"When sight returned, we had become faithless to our own eyes, for we did not believe what we saw. Before us were majestic meadows and dells luminous with blossoms, expansive oak and cedar groves—and everywhere we looked, fabulous beasts: elephants and camels wandered the fields with centaurs. In the dark portals of the forest, we glimpsed tigers, satyrs, and fauns. Nearby a river purled, with crocodiles lazing on the mudbanks and lamia swimming upstream.

"Soldiers appeared out of the forest, and the monks hailed them. They were swarthy men in topaz armor with long hair streaked like sunset and eyes green as weathered copper. At first we did not understand their language, but they had us drink of the nearby river—and afterward we understood them and each other.

"They informed us that we were in the kingdom of King John the Presbyter. The river from which we had drunk, they said, descended from a spring in Paradise, out of which Adam was driven, three days' hike from where we were. But journey there was fruitless, for a circle of fire walled in the Garden.

"Instead, the king's soldiers escorted us to the palace of their monarch. That journey took several days, during which we beheld numerous wonders. Chief among them was a waterless sea, a great expanse of billowing dunes with waves and tides and out of which we netted fish with golden scales, whose blood was purple dye yet whose flesh was very tasty. Down from the snowy mountains rolled a waterless river of stones, clacking and thundering into the sandy sea. The pebbles that came ashore gave light in the dark, and the longer one stared at them, the stronger one's sight became. Also, along the shore scurried ants big as dogs, which the people who dwelled nearby employed to burrow for gold.

"Prester John's palace emerged from a cliff face, carved from sapphire. We were met at the golden gates by a stately king dressed in crimson and wearing a gem-studded crown, and we fell on our knees before him. But he raised us up and informed us that, though he was indeed a king of Samarcand, he served Prester John as gatekeeper. Our amazement doubled when we learned that the palace's chamberlain and cook and even the stablemaster were kings all.

"Prester John himself greeted us on a high balcony, from where we could see across the extent of his kingdom, from the heights, where flames encircle Paradise down the far slopes to the ruins of Babylon and the tower of Babel. The monarch of this fabulous realm was not attired in finery but wore the simplest cassock the color of the raw earth. He was the most humble man I had ever met and declined to be called by any title other than presbyter, for he was a true servant of our Lord Jesus Christ.

"The days I remained in that kingdom are yet another tale, which I will save for another night. Suffice to say, we were well feted and spent long hours in conversation with the good and humble presbyter. His kingdom contained people of all races, yet none of them were poor. No thieves or liars dwelled in his domain, for only the good could find their way to this place.

"'But I—I have never been truly good,' I confessed to him, and he smiled most sweetly at me. He told me then that I had not found my way to his kingdom—the three monks from Hólar had carried me there not just on their shoulders but on their grace. And so I could not remain. After a hospitable stay to recuperate from the arduous journey that had brought me there, I was humbly but firmly asked to leave. A centaur would carry me to the limits of the domain.

"The monks who had come with me volunteered to accompany me, but I adamantly refused; they were kindly men, who did not deserve to be denied the comforts of that superlative kingdom. I chose to leave on my own, in the night when the monks were sleeping, for they would have come with me anyway of their own goodness. As I hobbled through the palace on my way to the gates, where the centaur awaited me, Prester John appeared to bid me farewell.

"The good king informed me that by my selflessness I had already begun to earn my way back into God's grace. He instructed me to continue on my pilgrimage to the Holy Land and once there to devote myself to prayer and fasting. Then he escorted me to the centaur and blessed me as I rode off.

"The centaur galloped at a tremendous speed, so that I had to cling fiercely to his mane and shut my eyes against the stinging wind. For a long time I was buffeted, and eventually I swooned. When I awoke, I was in a sugar cane field near the isthmus of Tyre. I was bedraggled, sores mottled my body, and most of my hair was gone, burned away by sandy winds. The Hospitalers found me there and brought me to Tyre, where they revived me.

"Even before I could walk again, I began my devotions. What had transpired in the kingdom of Prester John seemed no more than a dream to me. I told my tale to the Hospitalers. Some believed that I had indeed found the sacred domain of the presbyter king, for many had heard of that sacred place. But others tried to convince me that the Lord had merely sent me a dream to blot out the sufferings of my long and arduous pilgrimage.

"I no longer cared whether Prester John was real or a dream, though to me he was as real as flesh. The torment of my journey had purged my soul of selfishness. I was an old woman with only a short while left before my soul would quit my body. I determined to redeem my life by prayer, petitioning the Lord to have mercy on all of creation, for all that lives suffers. I had seen that most sincerely. Penniless in my wanderings, without the comfort or protection of my station, I had learned true humility.

"When our King Richard liberated Acre, I went there, to be

closer yet to Jerusalem, which was still in the hands of the Saracens. I spent all my days in prayer, fasting every other day and offering what crippled strength I had to nursing the wounds of the Christian soldiers. It was there that our king drafted me a charter to return to my barony and rule in his name, claiming that he had been instructed to do so in a dream. I humbly accepted the charter—one does not deny kings—and I thought no more of it.

"In September of 1192, four years after my pilgrimage began, King Richard won the right of pilgrims to enter the Holy City, and I went at once.

"For the next five years, I toured the Holy Land, devoting each day to prayer in the places where our Savior lived and prayed himself. On Mount Sion, where the old city of Jerusalem was destroyed by Nebuchadnezzar in the time of the prophet Jeremiah, I prayed in a church which has a chamber behind the altar wherein Christ washed the feet of his disciples. There, I heard Prester John's voice tell me: 'Return to Jerusalem and drink of the Cup.'

"I had been fasting that day and was weak from the crippling pain of my old age, so I dismissed the voice as the noise of my creaking bones. I journeyed the next day to the foot of the mountain, to the pool of Siloam, where Christ opened the eyes of the blind man. There, as I was falling asleep after a long day of worshiping God's grace, I saw a silver cup floating in the green air. I startled fully awake, and it was gone—but I remembered the voice on the previous day.

"The following morn, news reached me of a terrible battle to the south, where many Christian soldiers were left wounded and dying. I went there as swiftly as my aged body would permit, and I found many Christian men strewn in the fields outside Bethlehem. I aided the Hospitalers who arrived there with me, and after a strenuous day of tending the fallen, I lay down to rest.

"That night, I heard a boy's voice say, 'Father, behold the fire and the wood—but where is the lamb?'

"The next morning, a soldier whom I had helped informed me that we were lying on the place where Abraham dismounted and where he had taken his son Isaac as a sacrifice and ordered him to carry firewood. I knew then my death was near, for I believed that the cup from which I was to drink was the cup of my life and that Abraham's willingness to sacrifice his son for God pretold God's willingness to sacrifice His son for man. I, too, like all that lives, was a sacrifice, and I hurried back to Jerusalem to prepare for my death.

"Some few nights later, I was stricken with death chills. I asked to be taken to the Holy Sepulcher itself, that I might die near where our Lord was risen. The Hospitalers complied, and I was carried in a litter to the Sepulcher. The hour was very late, and no one was there but those who had borne my litter and a Canon Regular of the Holy Sepulcher, who had come to administer the last rite of extreme unction. That canon is now among you— Canon Gianni Rieti.

"After Canon Rieti performed the rite, a spasm shook me. An unearthly green fire leaped up from the Sepulcher, and a radiance shone. From out of that blinding light appeared, to my eyes alone, the figure of our Lord Jesus Christ—and he spoke to me in a voice that was the voice of Prester John, and I realized that the two were one.

"Jesus said to me, 'Daughter, you have won the favor of our Father by turning away from evil and embracing good. Now it is our Father's will that you return from whence you came and live in the world as I lived. Return to your domain and rule your people as a true Christian.'

"'But I am old,' I protested. 'It is time for me to die.'

"'No, child. You are not old. Your sins are old. But your grace is young and needs to live in the world. Drink of my cup, and you will have the strength to return to your people. Drink and live in the world as I lived—worship God as I worshiped Him on earth. Go and undo the wrongs of your flesh.'

"A cup appeared overhead in a fume of censer smoke of such a savor as though all the spicery of the world had been there. I realized at once that it was the very cup from which Jesus had drunk at the Last Supper. I took the vessel in my hands and I drank a liquor of cold fire. Immediately, I was enwrapped in the cloud of heavenly censer—and when it cleared, I had been restored to my youth, and I appeared to Canon Rieti and to the other monks as you see me now.

"The monks carried me at once to the Grand Master of the Templars, who lives close by, in Solomon's Tower. He marveled at the miracle and surely would have disbelieved had not the canon and the monks testified to what they had witnessed with their own eyes. All the rest of that night, we knelt in prayer and contemplation. All who had been there and the Grand Master prayed with me. And in the morning, it was decided that I must indeed fulfill the command that Jesus had imparted from our Father, the Creator Himself.

"I found a biblical scholar, David Tibbon, who is here among you, and I began that very day to learn the language and customs of our Lord Jesus Christ that I might live as he lived in the world and worship God even as he worshiped.

"Worldly gifts were bestowed upon me by the Grand Master and awestricken Crusaders who knew me when I was old and now saw me made young. But I refused all except for the few items I have brought with me as gifts for my household. Even the local caliph, who rules Jerusalem for his master Saladin, gifted me with my thrall, the Swedish Muslim, Falan Askersund. I accepted him, for to do otherwise would have insulted an infidel who had shown a glimmer of faith in our Lord. Within three days, I began my journey home with David Tibbon, Canon Rieti, my thrall, and the other monks and Hospitalers who had seen the miracle.

"In Rome, the Holy Father, who had been informed by a vision of my coming, blessed me, and we knelt in prayer together. At his insistence and by his own hand he drafted a writ, declaring his faith in my miracle. The very next day, I continued on my way—but, despite our prayers and the pope's blessing, our ship was storm-wrecked. All the monks and Hospitalers accompanying me drowned but for Canon Rieti and his dwarf, Falan Askersund, David Tibbon, and myself. We salvaged our baggage from the wreck and, after praying for those whom God, in His Mystery, had recalled, we went on.

"Now I am here, befuddled by the many deaths I have seen, awed that life lives only by what dies, and humbled that it is God's will that by living the full of our destinies we lose more than we are given."

Guy Lanfranc and Roger Billancourt ride out from Castle Valaise under the huge, stained moon. The sky is cloudless, the air silvery, and they gallop hard through the empty main street of the village. Soon they reach the forest, moving at a swift trot over the ancient Roman road that climbs into the hills. The stars gleam like ore in the black of the forest canopy.

Enshrouded by darkness, Roger thinks, *If the barbarians are out, there will be the devil to pay.* Two horsemen alone in the gloom of the night forest under a clear sky would be ideal targets for the Welsh, who love an ambush.

Guy thinks of nothing. Only fury fills his chest and spills over into his brain, leaving him numb behind his eyes.

The moon inches among the ragged trees as the riders hasten along the wends and curves of the hill road. At last, out of the igneous night, sparklights appear—the campfires of the siege party before Castle Neufmarché.

The castle itself is dark except for the ring of torches at the pinnacle of the high tower, where the Neufmarché standard lolls in the night breeze above the bodies of three attackers who had been captured and hanged. The siege party have lit numerous bonfires on the opposite side of the castle from where they have secretly excavated a mine beneath both the outer and inner walls. The war machines, underlit by the bonfires, rear imposingly against the night sky. The plan is to distract the defenders with these mighty war engines that the attackers have been building over the last few weeks while the miners work underground on the real assault.

Guy and Roger stop before the palisade of fire-hardened stakes that has been erected to stop sorties and succoring parties. The watch identify them, and the gate is opened. Inside, they ride to the largest bonfire, where the Griffin banner is displayed on a tall flagstaff.

Once dismounted, they are confronted by a thick-shouldered, long-haired captain with a furious hawk's face. His grin shows several missing teeth. "Got muzzled by your mama, eh? And at the last moment, too. The burrow's complete, the timbers are tallowed. We'd have dropped those walls at dawn."

Guy stares beyond the captain and sees the siege party's equipment gathered in heaps, many already wrapped in canvas in preparation for decampment. "What's all this?"

"We go back to Hereford in the morning," the captain answers.

"Word came before nightfall. The Griffin's been struck. The Swan flies again."

"That is a deception," Guy snaps.

"Aye, is it? My scout has seen the Swan over your castle. The baroness is returned. The siege is called off."

"Pay her no heed," Guy growls. "I am the master of the castle."

In the fire shadows, the captain's eyes look malevolently gleeful. "A master who cannot fly his own device? No, methinks not. The baroness is returned. Her messenger declares she is the king's legate. And we dare not defy the king, for eventually we must return to Hereford. There, his will has more steel than out here on the frontier."

"We'll pay you not a silver penny," Roger declares. "You'll go back lighter in the saddlebags unless you follow through with this war."

"Oh, we've already been paid," the captain replies, enjoying the ironies of the situation. "When Branden Neufmarché learned of the baroness's return, he sent us coin enough to reward our men. Truth be told, he even offered to treble the amount if we would turn our strength on Castle Valaise."

Guy and Roger reach for their swords and glance quickly about for treachery.

"Stay your hands," the captain laughs. "We fear the king's steel more than we covet Neufmarché's gold. Your lives are spared. Though soon enough perhaps you'll be wishing otherwise. The king's penalty must still be paid, and now you've no neighbor who'll pay it for you. I daresay, by summer's end, Branden Neufmarché will see you landless. From baron to vagabond. There's a troubadour's song in this."

Guy's arm lashes out to cuff the insolent mercenary, but Roger restrains him. He does not release him until he is on his horse. With as much stately dignity as they can muster, they depart before the remorseless smirk of the captain, but once clear of the palisade and open to vengeful attack by Neufmarché's men, they burst into a gallop that raises a silver cloud of moon dust behind them.

Clare closes the door of the bedchamber she has given her mother and pauses a last moment to look in. The baroness is lying on her back in the bed, her pale face luminous even in the darkness. The story she has told in the garden has touched everyone with a wonder that only silence could contain. No one could say anything when she finished. She drifted from the garden like an apparition, and when she was gone, each person—the knights, the children, the servants—sat silently regarding the space where she had been. Clare was the first to rise, to follow her mother; then came Dwn and the other maids.

Ailena had seemed asleep even as she was being undressed by the maids and wrapped in her nightgown: her eyes nearly closed, her arms limp. She said only, "See that David Tibbon is comfortable. Clare, do that for me." Then she was laid down, and her breathing went soft. Staring at her now, Clare sees a child with a face like a piece of the moon. Her mother has become a child. The thought sets her heart frisking like a bird in her rib cage.

She closes the door and nearly trips over the lanky legs of the Muslim Swede and needs both hands to keep from dropping her oil lamp. He is lying in the passage with a block of wood for a pillow and only a thin quilt between him and the hard flags. His turban has been removed, and his long, gold hair spills over his chest. Across his lap is the curved saber, his hand upon its hilt. Gazing into his celestial blue eyes, Clare feels her organs sliding over each other with surprise. She burbles an apology, but he says nothing.

Earlier, when her mother's chests were being moved in, she had caught him prying at the bolts on the clasp-plate of the bedchamber door with a thick knife, loosening the latch. When she told her mother, the young woman smiled and said, "He has sworn to Allah that he will not be separated from me until his thrall is fulfilled."

Down the hall, she finds the chamber that has been prepared for the Jew. The door is ajar, and within she sees him standing by the window, hands open before him, the top of his body moving back and forth in prayer. She walks away quietly.

Around the corner, she glimpses a shadow dash into one of the doorways. A moment later, a squat figure waddles from the doorway, the dwarf wearing a child's nightgown. "Mistress Chalandon." He greets her with a deep bow. "I thank you for this fine sleeping attire. Your maid has told me that it is all she could find that might fit me. I understand that it was once worn by your grandson and, before him, by your brother, the good baron Guy."

"You are welcome to it, kind sir," she replies in an awkward fluster, appalled that her maid has given a useful item to such a loathsome creature.

"Forgive me—you may not know my name. I am Ummu." He bows again and clicks, and his monkey prances into the hall and imitates his bow. "And this is Ta-Toh. We are both your humble servants."

Clare smiles uneasily. "Are your quarters to your liking?"

"Most decidedly, gracious lady," Ummu replies and steps closer into the yellow glow of the oil lamp. "My master the canon will be greatly pleased to rest his head here after many months with only the naked earth for a bed. He is this moment speaking with the padre in the chapel or he would warmly bless you himself. The baroness, I trust, is sleeping?"

"Yes." Clare's voice squeaks out, and she must clear her throat of her trepidation to speak audibly. "I have given her back the bedchamber that was hers when she lived here last."

"Her tale in the garden was enthralling, was it not?" The dwarf's large eyes gleam in the oily light. "You know, I was there with the canon in the Sepulcher when the Grail appeared. It came down from a luminous cloud, just as she told. But she was too modest to speak of the angels. They swarmed about her in motes of sunfire, writing Hebraic sigils in the air—the names of God."

Clare backs away from the dark-faced little man whose large eyes burn with ardent watchfulness. Her voice fails her, and she makes a gesture of good night. With a sharp cry, the monkey leaps up her leg and onto her extended arm, its primordial visage shrieking with devilish joy.

A scream cuts through Clare; she flares away so abruptly that she slams into the wall and spills oil. The flame sputters, and darkness narrows in.

"Ta-Toh!" the dwarf cries angrily, then reassuringly to Clare, "He mistook your extended hand as a beckoning."

The monkey flies back to the ground, and Clare retreats backward into the arms of her alarmed maids, who have come running at her cry. Falan, too, appears, unsheathed scimitar in hand. He stands aside for the maids, who huddle past with their mistress braced between them.

The dwarf shrugs and cossets the nervous monkey. Falan's severe face relaxes, flickers a smile, and he sheaths the scimitar.

Maître Pornic's spidery body rises from before the altar, where he has been kneeling in prayer with Canon Rieti. Gianni Rieti crosses himself and rises, too. The chapel is illuminated only by several tall candles and the broken moonlight in the rose window, and the two clerics are little more than shadows to each other.

"I will speak to the baroness about keeping you here as the parish priest," Gianni says generously. He is deeply impressed by the elderly cleric's simplicity and faith, having too often encountered worldly ecclesiastics. This small man in the coarse cassock seems more a rustic than a priest and reminds Gianni of the gentle friars who reared him. "You are better suited to tend this flock than I, a stranger."

"I have my place in the abbey. I will go there." Maître Pornic peers up resignedly at the taller man. "Has she changed the Mass?"

"The Jew reads from the Pentateuch, in Hebrew. He calls it the Law. The Law that Jesus knew."

"The bread and the wine?"

"Yes, there is still that. I bless the bread and the wine, and we share it."

"Even the Jew?"

"No, not the Jew. He declares his faith in God but says the Messiah is yet to come." When he sees the old priest recoil, Gianni is quick to add: "You must not think there is anything sacrilegious about the ceremony. We worship as Jesus himself worshiped."

"But our Lord and Savior passed authority to Peter, who founded the Church," the abbot protests. "As Christians, we are bound to God through the Church and our worship in the Church. This woman transgresses the teachings of the apostles."

"Jesus himself has spoken with her, padre. She has drunk from the Grail, even as Christ himself and his disciples drank."

"Your witness alone gives me the strength to believe this young woman's story," Maître Pornic says tiredly, stepping down from the altar and sitting in the front pew. He gestures for the canon to sit beside him. "You saw the Grail appear in the Sepulcher, my son?"

"Yes, padre, I did," Gianni answers and sits close enough to see the holy man's face in the soft darkness. "I will confess to you now, I was not worthy to witness such a miracle. I am a worldly man."

"You are a priest."

"My desires impelled me to the priesthood, padre—to escape the wrath of men who despised me."

"You were forced into the priesthood?"

"By my lust, padre. I have always been lustful, since manhood first came upon me. And the women—" Gianni shakes his head ruefully. "The women have always been drawn to me. I could never resist them. In my native Turin, the men of those women wanted to castrate me. I sought sanctuary in the Church, and the good fathers received me."

"What of your family? They let you flee to the Church?"

"I have no family but the Church. I was an infant left on the altar and reared by the holy fathers. The friars are the only parents I have known. When my troubles threatened my life, I returned to them. They arranged for me to be ordained, but that did not quell my lust."

Maître Pornic's face bows before this sinful admission, so that only the silver halo of his tonsure is visible in the darkness. He asks in a whisper, "You profaned your vows?"

"Yes, padre—many times. My penance was to go to the Holy Land, to fight for the return of the Sepulcher. Yet, even there I followed my lust instead of the Cross. There were many beautiful women among the *palazzi* of the Latin Kingdom, and they desired me—and I them. I was more discreet than I had been in Turin, but God saw each of my many amorous devotions. I coupled with maids and princesses, young brides and twice-over widows. And all with such chill spiritual composure, as though this was what God had brought me into the world to do."

Maître Pornic looks up with the staring eyes of a startled animal. "You are blessed! God has given you such vivid lust to be your Cross. Your lust must crucify you! You must hang in torment on the nails of your desire. You must suffer the pangs and convulsions of animal passion day and night, without touching woman's flesh, in deed or in thought, and without laying hands on yourself. You must hang in the raging burnings of desire until you go mad. That madness is Satan in you! When you face the Evil One, he will have his way with you. But if you persevere, if you accept your lustful anguish as an adoration of God, the madness will eventually pass— and in its place you will possess a wreath of flowing radiance, here—" He presses a splayed hand against his chest. "Light flowing round and round, a flowing light of infinite grace and beauty."

Gianni Rieti stares hard in the darkness at the wise face that has shed its peacefulness and stares back at him even harder, a keen devil. "I did not think such things were possible," he admits. "But then I was called down into the Sepulcher late one night to administer the viaticum. Frankly, I was selected because I happened to return to the chantry late from a midnight tryst and no one else was awake. I went down into the Sepulcher with the Eucharist and found there an old and enfeebled woman, nearly dead, lying on a litter in the crypt. She was surrounded by several Hospitalers and Templars, who had already performed last rites without the benefit of the oil or the Eucharist. I knew she must be some important personage to be there in the crypt itself, but I did not know who she was. When I gave her the viaticum, she could barely swallow it and nearly choked. In fact, her breathing did stop, and I thought her soul had taken flight. But then she shivered awake and cried out. That instant, the crypt seemed to burst into flame and a great trumpet blared. My eyes were blinded, my ears deafened. When I could see again, the old woman was standing and above her a luminous cloud descended. In fear, I retreated with the other knights, and we watched from the stairs as the Sacred Chalice appeared out of the burning cloud. We fell on our knees, all of us crying out as one. The old woman received the Grail and drank from it, just as she told us this night, she drank from it—and she was changed."

"Did you see our Savior?"

"No. I saw only the Grail and the tongues of flame wagging in the air about her. Then it was over. The Grail was gone. The flames and the luminous cloud were gone. And she was young. I wept. We all wept. I was not worthy to behold such a miracle, to feel the warmth of the Presence, to smell the fragrance of heaven. I was not worthy. Why did God choose me?"

Maître Pornic regards the young canon carefully and, even in

the dark, sees the sincerity in his mien. With an expression of profound sorrow, he lays a narrow hand against the side of Gianni's
face, and his touch is bright.

Gianni sits up straighter as the hand falls away. "I have
changed, padre. The miracle has changed me. I lust as much as
ever. Horror of horrors—I have even desired the baroness herself!
But I have locked my desires inside my heart. I will not sin again. I
have learned to fear the Lord."

"The fear of the Lord is the beginning of wisdom," the old
priest quotes from the Gospels.

"Padre, you are a true holy man. Have you ever seen a miracle?"

In the dim light, the bony highlights of Maître Pornic's face
seem to glow. "Yes, I have seen many miracles," he says, slowly.
"And, if you like, I will show you one, the greatest one of all. You
must come with me to the hilltop and stand with me under the
great cope of stars. And then soon, if you can bear the darkness
long enough, you will see the sun rise."

Dwn stares down at the sleeping baroness. The crone is too excited to sleep in the couch that has been set up for her at the foot of
the great bed. For hours, she has been sitting at the edge of the
large feather mattress, watching the young woman breathe, her
eyes darting wildly under her closed lids. "Servant of Birds," she
whispers. "You have come back. God has sent you back to us,
Servant of Birds."

When the presence of the miracle becomes too great for her to
bear, Dwn rises from the bed, walks to the door and opens it.
Falan Askersund lies at the threshold, his watchful eyes glinting in
the dark. She walks past him, and he does not stir.

Down the passage, she finds her way to stairs she would know
well even blind. No one is in the great hall or in any of the small
chambers she passes on her way to the large front door of the
palais. It opens soundlessly, and the huge blue stars and bloated
moon stare down at her as she wanders across the shiny flagstones
of the inner ward.

Though he does not recognize her, the inner gatekeeper lets
her pass: she is dressed in a silk bliaut and has obviously come

from the *palais*. The bailey is mostly empty. A lone dog drifts out of an alley between the shops. The guards on the parapet pay her no heed. At the outer gate, the porter, who is old enough to know who she is, asks where she is going.

Dwn holds up her hands, knobbed as thick roots, and the porter opens the gate. The long walk across the exercise grounds, through the barbican gate and along the great garden road is beautiful in the glossy moonlight. On the toll bridge, she holds up her knurly hands again, and the bridgekeeper lets her pass without a word.

The village is asleep. Cats flit among the squat houses chasing rats. No one sees the crone in her silk gown as she strolls along the dirt street. Above the stand of alder and ancient elms at the end of the village, bats whirr, circular blurs against the lunar glow.

At last, Dwn comes to the dungpile and stands a long time before it, gazing softly at its voluptuous mass. The small round windows gaze back. The slanted door of bleached wood opens with a cry, and she enters the acrid darkness. Among the familiar contours, she finds her way to the little hearth and kneels there. She reaches through the darkness and clutches the crucifix of lashed sticks. Placing the cross in the hearth, she opens her tinderbox and strikes a spark.

Dwn's eyes wince as the crucifix catches fire and all the wretched shapes of her hovel leap at her. In the sudden glare, she sees again the measureless old age of her bent hands and the delicacy of the filigree cloth at her wrists. Then the glow begins to fade as the cross falls to ash. The terrible incongruity of warped fingers and white silk startles her, and she has almost lost the opportunity to send her prayer off with the flamelight of the crucifix. As the glow fades into the straw-tangled wall of dung, she prays fervently so that the light of the most holy thing she owns will carry her message to God, "Thank you, Lord. Thank you for returning her to me—the Servant of Birds."

GARDEN
OF
WILDERNESS

*The Grail was fashioned by angels
from an emerald that dropped
from Lucifer's forehead when he
was hurled into the abyss.*

Lunel, Gascony, Autumn 1187

There was treachery in the colors of the season. The brassy oaks and feverish maples were pulling inward, away from the world. The brown eyes of chestnuts spied from among rotted leaves on the spongy floor, their lids hairy and somnolent, knowing what was to come. Gusts of mauve asters and wild jonquils burned brightly among the grassy verges, where vipers hid and pebble-sized spiders hung their webs. A lightning-split tree bubbled with mushrooms bright as embers, and poisonous gills rippled on the deadwood. Overhead, in the snow-valleys of the Pyrenees, purple bundles of thunder descended with that afternoon's storm.

But for now, the morning was blue and brisk. A girl named Rachel, who knew all the dangers that the colors of the season signified, sat peacefully on her secret knoll. She was twelve years old and serene with her knowledge of the terrain where she had grown through childhood.

Soon she would be a woman. Her older sisters had explained

the mysteries to her the winter before, and when in the spring her body had begun the awkward changes that would complete her, she was not alarmed. Not like one of the village girls with whom she played, who thought her first blood was God's punishment for missing Mass.

Rachel savored her time on the knoll. This was where she worshiped. Here, among the black currants and pink lychnis, she felt God's presence more strongly than in the temple or around her grandfather's sacred scrolls. When Father found her sitting dreamily in the gooseberry shrubs behind the cart sheds and the empty hay wains, a crown of hydrangeas in her hair and foxgloves twining her arms, he scolded her for squandering her time and called her a pantheist. Since then, she worshiped creation only in this secret place.

As she had gotten older, there was less opportunity to come up here. She had more responsibilities in her family, first as an assistant to her older sisters, who managed the household with Mother, and lately with duties all her own. Her charge as of this past summer was to oversee the maids who laundered the linens and garments. That duty was light: the washerwomen were a jovial lot who sang as they boiled the dirty clothes and lifted the steaming apparel onto the scrubbing boards, where they scoured them with pig-bristle brushes. They did not need her to oversee them, but Mother insisted that all her daughters know the workings of the household. And the washerwomen did not mind her company, for she was a playful child yet always willing to get her own hands dirty.

Mother frowned on playfulness in young women—managing a house so that the men were never troubled by any concerns but their own work was vital to the well-being of the family—and Mother wanted her daughters to be good wives. But Rachel was the youngest of the daughters, and lately Mother was intent on the upcoming wedding of the eldest in the spring. After that, Mother would have more time to attend to her younger girls' training, and Rachel knew that this would probably be among her last visits to the knoll.

This high place was secret even from her curious brothers, who had explored all the lands of the estate but were most content playing in the fields and creek beds. To escape them and her meddlesome sisters, Rachel had long ago trekked up the hillsides of wild mustard and squirmed through dense hedges to find this place. Over the years, she had discovered the dry rills cut by the rain in winding paths among the blue-green sedges and silver-branched thorn shrubs with their tiny white flowers. She alone knew those secret paths that led unhindered to the crest of the knoll.

There, scribbled with ivy and groundsel, were large blocks of weather-worn masonry carved with fauns and serene, muted faces. These toppled stones were the remnants of a Roman shrine that had stood here a thousand years ago. When she had first discovered them, she had sat for hours, day after day, studying the uncanny silences of those lovely faces and frisky satyrs that had been holy to another age. The sweet, moribund fetor of the knoll's vegetation must have smelled as dense long ago when these images were sharp and the faith in them alive. How strange it seemed to her then that glories could die.

Standing atop the fallen shrine, Rachel could see the vast expanse of her family's estate, from the vineyards on the cypress-spired terraces to the orchards by the brown swerve of the river Garonne. The stately house where she lived with its high-peaked tile roof twinkled with birds in a circle of shimmery aspen. Tiny blue figures, high on the steep hillsides above the thatch-roofed village, were swinging scythes. Down below, they were tossing long swaths of hay to cure in the sun, and, farther down, the little figures were carrying sheaves off in donkey carts.

In the orchards, the peasants came and went among the trees, harvesting the apples and pears to make cider and perry. Billows of perfume drifted up the hillside in waves, and Rachel breathed deeply of her happy solitude.

Bordeaux, Autumn 1187

They appeared first in the marketplace, drawn by the medlar fragrances of the fruit stalls. The fervent voices of the merchants and shoppers died down at the sight of them. Their faces looked charred, and they were trousered in dried blood. Their flesh hung like rags from their bones, glossy and raw where steel had bit them. Barefoot, bound in the shreds of their banners, without weapons or steeds, they had returned to their homes from the deserts, clinging to each other, leaning on broken spears, tattered fingers reaching for food, slobbery mouths hanging open, speechless with suffering.

After a stunned silence, the people recognized the disfigured semblances of their kin. These were men who, the previous year, had taken up the Cross and gone to the Holy Land. Appalled shouts pierced the market. Mothers screeched the names of their absent sons, and the husks that had returned shook their heads and wept black tears.

"Hattin," the broken mouth said. "They all died at Hattin."

Heads hung in shame, the surviving Crusaders listened to the one who had strength left to speak. Behind aged eyes, wise with pain, wicked with memory, the story shaped itself, and the broken mouth groped to speak.

The townspeople had carried the soldiers into the nearest tavern and soaked bread in wine to soften it for their cankered mouths. "Hattin?" one of the merchants asked. "Is that village near Jerusalem?"

"It is a vale—in the desert. We marched there in July, to meet the Saracens. In July, we marched—" The wicked memory could not fit his mouth, and he saw again the leafless skyline, the dunetops trembling like the roofs of ovens.

In a rage of madness, another of the survivors laughed with a sound that was no more than a putrid sob. "In July! The largest army ever—marching to fight the Saracens in the damned hellfires of July!"

"When the heat had crippled us, they came down from the dunes—they came down—they came screaming—"

The furies in their blackened faces silenced them, and they sat staring through their deafness, exhausted with what they could not say.

In dreamlike silence, the crowd marched to the church of Saint Seurin, where the Jews were hiding. The bishop himself met them at the steps in full vesture. "Go back to your homes," he commanded.

"Give us the Christ-killers and we will leave!" a voice shouted from the silent crowd, and murmurs ruffled through the throng.

"Go back to your homes at once!" the bishop replied. "King Henry and our Holy Father the Pope have forbidden the Jews to be harmed."

"Who will pay for Hattin?" someone cried out. "Only blood can answer blood!"

"Take your rage to Jerusalem!" the bishop called. "Go to the Holy Land and take Christ's home back from the Saracen!"

At a sign from the bishop, the clop of horses echoed on the cobbles, and soldiers from the fortress advanced slowly on the crowd, driving them off.

Fires blazed that night from the houses of the Jews, not only in the city but in the villages among the low hills of Larmont on the far side of the Garonne. The rage of Hattin marched south, burning its way back to the Holy Land.

Rachel knew whom she would marry. The arrangements had been made years ago with a merchant's family in a neighboring village. They were as wealthy as her family, and they were learned. The boy's father was himself not a merchant but a rabbi, a friend of her grandfather's famous cousin Judah, the renowned physician and linguist of Lunel. Rachel had met the family several times at festivals, and they were not much different from her own family.

Sitting on the ancient masonry atop her knoll, Rachel lately spent more time wondering what married life would be like. Of course, she would be happy in her marriage. She always strove to be happy. Her grandfather, the wisest man she knew, often said that happiness was a gift we gave to God.

She looked upward at the distant slopes of the Pyrenees, where her grandfather had his cottage. Long ago, when she was a small girl, he was the patriarch who managed the estate. Then, one day, that responsibility became her father's, and Grandfather let his beard grow and had a small house built for himself high on the flank of the mountain, where, closer to God, he could study the Torah and the Bible.

Rachel discerned Grandfather's white cottage on the amber

slope of the nearest mountain. How could one live there among the phlox and the ethereal deer and not be holy? Soon he would be coming down, to spend the winter in the great house with his family and to share all the wisdom he had learned during his summer retreat.

What would Grandfather say about love, Rachel wondered as she poked with her cloth shoe at the furry twigs of a dead shrub among the ruins. A brown whisper of spore vapored from a cluster of mushrooms, trailing a meaty aroma into the languorous breeze.

Rachel had heard the troubadours singing of true love at the annual fair. Recently, that was all she had been able to think about during her visits to her secret place. What would being in love feel like? What man could inspire such a powerful emotion in her? None of her brothers' friends did, neither did the rabbi's son to whom she was betrothed, though she was certain he would be a good husband. Mother and sisters had laughed at her queries about romance, and her father had assured her that such ideas were a gentile madness, not suitable for her, a daughter of Abraham.

From the village below, the clangor of bells whispered across the valley. Rachel climbed to the top of the masonry heap to peer down into the drowsy village. Today was not Sunday, so the liquid sound of the bells was not announcing worship or a wedding. Perhaps someone had died.

Once, with her peasant friend who thought her first blood was God's curse, she had visited the village church. Standing in the incensed dark, staring up at the saints with their long, narrow bodies, she was a trespasser. Or was God's thought here, too? That was another question for Grandfather, but she had not dared ask him.

Rachel noticed that the peasants on the hillsides and in the orchards had stopped their work. Something was amiss—and with that realization she recalled that the church bell was also rung to warn of fires and brigands. No smoke smirched the blue morning, and her heart panged with her mother's continual warning never to play far from the great house—wandering mountebanks and gypsies frequently stole children and disfigured them for display as freaks at the fairs.

No danger was visible from her high vantage. The quilted hills gleamed serenely, smelling of wild mint and cut hay. Clouds soared, and butterflies wobbled in the air. Yet the delirium of the tolling bell sent a chill deep into her chest.

A pulpy moon hung in the day sky, and Rachel noticed it as she picked her way down the hillside toward the village. She paused among the punky stems and waxy leaves of dead chaliceflowers to peer up at it. How serene that vaporous face looked in the teal of heaven. Under that benign gaze, nothing really serious could be wrong down below. Now, she could hear the commotion of the village inside the clanging of the bell, and it sounded like a festival.

The Christians had more festivals than she could remember—feast days, they called them, to honor their saints. Usually they were celebrated in the larger cities, and Rachel heard about them when the field workers came stumbling back to the orchards, oftentimes still reeking of wine. Lunel celebrated only one saint's day raucously, the feast of the Pentecost on the seventh Sunday after Easter, commemorating the spirit of God coming down as tongues of flame to the followers of the Messiah. That was the day of the village's annual fair, when hucksters came from all over Gascony to hawk their wares to the accompaniment of troubadours and jongleurs. For her family, that holiday was Shabuoth, which celebrated the revelation of the Ten Commandments at Mount Sinai.

Rachel spied women leaning from windows and standing in doorways beating pots, but where were the colorful jongleurs in motley? Instead, people ran helter-skelter in the streets, some carrying torches in broad daylight. She stopped abruptly on a slope of cinquefoil above a slope of evenly bound and piled sheaves.

Plague! she realized. She had read about plagues in the Bible and had heard from Grandfather about the scarlet death that had slain so many people in the northern cities that their bodies had been piled in mounds and they had to be buried in one grave. That was many years ago, when Grandfather was younger than she. Could that dread evil now be visiting Lunel?

A small figure scampered among the sheaves, then came sprinting uphill directly toward Rachel. She recognized the smudged and frightened face straining closer. It was her village

friend who thought God had cursed her with womanhood for
missing Mass.

"Rachel! Rachel!" she gasped and nearly fell to her knees. "I
was coming to find you."

"What's wrong?" Rachel steadied her friend. "Why is there
such a clamor in the village?"

"They're killing the Jews!"

Rachel gaped, bewildered.

"It's a Crusader mob from the north," her friend explained,
clutching at her, her eyes wild. "They're going to the Holy Land to
avenge the Christians that were killed at Hattin by the terrible
Saracen lord Saladin."

Rachel did not understand. She had heard of the Crusades.
Some of the men in the village had taken up the Cross and gone to
Jerusalem to wrest the sepulcher of Jesus from the Turks, and the
estate had lost some good workers. But Hattin—Saladin—she did
not know these names.

"The Crusader mob is killing Jews wherever they can find them,"
her friend sobbed. "I heard the men talking about it. The mob has
already slain all the Jews in Blaye, Agenais, and Auch! I've seen the
men from the north with blood on their hands up to their elbows!"

"Are you sure?" Dare she believe this naïf who thought her
womanhood was a curse?

"Rachel! They're charging through our village screaming
'Christ-murderers!' They've already set fire to your cousin Judah's
house and dragged him, his wife, and his children through the
streets by their hair! They're taking them to the church to be baptized. But he's spitting at them and I know they're going to kill
him! Rachel—you must warn your family."

With wide eyes, Rachel looked past her friend and into the village. Plumes of smoke had begun to rise from the village's affluent
center, where her cousins lived. Many of the people charging
through the streets brandished torches, and several held crosses
over their heads. Horror spiked through her as she recognized the
truth of what her friend had reported.

Rachel spun about and ran hard up the hillside. The shortest
route home was directly over the knoll and down through the
secret hedge paths. By the time she reached the crest of the hill, a

cold, sticky sweat had soaked through her chemise and her heart boomed in her ears. She threw her head back to catch her breath and saw again the day moon, shaped like a sleeping swan.

From atop the shrine stones, Rachel gazed down in a fright to see smoke piling into the sky. The heaped stacks of grain were blazing. Swarms of banner-waving men ran through the orchards and fields, smashing the harvest carts and setting their torches to the fruit trees. For a long moment, she stood transfixed, hardly believing her eyes. Then she saw how the swarms of men had converged on the great house, and terror jolted through her. She could not stand there and simply watch. She had to be with her family.

As Rachel leaped down from the jumbled stones and skidded along the steep rill paths that slashed through the dense hedges, she frantically considered what to do. Could she find a way past the furious mob? If she could, if she could find her way to her father and mother, she knew they would know what to do.

From on high, the rampaging mob had been a cloud of small figures. But as she descended to the rutted road that led to the village, she saw the gruff-faced, scowling men more clearly. They were strangers, grimed from their furious march, swinging crude banners with lambs and crosses scrawled on them. Many wore filthy gray blouses marked with streaky brown crosses that, with a start, Rachel realized had been smeared on with blood.

A group of these men singing a Christian anthem in shouting, angry voices strode down the path where Rachel hurried, and she barely had time to duck into the hedges as they bustled past. They brushed by close enough for her to see their mud-caked leggings and thick hands. They were dragging something behind them, and at first their legs blocked her view.

Rachel decided she did not want to see what they were dragging, but that instant the burdens swung by. Inches away the blood-clotted corpses of her father's brother Joshua and his two adolescent boys stared through her with crazed, sightless eyes. They had been stripped naked, and she stared with icy dismay at the first naked men she had ever seen. Where their genitals should have been was only mangled flesh, butcher-bright blood streaking their naked bodies, and sticking out of their mouths were some things like sausages.

The realization of what she saw surged through her violently, and she shrieked. The instant her cry retched out of her, she froze, icy terror locking her muscles. But the murderers, with all their vehement singing, had not heard her.

Rachel crawled through the hedge to a narrow mule path that ran parallel to the road and tried to stand, but her legs, void of tension, kept dropping her back to the ground. She crawled along the path until feeling returned to her legs and she could rise. Staggering along the hedgerows, she advanced to the edge of the apple orchard.

Her ashen face, beaded with droplets of sweat, swung side to side looking for a clear way among the green doors and shadows of the trees. The fires that the mob had tried to start in the trees had died out, smothered by the wet mulch and moist fruit. She stumbled, tripping on roots and slipping on rotted apples. When Crusaders appeared, she crouched behind the burly trees and studied the fragrant, amber sap oozing from crevices in the trunks, willing herself invisible.

Most of the mob had drifted away from the orchard. Some had gone off on the steep trails to the terraces, to raid the vineyards. Others had found the storehouse with the casks of wine and were jubilantly dousing themselves. Many more marched singing down the road to Lunel. Miraculously, the approach to the great house was clear.

Beside toppled and broken carts, several mules lay on their sides with legs sticking straight out. Rachel hurried past these unfortunate beasts, over the mustard-colored grass at the roadside, across the shimmering hay stubble and up the small, white stone path to the house.

The fire the rioters had set to the thatched roof of the servants' quarters had fallen in and gone out. None of the servitors, maids, or peasant workers was in sight. The great house itself looked empty, the shutters closed. She went around to the back, keeping a furtive lookout for Crusaders. The servants' entrance was closed, and the door would not budge. It had been barricaded.

Hope that her family had fended off the mob and were still alive inside flared through her; she called their names against the door as loudly as she dared. No one answered. She crept around to the side and tried to pull back one of the shutters, but they were tightly secured.

Unwilling to expose herself on the side of the house that faced the vineyard, where the mob had gone, she returned to the servants' entrance and pulled at the shutters blocking the kitchen window. A plank pulled off in her hands with a loud screech, and she stood jangling with fear of discovery, looking about desperately for a place to hide. Seconds passed, but no one came running, and she put her attention on the opening she had made in the kitchen window.

Squeezing through the tight opening, Rachel almost fell on her back in the washtub. Turnips sat in the tub, immersed in water. On the cutting board beside them, several white ones squatted in the nest of their peeled skins. The flensing knife lay on the reed matted floor. The cooks had left in a hurry.

"Mama?" Rachel called, stepping from the kitchen to the dining hall. "Papa?"

No answer came, and no one was in sight. Had the mob carried them off as they had Uncle Joshua and his boys? That thought set her breathing quickly again. She rushed from room to room, crying out her sisters' and brothers' names.

The door to her parents' bedroom stood slightly ajar. "Mama? Papa?" she called out softly, when she noticed a peculiar, sticky odor wafting from the room. She stepped through the portal and then reeled backward with the force of her horror. Her eyes felt a palpable stab of pain and her legs lost all feeling. There before her, her mother lay on her back on the big canopied bed, the bed sheets crimson under her shoulders. A big red grin gaped under her jaw. Beside her on either side, Rachel's sisters lay, their heads thrown back, their necks split open raw and red. The family Bible lay open at their feet.

Rachel slammed hard against the door jamb, trying to retreat. It was then she saw her brothers, sitting on the floor with their backs to the wall, heads slouched forward, glossy veils of blood soaking their shirts, puddled in their laps. Father lay on his side at their feet, a knife impaled in his gashed throat, his hand still clutching the haft.

Despair and panic thickened in her chest. She heaved herself from the room, the horrid stink of blood clogged in her sinuses. In the passage, she collapsed. A cold fire rippled up and down her body, and she convulsed several times as the terror stained its images forever into her soul.

She heard footsteps, felt them through the floor. They were coming back! Like an animal, she sprang upright, all senses bright and humming. The voices came next, laughing voices. "He killed them"— a big guffaw sounded from the main stairway—"the Jew locked his family in the bedroom with him and cut their throats! He killed them all, afraid we would baptize them. You have to see this."

Rachel flew away from the laughter, reached the servants' stairwell and, edging quietly down the squeaky stairs, lurched out of the kitchen. In the servants' dining room, she stopped, paralyzed inside the nightmare. Her parents' bedroom was directly above her, and she felt the pressure of their deaths weighing down on her, forcing the air out of her lungs. *No!* She shook her head violently. Laughter burbled from upstairs and heavy footsteps thudded on the floorboards. *No!* She had to force herself to breathe. She pressed her palms to her eyes so forcibly her head lit up with a radiance bright as blood.

In the kitchen, the servants' stairwell squealed, and the footfalls came thumping down. "Killed his wife and children with his own knife!" a thick voice said. "Crazy Jew!"

Rachel began to tremble. They would find her now. They would slit her throat, and she would be with Mama and Papa again, with her sisters and brothers.

No! She wrenched herself free of her paralysis and bolted into the dining room and the main hall. The front door had been forced open and lay hanging from one hinge, the white woodmeat of the broken jamb gleaming in the sunlight. She jumped into the blazing day without thinking to peek first.

A figure knelt in the courtyard below, and she stopped as though she had slammed into a wall. It was one of the gardeners, and he was bent over an old horse whose belly had been slit open. When he saw her, he stood and waved urgently.

Behind Rachel, the laughter and heavy footfalls boomed from the dining hall. She scurried down the steps and into the arms of the gardener. "Child, they will kill you!" She shot a frightened glance over her shoulder; the gardener glanced up and down the courtyard, saw nothing in the open space large enough to hide the girl.

The gardener knelt and with both hands pulled out the blue, ropy mass of the horse's bowels. He pried open the long gash. "In here," he rasped. "You must hide in here. It will only be for a short time. Hurry—or your life is forfeit!"

Rachel knelt down before she could think. Only as she jammed herself into the hot, wet interior and the gluey ichor washed over her neck and face did she dread what she was doing. The fetid fluid drooled into her nostrils, and she choked, believing utterly that she would drown in horse bile. She shoved her face forward, free of the enwombing viscera, coughed and was able to breathe shallowly through the gaping belly.

The gardener pushed the slither of bowels close to the horse to hide the girl's face from view and bowed over the creature, bemoaning the loss of a beast too old to be stolen.

In the gummy heat, Rachel wept, her eyes pressed closed to keep out the burning syrups, and her teeth aching with the sobs beating against her locked jaw.

"You can come out now." The gardener's voice spoke loudly, assuring Rachel that the mob was no longer within earshot.

Even so, she did not move. The slippery interior that held her had cooled and congealed. Its embrace had become comfortable, and she might have fallen asleep. She was not sure. Maybe she was dreaming now. Her eyelids, glued shut with the drying jellies, would not open.

"Come out now, young mistress."

She moved her face, testing her wakefulness, and felt the stiffening tissues pull from her cheeks. She must be awake, she reasoned. But what was this crimson cloud she was watching? Inside was her father's muscular face and his red hand clutching the knife at his torn throat. And there was Mama lying on the bed with her daughters at her side, the red pipes of their open throats gleaming and sparkling. Was that their voices she heard sparkling? They were singing something. She could not hear them clearly. The faces of her brothers made noises, too, bent forward, their heads lowered in prayer.

"They are gone now. You are safe."

The startle-eyed faces of Uncle Joshua and his sons were also in the fiery cloud, the bloody rags of their penises stuffed in their mouths. Trying to pry open her stuck eyelids, to stop seeing the horror, she felt as if she were ripping fire from darkness, and she screamed and screamed—but there was no sound.

The gardener pulled open the rubbery flesh and reached into the slippery entrails for the girl. She slid out in a glim of blood and oily fluid, her body cauled in blue membranes, her face clotted with black curds.

The girl lay on the ground curled in the shape that had hidden her in the beast's belly. She lay still as a thing born dead.

"Get up now," the gardener coaxed. "You are safe. The Crusaders are gone."

But she did not stir.

Pitying her, the gardener lifted her in his arms and carried her across the courtyard and down the path of white stones to the water trough before the stables. All the good horses had been taken, the stalls charred from the small fires set in the hay. The wood was damp from the autumn rains, and the fires did not do much damage.

He lowered the girl into the water, and she startled like a baby. With her neck braced in his hand, he used his other hand to cup water over her face and wipe the mucus from her eyes and face. When her eyes winced open, she looked up and seemed to stare through him. He stood her up in the trough, but her legs wobbled, and he had to lift her out and sit her on the edge.

Soaked, the drapery of her garments stuck to the contours of her body. The gardener stood back, roused at the sight of her. "You are out of danger now," he said. "Will you come back to the house for dry clothes?"

The girl did not answer him. She appeared nearly blind, and he passed his hand before her face. She blinked but did not look at him.

"Perhaps it is best we remove this grimy garment," he said and began unbuttoning her chemise. She did not object, and his fingers trembled as he tugged at the buttons. He had saved her life, he reasoned as he peeled the wet cloth from her small breasts. The others were dead, but he had saved her life—and now he would at least inspect what he had saved.

Then the air blasted from his lungs, and he shot forward, falling to his knees before the half-naked girl, his hands bracing himself against her shins. His surprised face jerked around, and he saw a man in an iron gray beard rearing over him, the stables' dung-turning spade in his fist.

"Old Master!" the gardener gasped and stood up, the narrow rectangle of pain on his back throbbing as the shock wore off. "I saved her life. Praise God! Your granddaughter is spared."

The peasants who worked the fields and the servants who had fled the great house when the Crusader mob attacked came from hiding at the sight of the Old Master striding out of the forest. He had heard the clanging church bell and seen the smoke of the burning sheaves from his cottage on the hillside and had hurried down the slopes. The sight of the looted storehouse, the dead animals, the scorched servants' quarters had set a chill in his bones. He remembered as a boy hearing about the slaughter of the Jews in Worms and how eight hundred were martyred with the declaration of the *Shema* on their lips.

The servitors, wailing with the grievous reports of the evil that had befallen the estate and its proprietors, flocked around the Old Master as he emerged from the copse below the vineyards. The Old Master's worst fears babbled in the air around him, and he bellowed for silence. The peasants cowed, and the servants covered their faces in grief.

In the great house, the old man entered the master bedroom and was felled by the gory sight. With a hand over his eyes, he quoted the *Shema*, his confession of his religious faith, and crawled out of the room of his ruin on his knees. Blinded with anguish, he staggered from the house and wandered drunkenly until he came to the stables where his granddaughter Rachel was being stripped.

Striking the gardener furiously with the spade, the old man

heaved the tool aside, and covered his granddaughter's nakedness. She blinked at him as if she did not recognize him.

"Did she come from inside the house?" he asked the gardener.

The servant nodded and explained how he had hidden her from the mob in the belly of the dead horse.

The Old Master gently stood Rachel upright and helped to balance her. The afternoon rain had descended from the mountains in towers of purple thunderheads, and he led her to the orchard and the shelter of the gardener's shed. As big dollops of cold rain began to fall, two of the maids came from the great house with towels and dry clothes.

While the maids dressed Rachel, the Old Master went back to the great house, taking the gardener and several other peasants. At the old man's command, they took axes to the furniture and broke them to kindling. Then the old man read long passages from the house Bible and set piles of kindling alight in all the downstairs rooms.

The blaze that roared through the passages and up the stairwells consumed the house, undaunted by the long veils of rain sweeping out of the mountains. From the sanctuary of the gardener's shed, the Old Master and his granddaughter watched the flames gush from the windows and doorways. When the tile roof collapsed in a vortex of flaming cinders, the old man lowered his head and prayed yet again. Rachel stared intently, her eyes keenly focused, seeing the dead tongued with fire.

Gévaudan, Winter 1187

Corpses lay heaped in the snow, the tips of their noses, their lips, their cheeks gone, devoured by rats, the eyes taken by the crows. The old man paused over them and recited a few lines from the Bible. He no longer bothered reading whole passages for the dead. There had been too many in the past thirteen weeks of their trek. At the outskirts of each village it was the same—corpses heaped in the forest for the animals to feed upon. At first, he had even tried to bury them. But there were too many. Then he read pertinent passages for the dead over their bodies. But as the weather grew colder and his granddaughter thinner, there was no time for that.

After the great house had been lost, with all the gold coins and valuables stolen by the Crusaders, the Old Master had taken Rachel up the mountain slope to live with him in his cottage. But more Crusaders came south, and when they learned that there were Jews in the high meadow, they came looking for them. He and Rachel escaped at night and headed east, to Muret, where the old man knew a holy man. He had hoped that the holy man might be able to break the spell of silence that had muted Rachel since the horror. But outside Muret, the leaf-fall covered mutilated corpses, and the holy man was nowhere to be found.

The old man cut his beard and used the ax he had carried from the estate to work as a woodcutter in the forest villages, earning just enough to buy them old bread and stale cheese. Staying in any one place too long was dangerous. Everywhere, fanatical Crusader gangs roamed, sacking synagogues, murdering Jews. The old man's satchel contained the scroll of the Law copied in his own hand, the Bible given to him by his grandfather, and his tasseled vestment with the blue riband. Even the suspicion that this drifter and his comely granddaughter were infidels would be their doom let alone these artifacts of their faith.

So they lived in wattle huts in the forested hills, shivering beside open fires, gnawing roots and woodbark when there was no bread. Occasionally, the old man managed to kill a squirrel or a rat. The girl ate whatever he presented to her, and he was sometimes grateful, sometimes dismayed for that. Surely it would be better if she were dead, but he had not the strength to be a martyr. Even chopping wood and freezing in the snowfall was easier than doing what his son had done.

"We will go south," the old man told Rachel, "to the big cities, Nimes, Avignon, Marseilles. Surely the synagogues there have not been sacked. The bishops will have protected them, and we will find a place among our people."

Rachel said nothing. Nonetheless, the old man spoke to her as though she understood, as he was certain she did. "The bishops have protected the synagogues because they need us. Their Christian law forbids them from lending money to each other at interest—and none of them is Christian enough to lend money to their fellow Christians without interest. Ha! So, you see, their own greed protects us. They need us to lend them the money to finance their wars. All the kings of Europe honor and protect us. It is only the rabble that loathe us, for they envy the affluence we have earned with the blood of our exile."

Rachel listened intently, hearing her grandfather as though his voice were warbling through water. His face, too, was lit in diamonded brightness, as though he were staring at her through a glare of water. Something was terribly wrong with her. She knew that. But she did not know what was wrong, and no words offered themselves to explain anything, only a humming silence like the pressure of water against her ears.

The old man sorrowed at the sight of Rachel's perplexity. "Life will be good again," he promised her. "You will see. You are young. We will find you a good husband. You will have children and know joy again. And that—" He squeezed his granddaughter's icy hand, "That will be good. For happiness is our duty to God."

The Old Master continued to talk with Rachel as they wandered among the villages. He related what he knew about the places they visited, why they were situated where they were, what famous personages had dwelled there. He sang her songs and he told her the stories she had liked as a child, about his own childhood and about his grandparents, anything but the terror they had endured. The girl seemed to be listening, but the melancholy glow in her face shone even in the dark—and she never spoke.

Rachel did hear her grandfather. She was glad for the comfort of his resonant voice. But somehow she did not understand him. Why was he speaking to her in another language? She wanted to tell him to speak langue d'oc or even the Hebrew that she knew sufficiently well from listening to her brothers' lessons. But her voice was so very far away, and she was always so tired and cold. It took all her strength just to stay awake, walking and listening, abiding the cramps in her stomach and the needling pains when she went into the bushes to void herself.

Other voices drifted along the slushy roads. They were easier to understand. They were the prayers of her brothers, mumbled because their heads were lowered. At night, she stared up at the blue stars, and her eyes ached to see the beauty of such flowers too far away to pick.

Castle Valaise, Spring 1188

The black branches of the fruit trees looked woolly with white blossoms, and the wood thrush trilled loudly from the forest. The baroness sat in her litter, the mild wind ruffling the canopy that shaded her and the wimple that protected her neck. She hated drafts on her neck, for they made the muscles stiff and painful for her to turn her head. Lately, she had been turning her head a lot, glancing over her shoulders to be sure her knights were still with her.

Ailena breathed deeply of the fragrant air that the physician from Hereford claimed would help clear the pain in her joints. For two years now she had been drinking his febrifuges to quell the hot ache of her bones, and she had listened patiently to his discourses on humors, hoping to gain some insight into the searing flashes of pain that had made walking nearly impossible. His lectures about the liver as the seat of honor and the spleen as the footstool of laughter sounded as nonsensical to her as Maître Pornic's mumblings about God coming down as a white bird to bless Himself as His own son.

Even so, twice a day she drank the physician's concoctions of dried and pulverized liver of toad immixed with he-goat blood and dog urine. She lifted her hands and turned them before her, amazed at her fingers bent and twisted at odd angles, the knuckles swollen big and round as oak galls. Her hands looked like crushed sea crabs. No swills of dog piss were going to heal these hapless bones.

"Do you see the family?" she asked her companion.

Dwn, sitting beside the canopied litter on a stool, looked up from her embroidery. "Hellene is strolling the twins in the garden and Leora is with them."

"And her swain? Where is Harold?"

"I saw him with William earlier. I believe they're off riding, hunting I think."

"With Guy," the baroness muttered darkly. "My knights should be at my side. Harold especially. He wants Leora's hand, so why is he not cozening me as he did all last year?"

Dwn returned her gaze to her embroidery.

The baroness held up her hand mirror, to see behind without having to endure the hurt of turning her head. Indeed, William Morcar, who had always been within earshot before, eager to cater to her every whim, was nowhere to be seen. Harold Almquist, too, who still required her blessing to take his place in this household as Leora's husband, was gone. They were both landless knights who, without her indulgence, would have to seek employment elsewhere. Always before they had been solicitous of her, but recently they had been spending more of their time with Guy.

"Their shift of alliance speaks more loudly than my speculum," Ailena said and glanced at the aged face in the mirror. The sight of her rumpled visage appeared almost fungoid to her, like some pale, wrinkly tree growth. She dropped the mirror in her lap and pressed her swollen knuckles to her eyes. "They plot against me, Dwn."

"They dare not," her old friend consoled. "In the eyes of God and king, you are the rightful ruler."

"Ah, but in the eyes of men, I am but an old, bent woman." She flexed her fists angrily, and the pain felt as if it was made of iron.

Languedoc, Autumn 1188

The old man watched Rachel carefully. Today was the anniversary of the massacre in Lunel. For a year, they had wandered the countryside, precariously eking out a living. In the spring, he had found work in the vineyards doing what he knew well, pruning and grafting. But with the girl they could not stay long anywhere. Her flowering womanhood attracted the men, who became too inquisitive about her aristocratic bearing, her melancholy glow and her silence, which had not dimmed with the passing seasons. In the cities, where they had hoped to find thriving synagogues but found only gutted ruins, men of the lowest stations approached and enquired about her. Sometimes her silent, tristful stare was enough to drive them off; other times, that only intrigued them more and the old man had to dissuade them with tales of a curse, disease, madness, whatever they feared.

Rachel's beauty had brightened despite the hardships of their roofless life. Though this was merely her thirteenth autumn and she had spent the prior year living in the brush eating acorns, beech mast, and nettle soup, she had grown taller, more stately and ample. There was no hiding in the girlish garments they had saved from the estate her vivid body, the fullness of her breasts or her long legs. He made her wear his mantle, yet the way she carried herself challenged the manhood in every peasant who saw her.

To earn a meal from a farmer, the old man and his granddaughter had cleared the fallen apples of a small, sunny garth. The brown and withered fruit had been stacked in two large piles, where the farmer would cover them with bramble and, in the spring, shovel the redolent mulch into his vegetable garden. Throughout the chore, the old man had eyed Rachel, looking for signs that she knew what today signified, what had happened a year ago near their own apple garth.

At day's end, Rachel sat in the hollow trunk of a willow tree, eating the black bread and milk curds the farmer had paid them. The jarred mass of her dark hair bunched over the collar of the bulky mantle, and she brushed it out of her face as the wind steepened from over the twilit earthworks and wall-steads. How many times had he tried to shear those loosened tresses, to make her appear less comely, but when his knife came anywhere near her, she pulled away and her eyes burned like opals.

She remembered—she would never forget. He knew: every day for her was the anniversary.

Castle Valaise, Autumn 1188

The baroness knew by the look on his face that her son had found a way to defeat her. A goat-eyed, simmering hilarity played on his swarthy face as he advanced into the great hall of the *palais*. Immediately, she looked about for her men, and they were in place: William and Harold flanked her on the dais and Neufmarché's soldiers stood casually at the back, chatting jovially among themselves.

No one stopped Guy Lanfranc at the entry or even seemed to notice him, but to Ailena his purposeful stride and his narrow-eyed grin were warnings. She signed for the soldiers at the door to detain him, but they did not notice her. They were not accustomed to watching her every gesture with hawklike vigilance. For thirty years, she had administered her domain by direct command, not furtive hand-signals, and she regretted now not having demanded more attentiveness from her guards.

The castle's guildsmen, their apprentices, and their families and villeins packed the great hall for the Saint Fandulf's day blessing of their crafts by the local holy man, Maître Pornic. This was also to be the day that the merchants paid their burgage, the yearly rent for operating their shops in the castle bailey. Everyone of prominence in Valaise was gathered here, milling about before order was called and the ceremony begun with the address of the baroness.

Several of the merchants bowed upon seeing Guy and attempted to engage him in conversation, but he brushed them aside and continued his advance, not taking his gleeful stare off the dais. The baroness did not like the mocking smirk on her son's dark face. Did no one else see it? What else would make him leer so vividly but her doom?

Ailena looked to William Morcar, but he averted his eyes, pretending to be watching a petty squabble between two merchants' wives in the front rank. By this she knew she was in serious trouble. Alarm caught her breath at the back of her throat, and her heart fluttered when she looked to Harold Almquist, who had married her daughter not two months ago, and he, too, looked away. The ingrate! What had become of his oaths of fealty?

The baroness looked frantically to Neufmarché's soldiers at the back of the hall, trying to catch the eye of at least one of them. Always before, they had provided sufficient threat to keep her son and her dead husband's acerbic warmaster, Roger Billancourt, from attempting physically to oust her. But they were oblivious to the threat, lumped together like laughing jays by the door of the hall, not realizing yet that they had already been caged.

In the arched doorway, the baroness glimpsed the square-headed silhouette of Roger Billancourt and, behind him, the fair-haired Denis Hezetre and some men with javelins. The terrible moment of defeat had come—and here in front of all the community that her father had gathered and she had maintained. She nodded to the herald beside the dais, and he blew an exultant note on his trumpet that silenced the hall.

Before Ailena could speak, Guy leaped upon the dais and announced to the assembly: "On behalf of my dear mother, the baroness Ailena Valaise, I am happy to inform you all that she has been deeply moved by Archbishop Baldwin's tour of our Welsh domain this past spring, and, after much consideration, she has decided to accept his call to take up the Cross. The baroness will be departing this very day on a pilgrimage to the Holy Land, there to live out her natural life in devotion and prayer to our Lord and Savior Jesus Christ!"

Amazement thrashed through the gathering, and Guy raised both of his hands for silence. Behind him, the baroness willed herself to stand, to refute this preposterous claim, but her shock had jellied her legs. How dare he presume to exile her, the rightful ruler of this domain? Her outrage guttered the next instant, when she witnessed the entry of Roger Billancourt and the men from the barracks he had armed with javelins. They swiftly surrounded Neufmarché's soldiers and began herding them out of the hall.

"At this moment," Guy continued, when the astonished voices in the crowd had subsided, "a bevy of palmers from Saint David's awaits in the lists with a litter to bear my mother on her holy journey. In keeping with the simplicity of our Lord's humble life during His tenure on earth, the baroness will forego all her material possessions and proceed from here rich only in her faith."

Ailena pushed her bent figure upright, inflamed at this callous treatment, but Guy turned and faced her lockjawed glower with a cold smile. "No need to rise, Mother. I've arranged to have you carried out."

The baroness sat down, and her angry eyes searched the assembly for allies but saw only startled faces and Roger's men elbowing through the crowd with a litter on their shoulders. Only Maître Pornic seemed offended, but Denis Hezetre had come up beside him and was speaking urgently to him.

"Everything has been thought of, Mother," Guy said through his insolent grin, bending close so that his pug nose nearly touched her long profile. "You are old. The knights are afraid that if we wait for our Good Lord to take you, Neufmarché will have time to make this castle his own. Now you may depart with dignity, a holy woman on pilgrimage, honored by Church and people—or you may depart noisily and without grace. But either way, dear Mother, you will depart."

Ailena's shriveled mouth sneered with disdain. "Your hatred could never touch me. Vengeance for your father's death is what you want. But you'll not have it unless you kill me."

"Say a prayer for me at the Sepulcher." Guy's smile of exultant bitterness settled into a grimace, and he signaled for the litter.

"I will be back," she moaned. "Unless you kill me now, I will raise an army and I will be back to retrieve what is mine."

"I think not, Mother." With his own hands, he lifted the baroness and was amazed at how light she was. Her old companion Dwn, who had watched helplessly from beside the chair of state, cried out in alarm and reached to stop him. William Morcar took her by the shoulders and pulled her away.

Ailena did not struggle or cry out as the litter-bearers carried her off before the stunned assembly. She sat upright, erect with indignation, facing the dais from which she had been usurped. And her son watched gleefully, expecting her to screech with fury at any instant. But the only mark of mortification he saw was the black glare in her strangled eyes.

The pilgrims wore coarse robes and many had shaven heads. They carried tall staves topped with palms knotted into crosses. When they received the baroness in the bailey, they cheered with pious joy and thanked the Lord for so noble a companion on their long trek. In the beginning, they carried her litter buoyantly on their shoulders. But by day's end, when she had refused to join in their psalm-singing and frequent prayers at the sites of the numerous roadside shrines, when she scowled at all their cheerful attempts to engage her in friendly discourse, they soured on her. Only their Christian charity obliged them to give her one of their spare robes that night when the chill descended from the drafty stars.

Ailena shivered and gnawed her aching knuckles. Virulent wrath twisted her stomach, and she could barely swallow the acorn bread the pilgrims shared with her. The next morning, the palmers agreed that she should walk the mile to the next shrine as a form of penance. That outraged her, yet, despite the spiked burrs of pain in her joints, she hobbled that mile under the gloating stare of the burly sergeant whom her son had thoughtfully sent along as her escort.

Three days later, her body braided in pain, her fine clothes bedraggled, Ailena reached the north bank of the Usk. There, in a Celtic chapel with a small bellcote, she had hidden a cache of gold coins several years earlier, after Roger Billancourt had almost succeeded in locking her out of her own castle. A faithful porter and several of Neufmarché's soldiers in the bailey spared her that indignity, but from that day on she arranged to have funds cached outside the castle in the event that she was ever exiled again. Most of the money she sent across the Channel as interest-free loans to her cousins in the Périgord. Her ancestral jewels she hid in a niche of her husband's vault, sardonically delighted that his corpse should become the guardian of her fortune. And to several local chapels she contributed small statuary whose wooden bases contained secret drawers in which she concealed gold coins.

At the Celtic chapel on the Usk, Ailena feigned remorse for her selfishness and lingered over her prayers in the candle-flickering dark after the others had left. The burly sergeant, impatient for supper, left her to finish her Hail Marys alone. As soon as he stepped out, she removed her gold, slipped the pouches into drapes of her robe, and unobtrusively joined the others.

With two of those gold coins, Ailena hired a bull-necked ferryman to accompany the pilgrims across the Usk and make sure that the sergeant did not arrive on the other side. During the crossing, the raft sweeled hard into the current, the ferryman lost his balance, desperately clutched at the sergeant, and the two fell overboard. Only the ferryman surfaced.

Ailena knelt with the others and prayed aloud for the sergeant's soul.

Arles, Winter 1188

The Rhône, gray as cold iron, harped on the gravel beds, singing with the soft, guttural voices of the dead. As usual, the dead sang morosely the Hebrew songs of the holy days. Rachel did not understand most of the words, but she knew they were chanting about God's love and the history of the people. The swollen vowels slurred among the reeds and the mizzling rain.

"Rachel, come away from the water," her grandfather called. He sat by the yolk-light of a small embering fire in a cobwebbed nook of a merchant's tomb. They lived here in the ancient graveyard of Arles, where Roman ruins lay scattered among the ladysmock and rushes of the riverbanks. "The rain is coming down harder. Come here and sit with me."

Rachel turned away from the singing river and climbed over stone nests and through tall tassels of grass. She sat beside her grandfather on the cold step of the vault and stared out over the tilted headstones weavy with creepers and vines. Her stomach hurt, and without the singing of the dead to distract her, hunger twisted sharply.

"Eat this," Grandfather said, handing her a waxy rind of cheese he had earned yesterday digging a grave. He had thought to share it with her, but seeing her hands fisted over her stomach he wanted her to have it all.

Rachel looked down at the cheese rind in her grandfather's hand. She took it, bit off one end, and passed the rest to him. She wanted to tell him to eat the rest. He was tired from digging all day. He looked skinny to her, and she wished he would grow his beard again. But her voice would not rise up from the far place inside her.

The old man touched her smudged cheek with his callusbarked hand. "We have shared everything so far, child. I will eat this. But you must speak to me. You must say a word to me."

Rachel stared at his beseeching expression with the plaintive glow bright in her face. She understood what he had said, though she had heard it through fathoms of depth. She wanted to speak to him, if only to say "Eat—" Her mouth opened, but the word would not come. Instead, the humming silence pressed more heavily on her, and her face closed.

Her grandfather patted her shoulder gently, took the cheese she offered and gnawed it disconsolately.

Arles, Spring 1189

Occasional mourners came to this field of graves by the river-bank, but for the most part the large tract of headstones, pillared vaults, and stone crosses was empty. A few scavengers drifted among the mounds, refugees like themselves who feared ghosts and the miasmal diseases less than they feared the scrutiny of the townspeople. But the old man's raised ax kept them at a distance.

Common sense as well as the ache of abused muscles and the dizzy spells that came with silver streaks of angels' wings in the air and shooting stars told the old man that he could not live much longer digging holes all day and eating scraps. Yet he refused to let the girl muddy herself with grave dirt. Instead, she plaited hats from the rivergrass. The hunchbacked yardmaster, who paid the old man in moldy bread and rancid cheese for the holes he dug, gave them an extra crust for the hats.

God of Israel, the old man prayed daily, hourly, *Creator of the world, break my miserable body but spare my granddaughter. Return her to her people, to a good husband, where she can fulfill your promise to Abraham and know the fulfillment of children.*

Once, he had ventured through the sprawling city with her bundled in his mantle, her head cowled, seeking others like them-selves. Casual queries to old women in the marketplace informed him that, in the autumn of '87, the Jews had been expelled from the Free City of Arles after Jerusalem fell to the infidels. The syna-gogues, some two hundred years old, had been torn down and their stones incorporated into the lofty cloisters and portals of Saint Trophime's Cathedral.

So the old man returned to the graveyard, grateful at least that there was work for him. In the evenings, he would read aloud from the Bible to his granddaughter. Since his hands were usually too stiff to turn the pages, she would hold the holy book in the firelight and follow him silently. As a girl, she had never learned to read Hebrew, but following her grandfather's black fingernail as it moved among the words, she began to learn. Now and then, to his utter surprise and her own, she would even try to pronounce phrases aloud.

This impressed the old man and gave him strength. Inside her hurt, she was awake and living, eating not just the scraps they earned but also the food of the spirit. At night, staring up past the bat squeaks, he found solace in the smoldering stars.

Arles, Summer 1189

Rachel sat on the ground by her grandfather while he dug graves, and she plaited hats and threaded their brims with wild flowers. He worked slowly, pausing frequently under the hot sun to lift the grass hat she had made for him and wipe his brow. Often after these arduous days, he fell asleep immediately after sharing their meal of dandelion soup and berries, too exhausted even to read from the Bible.

With the sun lingering over the ruins' broken parapets, Rachel wandered the lonely tracts along the river, gathering berries from the shrubs that flourished between the crypts. Not far from the graveyard, the pillar stumps and algal-blotched pools of the Roman baths stood among river willows and poplars. In the long, fanned light of sunset, the eroded faces in the stones watched her serenely. And the peace she had known on her secret knoll in Lunel glittered upward in her soul, like a silver bubble in the cold, pressured depths of her horror.

The baroness lifted her crabbed hand with its misshapen fingers to block the blaze of the setting sun, and she sat up straighter in her litter. At her signal, the bearers lowered her to the ground, and the knight she had hired to protect her stepped closer and blocked her view. She angrily shooed him out of the way and squinted into the red glare.

Ahead, at the end of an avenue of chestnuts, the ruins of the Roman bath held for a moment among its arches and vaulted spaces the bloated sun, gaseous and quavery. Ailena had been drawn here by the local rumor that at twilight the oily waters of the baths relieved the pain of hot joints. The torment of her gnarled bones had worsened with the difficulty of her journey south, and she was eager for relief.

A young woman stood silhouetted against the fiery sky. The sight of her regal bearing and intent profile assailed the baroness with strange and sudden memories, and she rose up on her knees, ignoring her pincering pain to see more clearly the shadow before her.

The surprised knight at her side took her arm and helped her stand. Glims of remembrance spurted through her as she gazed at the tall young woman and her halo of loosened hair. "Who is she?"

"A waif, my lady."

"No. Look at her."

"She is dressed in rags."

The baroness reached out her twisted hand toward the shade, and her wrinkled face went entirely slack, stunned by the brightenings of time in that dark shape.

When the shadow fell over him, the old man was bent over his spade, up to his shoulders in the dark earth, groaning over an impacted stone. He knew at once it was a doomful shadow, for it carried a sword. Tilting back his hat, he peered up at the sun-crowned stranger.

"Is she your daughter?" the shadow asked.

The old man looked at Rachel, who sat at the lip of the grave, her hands tangled in the ribbon grass she had been plaiting, her face unperturbed in the shade of her wide-brimmed hat. "My granddaughter," he managed. He spoke so rarely, his voice sounded strange.

"Come out of there."

The old man leaned his spade against the earth wall and obediently crawled out of the hole. When he stood up, he confronted a surly-faced cavalier in a short, lightweight tunic brown as old blood, with a belt of yellow leather around his hips, from which hung a dagger and broadsword. "Gather your possessions, bring your granddaughter, and come with me."

"Where are we to go?" the old man enquired, and the surly knight pointed with his chin for him to hurry.

Rachel rose at her grandfather's beckoning, and, after they had picked up the frayed travel bag that contained their few clothes,

the scroll of the Law and the Bible, they followed the cavalier.
They had no choice but to follow, though, for a moment, David
felt weary enough to consider defying the cavalier and accepting
the grave he had dug as his own. Only his concern for Rachel
made him comply.

The knight led them out of the graveyard to the chestnut-lined
avenue that ran directly into the center of Arles. A cart with a
sleepy driver awaited them at the cemetery gate. Nearby, the
hunchbacked yardmaster sat in the shade of a black cypress watching them and smiling toothlessly. The cavalier instructed them to
get in.

"Where are you taking us?" the old man asked cautiously.

The cavalier turned his back on them without answering and
strode to a horse tethered in the shade of a chestnut. The cart
trundled down the wide Roman road, past the ruins of the baths,
and through a gate in the truncheon-lined ramparts that opened
into the narrow, winding streets of Arles.

As in all villages and cities, the crown of the street rose above
the filthy gutters, into which householders dumped their slops and
refuse. In the summer heat, the stink stung eyes and sinuses.
Rachel and the old man, accustomed to the open air at the city's
edge, gagged.

Timber-and-plaster houses and open-fronted shops with large,
gaudy signs protruding from their lintels fell away, and the street
widened to an avenue. Stone buildings appeared, fronted by
ancient mammocked trees. Before one such stone house with a
small garden for a yard, the cart stopped, and the cavalier, who
had been following behind on horseback, ordered them out.

They passed under an iron-gated arch with a lionhead at its
keystone and followed a curved path of blue flags to a large wood-
en door strapped with iron. The cavalier led them past that, along
a pebbly path that ribboned among flowering hedges to a smaller
portal at the side obscured by shrubbery.

A well-groomed maid in an embroidered gown and tightly
braided hair received them into the gloomy house, and the cavalier departed. Through dark and fusty stone passages, the maid
guided them to a vaulted apartment with walls blackened by the
smoke from a vast fireplace. She opened the wooden shutters of

the tall windows, and the slashing sunlight revealed above the hearth venerable trophies of the hunt: antlers, the head of a bear, hefty boar tusks, and an array of hunting weapons used by departed generations.

The old man regarded his granddaughter apprehensively. This was the first large house they had entered since that monstrous day nearly two years ago when their own great house had become their family's pyre. Rachel stood before a sturdy chair, absently running her hand over its polished back and looking about with curiosity but not alarm.

"You are my guests," a husky, splintered voice spoke from the doorway. "Please, sir, be seated. Young woman, come to me."

Two servitors carried in an elderly woman seated in a riding chair. They placed the chair beside a window, on a platform built for it, and departed. Dressed in a wimple and a shiny emerald robe festooned with silk blossoms, the old woman seemed a noble personage. With a hand whose bones had been twisted by disease almost to a fist, she signed for David to sit in the bolstered chair facing her and for Rachel to approach.

"Do not be afraid, child. Come here."

Rachel looked anxiously to her grandfather.

"Obey me!" the dame said sharply.

Rachel started and approached the scowling woman.

"Stand here in the light. Turn around." The dame's dark eyes scrutinized her, gleaming with fascination. She pushed out of her chair, straightened painfully, and limped to Rachel. Her clawlike hands seized the young woman's face and tilted it back into the sunlight. A gasp of satisfaction escaped her. "Where are you from, girl?"

Rachel stared diffidently from the corner of her eye at her grandfather.

"Answer me! Where are you from?"

"Lunel," the old man spoke.

The dame frowned at him. "Is the girl dumb?"

"She has not spoken in two years—since she lost her family."

"Then she can speak." The dame nodded with satisfaction and clasped Rachel's hair in her bent fingers, examining the texture of the black strands and red filaments in the sunlight. "Gascony. You are a long way from there. Tell me, young woman, why have you come to Arles?"

"Your worship," the grandfather spoke, "we—"

"Silence! I want to hear the girl speak. You have a tongue in your head, child. Use it. What is your name?"

Rachel stared timorously at the dame, searching inwardly for her voice and finding only silence humming with dread.

The dame squeezed Rachel's cheeks in her fierce grip and stared hard into the back of her eyes, engaging the fear there. "You will speak to me when I address you. I will hear your voice now. What is your name?"

Rachel's mouth opened and worked but made no sound. Her eyes widened with alarm at the ire she saw in the old woman's face.

"Speak, you wastrel!" the dame shouted at her. "Speak or I will have your tongue ripped from your head!"

The old man shot up and stepped to his granddaughter's side. "Stop this, I beg of you. Why are you doing this to her? Who are you?"

"Be still and sit down," the dame commanded.

"No, my lady." The grandfather glared hotly. "Though we look no better than peons, we are not peasants to be bandied among your questions and ordered about."

"Shall I remove him?" a stern voice queried from the doorway.

The grandfather stared defiantly at the cavalier.

"No," the dame answered, more quietly. "I will call if I need you." She leveled a chill stare at the old man. "Tell me this girl's name and how she has come to be mute."

"Her name is Rachel. I am her grandfather, David Tibbon, a landowner from Lunel."

The dame offered her hand. "Help me back into my chair, David Tibbon. My bones are too weak to stand for very long, and I sense your story is a long one."

David complied, then took his place by his granddaughter's side. "Why have you brought us here?"

"I will tell you that after I hear your story. Please, sit down and tell me how a landowner from Lunel came to be digging graves in Arles."

David and Rachel sat, and the old man began to speak. Rachel heard his words from far away at first, as if they came warbling through water, but as the story approached the horror, the words rang louder. Her ears burned with the vibrancy of her grandfather's deep voice, and her heart beat in hot, hurtful blows under her collarbone. When he described what had become of their family, she saw them again—not as she witnessed them in her appalling and paralyzing memory of their deaths—she saw them again but differently. Her grandfather's pitying tale, with all the terrible loss and outrage spoken into words, stabbed her numbness alive and burst the cold pressure that had locked up her voice.

In a gush of impacted grief and rage, a raw, black, fiery cry ripped from Rachel's throat; she fell forward, sobbing, curled up on the floor amid her convulsive tears.

Rachel wept for hours. The dame had her servitors carry the young woman to a bed, where she lay wracked with sobs, draining the ocean of grief that had drowned her soul two years before. While she cried, her grandfather sat at her side, weeping with her, clutching her hand and softly calling her back into the world.

Slowly, the mournful spasms passed, the waves of weeping ebbed, and the girl plunged into a remorseless sleep. David lay down beside her and dozed, his curiosity and dread of this great house and its bone-warped dame overcome by exhaustion.

The dame remained seated in the vaulted apartment of hunting trophies, staring out the window with inward-seeing eyes, smiling to herself. Rachel's tears pleased her greatly. Where there was pain, there was feeling—and feelings could be shaped. Despite the terror she had endured, the girl was not dead inside, and so there was yet hope for a new life.

The chamber glowed amber with afternoon light when Rachel woke. The dense depths that had enclosed her had thinned away to layers of watery horizons. She felt lighter, more vibrant, cleansed. When she stood up, her limbs moved freely, unfettered by the weariness she had carried across France. Only her stomach ached, but that was the hollow pang of hunger, not the black, indigestible metal of suffering that had lain inside her belly all these months. She had cried herself free of that. Or most of it. Deeper inside, there was still an ugly weariness, but it seemed bearable now. Amazement glimmered in her: Was that all she had needed this whole time, simply to hear the horror spoken about in words that defined it as evil, that made her experience of the atrocity real, placing it outside of her and in the past?

She looked about the unfamiliar chamber at the wide bed where her grandfather slept, at the thick paned window and the pastel frescoes of a battle adorning the plaster walls.

"Grandfather," she called to David quietly, and for a bright, vital moment she felt dizzy with the freedom of her own voice. She lost contact with everything for that one precarious flash and felt the depths again widening under her. Quickly, she sat down on the edge of the bed, and the golden light of the room restored her newfound clarity. "Grandfather, wake up. We must find out why we are here."

David winced awake, sat up, and rubbed the sleep from his face with his thick hands. "I dreamed you were speaking to me."

Rachel smiled; that sight dropped the old man's hands into his lap. "God has restored my voice, Grandfather. I . . . I can speak again."

David seized her shoulders, peered into her face, not seeing the somnolent shine in her features anymore. "A miracle!"

"Oh, yes, a miracle," she said with a sad smile, feeling her voice in the roots of her teeth, hearing it echo across the horizons of death far back inside her.

David and Rachel returned once more to the hall with the vast fireplace and hunting trophies and found the dame still sitting where they had left her, her twisted hands locked in her lap. Rachel curtsied, saying in a slim, unsteady voice, "Your kindness— in bringing us here—has cleared my heart of much sorrow. I thank you—for myself and for my grandfather."

The dame nodded appreciatively, and a satisfied grin curved her severe lips. "You have both suffered terribly for no wrong. But now that you are rested, I would see you in a more fair countenance." The old woman rang a bell attached to her chair, and her servitors appeared. "See that my guests are bathed, clothed, and well fed. Then return them here."

David held up both of his blackened hands and bowed his head humbly. "Great lady, you have heard our story. You know now how terribly we have been reduced. What possible service can such unfortunates as we render you?"

"You will learn of that after I have seen you properly clothed and the famished expressions gone from your faces. Go, we will speak again at nightfall."

"Lady . . . please," Rachel spoke, giddy, emboldened by her new freedom. "We know not even your name . . ."

"That we may thank God for your munificence," David added.

"I am the baroness Ailena Valaise," the dame said, staring at her with half-opened eyes, trying to see Rachel without the tear-streaked stains on her face. "I cannot tell you my story, for it has not yet been told. I am what I cannot say. I tell you only this: that I have brought you here into my house because it is you, dear Rachel, who must help me say it."

The baroness sat with her eyes closed, her face lifted to the sun, feeling the heat soak into her bones. The journey from Wales had been a trying one, but now, all that suffering had been redeemed by Rachel. How poignant that she should be a Jewess! That only enriched the irony of the strategy she had been developing since last evening, when she first spied the young woman among the ruins of the baths. All night she had lain awake, amazed by her own amazement. It was not a delusion: the girl looked exactly as she herself had looked forty-five years earlier.

During the night, when the possibilities first occurred to her that there might be some use for this ghost of her childhood, she wondered if perhaps the child merely resembled a vague memory of herself in her last year of happiness, before her father died. But today, having examined the young woman in direct sunlight, she had seen the truth: Rachel had the same features, complexion, hair, and bearing. She had known at once the night before, even in silhouette, that this young woman was no peasant, her carriage was not that of a field worker. And she recognized immediately that the traits Rachel bore came from Aquitaine, very near the Périgord where Ailena had been sired. The long, straight nose, the swollen upper lip, the dimpled chin—those features were common there. But the combination of them all in the precise proportions of her own youthful countenance was nothing less than miraculous.

The baroness's creased face crinkled happily at the thought of God abetting her revenge. Since her son had ousted her from her castle, she had been planning to return. Originally, she had intended to hire mercenaries and besiege her own castle. But her bones had become more inflamed with each bumpy day of travel, and the cost of such a campaign would surely be her life. She decided then that the money she had been sending her cousins in the Périgord for years in anticipation of exile at the hands of her enemies should be sent to the king. He needed money for his adventures. In exchange, she would petition him to claim Castle Valaise for his own by escheat. That would turn Guy out into the world as landless as his father had been when he forced her to marry him.

But now, she had a more satisfying and sinister plan. The same God who had killed her father and who had surrendered her to a cruel husband had now delivered to her this veritable twin from her past. The justice of it, the splendid ingenuity of it all, made her show her teeth to the sun for the first time in years.

Rachel sat at the table of the dining hall fingering the delicate lace on the close-fitting bodice she had been given to wear with a delicate blue gown and soft shoes. Tears stood in her grandfather's eyes at the sight of her pleasure to be wearing again garments that, in happier times, she had taken for granted. But he swallowed those tears. He did not want her to see him grieved by their losses, fearing that that would again inspire her own grief. They had mourned enough. Whatever the baroness's motives, the joy that she had given Rachel was the answer to his endless prayer.

On the table lay the remnants of their meal: bread so fresh it steamed as they broke it, rabbit in raisin sauce, and buttery peas with onions. And, in goblets shaped like birds' heads, there was wine, which David recognized as the very finest, from Saint Pourcain in Auvergne.

The fragrant bath, the good food, and the wine thawed Rachel's numbness, and she looked at her grandfather with a brilliance in her eyes he had not seen since the horror. In the fresh green tunic he wore with the brown sash, he looked almost as she remembered him from before. His beard was shorn, but the wine had eased the fatigue and concern that had troubled his features, and she recognized the benign patriarch of her childhood.

The Bible lay on the table, where David had placed it after reading a psalm in gratitude. Rachel opened it and read aloud, "Isaac spoke to Abraham his father and said, 'Look, Father, here is the wood and fire for the sacrifice—but where is the lamb?'"

David laid his hand on Rachel's. "Yes, Granddaughter, where is the lamb? The baroness has cleansed us, dressed us up, and fattened us. What sacrifice does she have in mind?"

"Shall we run away?" Rachel looked to the doorway that led to the kitchen. "The cavalier is nowhere in sight, and the servants will not stop us."

"Where would we run, child? Even if we are not pursued, there is only misery awaiting us out there. Whatever the noble dame wants of us, the sacrifice can be no greater than what we have already offered the Lord."

"You will be mine for as long as I live," the baroness informed David and Rachel when they sat before her in the hall beneath the hunting trophies. Evening glowed purple in the tall windows, and bird songs tinkled in the cooling garden beyond. "In return for obeying me, you will have the very best food, clothing, and shelter. You will never again suffer persecution for your faith. And when I die, you will inherit a coffer of jewels sufficiently valuable to keep you in comfort all your lives."

David bowed his head humbly. "Baroness, for what service are you so generously rewarding us?"

Ailena's proud face tilted backward. "Complete and utter obedience during my lifetime."

"We are faithful Jews—"

"I will not ask you to murder or steal. Nor will Rachel's chastity be compromised. Menial work and hard labor will never be demanded of you. But, for whatever years are left me, you will conduct yourselves as I command."

David's brows knitted pensively. "And what do you command of us?"

"I will arrange for you to journey by sea to the Holy Land—to Tyre, the one city still held by Christian forces. You will bear letters from me that will enable you to acquire a house of stature equal to this one. There, you will await me."

David and Rachel exchanged amazed looks. In the silence, bird songs echoed in the darkening room. "Baroness," David finally spoke, "the journey to the Holy Land is a dangerous one."

The baroness's eyes seemed to glitter in the gloom. "Are your lives in the boneyard less dangerous?"

Ailena sat alone in the darkness, staring out her window at the dusty stars. For the first time since that cruel day nine months earlier when she was usurped, her mind toiled with more than rage. Strategies branched like lightning in the smoked dark of her brain, each bright fork lighting up new depths where smaller lightnings flashed, revealing all the tiny details that would have to be fulfilled for her grand plan to work.

For a moment, the complexity of the idea overwhelmed her. So much had to be accomplished—would there be time? Death gnawed at her bones already. And that was what most infuriated her: that her son—as hatefully as she had treated him for the sins of his father—would cast her out in her last days. The kingdom would have been his anyway; he had only to abide her malice a short while longer. But now that she had been humiliated, now she must live; now she must defy the sharp rats' teeth chewing on her tendons and live to create an enduring vengeance.

With that determination, Ailena relaxed. In the lightless room, a grandmotherly peace composed the wrinkles of her old woman's face. Her alert eyes clicked with starlight as she imagined the minute workings of her revenge.

o o o

Mediterranean Sea, Summer 1189

"God is punishing me for our deception," David moaned and clutched at the silken ropes of his berth. Through the gallery window of the cabin, sunlight glistened on the spume of the rolling sea. Flying fish skipped over the sparkling swells on translucent wings, and red robes of sargassum weed drifted by. David lay on his back, mouth lolling open, eyeballs rolling in his head.

Rachel comforted him with a damp sponge. The surging of the ship did not disturb her. "Grandfather, try to sleep again. Perhaps the sea will be calmer when you wake."

David lurched upright and sat with his head in his hands. "No more sleep. I feel I am smothering. Help me on deck, Rachel. Perhaps the wind will dispel this qualm."

Rachel unhooked the satin ropes of the berth and took her grandfather's arm as he lowered himself from the bed. Together, they staggered across the wide, handsomely appointed cabin and out the door. Rachel closed the door behind them and followed David up the companionway to the deck.

No sooner had the hem of her robe vanished through the hatchway than two barefoot men in torn trousers emerged from the hold. It led down into the vast cargo bay and the rowing benches. The two men, both rowers, had been taking turns watching the cabin, waiting for a time when it would be vacant. One rower was wizened and knotty, with a big nose and big ears; the other was dark, burned nearly black by the sun, with a weedy mustache and buckteeth.

"Watch the companion ladder," the hoary one said, entering the cabin and going immediately for the chest at the foot of the berth.

"And leave you to filch the best for yourself?" The charred one shook his head and followed. "We're in and out like the butcher's knife. Hurry now. They'll not be long on that pitching deck."

The chest they rifled contained only lady's garments, none of the coin or gems they had felt sure to find in so stately a cabin. "Be tidy, simpleton," the wizened one said as they returned the clothing, "or they'll know they was plucked."

"And they'll not know when their gold be gone?" The mustached one sneered and hurried to the other chest across the cabin. "Who's the simpleton?"

The second chest had only apparel and a sheaf of letters. The men searched under the carpet and the bolsters of the chairs. "Here's the goose," the dark one whispered, lifting the feather mattress from one of the two berths and exposing a tooled leather sack. He unthonged it, lifted the flap, and removed a scroll and a book bound in brown tawed hide.

The thieves opened both articles and squinted at the black, flame-shaped letters. "Is it Latin?" the mustached one asked.

"No. Not Latin. This be heathen writing."

"Turk writing? Methought those two looked queer for nobles."

"No, idiot. This be Jew writing. I seen it on their temples, whence they take the Christian babes to drink their blood. The captain must know of this."

On deck, David leaned over the rail with a dozen other pilgrims. Rachel stood behind him with a comforting arm on his back, watching shearwaters beat across the long, slow swells. To either side of them, two priests in black cassocks bent over the rail groaning, and David smiled to himself. Perhaps this illness was a blessing after all: because the Body of Christ was kept locked away so that it would not end up floating in vomit, David and his granddaughter were spared for now the ignominy of having to accept the gentiles' sacrament.

Water splashed the back of his neck, and he lifted a dizzy head to see another priest blessing the sea-sick pilgrims with holy water. Beyond the priest, on the high deck, the captain stood with his mates and two grimy sailors. David's eyes widened as he saw that they were examining the scroll of the Law from his cabin.

"Grandfather—what's wrong?" Rachel asked as he pushed away from the rail.

"Say nothing, Rachel," he mumbled, his mind churning. "Follow me now and say nothing."

David moved as quickly as his wobbly legs allowed and mounted the stairs to the high deck. "Captain, how have you come upon that scroll? Answer me direct!"

The captain, a narrow man in a black commander's vest and a velvet cap, cocked an eyebrow. "This is the writing of the Jews. It was found in your cabin by these rowers."

"What were they doing there?" David asked, not disguising the alarm in his voice or face.

"We was passing," the wizened one replied. "The door were open and we sees this scroll and book upon the bed. Were none of our concern but that the roll of the ship dropped it to the floor and opened it. When we spied the heathen writing we brung it here."

"Liar!" David cried. "That scroll and that book were both well secured beneath my mattress."

"Then you do not deny they are yours?" the captain queried. "What are cousins of the baroness Ailena Valaise doing with Jewish scripture?"

"Conveying them to the Holy Land," David answered hotly.

"Then you are Jews!" the captain shrilled. "You'll damn us all in the eyes of God!"

"You will indeed be damned," David agreed, "but not for us being Jews, for we are not. We are cousins of the baroness, as she herself informed you. But—" He hesitated, looking wildly at Rachel. "We are also envoys of the . . . archbishop. It was he who selected us for this dangerous charge, which we had hoped to complete in secret, with no jeopardy to any others but ourselves."

"What is this rant?" the captain demanded.

"What you hold is a Jewish talisman outfitted with a heathen curse that destroys those who are exposed to it for very long. The Jews—damn their eyes—the Jews have been using this for generations to sow strife among the Christian kingdoms. The archbishop got hold of this during the sacking of the French synagogues after Jerusalem fell. We are charged with conveying it to the Holy Land, where the Temple knights will use it against the Saracens."

The captain closed it gingerly and passed it to his mate. "Throw it into the sea."

"No!" David shouted. "No—that would only imperil your ship. The talisman must be taken directly to our enemy, upon whom its evil will work for the glory of Christ." He took the scroll from the mate, who eagerly gave it up. "No one else must know of this. Let the risk be entirely mine and this saintly woman's." He nodded to Rachel, and she bowed her head solemnly. "We are blessed by the archbishop himself and so protected."

The captain stepped back charily and raised a hand to block his face from the scroll. "Take it out of my sight. Should any harm even threaten this ship, I will burn it myself." He glared at the two rowers. "Have them tarred at once. They will be cast ashore on the morn in Sicily."

David ushered Rachel down the stairs ahead of him and hugged the scroll to his chest, chanting under his breath a prayer of thanksgiving to the one God.

"Your deception was wonderful," Rachel whispered jubilantly when they were alone in their cabin. "Your story saved the Torah *and* our lives."

David carefully stowed away the scroll and the Bible and then collapsed on his berth, his arm over his eyes. "That was no story," he moaned. "That was the sickness talking in me."

Rachel nodded compassionately and patted his head.

"It was so, Granddaughter!" David insisted vibrantly, peering out from under his arm.

"Of course, Grandfather," Rachel humored him.

"I would not lie about my faith—" David emphasized by staring intently at her before covering his eyes and groaning. "I dare not speak such blasphemous lies about the Law. I gave my voice to my sickness—and my sickness saved us."

David urged Rachel not to go on deck. The captain arranged to have food and water brought to their cabin, and David, groaning with nausea, enjoyed her comfortings. But when he slipped into deep slumber, she sat in the gallery at the rear of the cabin and opened the windows.

Rachel loved the sea. The crisp wind with its briny redolence filled all the chambers of her lungs with brightness and charged her limbs with vivid strength. Under her fingers, driven into the oak of the sill, sea minerals glinted with the same rainbow hues she saw in the spindrift lashing off the waves. But, best of all, she loved the embracing sensation of the ship's flight as the prow crashed into the swells and the sea picked up the stern so high she felt as if she were flying. Then the bow wave poured outboard with a rushing roar, and the ship reeled down into the sea's trough.

This was the only ship she had known, and she had learned all she could about it on the docks at Arles before they sailed. It was called an usciere and was among the largest transports in the world, thirty full strides long, eight wide, with two masts and two complete decks. On both sides of her bow, large eyes had been crudely painted, and on her flat stern a horse's head. In harbor, Rachel had seen the giant stern ramps lowered and horses marched into the hold. Often during the journey she heard them neighing, as unhappy as her grandfather with their flight over the sea.

The noises of the journey spellbound Rachel. The cricketing of the timbers, the rigging snapping and whistling, the cough of the waves all spoke to her of mystery, of everything that could not be known but could be spoken of in the near-speech of the sea and the wind. Only when the pilgrims began to sing and their dolorous hymns rose and fell among the sparking flints of the ocean breeze did the hollow roar of the crashing bow sound sinister. Death trumpets bleated in the broken swells. Whatever happiness could dwell on earth fled into the blue silence, and all the layerings of sound, full of ghostly speech, chilled, went cold inside her head; and suddenly she was again in the dark tunnels of the oak woods, numb under the frost-fiery rays of snow shooting through the branches, her stomach hurting, her eyes aching with frozen tears locked inside her by the gruesome sight of her dead family.

Rachel closed the windows on the pilgrims' praise of their god of love. Hands over her ears, she crept to her berth, managed one difficult sob, and lay there listening to the silence formed in her blood by horses crying.

Rome, Autumn 1189

Ailena sat still in her crux of pain. Every move sparked tiny searing fires in her bones. To minimize the painful jostling of her body during her travels, she had bound her joints with tight bandages and was obliged to sit rigidly erect, legs and arms stiff. But now her nose itched, and scratching it would cost her a moment's century of pain. To distract herself from the itch, she put her mind on the city outside the window and dwelled on all that it signified.

The baroness sat in a small fort in the Torre delle Milizie close to Trajan's market. Fortresses toothed the skyline, overshadowing the ancient buildings, which long ago had outlived their usefulness. Now rival gangs from those fortresses roamed the winding alleys and lanes of the tense, shadow-strewn city and clashed in the markets and piazzas. The Curia, representing the political power of the pope, fought for dominance with the Republic, who were Rome's aristocrats; and the commune, a powerful coalition of guildsmen and leasehold farmers, defied both the pope and the nobles. Almost daily, riots erupted on the hilly avenues, and partisans of all groups were garroted, or stabbed, or hanged from the skinny trees that sprouted on most street corners.

Ailena had come to this tortured city to fulfill a small but important facet of her strategy. If she survived the journey to Tyre, if she lived long enough to train Rachel to be Ailena Valaise, to know all that she knew, and even if she could successfully arrange an appropriate miracle to explain the restoration of her youth, still she would require the validation of a higher authority. So she had come to Rome to buy the pope's blessing.

That the Holy Father's blessing could be won with wealth Ailena had learned early from her father, whose family had gained title and land by supporting the house of Frangipani against the Pierleoni in their rivalry for the papacy. Alas, the current Vicar of Christ belonged to the rival family, so Ailena had arranged to meet with a powerful cardinal who had influence with the pope.

Giacinto Bobo-Orsini was eighty-three years old, a tiny, languid frog with bulbous eyes and knobby fingers. He entered the room briskly, his scarlet robes billowing, almost hiding from view his secretary, a young, blond priest scrupulously dressed in white surplice and black robes.

The baroness grinned like a painted mask, eating pain as she forced herself to kneel before the cardinal and kiss his ring. Her servitors helped her back into her chair and wiped the pale sweat from her creased brow and tremulous lips.

Bobo-Orsini sat in a grand chair, his secretary close at his side, translating the baroness's langue d'oc into Latin.

"Your Grace, I am bound for the Holy Land, where, at my advanced age, I will almost certainly give up my soul to God. Thus, having little further need of my worldly possessions, I am surrendering my wealth to those of this world who can best use them." Ailena took a pearl-crusted jewel box from one of her servitors and opened it, displaying an oblong emerald and three rubies large as hazelnuts. She had spent half her fortune on these jewels, determined to make an impression in the Curia that would persist until she needed their help. "I know that your Grace is much beloved of our Holy Father. I know that you strive daily against the secular powers of the world to assure that our Holy Father's influence is not diminished in this world. I want to offer you these few insignificant baubles that I possess, to further your efforts on behalf of our Holy Father—and to remember me should I need your counsel during what little time is left me in this world."

Bobo-Orsini accepted the pearl-studded box with a lugubrious smile and, not even glancing at the gems, passed the gift to his secretary.

"Surely your pilgrimage will win favor in the eyes of God," the secretary translated, and the Prince of the Church rose and briskly exited from the room.

Alone with her servitors, Ailena felt her disappointment wince like a bubble in her heart. The cardinal was older than she and, no matter his influence, would probably depart this life before she reached Tyre. Had her wrath deluded her? Was her unholy pilgrimage God's final mockery of her life?

She signed for her bearers to remove her from this fort. She would not spend another day in Rome. This was the city of defeat, its corpse fought over by jackals for the last thousand years. She would leave at once for the Holy Land, where victory had once been won over death—and where she would win that victory again.

Tyre, Autumn 1189

The city extended like a hand spread upon the sea, attached only at the wrist, an island approached by so narrow a spit that it was easily defended by the arbalisters on the Christian barges. The deep moats and sturdy ramparts gladdened David, for the long sea journey had left him weak and he wanted to rest untroubled by fear. With the baroness's letters in hand, they were immediately received at the fortress of the town's commander, Conrad, the Marquess of Montferrat. Well pleased by the baroness's promise of gold coin and a tallage on the lands she proposed to purchase and farm in the area, he installed the Tibbons in a spacious palazzo on a palm-crested terrace overlooking the green sea.

David sought out the city's synagogue and found a small, black-stone building wedged between the sea wall and the monolithic rocks buttressing the terrace slopes. The narrow building was so far out of the way, there was no road leading to it and was accessible only by boat or by a precarious footpath on the sea wall. David and Rachel had braved the footpath, and he had kissed the threshold of the temple in gratitude for his safe delivery, praising God for sparing him and his granddaughter from the slaughtering Crusader mobs.

Rachel listened to his prayer of thanksgiving in silence, until she could stand it no more. "What of your children and grandchildren, my parents and brothers and sisters?" Rachel challenged hysterically when he invited her over the threshold. "God let them die. Uncle Joshua and his sons, too. They died horrible deaths and God did not save them. How can you thank God?"

The worshipers in the temple covered their faces and turned away. "God creates calamity as well as blessings," David said to her quietly. "Isaiah says so: 'I make peace and create evil: I the Lord do all these things.'"

"I will not thank such a god." Rachel turned away, gazed out over the emerald water shading to hard blue under the high morning cumulus.

David waved aside the rabbi, who had emerged frowning at the disturbance, and stepped up behind his granddaughter. "Look at the land." He gestured at the saffron hills of the coastline splotched with virid hues. "This is the land that God has given our people. He has blessed us by returning us here."

Rachel passed her grandfather a dark, sidelong stare, then pointed at the lofty tower of Gibeleth that rose from the sea haze above an unseen fortress far to the south. "This land is not ours. It belongs to the Saracens and the Christians. If this is our land, why do the unfaithful possess it? Why did God let the faithless kill my family?"

"Why? Why?" David shook his head. "Shall the clay question Him that fashions it?"

Rachel said nothing. Her words had opened a jagged darkness

inside her. Was that God's wrath? The rustling busyness of the fronds on the terrace above her filled with half-heard voices—the sibilant laughter of her sisters. *No!* She would not listen to the dead again. With forced animal clarity, she looked down at the white juts of ocean limestone where the sea sloshed and black crabs scuttered.

David pulled at his shorn temple locks and turned away. God alone could retrieve her from where she had gone. He returned to the synagogue and joined his people in praising the Creator. Afterward, when he had told them his story, they advised him to leave Tyre before the baroness arrived. They told him of the numerous Jewish settlements throughout the promised land and urged him to flee there with his granddaughter before the gentile found them again and bent them to her will.

But David had given his word. The baroness had retrieved them out of abject poverty and had promised that their servitude would not be menial, and that Rachel would not be molested. He would not break his word.

Later, on the way back along the footpath atop the sea wall, David twisted his ankle and very nearly plummeted into the tropic tide. He limped a short way to a sand bank littered with coral skeletons and old conchs, while Rachel searched about for a crutch. She came back with a smooth staff of driftwood and helped him to his feet. When their eyes met, he countered the mocking flatness of her stare with a shrug. "Sometimes God hides—and then we fall over Him." He sighed. "And often break our necks. We must trust God knows what He is doing."

Tyre, Winter 1189

Each night, Rachel woke when the ocean clouds crashed into the mountains and the rain drummed on the tile roof and rattled in the fronds of the palms. She would lie there breathing the coolness of the washed air as it streamed through the lotus-shaped windows of the palazzo and billowed the diaphanous curtains. In the sounds of the rain dripping off the roof and rushing down the gutters of the street, voices whispered in Hebrew. The dead swarmed through the mauve lambence of the night and circled her as she floated under the damascened bedspread, her arms folded over her chest as though she were one of them. As she tried to understand them, everything began to deepen again. The harder she listened, the more she forgot where she was. What were they saying?

Never and always.

Each night, she became convinced they were praying for a place and time to be heard, and she listened hard for their voices in the coughing rain.

Never and always.

And then the rain passed, the thunderish atmosphere chilled, and through the windows she saw wisps of the storm floating among the bright, crepitant stars. The voices departed. Watching the wheel of stars revolve in the dark tempestuous night, she drifted back to sleep.

The bells of the churches spoke at dawn. Rachel woke to aromatic fumes from the sailors' taverns along the seafront below the terrace of the palazzo. Spicy wafts of cuttlefish, blistering entrails, and braised pigeon and squid invaded her bedroom with first light and with the shouts of the fishermen gathering their nets.

David was already awake and in the garden, hands open before him, praying to the Creator as He wove a new day. The servants, too, were about, brewing their fragrant teas, mashing sesame seeds to strew in the fig paste they served each morning with dates and winter plums.

The baroness would not arrive until the spring. No large transports would cross the sea until then, and she would winter in Sicily. Several small skiffs had dared the crossing and delivered letters from her. They arrived each time by the same courier, a tall, bald man in a burgundy caftan. With the alert hairy face of a monkey, he called out from the iron gate in Arabic, and the servants came scurrying from wherever they were in the palazzo. The letters bore the signet impress of the baroness and the wax seal of the marquess, who had received them, and they were always accompanied by a pouch of bezants, the thin gold coins that were distributed to the servants as payment.

The letters were assurances to the marquess of the baroness's intentions to reimburse him, and they were also accounts of the political developments on Sicily. There Tancred, a petty despot, fancied himself a king, and the baroness was using her monies to prepare for his overthrow by the new English monarch, Richard Coeur de Lion. The letters provided no instruction to the Tibbons other than to await her arrival in the spring.

David's imagination had exhausted itself trying to surmise what the baroness wanted of them. After the morning meal, he went each day to the synagogue, by boat and not the precarious footpath, to pray and confer with the leaders of the Jewish community. The oriental Jews, headed by Rabbi Ephraim, whom everyone called the Egyptian and who could not fathom what a Norman baroness would want of the Jews, eventually convinced David to seek counsel from the European Jewish community who had established settlements outside the fortress city of Tyre.

During the winter months the Saracens disbanded, returning to their wives and children in Mesopotamia and Egypt, and there was little danger in roaming the countryside. The Tibbons rode out of the city astride donkeys among a group of pilgrims on a tour of the local holy sites. They passed through rustling fields of sugar cane and black fields dusted green with the early buds of winter barley. Gulls wheeled overhead until the land became stony and the road a rivulet of dust among the citron rocks.

Here and there scraggly carob trees crowned low hills and a stone house glowed limewash-white in the brash Levant sunlight. Beside wooden scaffolds for drawing water from deep wells, drowsy palms and the green slither of gourd vines sprouted, a crooked field fluttered verdantly, oxen lumbered, a black-faced farmer stared at the pilgrims from under the hood of his white robe and smiled, showing blue gums, amused by their dusty progress. Then the terrain turned to rock and sand again and shone like tin.

In a village of cluttered square houses on a hillside of lion dust and pearl-shadowed shards, the Tibbons found the community of European Jews recommended by Ephraim the Egyptian and were warmly welcomed. Rosh ha-Qahal—"Head of the Community"—Rabbi Hiyyah, a fleecy-haired old man, introduced them to a robust, bronze-fleshed farmer, Benjamin of Tudela, and to a waxen little weaver, Rabbi Meir of Carcassonne. Their wives and daughters embraced Rachel and sat her and her grandfather on a reed mat under a sprawling fig tree, where they were served flat bread, olives, and small red oranges.

After hearing their story, Rosh ha-Qahal nodded sagely. "You will buy your freedom," he decided. "You will pay to the Norman baroness the full cost of the clothing she has given you, the transport on the usciere, the food, the shelter during your time at the palazzo, the use of her servants, and a generous amercement for breaking your pledge. Then you will be free, and you will both come and live here among us." He looked to the large, bronzed farmer. "How much should that be, Benjamin?"

Benjamin scratched figures in the ocher dust with his finger, said, "A hundred and twenty bezants for cost, half that for an extravagant amercement—a hundred and eighty bezants."

"Good," Rosh ha-Qahal nodded. "You will pay the baroness two hundred bezants and be free of her."

"Two hundred bezants," David despaired. "I haven't even one."

Rosh ha-Qahal dismissed his concern with a backhanded wave. "That is only gold. We will lend it to you."

Rabbi Meir slapped his waxen hands together. "It is done. I will collect the sum from the community after the winter harvest. You will have it in hand well before the baroness returns."

"But how will I repay you? I am an old man."

"Your experience will repay us," Rosh ha-Qahal replied. "Your knowledge of vineyards and orchards will enrich the community many times over what we are lending you. Think no more about it. Let us eat. And afterward we will sing and there will be dancing."

Throughout the remainder of the day, the Tibbons were hosted by one family after another, each hearing their story anew and telling its own while the others took their places in the buff fields and in the hillside orchards of smoke-silvered olive trees. David glowed with joy, and Rachel hung between desire and dread, wanting the affection the families laved over them and yet fearing the emptiness these people widened in her. The young women were so like her sisters, the boys remindful of her brothers—laughter and happiness came only so far in her, then brinked on this black chasm of memory.

The community sensed the young woman's reserve and queried her grandfather. "She is grieved because she saw the martyrs," he explained. "I think she sees them still."

At sunset, Rachel went alone into an open field to find the expanse that complemented the emptiness that had been opened in her. Vast octaves of violet and indigo vaulted the sky. Starscapes burned magnificently over the dark sand faults and ancient hills.

"Sadness grows its own body, you know," a melancholy voice said behind her. She turned and faced Rosh ha-Qahal, whose woolly curls shone like the silver outlines of a cloud. "It sees with its own eyes, hears with its own ears. You must live with this other body, Rachel. It belongs to God as surely as does your flesh. But you must not let this body of sorrow live for you."

The Head of the Community retreated as silently as he had arrived. Rachel watched the last vertiginous hue of day vanish in the cope of heaven, then returned to the village to sleep. Hours later, she woke and stepped out of the woodsmoke-scented house into the deep chill of the desert. Her breath smoked luminously. She stared west and saw, far off, the giant swells of cloud blotting the starlight, releasing their rains over Tyre on their way to the mountains. Distantly, the dead whispered, *Never and always.*

Tyre, Spring 1190

Rosh ha-Qahal and the others in the community wanted the Tibbons to stay with them, but David insisted on returning to Tyre, to await the baroness in the palazzo as he had promised. He spent most of his time at the synagogue, occasionally hosting Rabbi Meir or Benjamin of Tudela at the palazzo when they visited the city. He grew his beard and his temple locks long and became active in the Jewish community, even contributing to the correspondence with the famed Maimonides, who was then living in Cairo and who communicated frequently with the Tyre community, on one occasion writing, "It is because of your dwelling in this place that God assures us a Redeemer even today."

Rachel waited in the palazzo as a very old woman might, watching the sea mix her pigments, puttering in the garden among the lurid cactus flowers, the black moon-pearls of the pepper tree, the violet shadows of the jasmine hedges, or just following the servants around, the swarthy women in their long oiled plaits padding bare-foot among the rooms, wiping the peach-colored dust from the sills and the polished chests.

Sometimes her grandfather took her with the servants into the brazen sun of the marketplace. There, under crisscrossed palms and bright domes, against limewashed walls that had peeled to oyster-colored patches, stalls offered early spring crops, sparkling fish, live animals, seabird eggs, bolts of baize and silk, all hawked by dark-faced men with chalk streaked under each eye and their heads wrapped in cloth.

On the return from one such outing, the hairy-faced courier in the burgundy caftan awaited them at the palazzo with a letter from the baroness. In it, Ailena commanded them to leave the palazzo with its servants and to wait outside of Tyre until she sent word for them. David and Rachel returned to the Jewish settlement and lived there several weeks before the courier sought them out and took David back to the city with him before nightfall.

On the patio overlooking the garden, the baroness awaited him, looking more wan and shriveled in the illumination of the oil lamps than he remembered. Her formalities were brief; she directly informed him of how, having been exiled by her son, she intended to train Rachel to do what the baroness herself could not do—return to Wales and exact revenge.

David listened simple-eyed, hardly believing his ears. "What you ask is impossible," he said. "Rachel is just barely a woman."

"Who looks exactly as I myself looked as a young woman. With the proper training, she will know all that I know and no one will be able to doubt that she is me."

David's stare widened as he perceived the madness of the baroness's plan. "If she claims she is you, they will kill her for an impostor—or a witch."

A cold grin lit up the baroness's face. "The beauty of my strate-gy will protect her. You see, David, I will convince them all that I have been made young not by witchcraft but by God's grace—by a holy miracle."

David staggered backward as if punched. He raised both hands palm-outward to protect his face. "That cannot be. Not with my granddaughter. That would blaspheme God."

The baroness's eyes narrowed lethally. "You and the girl are in my charge. You will do as I say."

"I will not blaspheme God."

"Not *your* God, you fool. The Christian god. She will declare that she has been restored to her youth by the Messiah—by Jesus, who is a false messiah to you. No blasphemy there!"

"No one will believe. They will kill my granddaughter. You swore she would not be molested."

"And she will not be. I have thought of everything. I will take every precaution in executing my plan. I will not have it fail. Rachel will return to Wales as Ailena Valaise, baroness of Epynt."

"But why?" David's voice rose woefully. "To what end must she effect this ruse?"

"To usurp the usurper!" the baroness snapped. "I want my revenge, even if I must grasp for it from the grave!"

David lowered his head, unable to face the hatred in her stare. He reached into his robe, removed a pouch heavy with gold, and laid it on the taboret beside her. "Here are two hundred bezants," he said. "This is compensation for the money you have spent on myself and my granddaughter. We will have no more to do with your revenge."

The baroness stared fiercely at the pouch, then picked it up in her crabbed hand and heaved it back at David. "No!" Her shout rang so loudly it echoed from the sea wall. "Money cannot buy what I want. Rachel is mine. She will learn what it is to be me. And she will go back and finish my story as I want it told. Or her story will end here."

David rose and dropped the pouch in the chair where he had sat. The baroness's loud cries pelted him as he rushed from the palazzo.

With the city gates locked for the night, David waited for morning at the home of a fellow Jew. The memory of the baroness's wrath kept him awake until dawn. Then he borrowed a donkey and hurried from the city. On the way, several horsemen in chain mail and greaves charged past him, and he followed the dust plume of their horses to the Jewish settlement.

When David reached the hillside, the Norman knights hired by the baroness had arrived before him and were trampling the fields, hacking at the branches of the fruit trees, and stampeding the herds on the hills. One of them hailed him, and threw the pouch of bezants at his feet. "Tomorrow we will return and level this village," he warned menacingly, then waved his men off and rode back toward Tyre.

The village elders were furious. Benjamin of Tudela prepared to ride to the neighboring villages to rally enough men to fend off the Normans when they came back. But David would not have that. He returned the pouch of gold coins and, with a shamed head, shrank from their protestations.

The next morning, while Rachel eagerly pressed her grandfather for what the baroness had wanted of them, he placed a thick finger against her lips. "We have given our word—that is enough," he said wearily. In a letter he left with Rosh ha-Qahal, he apologized to each of the families for the damage the knights had done to their property, and, with his granddaughter riding atop the donkey, he and Rachel returned to Tyre.

The baroness's throat felt blistered with her yelling. Her fury at David's rejection of her plan had almost killed her. Hobbling after him, screaming threats, she had nearly broken her neck on the stone stairs that led from the patio to the garden exit, where he had fled. Blessedly, the servants, alerted by her shouted imprecations, had come running and stopped her in time. That night, with her pulse beat knocking furiously under her jawbone, she had sat with the bristly jowled courier, whom she had hired through the marquess to watch the Tibbons, and she had learned of the Jewish community.

Ailena had already exhausted her fortune, money she could have spent raising a mercenary army in France. Instead, for her money, she now had recognition in the Curia, had invested in Tancred's submission to Richard Coeur de Lion in Sicily, and, through the marquess of Montferrat in Tyre, had purchased two farms, whose rent would help pay her daily expenses. After all her effort, she was not about to let Rachel slip away.

Under a crown of sunshafts raying through the date palms of the garden, the baroness met with Rachel and David. The baroness looked triumphantly at David, who sulked on a stone bench beside the prongs of a large cactus. Then she faced Rachel, seated on a stool before her, and smiled lavishly to see again the likeness of her youth. She explained the broad outlines of her strategy to the girl, speaking gently and confidently in a voice still hoarse from the previous night's tantrum.

"I have even conceived of the miracle that will transform me into you," Ailena said. "You will drink from the Holy Grail!"

Rachel looked to her grandfather, and he opened the palms of his hands to show his ignorance.

"You do not know of the Grail?" Ailena asked, incredulous; then stroking her chin: "Of course—you are Jews. What would you know of Christian superstitions? Well, you will be amused by this one. It is utterly charming." The webs about the baroness's eyes darkened with malicious glee. "The Grail is the chalice that Jesus drank from and passed around at the Passover feast, saying to his disciples, 'Drink, for this is my blood.' And the next day he was crucified, and, as prophesied, Joseph of Arimathea used that very chalice to catch the Savior's blood as it poured out from his wounds. Over time, the Grail was lost. But now and then it appears to the faithful—and, as legend would have it, those who drink from it are restored to their youth." Ailena smiled chillingly. "I shall drink from the Grail."

The fifteen-year-old girl received the baroness's idea with a soft nod, which both surprised and relieved Ailena.

"What if we are not believed?" David queried.

"*I* will be believed, for Rachel will be speaking as me. And in Wales the legend of the Grail is renowned. The people there believe that Joseph of Arimathea carried the Grail to their heathen lands with the good news of the resurrection. They believe Saint Joseph brought the Grail to their wilderness, where a great warrior, Uther Pendragon, who drove the Romans from Wales, built around it the famous Round Table in memory of the Last Supper. Many people have claimed to have seen the Grail. To them it is quite real."

"What happened to the Grail?" Rachel asked.

Ailena's withered face brightened, pleasantly surprised at the girl's interest. "It was lost. You see, at this Round Table was an empty seat, the Perilous Seat, where no one could sit without peril of death unless he could answer the question, 'Whom does the Grail serve?' Upon Uther's death, his orgulous son Arthur sat there. He had no idea whom the Grail served. He thought that all in his kingdom served him—his wife was his passion, his knights were his strength, his land was his sustenance, and the Grail was a mere emblem of his authority. Shortly thereafter, he was gravely wounded battling the pagan tribes. When he was carried back to his castle, the Grail was gone. Arthur's wound would not heal, and as he lay dying, his wife abandoned him, his knights lost faith, and his kingdom withered to a wasteland. He lost everything. Only a few of his knights remembered the glory of his father Uther, and they began a quest for the Grail."

"Did they find it?" Rachel wanted to know, intrigued.

Ailena smiled at her childish interest. "One did. But that is a different story."

"Whom *does* the Grail serve?" Rachel pressed.

"The Grail king, of course."

Rachel looked puzzled. "Who was that?"

"That was Arthur."

"But he was gravely wounded for sitting in the Perilous Seat."

Ailena stared shrewdly at the girl. "Because he thought all in the land served him. He did not realize that the king and the land are one."

Rachel's eyes glazed over as she pondered this.

"To rule is to serve," David explained. He faced Ailena and sighed. "If you send my granddaughter back to your domain as a baroness, she will have to serve your people."

"Bosh. My plan is far more simple. You will return merely long enough to unseat my son. Then you will collect the jewels I have promised you, and you may go where you please."

David frowned darkly, but Rachel merely nodded. Having seen the horror, having since carried the seeing with her through two years, Rachel could not be astonished anymore, only informed. So now she would learn to be a baroness. If that pleased this lame old woman who had lifted them out of want and despair, who was she to object? From the look of her skull-tight face, the baroness had little time left in this world anyway. Why not humor her and enjoy the privileges of the palazzo?

Ailena, gratified by Rachel's ready acquiescence, finally allowed the fatigue of her sea journey to claim her. She beckoned the girl closer, kissed her cheek, and waved her off. When Rachel and David had retreated to the edge of the garden, the baroness croaked, "Stop." The girl turned, her lean figure in her luminously pale robe a sand lilac among the umbrageous creepers and clicking fronds. She was the beautiful wraith of Ailena's past, a burning doorway into the enormous vista of the future. The baroness smiled and closed her eyes.

Tyre, Summer 1190

Ailena installed the Tibbons in the north wing of the palazzo. Every morning she sat with Rachel in the garden and told her something about her life, beginning with her childhood in the Périgord. During the afternoon, while she rested, the baroness let Rachel and a servant roam the white scar of the wide beach below the terraces of the palazzo.

David spent his days at the synagogue and sometimes in the marketplace, garnering news of the war between the Christians and the Saracens. That summer the great Saracen commander, Saladin, was busily defending Acre, the next large city south of Tyre. In July, Henry of Champagne had landed with ten thousand men and a large number of knights, nobles, and fighting priests. As fast as he built his siege engines, Saladin's forces destroyed them, using a sticky, fierce-burning explosive tar called Greek fire, invented by a young coppersmith from Damascus. The Christians had never seen the likes of it, and it thwarted all their traditional attempts to invade Acre. In frustration, Henry made the fatal error of marshaling his forces head-on against the defenders. On the feast of Saint James at the end of July, six thousand Christians were slain, among them women in armor who had fought valiantly beside the knights.

What sifted down of these gory battle tales invaded Rachel's heart, and she could restore her sense of well-being only by walking the beach under the hard sun and the spray-feathered wind. Only then, after sitting on rocks crusted with red splotches of coralline algae and staring into the purplish silver horizon could she turn about again and face what the Arabs called the "kiss of thorns"—the towers and garret walls of the city.

The story of the armored Christian women who had died among the knights anchored Rachel's wits in her own fate. So the world was cruel to everyone, not to her alone. The baroness's continuing history of grief affirmed that dark truth. Day by day, Rachel heard gruesome accounts of what happened to Ailena after her father died. She had been the same age as Rachel was now and had been forced to marry a brute who delighted in beating her.

Understanding the precarious beauty of life for the first time, Rachel realized that the happiness that both she and the baroness had known as children was a rare gift. From God, as Grandfather believed, or from nowhere, as the baroness had become convinced; the gift of life's beauty did not last long, and if grasped after its time had passed, such beauty darkened to a grief that distracted the heart from everything else that must be lived.

Tyre, Autumn 1190

Baldwin, Archbishop of Canterbury, and Hubert Walter, Bishop of Salisbury, reached Tyre in September with news that the kings of England and France were on their way to the Holy Land. The prelates conveyed from the English king a terse but grateful acknowledgment to the baroness for her financial assistance to Richard's supporters in Sicily. With that small but vital piece of her strategy in place, Ailena addressed herself to Rachel's training with more zeal.

The girl seemed to resemble her youthful self more each season as she bloomed into womanhood, but the horror she had witnessed still haunted her with spells of distraction and gloominess. Ailena despaired of conveying all the small details of her life to so dreamy a pupil, and for a while she became gruff with the child.

Then, from one of her tinsel-robed maids, the baroness learned of a Persian magician who could put people to sleep with the pass of his hand, and with a whisper in their ear convince them they were camels or monkeys. Ailena went at once with Rachel to find this magician. The warmth of the Levant had penetrated to her bones and relieved some of the miserable pain that had polluted her life, but what sustained her was the work her revenge required.

Eager to find the magician who could help her, she was able to walk the twisted warren of streets herself, guided by her maid through cramped lanes of narrow and verminous rock houses lit by flickering rush lamps. A dirt path meandered among the jammed buildings, passed through a stone gate, and arrived at an inelegant wooden hut leaning against an embankment of red earth.

The interior was unlighted, but upon their arrival a skylight of woven rushes was lifted, and a silver shaft of daylight illuminated wicker chairs, a floor of tamped earth, and a back wall that was the dirt slope. The man who greeted them wore a leopardskin mantle over a sinewy body of blue-black skin. From under a dark red headcloth, his austere face gazed impassively, his bright, tapered eyes chilling all who stared at him.

The Frankish soldier whom the baroness had hired to accompany them cursed at the sight of the heathen, and Ailena motioned for him to wait outside. She introduced herself in the halting Arabic she had learned from her servants, until the amused magician replied in a spiced but fluent langue d'oc, "I am Karm Abu Selim. Why are you surprised that I speak your language? Your people have occupied this land for more than a century. I have stolen the nightmares from their souls and given them sleep. I have instilled obedient rage in their arms so they could fight without fear. And, when they came back, I dulled their harsh memories of war like a dwindling star, so that the sun of a new day rose in their breasts. With me, longing and pain can be silenced, the voices of the angels made loud. I know the way through the crooked holes in the heart. I know where to find the chances heaven has strewn around us. How may I help you?"

Tyre, Winter 1190

David remained secretly defiant of the baroness. In November, when Baldwin, the aged Archbishop of Canterbury, died and

Conrad of Montferrat returned from the siege of Acre with a wife stolen from another noble, David took advantage of the grief and outrage in the city to absent himself for a tour of the local holy places. The baroness, busy with her own intrigues among the nobles of the city and her indoctrination of his granddaughter, did not miss him.

Saladin's army had dispersed for the winter, and the real danger in the land was not warfare but starvation. The ferocious battles of the last season had destroyed numerous farms and fields, and many people were reduced to slaughtering horses and mules for food. David traveled on foot to the hillside Jewish village where Rosh ha-Qahal dwelled, and he beseeched him for help in finding a husband for Rachel.

"He must be willing to flee far," David insisted, "to Egypt, where the baroness will not be able to find us."

Rosh ha-Qahal, approving that David had found the courage to defy the baroness, set about finding an appropriate husband. Within a few days, he presented to David a curly-haired young man of intense paleness with dark eyes of penetrating lucidity and a wide, guileless mouth. His name was Daniel Hezekyah, a carpenter who had learned the trade from his father and grandfather. But it was books, not wood, that held his passion; at nights he studied with Rabbi Meir, hoping soon to become a rabbi himself.

David returned to Tyre with Daniel and his father, so that he might show them to Rachel. They knew David's story and were willing to break with tradition, traveling to meet the prospective bride because her virtues had been so well lauded by Rosh ha-Qahal. They were not disappointed. Rachel met them in the synagogue, dressed in the silken finery the baroness had bestowed on her, her heart's blood in her face at the prospect of being a bride. Daniel had to force his voice to speak to her: the avidity of love had opened in him so fully that there was barely room in his lungs for breath. David caught the eye of Daniel's father and received his nod.

After the formalities of their introduction, Rachel and Daniel strolled by the sea, most of the congregation following at a respectful distance. He talked in long scholarly sentences about their lives as a block of wood, to be shaped with the grain, which was the dark striation of griefs she had endured, and that now necessitated their flight to Egypt. The compassionate tenderness of his voice convinced her to speak of the emptiness her sorrow had hollowed in her, and of the voices of the dead that echoed there, with their chant *Never and always*.

Daniel could have known then that their love was doomed. But he had faith in the restorative power of the fluid, warm strength that swelled in his chest at her nearness. When he left with his father, he promised that in the spring they would be wed and then leave at once to find their happiness in Egypt.

Tyre, Spring 1191

The winter famine had worked to the baroness's advantage. While the fields around Acre had been ravaged by the war, the farm and fields she owned near Tyre enjoyed rich harvests, and she was able to sell each sack of her cereal grains for a hundred pieces of gold, each egg for six deniers, and the sale of her small herd of cattle made her more money than she had possessed before she sailed for Rome. Even after paying the tallage she owed the marquess, she was a rich woman.

The continual winter rains had dampened her bones and crippled her with pain, but her accruing wealth and the profound usefulness of Karm Abu Selim in the training of Rachel eased her suffering. She had brought the Persian magician to her palazzo and given him his own suite and servants. Each morning and evening, he immersed Rachel in a trance, in which she sat openeyed, not only listening to the baroness's life story but experiencing it with all her senses. Karm Abu Selim masterfully re-created sensations with perfumes, textures, and sound effects garnered from a multitude of improvised instruments. Gradually, the whole of Ailena Valaise's remembered life was being lived again in Rachel's mind.

Ailena, thoroughly pleased with the girl's progress, happily put more of her attention into increasing her wealth, and did not notice that, between the magical sessions, Rachel spent less time at the seashore and more time at the synagogue. Secret arrangements for her wedding and the escape to Egypt were worked out in detail. Letters were dispatched to contacts in the Jewish communities of Alexandria and Cairo, and several members of the groom's family, who were disgruntled at the bride's lack of dowry and the necessity for such a distant move, had to be mollified.

By Passover, everything was in order. Daniel and Rachel had met several times, and their affection for each other had become ardent. But at the Pesach ritual, when the rabbi pulled back the Paschal lamb's head and cut its throat, Rachel fell into the emptiness of its gaping wound. The spurt of blood draining into the sacrificial cup drained her strength with the lamb's, and her senses teetered into delirium.

Karm Abu Selim had implanted in her mind the image of the Grail; whenever she wished to intensify the memories of the baroness, she had merely to imagine the Sacred Chalice, and the memories the magician had given her would leap up in her. But now, seeing the ceremonial chalice catching blood, she witnessed again in her mind the gruesome image of her family's slashed throats: all of Ailena's memories scattered like smoke in a blast of wind.

Rachel experienced herself collapsing into a cavernous chill, a huge, icy darkness, in which the lamb's blood was the only warmth. Her bones knocked with her shivering; an incandescent terror flared through her as she realized she was dying. Her throat had been cut; all life was spilling out of her. A monstrous cold wreathed her heart, and she heard distantly, growing louder, the pulsing sound of some horrible fate approaching, inevitable, final.

Iron hands had seized her, tearing her apart—shaking her awake as sight snapped back into her bulging eyeballs. She saw David's worried countenance looming close and heard the gloomy, pulsing sound of her own voice shouting again and again, *"Never and always!"* She had collapsed, and her grandfather was crouched over her, shaking alertness back into her. Over his shoulder, she glimpsed the appalled grimaces of the congregation surrounding Daniel Hezekyah's pallid, horror-stricken, and inconsolably grieved face.

Daniel Hezekyah waited at the synagogue for Rachel to return to the seashore. He wanted to speak to her again before he left Tyre, to tell her himself that he still loved her, no matter her madness. Who would not be mad who had seen that horror? He waited three days to apologize for letting his father hold him back from where she had fallen during the Pesach ritual, afraid like the others of whatever virulent *dybbuk* possessed her.

But afterward, when David had swathed his granddaughter in his mantle and had huddled her off back to the gentiles' palazzo, Daniel realized he loved her more than he feared any *dybbuk*. So he stayed at the synagogue when his father returned to their village. He waited at the large window of the temple, watching for her to stroll down to the sea as she had been wont to do.

Daniel wanted to tell her that he loved her in body and soul, that the flaw of her soul was the flaw of all their people since the Diaspora, and that it was not wrong to be mad in a mad world. He could not marry her. The Law forbade that—for, as was written in Deuteronomy 28:28, those who did not obey the commandments of the Lord God, the Lord would smite with madness and astonishment of heart. What she had done wrong he could not say. Though others claimed she had been struck mad for serving the gentile, he did not believe that. Perhaps there was some ancestral crime for which she had to pay. Whatever the crime, he could not break the Law and marry her, but neither could he stop loving her.

On the fourth day, Daniel went to the palazzo and asked at the gate for her, but the servant claimed there was no such person in the house. Back at the synagogue, he waited another week, twice more returning to the palazzo and twice more being turned away. Finally, he wandered the strand alone where they had strolled together. He wrote her name in the sand but, haunted by an incipient and tenacious remorse, returned to his village.

Rachel never again returned to the beach or the synagogue. After her collapse and humiliation before her own people, she wanted to forget herself and all the grief of her past. Karm Abu Selim found her a more eager devotée of his magic and was able to steep her in trances so deep that even upon awakening she walked about dazed for half the morning believing she was Ailena Valaise, bewildered to find herself in a garden of vine and jujube, pistachio and apricot, the sea-salt air tainted with desert dust.

David mortified himself before God, covering his head with ashes, and fasting until his vision blurred and he could no longer stand up for his prayers. The Persian magician fed him a pellet of opium, guiding him to the throne of God, where tongues of fire lashed him and purged him of his transgressions. When he recovered, a childlike hesitation seemed to wrap his body and unfathomable resignation shone out from under the silver hair. From then on, he conspired no more to remove his granddaughter from the baroness's influence. When his friends at the synagogue enquired about Rachel, his unvarying reply was like a chant, "All that is is God's will."

Acre, Summer 1191

On July 12, Richard Plantagenet, the Coeur de Lion, captured Acre, massacring twenty-five hundred of the Saracens after they had surrendered and he had assured them of no reprisal. When the baroness moved there in August to invest heavily before all the worthy properties were sold, the field where the slaughter had occurred glittered with mounds of bleached human bones, and the hills were strewn with the remnants of the horrid orgies of the carrion birds and jackals.

The sight dizzied Rachel, and Karm Abu Selim tranced her with a tap to the center of her forehead. "Behold this field of lilies," he intoned and she saw what he said. "How radiantly they shine in the sun."

Ailena Valaise knew joy in Acre. She moved into a large manor house on the Street of the Three Magi near the central blue-domed mosque that was the city's palace. There she mingled with royalty, winning their favor with her generous gifts. King Richard, pleased with her financial support of him in Sicily, renewed in his own hand her charter as baroness of Epynt. Ailena exulted to learn from the king that, on Easter of that year, he had been wed in Sicily by the new pope, Celestine III, born Giacinto Bobo-Orsini.

Occasional letters from the baroness's daughter Clare informed Ailena of her son's despotic rule of her domain. But she was now in no hurry to exact her revenge. The anguish of her twisted bones had been held in check by the dry clime as well as by her Persian magician's charms and medicines. And Acre offered new opportunities to expand her wealth. She owned an oven in the city that earned her over two hundred bezants a year, and, in the countryside outside the ramparts, she purchased Kfar Hananya, a village replete with orchards and extensive fields. She also acquired two nearby gardens, where she could meet in private with Rachel, for, now that Ailena had become a local favorite among royalty and the knights, she could not be seen with the woman she had destined to take her place.

Rachel and David lived in Kfar Hananya with their own servants. David spent his time overseeing the care of the baroness's fruit trees and praying in the temple, where he told all enquirers that his granddaughter was already spoken for.

Each day, Rachel rode her horse through a stone valley of red sandstone needles and across a scrubby wasteland of rosy shale rubble, where butterflies tippled among the desert flowers. No one but peasants saw her as she arrived at the small oasis garden of Quasur el Atash, the Fortress of the Thirsty. There, she met with Ailena and Karm Abu Selim and continued her trance-education.

Sometimes Rachel lingered at the oasis all day, long after the baroness had finished relating the next episode of her story in company with the magician's magical rapport. She replayed in her memory all she had learned of that distant and cold land of Wales, imagining among the red basalt rocks the verdant cliffs and mountains where she was a baroness.

In the evening, riding back to Kfar Hananya, the hooves of her horse ringing on the shingle floor, the sky ablaze with stars, Rachel brooded on all the small details of her new life—the name of her favorite boarhound, the arrangement of rooms in her castle, and even the numerous brutalities her husband had inflicted on her, the remembered pain and rage a vivid part of the world she carried inside her.

Jerusalem, Autumn 1192

As soon as King Richard won the right of pilgrims to enter Jerusalem, Ailena moved David and Rachel into a Jewish settlement within the Holy City's Syrian quarter. In a tiered house of stone blocks at the corner of Jehosaphat and Spanish streets, they lived simply with their servants. David remained immersed in his worshipful life, assuaging his onerous foreboding with prayers, and Rachel continued her tutelage with Ailena in a walled garden behind Saint Elye's chapel.

Now that Rachel knew the salient features of the baroness's life, she had to learn Welsh as well as Ailena's handwriting. But these disciplines were easy compared with the training necessary to overcome her docile habits and assume the flinty, strong-willed temperament of the baroness. In her trance, she practiced the hostile mannerisms that would be necessary when she finally confronted Guy Lanfranc and the knights of the frontier.

"These men understand only one thing," Ailena whispered to the mesmerized girl. "Power. The power to assert your will is the power to restrict freedom, to inflict pain, to kill. Power is not your right or your privilege. Power belongs only to those who can command it. And the secret of command is voice and bearing—and, above all, cunning."

With the baroness and the Persian magician, Rachel went out into the desert often and worked endless hours ordering the wind and the rocks, hardening her voice to the temper of iron with her indignation at the insolence of the sun and the audacity of the clouds. She learned to stand unquailed, defiantly staring down the magician's lion-shouts and the baroness's degrading insults.

In the evening, back in the palazzo, sipping cool, minty sharbat, Ailena instructed her in the philosophy of the wolf. "You need the pack, yet you must stand alone. You are the leader. If you show any weakness at all, you will be eaten." Ailena's bony face quivered with remembered rage. "I swear to you. Show weakness and you will be devoured."

"Yet the ruler and the land are one," Rachel reminded the baroness. "Who rules must serve."

The old woman's upper lip curled contemptuously. "That is a fairy tale. In the real world, the sword rules—and it serves only power. Learn these lessons well!"

Even with Karm Abu Selim's help, these difficult tasks required arduous efforts. Rachel lost herself in them. She began to speak Welsh almost continually, and, to the exasperation of her grandfather, she began comporting herself with imperial arrogance. David feared for her soul and confronted the baroness on the worn steps of Saint Elye's: "What you are doing offends God."

The Frankish soldier who escorted the baroness among her numerous properties moved to seize the impertinent Jew, but Ailena stopped him and had the knight wait for her in the doorway of the chapel, out of earshot. "David," she said kindly and sat on the sun-warmed steps. "What happened to your faith that whatever is is God's will?"

"What you are doing offends God," he repeated. "My granddaughter believes she is a baroness."

Ailena's crumpled face crinkled with a satisfied smile. "She *is* the baroness. When I die, she will take my place."

"She is Rachel Tibbon. She has her own soul. She cannot carry yours. What you are doing to her offends God."

Ailena's smile slid from her face. "There is no God, David. Don't looked so shocked. Have you been blind the whole time you've been here? The Saracens and the Christians have been killing each other for their gods for a hundred years now. And the Jews, the Chosen People, have been crushed in between. Where is God in all of this blood-letting? Smug in His heaven, perhaps. But down here, David, down here in the suffering, in this boneheap of life, there is no God." She offered her hand. "Now help me up. Mass is about to begin. There are so many tiny details I must sort out, and church is the only place I can think clearly—the music is so soothing."

Jerusalem, Spring 1197

Years passed. With each season Ailena shriveled smaller, and her joy at soon fulfilling her wrath on her son seemed to burn brighter as she watched Rachel grow to a tall, imperiously beautiful woman. Daily they shared the magician's trance, seeing as one their domain in the hills of northern Wales. And when not under his spell, they spoke to each other in a mélange of Welsh and langue d'oc about their feelings and perceptions, more intimate than mother and daughter.

To appease her grandfather and to earn his blessing for this endeavor which she had embraced with her soul, Rachel read the Law with him in her spare moments. She assured him that when the baroness died, they would collect the treasure she had promised them and return to Kfar Hananya to live as dutiful Jews. But as that day approached, and the baroness shrank even beyond the help of the magician's potions, Rachel's sleep was mocked with nightmares. She dreamed over and over again of the Paschal lamb, its throat slashed, severed veins spurting blood—and always it was her mother's eyes looking out at her from behind the beast's startled face.

"This is the last time we will speak," Ailena said when Rachel appeared beside her bed in the gaunt house that the baroness had rented behind Saint Elye's. For days, Ailena had been too enfeebled to walk, and she had to complete the final arrangements of her vengeful plan through Karm Abu Selim. "All is in place, dear Rachel. All is in place."

Rachel clutched the shriveled woman's bony hand, her eyes lustrous with tears. "Everything will be as you have foreseen, my lady."

The old woman nodded, and closed her eyes. For a long while she lay perfectly still, sipping thin air through her parched lips, unable to draw a full breath for the pain that shackled her. Rachel looked to Karm Abu Selim, who sat at the corner of her bed. He shook his head at her appeal.

"Remember," the baroness rasped. "My wealth here belongs to the Templars. I have already drafted them a will, which they will receive tonight. There is nothing for you here. You must return to Wales, to Gilbert's vault. That is yours." Her eyes hardened in her shriveled face. "Remember what is required of you. Unseat my son, as I have instructed! That is the only way to satisfy my ghost. Unseat him!" She gasped and held up a finger to indicate she was not done. "One more task before you flee Wales with the gems you have earned—one more task you must accomplish to ease my ghost. My daughter Clare writes me that her son Thomas fancies to be a priest. Stop him. No grandson of mine will serve the

Church. God will get his sycophants elsewhere, not from my blood. Do you understand?"

Rachel squeezed her hand. "Fear not, Servant of Birds," she said in Welsh. "All that you have planned will be fulfilled."

Ailena smiled wanly. She raised her free hand and painfully opened it, revealing in her clutch a green and gold signet ring. "At the last moment, take the ring. My soul will come with it."

Rachel shivered in the dark of the narrow rock corridor. Ahead, in the glaucous light of a wax taper, she could discern the furtive shadows of the Mesopotamian magicians Karm Abu Selim had hired. Their whispers sounded like trickling sands. She pressed her back against the hard rock wall, needing its solidity to calm herself. Only a few strides away was the ladder that led up from this tunnel to the Holy Sepulcher, where the gentiles believed that their messiah had risen from the dead.

She wished that David could be here with her, but he had to wait for her in his house on Jehosaphat Street. She was entirely on her own now—alone with the lifetime of living memories that the baroness and the magician had bequeathed her.

Though the tunnel's heat stifled her, a clammy cold dewed her body. She was afraid that when the moment came for her to climb the ladder and take her place as the baroness she would make a mistake. The grotto above her was jammed with Hospitalers, fanatical warrior-priests who would cut her to pieces if they suspected her of blaspheming their sacred shrine. She could hear their droning prayers as they administered the last rites to Ailena and the irreversible act drew nearer.

The shadows in the tunnel's dark recesses stirred, and black figures appeared, men in sable robes and headcloths, their faces charcoaled. They carried unlit torches, pouches, and vials, and brushed past without looking at her. One shadow stopped in front of her and held up a chalice that glistered in the dull light. "The Sangreal," the shadow whispered, and she recognized Karm Abu Selim's voice. "This is the image of your new life. See it in the dark behind your eyes whenever you must drink of the memories I have given you. This is your new life."

He turned the golden chalice before her, and its mirror finish reflected her frightened face. "When you stand in the crypt above," the magician continued, "and this comes to you out of the smoke, drink from it. The potion is sweet and harmless. When you are done, let it go. And if any one of the knights approaches, let it go quickly. Do you understand?"

Rachel nodded, and the magician touched his finger to her brow. "You are serene. You are strong. You are the brow of a lioness." A warm radiance dispelled the clamminess on her flesh, and a sigh she had locked in her chest escaped through her nostrils.

Karm Abu Selim took Rachel's hand and guided her to the foot of the ladder, where the wax tapers tainted the air with a papery light and a purple scent of incense. "Wait here. When I call, you will rise like a bubble from the bottom of the sea." He ascended the ladder, a waft of black smoke.

Rachel clutched the smooth wood of the rung before her and looked up at the dark hole where she would go. A sharp flash of silver light drove needles into her brain, and she nearly collapsed. Amazed shouts sounded above her, and through her aching sight she beheld billows of luminous smoke.

"Rachel, come now," Karm Abu Selim's voice called.

Rachel's heart quailed, and she craved a moment of reprieve to clear her sight and gather her wits.

"Quickly!" the magician hissed.

With an ache of effort, Rachel climbed the ladder and found herself inside a cloud. Men in ebony robes dashed about touching torches to trivets that held pans of yellow powder. The powder ignited into brilliant coiling fumes that scorched her breath with their spicy pungency. Mutilated music jangled through the curtains of smoke, eerie pipings and echoey chimes floating above the mightiness of a deep roar.

Karm Abu Selim took Rachel by her shoulders and turned her about so that she faced the grotto. Illuminated by torches set in iron sconces, a dozen men in white robes, some hooded, huddled against the back wall and the rock steps, their faces gaping like fish. From where she stood within a rock alcove, she could see them without being seen. They stared in terror and exaltation at the smoke-coiled space three paces from Rachel, where the baroness had lifted herself to her knees to reach for a gold chalice floating in the air before her.

From her vantage point in the dark nook, Rachel saw the black silk threads suspending the chalice. Then the black-robed men in the alcove across from her touched their torches to the throats of vials they had set in wall niches. Flames gushed from the vials and dissolved into bright blowing motes that wafted over Ailena.

Rachel gasped, not for the holocaust of sparkling vapors but for the bone-wracking pain Ailena endured to lift herself to her knees. Blinding flashes gouged sight, forcing Rachel to look aside. In a wincing blur, she glimpsed a black shadow snatch Ailena and whisk her away from her litter—toward *her*. As the old woman hurtled by in the arms of the shadow, Rachel glanced at her, saw the bulging lifeless eyes, the sagging mouth with a black thread of ink drooling from it.

Not ink—but poison, Rachel realized as she herself was seized and thrust forward. She felt something hard pressed into her hand. *The ring.* She slipped it on, obeying the hours of rehearsal she had enacted with Ailena in a trance. And then, the golden chalice was in her hands. She brought it to her lips—afraid to drink, fearing the poison.

The dense smoke parted; from the corner of her eye she saw the knights on their knees reduced to stupefaction. She drank from the chalice, and cool sharbat soothed her parched throat. As she released the chalice, it sprang from her fingertips so swiftly it appeared to vanish in front of her eyes.

The bizarre music stopped abruptly. Rachel looked to the alcove for Karm Abu Selim—but he and all the shadows were gone. The trivets, the pans of incense, the torches and vials all were gone, vanished in an instant, as though she had only imagined them there. Even the hole from where she had climbed up had somehow sealed over. She was alone.

Heart banging so furiously it hurt her chest, Rachel turned to face the knights, the last fumes of magic vanishing around her.

Rachel fell to her knees and intoned aloud the Christian prayers the baroness had taught her. A small shadow slinked across the grotto and leaped onto the litter beside her. Her breath failed, her prayer faltering, as she realized it was a monkey dressed as a squire, with a tiny brown tunic cinched by a yellow sash.

A resentful shout came from the crowd, many of whom had begun to pray aloud in fervent voices with her. A dwarf with the face of a goblin, his head flat and triangular as a serpent's, wobbled over to the litter, and the monkey bounded onto his shoulder and clutched at his curly black hair with one hand while making signs of the cross in the air with the other.

The knights clambered forward, moaning protests, as the dwarf scurried around, looking under the litter, peering into the alcoves, tasting the air with his long purple tongue, obviously suspicious. Then one of the Hospitalers grabbed him by his belt and carried him back across the grotto like baggage, depositing him on the stone steps. A tall, blond-bearded man in a white headcloth with a curved saber at his hip—the only armed man in the tomb—put a curved-toed shoe on the dwarf's shoulder and forced him to sit.

The other Hospitalers had prostrated themselves before her. She finished her prayer and lifted her face to the writhing torch-shadows on the ceiling. "God's will be done," she intoned in Latin.

The Hospitalers were staring intently at her, their faces streaked with tears. Two jabbered at her in Latin, touching the hem of her dress and shaking violently with sobs.

"I do not understand," Rachel said, her voice splintering at the edge of meaning with thirst from the vapors, whose effluvium still reeked in the air. "I speak only langue d'oc and Welsh. Please—" She removed the knights' callused hands from her robe. "Do not worship me."

A man in black with an odd-shaped crimson cross over his heart knelt close beside her, his tousled hair in his eyes, tears running down his shaven cheeks and glittering like dew in his precisely trimmed beard. "I speak langue d'oc," he gasped. His face was so extravagantly handsome it looked evil. "I am Gianni Rieti. Do you remember me?"

Panic flared in Rachel, for she had never seen him before and could not recollect the baroness ever mentioning him.

"It was I who administered the viaticum."

Viaticum—traveling money. Rachel recalled that this was what the Christians called the holy bread they fed the dying. This was the priest who had administered Ailena's last rites.

"I stood with you at the threshold of death," Gianni Rieti said. "The light drove me back and blinded me. Even now, my eyes ache from the glare of heaven's glory. Blessed woman, tell us— what did you behold in the light?"

Rachel sighed in gratitude for that cue and spoke the words she had memorized: "I saw our Lord Jesus Christ." At the mention of that name, all heads bowed. "He restored my youth—but not as a saint, as a sinner. I have been rejuvenated to undo my sins. I am not to be worshiped. I am not worthy. And no one—" She emphasized this by gazing into each of the impassioned faces regarding her, just as she had been instructed to do. "No one is to speak of this miracle, which you have been chosen by God to witness."

There—her seared throat had said it exactly as the baroness had insisted.

"But the bishop and the king," Gianni Rieti said after translating her message to the other knights. "*Surely* they must know! This is too glorious an event to keep secret. The whole world must share our joy. You are living proof of God's love and power."

Rachel shook her head, put her hand on the crimson cross of the priest's black robe. "That living proof is here or it is nowhere," she improvised. "Now, please, take me to Solomon's Tower, to the Templars' Grand Master. He is the executor of my last will. He should know there have been some changes."

David Tibbon waited at the window in his tiered house at the corner of Jehosaphat and Spanish streets. This, he knew, would be his last day in the Holy City, the city of drunken walls tilting over the shrieks and clangs of the waterbearers in the dun mud streets, the honks of the camels, the shining voice of the muezzin, and the cries of human joy and misery swarming from the shuttered balconies. He breathed deeply the aromas of spice and fish, brick dust and sandalwood and gazed down at children dashing by, some with pockmarked faces, all, he knew, with hair full of blood-ticks.

Once, three or four years ago, from this window he had watched an aged donkey collapse in the street from exhaustion.

Since it was too heavy to drag to the slaughterhouse, men in head-cloths came with axes and cut it into pieces right there while it was still alive. Its brays rang out, and it stared with squirming, startled eyes as its legs were hacked off, its haunches torn away like limbs from a tree. He had watched with such grim fascination that he had not noticed Rachel standing behind him, transfixed.

For days afterward, for as long as the street remained dark with the donkey's blood, Rachel would not eat or speak. Even the panther-faced magician could not bring her around. When she did speak again, she told David, "I die with everything that is dying. I go with them."

Now the baroness was dead. Would Rachel go with her? *No— that cannot happen.* Her training with the old woman and the magician had been so thorough and had endured for so many more years than David would have guessed that now he was sure she would stay for him. The plan would go forward. They would not even have to think for a long time. The plan would think for them.

Right now, with the tempera of early morning washing the sky in the colors of lemon and watermelon, Rachel was completing her nightlong vigil with the astonished Grand Master. The baroness had been shrewd to give the Grand Master her last will before she died. The will converted to the Templars all her extensive holdings in the Holy Land. If she had left them intact, Rachel and he would have had no incentive to leave and fulfill her revenge. But now, they were as penniless as when she had plucked them from the black mud of the graveyard in Arles. The treasure she had promised them was a cache of jewels in some crypt deep in the wild hills of Wales.

David shook his head ruefully, thinking of the long journey and frightful dangers ahead. Below, a small creature screamed from the butcher's stall as it was disemboweled. Black beads of flies hovered over the scream like smoke. He watched a flight of doves climb above the minarets into the first rays, and he heard the muezzin sing from the *Ebed:* "I praise the perfection of God, the Forever existing."

∘   ∘   ∘

Falan Askersund had come to the Holy Land fifteen years earlier as a squire to a Swedish knight who had refused to destroy the old sanctuary of idols on his land and had been exiled in penance to Jerusalem. Falan had been only twelve when he arrived, eleven when he had left Björkö, the Isle of Birches, where his own family had been forced at swordpoint to worship the cross. He had been captured in battle two years later and carried off to Damascus, the city the Arabs called "The Bride of the Earth—the Garden of the World." Even that first day that he saw her from the chattel cart, with fear chafing his heart as chains rubbed his ankles raw, he loved her: she was as beautiful as he had always imagined Paradise to be, the immense level plain of the Ghuta emerald with gardens and orchards of orange and citron and jessamine. And rising from the midst of these fragrant groves in a babel of gurgling brooks were the Roman gates of polished red sandstone, the yellow sea of clay houses, the forest of minarets, and the great golden dome of the Omayyad Mosque.

For two years, Falan lived as a harem boy to one of the Sultan's viziers, pomading his buttocks, pleasuring him with his hands and mouth. For his compliance, he was treated kindly and dwelled in shaded courts and exquisitely carved and painted rooms in the vizier's palace. He learned Arabic, he read the Qur'an and was deeply moved by its simple yet profound wisdom as accessible to all as the clear water of the Golden Stream that flowed through a carefully planned network of channels to every street, even to the poorest homes.

At sixteen, he had grown too old for the harem, and the vizier offered him his freedom. But Falan did not want to return to the mongrel society of Christians who trampled their poor, forced people to worship their three gods and their endless icons, and mocked the teachings of their own prophet by slaughtering each other. Falan's love for Islam glowed like a lantern in his chest, dispelling all the darkness of doubt about life and death that had haunted him since he had left Björkö.

Falan begged the vizier to test his faith by the sword that had brought him to this land, and the vizier turned him over to the generals. That was in 1187, when Saladin sounded the tocsin for the *jihad*, a holy war of extermination on the whole Christian plague. Falan learned the skills of a warrior in battle, his loyalty as an outsider continually tested in the front ranks against Christian knights and footmen. He fought valiantly at Hattin, where thirty thousand Christians fell under the Muslim sword on the very Mount of Beatitudes where the Messiah had taught the people the blessedness of peace. He cried, "There is no god but God!" at the walls of Jerusalem, and wept to see the thousands of Muslim slaves liberated from the rapacity and tyranny of their Christian masters. He fought at Toron, Beyrut, and Ascalon and wept again at the clemency and even-handed justice Saladin administered to the Christian warriors who killed so many of the faithful.

After the Peace of Ramla in September 1192, the Holy War was over, and all of Palestine west of the Jordan that had been Christian five years before was in the Muslims' hands except for a narrow strip of coast from Tyre to Jaffa. When Saladin died of fever six months later, Falan returned to Damascus and mourned for a year. Afterward, he pilgrimaged to Mecca and on his return immersed himself in the noble simplicity and austere self-sacrifice of Islam. He married and had children, but Allah took them in the fevers that swept Damascus in the summer of 1196. From that time, he no longer had the heart to reside in the Garden of the World. He went to Jerusalem to study in the House of God.

Falan served the emir of Jerusalem as an emissary with the German and Danish Christians, whose languages he spoke. He was assigned to help keep Saladin's promise of protection to the Christian pilgrims who flocked to Jerusalem to see the place where their Lord died. Occasionally, he had to fend off rough Saracen soldiers, hungry for vengeance. Some in his own ranks doubted his faithfulness because he defended the polytheists, and though the emir himself commended him, Falan determined to prove to all that he served only Allah.

When the emir sought a warrior to help fulfill a jape that a Christian baroness had determined to work on her own kindred, Falan volunteered. He would escort the sham baroness back to her kingdom in the very heart of Christendom and, after installing her among the faithless, he would return, his devotion to Islam unscathed.

Later, standing at the taffrail of the large ship that carried him out to sea on his way to the cold domain of his enemies, he ached with sorrow at watching the Holy Land set into the vermilion morning sun, horizons of clouds rayed with dawn above the spires and towers of Acre. The soft air carried the sweet rot of market smells, fish, blossoms, and the dusty tang of the desert.

Beside him stood the young Ailena Valaise, whom he was sworn to protect with his life. She was a long-nosed woman of sullen aniline beauty, with a complexion of solitude that he had seen before in the faces of war orphans. Her candid eyes dauntlessly watched the shore retreat, and he wondered what she was thinking—and realized only then and with a start how implacably, from this time forward, his survival depended on interpreting the silence around him.

Rachel heard David groaning with seasickness below deck in his berth, but she ignored him for a moment to fill herself with a last view of the Levant. She watched the land fold its few bristly trees into the shoreline, the shore into the jumbled city, the city into the hills, and all into the purple shadow of the mountains. The silent desert with its huddle of gray forts stretched out languidly before her as the ship wallowed and yawed, the rowers turning her into the wind. There was Tyre to the north, the coastline stretching beyond it as far as she could see. How small the world looked from out here.

All of creation is a garden, she thought. *The Holy Land is but a sandy fringe in a garden of forests and grasslands.*

The ship heeled upon the racing wind, the sails snapped out, and the bow hissed through the beryl sea. Spray dashed Rachel's cheeks, and she looked north toward the dark horizons of her destiny. *God did not expel us from the Garden after all,* she understood silently. *He exiled us in the Garden and made it as wild as we are—a garden of wilderness.*

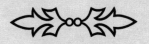

TREE
OF
WOUNDS

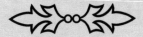

*The Grail is the spring of life—the
womb—the vessel containing the
promise of immortality—the
receptacle wherein the constant cycle
of death and rebirth takes place.*

Rachel Tibbon wakens with a start and stares hard into the darkness, trying to remember where she is. Memory sifts back: she is Ailena Valaise, and this is her first night in her castle. She sits up and sees that the curtains of her bed are drawn and that the couch where Dwn sleeps is empty.

Fear tightens her body. Where has Dwn gone? Does the old woman doubt her? How could she have hoped to fool such a life-long friend? The baroness had been mad with rage at her son—but perhaps she had been simply mad, befogged entirely beyond reason. If Dwn doubts her, no one will believe. She and David will be tortured to extract their confessions, and then stoned or burned.

Rachel clutches at her bedsheets and brings to mind the golden chalice that carries the baroness's memories. The glimmer of the bright goblet leaks out into the darkness of the room, and she sees again, in the refulgent light of remembrance, Ailena's withered body, her cobwebbed hair, her knobby hands rasping incessantly together. "My lady—they know I am an impostor."

Nonsense, the ghost whispers. *The living do not know what they see—only what they believe.*

"Dwn is gone."

She will be back. Fear not.

"I do fear, my lady. I fear for my life—and for my grandfather's life."

The ghost laughs silently, her thin hair and white robe blowing in an unfelt wind. *You are dead already. Everyone is dead when they are born. Life is a dream, dear child. Don't you remember? Come now—after all I've taught you, you cannot pretend to be so innocent. Only death is real. Why else do the living pray to their saints? Why else would you turn to me? The living depend on the dead!*

Darkness rays through Ailena's silent laughter, and Rachel is alone once more, shivering in the lambent warmth of the summer night.

Rachel drifts back to sleep and dreams of the shipwreck, which befell them only two days after leaving Rome. The pope himself had received them in the Basilica, and, to the proud joy of the Hospitalers who had accompanied her from Jerusalem, the Holy Father had embraced her and kissed her on both cheeks. With trembling fingers and traces of tears in his eyes, Celestine III had penned in his own hand the writ of authentication that confirmed the miracle of her rejuvenation.

There was no doubt in Rachel's mind that the gale that swooped down on them off the coast of France was God's punishment for duping the pope. That night, she had huddled in her cabin with her grandfather as the squall buffeted the usciere. Timbers squealing, the ship lurched among the storm swells, and rats scurried from their hiding places. The wailing scream of the wind even smothered David's loud prayers.

The cabin door had burst open, and Falan Askersund stood there. He grabbed Rachel by her arms, pulled her upright, and staggered out of the tilting cabin with her. David followed them up the gangway and onto the rain-lashed deck. Black claws of rock suddenly reared out of the thrashing mists, a cyclopean landscape of exploding waves and shrieking wind.

Several of the Hospitalers stood on the foredeck, their swords drawn, hilts raised against the tempest, warding off evil with the crosses that had defended the Holy Land. The black sea indifferently towered above them and fell on the ship. Falan deftly hooked an arm around a rail post, and pulled Rachel tight to his side as the foaming water surged over them. Gasping and struggling, the Hospitalers flew by and then vanished overboard.

David had been hurled back into the companionway, and he emerged soaked, seeking desperately for his granddaughter. The Hospitalers appeared alongside the ship, bobbing in the raging channel until a massive comber hurtled them onto the rocks. Another great wave struck the ship broadside, submerging the deck, and the wash sucked David away. Rachel's cries flapped emptily in the slashing rain.

With a tormented groan and shudder, the keel struck the reef; the oak timbers burst apart, and the deck tilted sickeningly as the sea flooded in. Muscles knotted, Falan strained against the cascading water on the sloping deck, carrying Rachel to the bow. Several men had lowered a smaller boat, hoping to ride the maelstrom to shore. But before all could reach the boat, it dipped over the side, and the current flung it into the rocks, shattering it to splinters and flying bodies.

Rachel clung to Falan. Over his shoulder, she saw another breaker loom high above the ship and shouted to warn him. The howling wind swept her cry away, and the next instant, the great wave smote them. Like a giant's hand, it lifted them high above the ship. And the hungry sea received them.

Again Rachel wakes with a sweaty shudder. Dawnlight stands in the tall, spired window, the river Llan glinting behind it, shimmering in a band of bright snake scales. She remembers where she is. Miraculously, the shipwreck had not killed her. She had regained her senses in Falan's arms, washed ashore with Gianni Rieti and his dwarf and monkey. Later, they found David floating on his back in the shallows, still alive. But no one else survived. God's wrath had taken them all—and had left her and the few others alive for further torment.

Sitting up in bed, Rachel can still see in her mind the wreck of the ship wedged fast among the black rocks, aswarm with local fishermen zealous for plunder. If not for Falan, they would have slit her throat for her gold signet ring. With Gianni Rieti's help, they found his Arabian stallion and two of the six camels still alive in the hold and got them to shore, together with Rachel's sea chests.

David had wanted to dismiss the two surviving knights, take the small treasure in the chests, and make a new life for themselves in Provence. But too many had died to bring them this far, and for Rachel the voices began again with unabated relentlessness. She was afraid of the ghosts of the drowned, afraid they would join the wraiths of her family to torment her all her days.

Most impelling was the voice of the baroness: after seven years of training, Ailena would not give up. She clung to Rachel's soul, inflaming her with the zeal to fulfill her bargain and claim her treasure. And even David had to admit finally that his grand-daughter knew more about being the baroness than of being her-self. So with great reluctance, he submitted to the final, audacious act of their unknown destiny.

Gingerly, Rachel steps out of bed, kneels before the largest of her chests, and presses her face to its carved lid before opening it. Inside are the baroness's silk and damask garments purchased in the Levant. Here, too, she has carried her grandfather's scroll of the Law, and the Bible, side by side with the pope's writ and the king's charter. Now that most of the gifts have been distributed, all that remain are a velvet-wrapped present for Guy, and five vessels of hardened red clay.

The oblong vessels are the baroness's last gift to Rachel—grenades, hand-bombs the size of wine carafes purchased from the Saracens. They are filled with the mysterious Greek fire, waiting to be ignited by burning the stubby fuses that plug their short throats. The baroness had thought them a useful gift to the alchemists at the king's court, should the occasion ever arise.

Rachel takes out her present for Guy, a Seljuk Turk dagger with a gold-braided ivory hilt, a ruby-set crocodileskin scabbard, and a curved blade of the finest blue damascene steel. She unwraps it and holds it in her hand, feeling its lively heft. "Why such a beautiful and deadly gift for one whom you hate and who hates you?" Rachel had asked the baroness.

The old woman had been close to death then, unable to get out of her bed, her skin shrunk close to her skull, but she had laughed huskily at Rachel's ingenuous question. "You should know by now. You are almost me."

Rachel, fingering the smooth hilt as she fingers it now, had answered, "He sent you out penniless and yet you return with a princely gift. A Christian gesture."

"Yes," she had answered, satisfied. Her closed eyelids were creased like walnut shells. "He must know that I love him. He is, after all, my only son. How can I really hurt him if he doesn't think I love him?"

Rachel lays the knife back in the chest, frightened at the hatefulness of that memory. She stands and looks around at the bedchamber that, until now, has existed only in the images woven by the baroness. The room appears smaller, the frescoes painted on the walls duller than she had foreseen.

She presses her fingertips against the fresco of the stag hunt on the wall opposite the bed. The stucco feels dank, and the air smells mustier than she would have guessed. In the palazzos of the Levant, the rooms had been continually charged with sweet incense and the floral spices of the surrounding gardens. Mildew taints the air here.

Trailing a hand along the stone sill, she paces the breadth of the chamber. The space is as large as the baroness had said, yet it feels more confined. She winces, and shivers at the thought that this is the reality of her years of dreaming. Since the destruction of her family, she has lived simply as an observer, staring out at the world as though it were a desert mirage, obediently accepting Karm Abu Selim's trances. But now those dreams have become real. Now she must act. And that frightens her.

Yesterday, the acting had been so well rehearsed, she did not have to think. But today—what will she do when the others question her, when decisions must be made?

Panic chills her down to her viscera, and she sits on the bed and calls forth the golden chalice. Instantly, vividly, it appears in her mind; relief saturates her. Karm Abu Selim's sorcery still works. She can still escape being Rachel by drinking of this magic goblet. The baroness's memories and her very spirit brim in her. Through the image of this aureate cup, she can die as Rachel and be reborn as Ailena all on her own—again and again.

Dwn returns at dawn from her prayer of thanks to God at the shrine of her old home in the dungheap. She passes Falan Askersund in the passage, on his way to relieving himself in the privy. Quietly, she opens the door, hoping her mistress is still asleep, and she finds Rachel sitting on the edge of her bed staring dreamy-eyed into space. One of the sea chests is open, and sitting atop the garments is a wicked-looking dagger, a work of such intricate beauty that only the devil's children could have shaped it. With a soft knock, she enters. "Forgive me, my lady, for not being here when you awoke."

Rachel looks about like a startled animal, searching the crone's face for any sign that she has been found out. When she sees that the old woman regards her kindly, she rises, summons forth the baroness's spirit, and presents the dagger. "For Guy. Will he accept it?"

Dwn looks wary but does not touch the satanic instrument. "It is truly handsome, in its frightful way. It will appeal to him. But he is wroth at your return. You hit him hard when you struck the Griffin and flew the Swan. The miracle of your transformation does not move him."

The old servant steps to the open chest and peers in. Her eyes widen at the sight of the delicate garments, and, with a gasp of pure joy, she kneels to touch them.

"What will Guy do?" Rachel asks.

"Certainly he will rally the men he's brought from Hereford. He'll not sit by idly, that much I know."

Rachel kneels beside the old woman and clutches her thin, taut arm. Her features have become fragile with fear, pathetically young, delicate as frosted crystal. "Dwn, I am frightened."

A surprised expression flits over Dwn's wizened face. She takes the young woman's hand in hers, rubs the smooth knuckles with her coarse fingers. "Servant of Birds, you *have* changed. Your heart has changed with your flesh. You have seen the Grail! You need never fear again, my lady."

Rachel closes her eyes. "Of course. I am not afraid for my soul. But the miracle has changed me—and I am afraid that I have lost the spirit to rule."

"But our Savior sent you to rule in His name." Dwn's face quivers with puzzlement. "You *saw* our Lord. How can you ever be afraid of anything again?" The old woman traces Rachel's lineaments with a quavery fingertip, her amber eyes shining with awe. "You are a child again. You have the face of a child. I remember you well when last you had this face. But there was far more bitterness in it then than now. You have shed much ire with your years, sweet lady." She touches her own weathered face. "Do you remember how I looked?"

Rachel blinks. The dark spur of hair on the old woman's chin is the cue the baroness had taught her to identify, if the old servant were still alive. But she cannot bring forward any image of the youthful Dwn. She shakes her head. "I'm sorry, my friend. I'm far too anxious to look backward. I cannot take my eyes off today and tomorrow."

The concern in Rachel's gaze troubles the crone. The baroness had never admitted to fear, even when her husband had beaten her to within an inch of her life. Dwn looks deeply into her face, trying to read what calamity her friend foresees. Awkward and perplexed, she then releases the soft hand and turns her attention shyly to the contents of the chest. "Show me the gowns you have brought from the Orient."

The two women are sorting through the bright apparel when Guy appears in the doorway, his topknot undone, his lank black hair framing a furious countenance. All night long he has sat in the stairwell, waiting for Falan to leave his post—ample time to nurse his rage at losing his Hereford mercenaries. Dressed in the same green cotta he wore at last night's feast, he stalks into the bed-chamber. The Griffin device on his breast is dulled with the dust of the road. "How came you to wear my mother's signet ring?" he demands.

Dwn screeches a Welsh imprecation at his intrusion and covers her mistress's dishabille with a blue samite cape.

Rachel draws the cape about her and gently moves her servant aside with a reassuring nod. "Dear, dear Guy—my son—" She manages a cool smile though her pulse beat roars in her ears. "This is *my* ring." She lifts her hand to display the green chalcedony embossed with an ebony V.

"Liar!"

Rachel lifts her chin and fights to steady her voice: "Your faithlessness ill serves you, Guy."

Guy strides across the chamber and presses close to Rachel, sensing her fear. There is a tremor in her upper lip, a startled alertness to her stare. "You are not Ailena. You are not even a good semblance."

Facing Guy's contemptuous sneer—with his pug nose and swarthy, pinched frown, he looks like a bat—Rachel thinks, *This is the same brute who came in hundreds to Lunel to kill my family.* The frost shivering in her hardens to a cold fire. Suddenly, she is not acting anymore. The baroness is gone, and she is Rachel, watching him through her plundered and furious soul. When she speaks, her voice is edged with iron: "Get out of my chamber. Get out this very moment."

Guy's mouth widens into a cruel grin, certainty affirmed now that this quivery young woman is an impostor. Mother would simply have slapped him. "Who are you? How did my mother get you to come here and throw your life away on this laughable scheme?"

Years of standing up to the shouts of the baroness and the magician during her desert training make Rachel set her jaw. Defiantly she pushes her face close to his until she tastes the sourness of his breath, sees the filaments of blood tangled in the whites of his eyes. "You've not changed one whit, Guy. I had hoped you would be a more gentle man as you gained in years and experience. Why are you so loath to have your mother back?"

"My *mother!*" Guy's face twists with derision. "Am I wearing cap and bells? Do I look foolish enough to believe you are my mother? Deceiver! God—if there is a God—permits even the sainted to suffer and die in famines and war. Why would He spare my mother, who was never good except to herself?"

Dwn snaps, "You dare question God? You who have murdered the rightful people of this land?"

"Shut up, old woman, or you'll join those rightful people."

Rachel puts out an arm to hold her servant back. "God has spared me for I need to undo what evil I have done."

"Undo how? What are you going to do?"

"I will address you when I address the other knights in the *palais*. Go there and await me."

Unable to contain himself, Guy lunges forward. With sudden fury, he seizes her cape with his left hand and twists it tight about her throat. "I swear—tell me now or you'll not speak again!"

Rachel twists loose of Guy's grip. A needle of anger stabs into her heart. The baroness's voice rises without her volition. "The siege of Neufmarché's castle is lifted! That is my decree. And, dearest son, you shall pay reparations."

"Never!" Purple veins throb at Guy's temples as he draws his dagger.

Dwn clutches at his knife arm, but he slaps her free. She rebounds to heave herself at the furious man, but Rachel grabs her servant's arm. "Stand back, Dwn. He will not cut down his own mother." Rachel backs away carefully, looking him steadily in the eyes. "Am I not the same woman who mended your wounds after your first brawl? Yes—do you remember that, Guy? What were you—I think but fourteen that summer, the summer you loved Anne Gilford, the cobbler's daughter? You fought three grown men for her honor, wounded them all and took your cuts without crying. But how you did cry when pretty Anne rode off with the miller's son to make their fortune in Gloucester! I rocked you in my arms then like a newborn babe."

Guy's knife arm freezes; he stares hard at this woman, seeing then—or is he imagining?—the beautiful features that had awed him as a child, even as he had hated her for betraying his father. *Is this truly she?*

Suddenly, a lash of white silk snags his knife arm and jerks him off balance. Behind him stands Falan Askersund, his blond hair fallen in a long braid over his shoulder, his unraveled turban stretched taut between his hand and the captured arm. With a simple twist, the headcloth snaps, and the coin-weighted loop around Guy's wrist unwinds. Sternly, the Muslim knight turns aside, hand on his scabbard, and jerks his head for Guy to depart.

With a last bellicose look at Rachel, Guy stalks out of the chamber, chewing his rage. Falan, too, departs and closes the door after him. In the tense silence that follows, the crone clutches her Servant of Birds, afraid for what is to come.

David is wearing the ritual leather strap on his left arm with the small square leather box on his forehead and is in the middle of his prayers when he hears the knock at his door. "Who is there?" he asks nervously, and prepares to remove the phylactery, then restrains himself. Though his granddaughter's status as a baroness has afforded him protection from the gentiles since they left Jerusalem ten months ago, the old habit of fear has made a nest in his bones. He has prayed about this many times and has always come up with the same answer: the fish that leaps out of the water is a dead fish. It is true; he belongs among his people, not here in a gentile fortress in the northern wilderness, his granddaughter pretending to be someone she is not. How he hates that—but he is strangely proud of her. Though she nearly slipped into a trance during her questioning in the *palais* yesterday, she has been convincing in her role.

"Rabbi, it is I," Rachel's voice calls through the door, and he opens it. She looks tall and imposing in her dazzling white robe of sendal silk ornamented with gold embroidery and pearl beadwork, her hair swept up in ring-braids under a gold chaplet. "May we come in?"

David stands aside, and the two women enter and go immediately to the window, where the scroll lies open on the broad stone sill. Falan Askersund, who has accompanied them, closes the door and waits outside.

Dwn moves close to Rachel and does not disguise her uneasiness at the sight of the bearded Jew in his religious attire. In her whole life, she has never seen anyone who is other than Christian.

In Welsh, she queries, "What are those leather straps on his arm and head?"

"*Tefillin,* they are called," Rachel answers. "Within, they contain Holy Scripture, and are worn as reminders of God, except upon the Sabbath, which itself is a reminder. The prayer shawl he wears is called a *tallit*. The tassels advise us of the commandments given to Moses."

"You speak as though you are a Jew already, my lady."

"Jesus was a Jew, Dwn, so that has become my faith as well. That will also be the faith of this castle while I am here. We will worship as our Savior worshiped."

Dwn puckers her creased lips and shakes her head. "Maître Pornic will find little favor with that."

"Maître Pornic is no longer our parish priest," Rachel says matter-of-factly, regarding the open scroll. "Gianni Rieti will minister to the castle for now. He has been studying with Rabbi Tibbon since Jerusalem."

Dwn clucks knowingly. "Now I think he is studying with Maître Pornic. On my way back to the castle at first light I spied them together atop Merlin's Knoll deep in prayer."

David and Rachel exchange nervous glances. "I will address that in the great hall today," Rachel says. "That is why we are here, Rabbi. I will formally introduce you today during my installation in the great hall. These first days will be difficult, for as many disbelieved our Lord in his time, so many will surely disbelieve me."

"You are always in my prayers," David answers sincerely but adds, looking at her sharply, "Though perhaps it is best if you do not impose the original faith of Rabbi Yeshua so quickly upon these people. Let them keep their own worship and you keep yours."

"That is wise, Rabbi," Dwn agrees, with some relief.

"That shall be so in the domain," Rachel says flatly. "But in this castle, where I dwell, we will eat and praise God as did our Lord Jesus Christ."

"Eat as did our Lord?" Dwn echoes hollowly and plucks at the hairs on her chin mole. "The castle swineherds will marvel over that news."

"And the cooks will marvel at our new disdain for swan and heron and hare—and no more meat with cream sauces. Will you instruct the cooks, Rabbi?"

"I should be more at ease to do so in your presence, my lady," David answers, eyeing her pointedly.

"Then let us go to the cookhouse," Rachel says. "But first,

Rabbi, lead us in a prayer as Jesus—or, as you call him, Yeshua—would have prayed."

David nods. When Dwn drops to her knees, he gently lifts her up. "Friend, Yeshua prayed standing up, with hands open to God, to receive his blessing. Let us do likewise."

And so they pray—and David's voice issues from him in the language of his ancestors, proud in the strength of his granddaughter, strong in the hope of life, and alive with God's splendor that was, is, and always will be.

Rachel requests a moment alone with the rabbi, and after Dwn departs, she clutches his arm and says in a hot whisper: "Grandfather—he tried to kill me!"

"Who, Rachel?"

"The baron. He *knows* I'm not his mother." Her eyes are desperate. "I'll never convince him."

Though alarmed by the panic in Rachel's expression, David keeps his face passive. He pulls her close. "We need not convince him at all. The jewels the baroness promised are waiting for us. We have only to retrieve them quickly and quit this place."

Rachel breathes deeply of her grandfather's body heat and is calmed. "Yes. I will go to the abbey to get our treasure soonest. We will return to Jerusalem and be there for Passover."

David pulls away to face her. "During the short time we are here, we must not make too much of worshiping as Yeshua did. Let the gentiles have their pork."

Rachel shakes her head, and the fear in her face slips away. "No, grandfather. My father—your son—sacrificed his whole family for his faith. He would have sacrificed me, too, if I had been there. I have forsaken everything else to play this role, but I will not forsake our faith."

David puts a gentle hand to her cheek. "I understand." He leans closer, peers at her beseechingly. "But you must be careful. You are right to be frightened, and fear makes you vulnerable to the frights of your past. When you dwell on those frights, you say troubling things. What was that you said in the great hall about fire? That did not sound like the baroness."

Rachel looks at him blankly. "I don't know. The young knight Thierry made me think about fevers and death, and the words just came to me."

"You must watch that," David warns. "The Persian magician has not healed your grief. He has merely hidden it—and when it finds your voice, it speaks from Rachel, not from the baroness."

A loud blast on trumpets assembles the household in the great hall. The rushes and flowers on the floor have been replaced with fresh blooms, and the tall, arched windows are open, admitting sunshafts, spurts of wrens, and summery breezes. Guy Lanfranc and Roger Billancourt have sat in their chairs long before the herald's call, sulking and glowering as they watched the servitors change the Griffin trappings to ones embossed with the baroness's device.

As Clare and Gerald, with their children and grandchildren, take their seats on the cushioned chairs of the front rank, the other castle dwellers arrange themselves on the settles behind them: first the knights, with their sergeants and squires; then the guildsmen and their families; and behind them the castle villeins on the benches at the back. The dwarf, Ummu, and his monkey familiar, Ta-Toh, cause an excited stir as they somersault in, prompting an irate sergeant to raise a quarterstaff at them.

At the foot of the dais, on a cushioned settle that faces the assembly, Gianni Rieti sits between the gaunt Maître Pornic and the bearded and shawled Rabbi Tibbon. Gravely, they watch as Rachel enters the great hall at the back, escorted by Dwn and Falan Askersund, and they note the rapt wonder in the faces of the villeins as she nods to them and to the older servitors—the attendants, maids, and guildsmen whom the baroness knew before her pilgrimage.

Gerald Chalandon, as castle steward, greets Rachel in the sunlit front of the great hall, drops to one knee and kisses her signet ring. His large, sallow skull glows amber in its cuff of silver-streaked hair, but it is his stout wife, Clare, who beams most beatifically at her youthful mother.

Rachel curtsies to the holy men before ascending the dais and taking her seat in the canopied chair of state. Behind her, on a stool, sits Dwn with Falan farther back, obscured from view by large banners embroidered with silver-threaded swans.

The array of staring faces chills Rachel. These strangers gaze at her with open-mouthed reverence as though she were some holy icon—except for the hard-eyed Guy and his warmaster and the abbot whose face is lowered in prayer. She wants this presentation to be over and done, but she dares not reveal her trepidation.

At Gerald's signal, a herald blares his trumpet, and the hall falls silent. "Will you have Ailena Valaise, lately returned in blessed guise from the Holy Land, as your present undoubted baroness and suzerain?"

Cries of "Fiat!" rise up from the assembly of knights, though Guy and Roger remain ominously silent.

"All those of knightly rank who will serve in liege and life the baroness Ailena Valaise come forward and do homage," Gerald demands loudly.

Denis Hezetre rises and stands before Guy. "You should lead us in this, as you've led us in all else," he says quietly.

Guy glares darkly at him. "I'll kiss the Devil's buttocks first."

Denis does not even look at Roger. He mounts the steps of the dais, goes down on one knee before Rachel and kisses her ring. He is followed in turn by Harold Almquist, William Morcar, and his son Thierry, who pauses first before Guy and receives his nod. When they are done, they stand to the right of the chair of state and face the assembly.

"These are my knights," Rachel says in a strong voice. Her strength surprises her, for she trembles to see the Frankish warriors whose kind destroyed her childhood home. To go on, she must call up the Grail and stare into its gold luster. Then she knows what she must say. She looks down at Guy. "They honor me with their lives. Why has my own son refused me this honor?"

Guy rises, hands on his hips. "I do not recognize your right to rule this domain," he says sourly, and anxious murmurs flare through the crowd.

"The pope and the king recognize her right," Clare announces angrily, pointing to the lecterns on the dais where the two vellum documents are posted. "Behold. They are there for all to read."

Guy returns his sister's scowl with a sneer. "Dearest sister, perhaps you have not heard, but the pope who signed that writ is now dead."

"Be quiet, the two of you," Maître Pornic interjects abruptly. "Celestine the Third surrendered his soul to heaven in January. It is our intention that our new Holy Father, Innocent the Third, shall study the writ and confirm that a miracle could indeed have been performed for one as worldly as the baroness."

"My mother was no more worldly than Saul before he became Paul, or the tax collector who became Jesus' disciple," Clare protests. "Are not all sinners subject to grace through penitence, Maître?"

"Celestine the Third was ninety-two when he signed that writ," Maître Pornic adds patiently. "The new Holy Father has the sensibilities of a younger man and should review that document."

"I say the pope's age makes no difference," Clare persists. "The Holy Father is infallible."

"Lady Chalandon is correct," Gianni states. "The authority of the Holy Father can never be impugned."

Guy ignores the canon and bows to the holy man. "Thank you, Maître. Your reservations are sufficient for me. Moreover, within this past month, the king has officially changed his seal. Malchiel, the king's seal-bearer, was drowned off Limassol on the journey to the Levant. When his body washed ashore, a peasant found the seal on the corpse, and the king bought it back from him. I know the story, for I had to pay the heavy fee for use of the new seal."

"Which," Clare adds mockingly, "was used to decorate a penalty decree for your rebellious support of John Lackland against his brother, our good King Richard."

As hoots and catcalls resound in the hall, answered by gruff challenges from Guy's sergeants, Rachel feels the baroness's presence stirring within her, gathering words that swell with a pressure in her lungs.

"Children," she calls down suddenly from the dais. "Silence! I am the rightful ruler of this domain, and my rule has been and will again be affirmed by both the new pope and the king. In the meantime, I will not hear my status debated any further. I owe faith and loyalty to my knights and my people as much as they to me." She looks cunningly down at Guy and the warmaster. "And to that end, I herewith declare that the siege of Castle Neufmarché is concluded."

The back ranks, who have just learned of this, erupt into amazed and disappointed shouts: "God's blood!"—"Unfair!"—"We've won that prize!" At Rachel's signal, another blare of the trumpet silences the crowd.

"Guy," Rachel addresses the scowling baron, who is still standing. "As you will not pay me homage, I cannot assume your debts. The damage you have wreaked on Neufmarché you will restore in full, the exact sum to be approved by the seigneur you have assaulted."

Again, the hall reverberates with astonished cries and harsh laughter from the back ranks, eliciting yet another trumpet blast.

"Hostilities will also desist against the Welsh," Rachel continues. "The lands taken from them during my absence will be restored forthwith, and the fortalices on those lands given over to the local chieftains." For response to the ensuing outbursts of disbelief, Rachel looks over her shoulder at Dwn and catches the old woman's secret smile.

The baroness raises her hand, and the hall quiets at once to hear what her next decree will be. "Today, the swine will be driven from the castle, to be divided equally among the villagers. Pork, swan, and hare will henceforth no longer be prepared or eaten in the castle. Neither will frogs and snails and all fish without fins and scales. Those who wish to eat these foods, which our Lord and Savior considered unclean, may do so in the village. The cookhouse will be instructed by Rabbi Tibbon in the methods of food preparation that our Savior himself honored."

Rachel gazes out over the great hall with the unique emotion of power. She has experienced something deep in her change. The chill that she had first felt upon facing this crowd of Normans has become a flutter of heat. The spirit of the baroness flexes in her like cleverness. She is no longer afraid of these Christians: she commands them. An exultant smile trembles in her to see the puzzlement on Clare's chubby face, the futile anger in Guy's locked brow, and the awe drenching the scores of people watching her, adhering to her every word. And there, among them, is Grandfather David, looking anxious, appealing to her with an upglancing look from his bowed head to conclude this assembly.

"Tomorrow," she says, and the hall is instantly silent, dappled only with the twittering of the wrens. "Tomorrow, I will leave the castle to tour my domain and to seek counsel in prayer at Trinity Abbey."

Whispers glitter in the hushed hall. Guy turns on his heel and, with his warmaster trotting close after him like his shadow, he strides out of the hall. Rachel considers stopping him; but just knowing that she can, with one word, is enough.

After Rachel's accession to the barony of Epynt, her grandfather reads from the Torah in blessing of the assembly, before Gerald Chalandon dismisses the gathering.

"'Take heed to yourself, lest you make a covenant with the inhabitants of the land where you go, lest it be for a snare in the midst of you—'" David intones from the thirty-fourth chapter of Exodus as the rowdy crowd presses toward the dais. As the villeins reach out deliriously to touch this woman who has drunk from the Holy Grail, the guildsmen, apoplectic with indignation, surge forward demanding compensation for the funds and goods they have invested and now lost in the siege of Castle Neufmarché, and fistfights break out in the great hall.

Above the cacophony, Rachel stands on the dais surprised by the violent reaction of the crowd. Her sense of command evaporates, and she feels suddenly frail and spent. The melee confounds her, and she doesn't know where to focus her attention. Squinting in the sugar-white morning sun, she searches desperately for her grandfather's face in the angry crowd.

She watches with mounting panic as the crowd swallows her grandfather and spirits him away, and for a moment she feels once again all the stupor of horror that she felt eleven years ago, watching helplessly as a similar mob destroyed her home. The hive noise of the crowd rises up, urgent and implacable, and jars her to within a hairs breadth of falling out of herself—falling and being swallowed by the mass of red faces struggling angrily toward her. There is nowhere to go at all, nowhere to hide. The power she had enjoyed a moment ago has fixed her in eternity at the center of this patchwork of inflamed faces.

Softly, she speaks to the surging crowd: "Good people, I cannot restore old policies. You must understand. I . . . have become renewed, transfigured. Another pattern cuts our fate and binds us to the strife which divides us. Do you understand? You must understand . . ."

Her voice trails away, and an uncontainable panic flails through her. In despair, she sits down and strives to see the golden chalice, to drink deeply from the presence of the baroness. But the enraged shouts pummel her too fiercely for her to focus on anything. Her alertness smudges, blurs toward blindness, and imminent madness knots tightly in her throat. Suddenly, gentle hands take her by the shoulders and turn her away from the seething throng. "Mother, are you all right?"

Clare's concerned face looks down at her and fills in the gaping emptiness with her fleshly presence. Rachel nods, rubs the numbness from her temples. "Where is Grandfather?" she asks.

Clare returns a baffled look.

"The rabbi—where is he?"

"Maître Pornic has summoned him," Clare answers and coaxes her to stand. "Come, Mother. Let us away from this shouting rabble. Merchants!" She sniggers with disgust and waves for Gerald to come and help her. "Money is their soul, cold and dirty."

Rachel gratefully accepts Gerald's offered arm. All her strength has washed away, leaving her hollow. She closes her eyes and again invokes the Grail. Now it appears, bright as a piece of the sun behind her lids, and her anguish dwindles, but it does not go completely away. She has come too close to losing everything: she realizes with icy clarity that she is too fragile to go on. *Yet—how can I stop? I must play this role just a little longer. I will go on. I must.*

"Tell me, Rabbi, is Jesus the Messiah?" Maître Pornic asks. He is seated in a sturdy oak chair whose high back is carved with a lamb bearing a crosier. Facing him, in a chair backed with the carved heads from Ezekiel's vision of a bull, an eagle, a lion, and an angel,

David sits, the scroll of the Law in his lap. They are in the apse behind the altar, where light from the stained glass windows breaks the woe-dark of the chapel into fiery bits. Gianni Rieti stands, arms crossed over his chest, leaning against the back of the altar.

"'Shall a man make gods unto himself and they are no gods?'" David answers. "Why do you make Jesus a god?"

"You quote the prophets?" Maître Pornic assesses the man before him with cold-eyed dispassion. "Did not the prophet Isaiah foresee the coming of the Messiah?"

"I quoted Jeremiah, chapter sixteen, verse twenty. As for Isaiah, he wrote, 'And the sons of the stranger that love the name of the Lord, even them will I bring to my holy mountain.'" Watching the quiet darkness in the shriveled man's keen eyes, David's emotional balance swings from fear to respect and back again.

"The name of the Lord is Jesus Christ," Maître Pornic says with great tenderness. "Do you believe Jesus is Christ the Savior, the Anointed One, the Messiah prophesied by your people?"

"There is no Jesus in the Bible of the Jews."

Maître Pornic closes his eyes and shakes his head. "'He came unto his own,'" he quotes from the first chapter of John, "'and His own received Him not.'"

"Surely, Maître," Gianni Rieti intervenes, "you did not summon the rabbi here to question his faith. The baroness has elicited his aid in learning the language and customs of our Savior because he is a scholarly Jew."

The holy man's face condenses brutally. "He blessed the assembly!" His fingers shake. "This—man, who has no faith in our Savior, blessed an assembly of Christians. What mockery do we make of our Lord's suffering?"

"I blessed the congregation as any rabbi would bless," David answers, experiencing a cold wind through his chest, "even the rabbi you worship."

"I worship the Son of God!" Maître Pornic shrills, his voice clattering back from the dark heights. At the sight of the alarm in the Jew's face, the fury passes, and the abbot raises a dispirited hand to pinch the flesh between his eyes. "Forgive me." He stands and staggers as if he has been struck. "These are my people, my flock." He waves that thought aside. His starved face has the serene ferocity of an eagle. "The miracle of the Grail—the miracle that transformed the baroness from an aged, bent, and bitter woman to the beautiful youth who rules Epynt today—does that not stir faith in you that Jesus is indeed the Messiah?"

David's mouth opens and hangs open like a mousehole in the shag of his beard.

"The rabbi did not know the baroness before the miracle," Gianni replies for him.

"Did you, my son?"

Gianni shakes his head.

"She was an entirely godless woman," Maître Pornic recalls in a calmer voice. "It was the death of her father, Bernard, the first earl of Epynt, that rotted her faith. He himself had been an assiduously religious man. I knew him well—many years ago." Weariness thins his voice. "We pilgrimaged to Saint David's together. He loved the Welsh, with their fierceness and their music, and he did not take any more land from them than was needed for his crops. 'They're Christians same as we,' he'd say. 'Let's worship together.' And he built this chapel as much for them—though they stopped coming when he died. The Lord took him away in a fever. And his daughter, our baroness, lost her faith with him."

David strokes his beard and looks haplessly to Gianni Rieti.

"Certainly, you would keep faith in your God," Maître Pornic asks, "if He assailed you as He did Job."

David bows his head. "Eleven years ago, I lost my entire family to the Crusader mob—my two sons and their families—"

"And so God tests our faith," the abbot affirms.

"Is it a test?" David asks, looking up, stricken. "I do not think so. We test ourselves, because we know of good and evil. But the Lord *is* good and evil."

"No." Maître Pornic rejects that thought with a wave. "Satan is evil, and God has cast him into the abyss."

"Yet who created Satan?" David asks. "And the abyss—who created that? And the pox and the drought and all manner of calamity, from whence do they issue? They come from On High."

"Not at all," the abbot says. "They come from Satan to try our souls and wrest us from God's grace."

David shrugs. "That is your faith. Mine tells me that Jehovah is more than we can know. In darkness, in suffering, in human failing—He is there, too. Who are we to question Him? Yet we must question, for that is the strength He has given us. We must doubt and we must question. And when we have reached the limit of our strength to question, we remain what we are. For we are never more than we are. We are never more than what He has made us."

Maître Pornic's wispy eyebrows go up and down slowly as he thinks about this.

"I saw the Grail," Gianni blurts out. "I saw the old and sickly baroness drink from it and be changed. Her withered flesh fell away, her bent bones straightened, and she was made young. I saw this with my own eyes."

"Think on this," Maître Pornic says to David. "Miracles open the way to faith."

"Do you believe this miracle?" David asks him.

Maître Pornic moves his harrowed visage into the warped light of the stained glass and stares at David with red-slashed eyes. "The way opened to me long ago, Rabbi. I found Jesus in a blade of grass. And now I believe only in the miracles I see."

Guy Lanfranc sits on a trestle table in the groin-vaulted chamber behind the great hall. As a boy, he had often come here to watch his father ready himself for his forays against the tribes. What he remembers best are the smells: of the vinegar that cleaned the chain mail, the horse sweat that clung to the musky leathers of boots and gloves, and best of all the solemn scent of the flaxseed oil that the varlets daubed on the joints of the armor. To this day, he cannot help feeling a tenacious nostalgia, a stirring, puerile thrill whenever he smells its tan fragrance.

As for his father's armor, Guy would have kept it here had not Ailena disposed of it unceremoniously the day he died. Instead, his own helmet, cuirass, greaves, and chain-mail shirt and cowl lie on the boards against the wall, where his father's had once hung. Remembering how often in the past he has come here to gird himself for countless raids, he feels a surge of confidence borne of combat-tested experience. He must not forget, he scolds himself, that he has triumphed in too many battles to be concerned by the threat of a mere woman.

"What are you dreaming on?" Roger Billancourt asks as he strides in.

Guy smiles wanly at his mentor. "I was wondering what Father would have done in my place."

The warmaster blows a laugh through his nose. "He'd never have let the wench into the castle to begin with."

"That was a blunder, wasn't it?"

"No sense grieving what can't be changed." Roger leans against the wall beside the window, strokes his stubby beard and assesses the baron. *He has the steel of his father,* he thinks, *but not the edge. He's hard enough to endure, all right, but not sharp enough for quick decisions—or keen enough to cut through his moods.* "Don't look so melancholy. Your knights will be here in a moment. They must see you in command or you'll lose them to the Pretender."

"She *is* an impostor, isn't she, Roger?"

Roger's jaw rocks loose. "You actually doubt it?"

Guy pinches his lower lip, then throws up his hands. "In her bedchamber, when I confronted her, she spoke of my childhood and Anne Gilford—"

"Your mother prompted her," Roger says with sharp certainty. "I'm sure the old harridan has arranged this. It stinks of her scheming."

"Yes—that must be so. But briefly, I believed her—believed she was actually Mother." He laughs at himself and looks around fondly at the walls, where shields and crossed lances are hung. "For years after Father died, I came here every day and stared at these weapons, imagining the vengeance I'd have on Mother when I grew up. I didn't realize how strong she was then—didn't think I'd have to wait until she got old and feeble before her knights would rally around me and I could unseat her. I thought I could just lop her head off and be done with it, just like that."

"Those were long years," Roger agrees. "If I had not made myself useful helping her defend against the other lords of this lawless frontier, the March, she'd have lopped *my* head off, to be sure." He straightens. "Your men are coming. Show your mettle."

The knights William, Harold, and Denis enter and nod to Guy and then to Roger. The baron stands, his face set like a snake's jaw, with a hard, joyless smile. "Who is this bitch Ailena has sent to harry me, this bitch who pretends to be my mother? This bitch to whom you have sworn homage? Answer me!" He passes a slit-eyed stare among the knights, leaning forward, arms locked straight, fists knuckling the trestle table, where the banners for the dais had been stitched. Roger Billancourt stands behind him, arms akimbo, square, grizzled head cocked belligerently.

William Morcar tugs at his bushy mustache, elbow in hand, arm across his chest, tilting back on one leg of a stool, staring up at the narrow window. Harold Almquist leans in the doorway, bald head lowered, studying his boot tip. Only Denis Hezetre meets Guy's hard gaze from where he sits at the far end of the trestle table, square hands splayed flat before him. "What if, indeed, she is your mother? What if God has worked a miracle on her?"

"Then she belongs in a nunnery," Guy responds sharply.

"Her father, Bernard, your grandfather, carved this domain out of wilderness," Denis reminds him. "For thirty years, she ruled from this castle herself before we packed her off on her pilgrimage. She has the right of blood, Guy—and she is capable."

Guy looks to Roger Billancourt with his mouth open, incredulously, wondering what is wrong with his friend, and the old master-at-arms grimaces at Denis reproachfully. When Guy faces Denis again, his gaze is quizzical. "So you believe her? You believe this kitten is my mother?"

"Who else could she be?" Denis asserts.

"There were witnesses to the miracle," Harold mumbles.

"Only two survived the journey here," Guy says, "one with a dwarf in his shadow and the other a treacherous Muslim."

"The pope himself authorized—" Harold offers tentatively.

"Bah!" Guy cuts him off. "Was he there? I say he was bought."

"By God's beard, Guy," Denis protests, "the old servant Dwn recognizes her."

"God's balls! The hag recognizes a chance to help herself and her own people. You heard the impostor. She wants to give our land to the Welsh!"

"But that is exactly what Ailena Valaise would do," Denis protests. "She grew up with a love for them, inherited from her father, is that not true?"

"Denis—" Guy stares imploringly at his friend. "Are you with me?"

"If you are right, Guy, I am with you. I have always been so. But, in truth, I do not see that you're right here. God has worked a miracle! Can you be so faithless as to deny your own mother? Almighty God has returned her to us for His greater glory!"

Guy snorts angrily but, though he flashes sharp looks at the others, experiences a queasy uncertainty. "How do the rest of you stand? With me or with the Pretender?"

"The point is moot," William Morcar ventures. "We backed Count John. Now Richard is king again. Unless we can meet the king's penalties for our service to John, this domain will belong to the king's men."

"Aye—" Roger speaks up for the first time, and squints craftily at the men. "But the king's penalty is not due till Saint Margaret's. We've a month yet. If this deceiver can be discredited quickly, there'll yet be time to break Neufmarché and seize the coin to pay the king."

"The Hereford troops are gone," Harold states. "The siege is lifted. We'll not crack that nut this season."

"Then we must be swift," Roger insists. "We must unseat this deceiving kitten soonest."

"And if she is not a deceiver?" Denis demands. "If she is truly Guy's mother, the baroness Valaise herself?"

"Then let God decide," Roger says, stepping to Guy's side. "A tourney has already been planned to celebrate our victory over Neufmarché. That tourney will be held instead to honor the baroness's return. Let us announce an *assise de bataille* and challenge the impostor's authority on the tourney grounds. I myself will best the Italian priest-knight and Guy will take the heretic Swede. We'll be done with this pretense quickly."

Denis objects with a shake of his head. "Such an *assise* cannot assert right of rule if the king and the pope affirm her charter."

"Both vellums are questionable," Guy answers quickly. "That

much was made clear in the great hall. If we best her knights, the guildsmen will accept me as baron. They've invested too heavily in our siege to forsake me."

"And we need not sack Neufmarché," Roger adds. "The threat alone may be sufficient to inspire him to pay our penalties."

Guy nods, satisfied. He peers down at Denis. "You will not stand against me at the tourney?"

"No. I have sworn homage to the baroness and will defend any threat to her with my life. But I will not champion her in games the pope has declared illegal." Denis rises and leans forward on the trestle table. "The tourney has no authority in the king's court. It is only a game, Guy, a mock battle."

Guy's thin smile stretches straight back, a viper's grin. "A mock battle to unseat a mock ruler."

"I notice you said little," Roger Billancourt addresses William Morcar. They are in a cramped and windowless anteroom, where the tapestries are stored in rolls on wooden shelves. Reluctantly, William has let the older man lead him here, knowing the bow-legged, iron-whiskered warrior requires him for some devilish work. He is afraid of the old warrior, for in battle he has often sacrificed men to win small victories; William dreads what sacrifices the warmaster will demand now that Ailena has returned to threaten him.

"Guy needs no empty words from me."

Roger places his hard fist with its square knuckles on William's chest. "Your heart is an eagle, William. It screams only when it's hungry."

"What mischief is in *your* heart, Roger?"

"Mischief?" Roger shakes his dented head. "None. Only loyalty to our baron, who is your wife Hellene's uncle as well as your son Thierry's godfather and patron."

"Roger, don't harry me with loyalties I know too well. I've proven my allegiance time and again in the field."

"Then why have you sworn homage to the kitten? What sorcery won you to her side?"

"No sorcery but God's own hand, who restored her to us."

"God's hand—or the Devil's?"

"Only priests see a difference."

The air goes dark when the warmaster smiles, and William regrets speaking in anger. "By God or the Devil, the kitten sits in the chair of state and you have sworn your fealty. That cannot be changed. So what will we do about Thierry?"

William's anger swells again. "I do not want my son's name in your mouth."

Roger pushes his face closer. One eye is larger than the other, on the side of his head where, years before, in service to Guy's father Gilbert, a mace crushed his skull. His imbalanced stare has a crazed intensity. "Thierry," he says in a flutelike, mocking voice. "Thierry was to inherit the realm when his godfather returned to God or the Devil. But now—" He moves his lips with cruel deliberation. "Do you not understand? Thierry will inherit nothing. The kitten is barely older than he and will outlive him and his children because she is the Devil's kitten."

"Then that is the will of God or the Devil," William mutters tersely.

"You want your son to live landless, to wander as Gilbert and I wandered, fighting for whomever would give us a meal? Do you want him to marry some legate's niece, like you, so he'll have someone else's roof over his head and someone else's laws to live by? Think, man! He could be his own law in his own castle! God or the Devil has given it to him. The same Devil-God who cut off Guy's manhood has *given* it to him!"

"The lineage belongs to Thomas," William says tonelessly.

"Clare's son?" Roger hisses through his brown teeth. "Thomas is a Chalandon, and like his father Gerald he is a flower, all fragrance and delicacy. His place is rightfully in the abbey studying the old texts, so that he can be a priest and make his foolish distinctions between acts of God and the Devil's work. Already, he has forsaken his place in this world. The chair of state belongs to Thierry. The Devil-God has given it to him."

"But, Roger, need I remind you—Thierry has already sworn his homage to the baroness."

"Only at Guy's nod. Guy loves Thierry like his own son; surely you can see he has been training him to rule since he was a boy. I know he would deny him nothing. Thus he gave Thierry the nod to serve the Pretender. Why exile him with us? If we fail, he at least should not suffer."

William tugs thoughtfully at his mustache. Though he dislikes the warmaster's cruelty on the field, he cannot deny the truth of what he says. God or the Devil has left men with the power to lift themselves from their miseries and shape their own lives. He learned that early, as the son of a mercenary; his father had died on the field and his son had no God-given opportunities. Were it not for Hellene, William would have lived an entirely aimless life. "What is there to do?" he asks wearily.

Roger steps back and rubs his stubbly chin. "Two things must be done. And Guy must know about neither of them, as these are acts we must do for him, not by him." He waits to receive William's nod of assurance. "First, an alliance must be struck with Branden Neufmarché."

"Alliance? Two days ago we were poised to sack his castle."

"But today the Pretender sits in the chair of state. You heard her surrender our outlying lands and fortalices to the barbarians. That is a danger to all the barons of the March, including Branden Neufmarché." Roger's scarred face crimps into a one-sided grin. "The old warrior Howel Rhiwlas and his crazy son Bold Erec have been making new alliances among the tribes. The Welsh are slovenly but fierce, and with them banding together like this any marcher lord would rightly be alarmed. Branden will ally with us, thinking to protect his interests. We will even promise him some of the land we will recover, to goad him with greed as well as fear. In return, we will have the advantage of his troops if we need to move against the Pretender and those in this castle who may try to defend her."

"Attack our own castle and knights?" William whispers with horror.

"Yes, we must prepare for that eventuality. But if we do the second thing well that we must do, we'll not need the first."

"Murder," William says somberly. "If we murder her, we will not need Branden's men to fight our own people."

Roger allows the faintest smile to touch his cracked lips. "In the beginning was the word, eh? In the beginning of every enterprise we must choose carefully what we will call it. Murder is too heinous a word, William. Choose again."

William lowers his head. "Accident, then."

Roger smiles and puts his fist against William's chest. "The eagle screams in your breast now, my friend. Accidents are acts of God and ploys of the Devil. God or the Devil are given the credit for bringing the kitten here—let them take the blame for what happens to her."

The women sit on stone benches in the court garden as the youngsters, Joyce and Gilberta, frolic among the rose arbors and the children, Blythe and Effie, lie among the foxgloves, sharing pastries. Rachel gazes up beyond the leaf-dazzle and the castle ramparts to the blue clouds in the high silence. Being someone else is both easier and harder than she had imagined. The comforts are easy: enjoying the rose-blooms under those mountainous gorges of clouds feels natural. But the pretense of caring for strangers is difficult. Listening to the roistering voices of the women and answering them in the ways they expect requires all her training.

"Mother," Clare calls insistently. "Shall we hold court, as we did when I was Madelon's age?"

Rachel drops her stare from the cloud mass and faces Madelon, Hellene's fifteen-year-old daughter. Skinny as a boy and fleecy blond, with pink eyelashes and a lusty little mole beneath her lower lip, she is Thierry's twin, but she somehow lacks his dark features and stocky frame.

"Grandmère has told me about the court," Madelon says in a breathy, petulant voice, "but Uncle forbade it."

"The court of love—" Rachel feels a prickle of warmth at the sides of her neck, exerting herself to remember the baroness's explicit instructions on the nature and fulfillment of romance with the beau ideal.

"Grandmère, you blush!" Leora squeals, and all the women laugh.

"I am too old to conduct the court," Rachel protests mildly and looks sideways at Dwn for support, but the old servant smiles slyly.

"On the contrary, Mother, you're too young not to." Clare leads the others in another gust of laughter. "Tell us now, are you going to love again?"

Rachel looks down at her hands and the white knuckles of her locked fingers. What would the baroness answer? "To love in the courtly manner, a woman must rule."

"There are knights even here in the Marches who would fall to their knees to be ruled by you," Clare says.

"But to rule properly," Rachel quickly adds, "one must serve. I must first find a man gentle and wise enough to serve before I would hope to rule him with my love."

"You'll have to search hard in the Marches to find a creature as rare as that," Dwn clucks.

"Let us hold the court again, Mother," Clare presses. "Dwn is right. Since you left, there has been only the tilt and the hunt, dice and hawks, only boorishness and fighting cocks, stable-talk and war plans."

The other women plead beseechingly, and Rachel silences them with an agreeable nod. "We will hold a court of love—but only if there are men enough to attend. Besides your Gerald, Clare, who among this rabble of soldiers would know how to conduct themselves in the court?"

"Your Italian knight would," Leora says and tangles a suggestive finger in her red locks. She points with her eyes to the arched doorway of the great hall, where Gianni Rieti is passing on his way back from the chapel. "Call him over, Grandmère. Let us see if he requires instruction."

Hellene finds her sister Leora's coquettishness trivial beyond all forebearance and her talk of courtly love sheer foolishness. Her William would scold her for sitting here without objecting, but formality is vital to Hellene, and so long as the baroness attends to such customs, she will abide them, too. But including a padre in this nonsense—to that, she objects: "He is a priest."

"A knight-priest," Leora counters, "and more comely than a priest should be."

Relieved to have the focus removed from herself, Rachel signs to Falan, who is sitting nearby under a red maple, his saber in his lap.

Gianni Rieti is surprised by Falan's summoning hand on his shoulder. He has been deep in thought, contemplating his responsibilities to the Church and to God. After witnessing the miracle of the baroness's transformation by the Holy Grail, God's power had seemed evident, and serving Him had seemed straightforward. He would follow and obey the baroness, the object of God's miraculous love. But now the fast-shriven, mystic abbot, so unhappy with the baroness's devotion to Christ's ancestral faith, has troubled him. He has to think this through, and he does not like thinking about such supernal matters.

As Rachel introduces him to Clare, her daughters, Hellene and Leora, and to their daughters, adolescent Madelon, and the girls Joyce, Gilberta, Blythe, and little Effie, he greets each cordially, but it is Madelon his gaze lingers on. He cannot help observing, almost despite himself, the elegant curve of her throat, the gypsy mark under her reckless mouth, the demure downcast of her pale eyes that makes her beauty enigmatic.

When his attention is abruptly drawn away from Madelon by Clare asking if he is aware of courtly love, he professes ignorance. He remembers hearing of some frivolity going on in the court of Poitiers, where women took the upper hand in commanding men. He could scarcely believe that such a trivial game has penetrated this deep into the wilderness.

Clare explains, "It began thirty years ago, Father Rieti, around the time I married Gerald. It was he who brought the notion with him from the Limousin."

"Remember how it scandalized the old knights?" Rachel asks, almost hearing the baroness's laughter when she first told this anecdote, "especially when Gerald told them that chivalry had begun here in Wales centuries ago in the court of King Arthur in Caerleon on Usk? After that, those stable-stinking knights fell over themselves in the bathing tubs, purging the odors of the kennels and the highways."

Clare brays with raucous laughter. Then, to show the canon her refinement, she adds, "Chivalry was actually devised by the Countess of Champagne, named Marie, the elder daughter of Louis Capet and Eleanor of Aquitaine. She had a clerk named André the Chaplain, and she set him to work translating Ovid's *Art of Loving* and *The Remedy for Love*. You know those works, Father?"

"Of course, my lady. *Ars Amatoria* and *Remedia Amoris* poke fun at illicit Roman love affairs with the pretense of taking them seriously."

"A pretense indeed," Rachel continues. "A pretense André turned about. In his *Book of Love,* man is not the master, employing his arts to seduce women for his pleasure, man is, instead, the property, the very thing of woman."

"And the courts of love?" Gianni enquires, feeling Madelon's eyes upon him and daring to pass her a white-toothed smile.

"An assembly of men where women hold sway," Rachel answers. "In the court of love, women set the rules, the rules of chivalry."

"Will you attend our court of love?" Madelon boldly asks, feeling her heart trip nimbly as Gianni's dark, level stare plays over her.

"Yes—" he answers and turns his handsome regard on Rachel. "But only if the baroness will define love for me."

The challenge tosses Rachel's head back, and she watches ponderous clouds shouldering heaven. The answer comes easily, for the baroness was fond of mocking love: "Mortal love, dear knight, is like licking honey from thorns."

Denis Hezetre drifts like a bronze panel of sunlight in the dark archway of the great hall at the edge of the garden. After catching Rachel's eye, he bows and beckons her away from the giddy other women. Rachel excuses herself. Clare rises, too, and sends her daughters off to their tasks—no-nonsense Hellene to oversee the servants and freckly Leora to monitor the children's day-lessons. Clare, herself, will tour the cookhouse, sample the day's fare, and mollify the outraged staff, whose talents have been stinted by the baroness's dietary restrictions.

Gianni Rieti bows as the women disperse and turns to seek out his dwarf companion, Ummu. The little man, lacking respect for all religions, will delight in hearing of the clash between the abbot and the rabbi, Rieti thinks, smiling to himself. Neither of those holy men witnessed the miracle of the Grail, and so both doubt its veracity. But Ummu had been at Gianni's side when the Holy Chalice appeared; he had seen the dying crone transformed into the nubile maiden—and, yet, his disdain for everything spiritual obliged him to doubt his own eyes. *What a wonder the dwarf is,* Gianni smiles to himself, pleased and amused to have the companionship of one so monstrously faithful to the earth.

"Padre."

Gianni glances over his shoulder and sees Madelon standing under a trellis of sugary blossoms, a finger of sunlight in her golden curls. She had purposefully forgotten a hair ribbon on the stone bench, so that she might hurry back without arousing the suspicions of her mother.

Staring at him impudently, with a mixture of defiance and mischief, Madelon says, in one breath, "Meet me in the outer garden by the willows, after the blessing of the holy water, so that we may talk unimpeded." Then, with a half-giggle, she turns and is gone.

Gianni blinks. He had recently learned from Maître Pornic that the villagers traditionally gather in the chapel at this day of the month for noon Mass and the consecration of vialed water—ceremonies he is obliged to perform now that the baroness has dismissed the abbot from castle services. Gianni runs both hands through his dark mane, flustered, knowing well what the woman-child wants. This Mass, his first in the castle, which was to be so simple and pure, and in which he would have performed the sacrament of the Eucharist with the unblemished cleanliness and sincerity of soul deserving of the occasion, takes on profounder resonances now, he realizes: his prayers will be as much for his own soul as for the souls of his new flock.

Denis Hezetre ushers Rachel into the great hall, to a corner away from where the servants are straightening the toppled benches and gathering up the crushed mint and rushes. Falan watches from the doorway while the two sit on facing settles in the silver, oblong fluorescence falling from a high window. Denis is momentarily breathless, facing this young woman of moon-cold skin whom he remembers only as ancient, haggard flesh mottled with broken blood vessels.

"Your son plans to unseat you, my lady."

She watches him with ambiguous eyes vibrant with searching and fear. Never had he seen such a look in the old baroness's eyes, which were always morose but shrewd. "So I would expect. You know his strategy?"

"An *assise de bataille*."

"That is illegal."

A glimmer of bewilderment troubles his blond face. "I need not remind you, Guy has never heeded law, only power."

"But he will heed this law. I will not accept such an *assise*. Why should I risk what is already mine?"

"He will challenge your knights at the tourney to be held in your honor."

"Then cancel the tourney. The pope frowns on them anyhow. If men have ferocity for battle let them not spend it in the tilts when there are Saracens to challenge in the Holy Land."

"This tourney was announced across the March in the spring, my lady. There are barons on their way here already. But, more importantly, there are the guildsmen to consider, many of whom have invested heavily in the siege you called off. They are not pleased, and see the tourney as providing a means of recovering their losses. If you deny them, your position will be in even greater jeopardy."

With a lachrymal smile, Rachel says hesitantly, "In former times, Denis, I daresay you'd not have to think this through for me. Since the Holy Land, I've lost my head for strategy."

Denis regards her quizzically; her candor is unexpected. "Strategy is all that will hold your chair of state so long as your son is your enemy," he says gently.

"There is more and better than strategy to help me, kind Denis—there is faith. I learned its power well in Jerusalem."

Denis bows his head. "You have been glorified by God. He will defend your right of rule."

Rachel nods absently. *Time is my only defense. The time it takes to claim the treasure I've earned and to flee this nest of vipers.*

"You have changed more than I can say, my lady. Truly you are not the same baroness who ruled this domain for thirty years. The gentleness I recognize in you now ill serves a ruler on the frontier. Even as I believe that God stands behind you, I . . . I fear for you."

Rachel's eyes sharpen. "Then perhaps I should return to the Holy Land and leave this domain to its natural succession," she replies anxiously. "Tell Guy that, and he will sleep better."

"The innocent are fools, the wise are cowards—so sing the ancient Welsh bards."

Rachel smiles. "A fool if I stay, a coward if I leave. Since you think so ill of me, why did you kiss my ring?"

Denis closely regards the soft-lipped woman whose dark, clear eyes seem as troubled as a seer's. *Is Guy right?* he wonders. *Is this woman not his mother at all? Is she, perhaps, so utterly changed by the Grail that she has become an impostor even to herself?* "Devotion is all I've known, my lady."

"True, your devotion to Guy is famous, even as he bullied you when you were boys. Because your stepfather was my warmaster, Guy hated him—hated all men who were close to me after Gilbert died. He was a spoiled, pugnacious boy, my son, and still is. I saw then that he could not resist pummeling you, because that was simply the only way he could hurt your father. Yet, I seem to remember, when he went to Ireland for adventure in his seventeenth summer, you went with him. Has that devotion never wearied?"

The sudden mention of that summer takes Denis by surprise. "Never," he stammers. "I am still Guy's friend. I will always be."

"And there is yet no woman who has won your devotion?"

"*You* have, my lady."

Rachel sits back, suddenly lonely in her shoulders and elbows, fingerjoints and knees for the pain that should be there. The old baroness alone has the right to this loyalty, and suddenly, Rachel feels deceitful. She remembers Ailena telling her, "The archer, Denis Hezetre, with the boyish face—my son did more than beat him when they were youths, he abused him as if he was a village girl and broke his lust on him. I caught them at it once in a hay rick behind the stables. Guy never looked more malicious than when he had that poor boy under him. But Denis, the mistaken fool, thought it was love and has loved him ever since—though the wanker that tamed him was lopped off in Ireland."

"I do declare myself unworthy, Denis," Rachel confesses. "You are right—I am not the woman I once was. I can never be again. Your devotion to me will set you at dangerous odds with Guy. Be warned."

The pollen-glinting space between Denis's eyes twitches. "I . . . I want to tell you—I know your son has never loved me as I do him." He pauses, gnaws his upper lip; Rachel, seeing his distress, wishes he would say no more. But he goes on. "As a young man, I had foolish hopes, apparent joys that were illusions. Since Ireland, a lifetime ago, my heart has been dumb." His gaze drops to his clasped hands. "After that loss, there was no hope of winning his love as I wanted it. Only now, with your return—to see you so marvelously changed by God's own hand—" He faces her brightly. "Only now have I felt sincere joy. For now I know, there is something timeless in us. Something that is worthy of homage. Even if you are not half the ruler you were, I look at you and I know this devotion will return my love somehow."

"He was so sincere, grandfather," Rachel says in a faltering voice. She sits on a faldstool by the keyhole window of David's room. "I had to bite my tongue not to blurt out the truth."

David looks down at Rachel, his bearded face drawn with astonishment and growing fright. "Your heart must be a battlement, Rachel. You must feel no pity for them. Or our lives are forfeit."

Rachel holds her hand to her face and weeps. "They see God's hand in me. Grandfather, am I blaspheming the Lord?"

"No, child. If anything, you are exalting Him in the hearts of these polytheists. Now their faith is stirred." David walks over and caresses her hair comfortingly. "And soon we will be gone from here, Granddaughter. Tomorrow, we will retrieve the jewels that are our rightful payment for our long service to the baroness, and we will leave. We will return to Kfar Hananya and we will live as the Lord intended us to live. We will never return. And the people here will be left with a wonder that they will believe has come from God."

* * *

Gianni Rieti leaves the chapel with the villagers and strolls with them through the bailey gate and along the tollhouse road to the bridge. They are happy with him, for the ingenuousness with which he performed the mass made the air around him seem to shine with holiness. At the bridge, he blesses the last of them, who hold their clay vials of holy water to their breasts and depart singing a joyful hymn.

Beyond the tollhouse road are the extensive garden and orchards, where Ummu already awaits him. The dwarf beckons to him from among the bearded hazels. During the Mass, Gianni had actually convinced himself that he would return immediately to the castle. But now the memory of the slender, flaxen-haired girl with the gypsy-mark of a mole on her lower lip lures him into the trees.

"Is that a hesitant step I see?" Ummu taunts. "Or is it just that you are so heavy with unspent seed your gait is slackened?"

"I am sworn to chastity, evil dwarf." Behind Gianni's scowl, he is glad to see his dwarf, for the little man often provides good counsel though his wit is barbed.

"How long have you been chaste now, padre? Nigh ten months. Surely even the angels are amazed. Ah, but your dreams must be sinful indeed. Too bad I cannot peek at them. They must rival all your exploits. "

"Too sadly true, stump. I wake fevered each night, salacious as a schoolboy. But I've lived as Maître Pornic instructed. I am keeping the lust within me, though it burns, Ummu, like rampaging fire."

"A veritable Saint Anthony! But this is no dream that awaits you in the willows."

"You've seen her?"

"While you've been turning water into water, I have indeed watched her. She paces restlessly—and alone. Her horse is bridled to a shade tree not far away but out of sight, where her complicit maid keeps a watchful eye. No doubt for the young sport's mother, Hellene, her own name's irony, stony-eyed as a Medusa."

"She would have no cause for concern if she knew," Gianni

says. "I intend only to speak with the maiden."

"Speak all you please, padre. I am sure the lady's replies will please you more than you intend."

Through the hazels, Gianni spots the shaggy willow copse. "Try to spend at least as much time watching out for me, please, as watching what I do," he begs.

"I will—if you at least promise to do something worth watching. I've been bored these past ten months."

"Where's Ta-Toh?"

"In the cherry trees, I suspect."

"Keep him close. I don't want him startling the maid, or the horses."

Gianni Rieti brushes the creases from his black tunic and advances into the willows. Madelon stiffens when she sees him, but his easy smile and flagrant bow set her at ease.

"You summoned me here, sweet lady, and I am happy to come."

"You honor me, padre. I was not sure I was worthy of your attention."

"Your charm is worthy of far more than I have to give." In the dappled light, parts of him glow more vividly—the clean line of his jaw with its thin-edged beard, the soft coils of his blue-black hair, the bright energy compacted in his eye. "Please, do not call me padre. I did not come here as a priest."

She glances at his tapered sword, the onyx-hilted weapon he has worn at every Mass he has performed since taking his vows to free the Holy Sepulcher. "Are you here as a knight, then?"

Gianni stares down at his boots, ashamed. "I am here as what I am."

Madelon steps closer and lays a hand against the scarlet cross above his heart. "Will you walk with me and tell me about yourself and the wonderful lands where you have traveled?"

Gianni parts the curtains of willow, and they stroll up a grassy hill toward a slope of venerable elms, talking about the Crusades that had begun when these elms were saplings more than a century before. Beyond the elms, flowerbeds pattern the fields between the fruit trees, and peasants stoop here and there among swaths of lilies, marigolds, poppies, daffodils, and acanthus plants.

Madelon enquires how such a striking man came to be a priest, and he tells the story of his orphaned childhood among the friars, dwelling particularly on the peccadillos that obliged him to become ordained. *If she knows the truth of me, of my lust, she will protect herself,* he reasons, *and my vows will remain unbroken.* He describes his dalliances in almost lewd detail, interpreting her wide-eyed pallid expression as revulsion.

Crooked Simon, the hunchbacked gardener, ignores the couple as they drift by, and he works assiduously at his grafting, marrying plum to pear, quince to peach, looking up only once when an evil-faced imp dressed as a squire scampers through the trees followed by a garishly garbed monkey.

In an herb croft lush with lettuce, cresses, and mints, Gianni completes his sordid story with a thorough recounting of his debauches in Jerusalem. Done, he bows to the open-mouthed maiden and turns to depart, proud and propitiated.

But Madelon is not alarmed so much as astonished; here, in her own castle, among the lummox warriors and rude varlets who care more about horseflesh than women, is a handsome knight who knows the mysteries of romance, who can satisfy her unslaked curiosity about the riddles of love, and initiate her into womanhood before her mother succeeds in marrying her off to some wealthy but crotchety earl! That this charming knight is a priest had seemed an insurmountable problem—until she heard his story and realized he had not been called by God but had become a priest by default.

She seizes his arm and leads him around a dense hedge to the wild end of the garden, where wreathe woodbine and hawthorn flourish, out of sight of the field workers. "How you have suffered," she whispers, pressing close to him. "God does not want you to be a priest. Don't you see? That is why He chose you to be in the Sepulcher the night of my great-grandmother's miracle. He wanted to bring you here, to me, to be healed of your suffering."

Gianni's mouth sags. "I—I had not thought—"

"How could you have, poor fool, victim of your passions. You have been led by error and deception your whole life, knowing only lust and never love. But now, here, with me, another miracle can be worked. You can be healed, here in my arms. You can put

aside the sword and the cross. You needed them to protect yourself out there. But in here, with me, you are safe at last. You can
be yourself now. You can be mine."

Gianni struggles to breathe without gasping. "I am a . . . priest!"

"In name, yes, but in spirit you are a man of the world, with all
the desires of such a man. Your story has told me so." She looks
anxiously at him. "Am I too bold? Perhaps you do not find me
beautiful?"

Gianni's mouth works without sound before he blurts, "You are
most beautiful."

"I cannot expect you to save me from my fate," she says with
downcast eyes. "I am destined to marry some stodgy nobleman
with bad digestion. But before then, before I must spend the rest
of my days knowing only the rituals of love, I would hope you
could show me love's passion." She bites her knuckle and looks at
him with frightened eyes. "I am too bold. You must think me
without virtue. But that is not so, Gianni. May I call you Gianni?
You are the first man who has stirred in me the hope of
romance—"

A woman's reedy cry penetrates the hedge. Madelon pokes her
head around the corner, and when she looks back at Gianni, her
face is ardent. "My Aunt Leora is coming to pick flowers with the
children. We mustn't be seen together yet. I will call for you when
we can be alone again."

Madelon kisses his cheek and softly runs away. The next
instant, Ummu tumbles from the hedge, biting his knuckles to
keep from bursting into laughter, and Ta-Toh leaps into Gianni's
arms and kisses his pale cheek.

An owl hoots mysteriously from a cypress tree at midday, and
Dwn, who is in the garden outside the castle walls gathering flowers for her mistress's chamber, stands tall, alarmed by the evil
omen. Blythe, the young girl whose knitting the old woman is
supervising, does not notice; with her tongue sticking out of the
corner of her mouth, she knits and purls with fierce attentiveness.
Dwn turns to call her from her work when a shadow stirs under
the cypress and whispers her name.

Erec Rhiwlas beckons the maid. He sits on the far side of the tree atop his roll of hides, still dressed in the worn garments of a tanner from the hills.

"You should be long gone from this place," Dwn scolds with a hand over her chest to still her heart. Though she sees now why the owl hooted by day, its sleep disturbed by a prowling Welshman, to her this is still a bad portent. "If the gardener sees you, he'll call the sergeants."

Erec opens his arms before him with mock innocence. "I'm just your simple cousin." He stands and leans against the tree, his green eyes large with amazement, and points with his face to the banner of the Swan fluttering over the castle: "Is it true then, cousin, what I hear in the village? The baroness has unseated Lanfranc?"

"It is true. And she has lifted the siege on Neufmarché. And restored the river meadows to the tribes."

Erec smiles broadly and slaps his hand against the tree. "She is the miracle of our prayers! I must meet with her—my father, too. Howel knew her in the old times."

Dwn wags a knobby finger. "Not here, not now. Guy did not surrender his chair of state gladly. He swears she is not his mother."

"He's the Devil's son!" Erec acknowledges. "Has he no love for God? This miracle must seem a curse to him."

"I fear for my lady," Dwn whispers. "I know Guy and his war-master are already plotting some grief for her."

"Then I must see her and offer her my sword."

Dwn watches him shrewdly, still and attentive as a heron. "Is it her amity to the tribes or her beauty that moves you, Erec Rhiwlas?"

"That is a happy union, isn't it, Old Mother?" Erec smiles rakishly. "You must arrange a meeting."

Dwn shakes her head. "Not I. In all our years together, I have never presumed to guide Ailena in either statecraft or love. You arrange your own meeting, Bold Erec. She leaves for Trinity Abbey on the morrow."

"I will tell Howel." Erec leans closer. "But now tell me, Dwn. You have been with this young woman a whole day: is she truly the baroness Ailena?"

"Oh, yes. Indeed, she is the Servant of Birds. But she has changed more than in the flesh."

"How? How is she changed, Dwn?"

The old woman's amber eyes darken. "This I don't know exactly. She looks and sounds the same. She carries herself as before. But there is something more quiet about her—as though, even awake, she is on the verge of a dream."

The sky is a dragon's mane when Dwn returns to the *palais* from her long day with the children. Feeling airy with joy, she practically floats up the winding stone stairs. Clare and her daughters Hellene and Leora have accepted her back so graciously and completely, her ten years in the dungpile seem little more than a foul dream, though the dirt still grains the cracks of her hands. Today, she has helped the young ones knit and dye, and, after meeting unexpectedly with Bold Erec, she has gone flower-picking with the youngest and shared a dinner of braised quail in cherry sauce outdoors under the elms with Clare and Gerald.

But now at the door to Rachel's bedchamber, she pauses, sensing something awry. She is not perturbed to see Falan Askersund with his brow pressed to the flagstone, haunches in the air, praying to his heathen god. But something is amiss beyond the closed door. She feels it somehow—the air so close and still her head feels heavy with the smell of it.

Falan opens the door for her, and she clears her throat softly before entering. The orange flames of evening in the majestic windows light the chamber brightly. The bed curtains are open, and Rachel lies at the foot of the mattress, curled up, her face glossy with tears.

"Servant of Birds, are you angry at me for being away from you all day?"

The Welsh words must travel a long way to reach the place in Rachel that understands. Since her encounter with Denis Hezetre, a dumbfounded anguish has possessed her. As if a fog has momentarily lifted in her head, she realizes she is only a woman. Who is she to pretend to be God's miracle? Overwrought with shame, she has lain here for hours, returning to the moment when the sham all began, years ago, when she was just entering her womanhood, returning to when she had crawled into the belly of the dead horse and had lain there pretending to be alive when everyone else in her family was dead.

No, not everyone, she kept repeating to herself. Grandfather had survived, too, and he had said God was not offended by her pretense. Laughter at that thought had broken into tears several times already, and now she is left with the wonderful arrogance of being alive, naked Rachel beneath all her fine clothes, and alone with death.

A huge music moves through her, like the sound of the sea, waves of clarity ebbing to grief. For long minutes, she is lucidly calm. In that blinding lucidity, she sees no other path: she knows she has no other choice but death or life. She must pretend to be the baroness or there will be death, either at the hands of these Christian warriors or, more slowly, by poverty and long wandering. The thought of her grandfather suffering, after he has suffered so much to bring her this far, pulls her away from her senses into a deep grief.

Tears burn on her face. She does not want to be Rachel anymore. Behind her closed eyes the Grail appears, scalded with gold light, hurting her brain with its radiance. The goblet tilts toward her—and *blood* pours out rayed with sunbeams. She startles alert, her eyes snapping open, and she sees an old woman standing before her.

"Ailena?" Dwn sits beside her and strokes her hair. In langue d'oc, she asks, "Is it I who have hurt you, Ailena?"

"No." Rachel unfurls, wipes the blurriness from her eyes, and sits up. "No, you have not hurt me, Dwn."

"Then what is wrong? Why are you crying?"

Rachel flings her gaze out into the purpling sky. "I am . . . wrong, Dwn. I am all wrong."

Dwn clucks, wipes the damp strands of hair from the young woman's chill brow. At that touch, she feels that something is indeed wrong . . . some error of the soul that wracks this body and shadows the blood with the chill of death on this warm June night. "You are troubled because everything is changed. Look at me, look what the hard, wild earth has done to *me.*"

"You are beautiful," Rachel says with conviction, and clutches her crusty hand. "You are true. You are yourself."

"As are you, my lady."

"No, no. I am . . . a lie, Dwn."

Dwn stares hard in the gloom and again recognizes all the details, the dented chin, the swollen overlip, the long nose, and broad brow limned in last light. "You are the very Servant of Birds I remember well, those long years ago."

"But I am not. I am someone else," Rachel says fitfully, throwing herself weeping upon the bed.

"Who are you?" Dwn asks kindly.

Rachel closes her eyes. The Grail is gone—but the blood remains. A crimson puddle mirrors her face and, beside her, that of Grandfather. His woe-carved features plead with her to say no more. A spasm of fear bends her forward; she feels the sticky warmth of the blood on her face. This is the blood from the Grail, the blood that has purchased her lie, that has made her the baroness. She knows it is the blood of her family and the blood of Ailena Valaise, inextricably mixed. Disgust pulls her away, and she sees again her grandfather reflected in the spilled blood. In a sharp flash, she recalls his years of splitting wood, digging graves, soliciting her a husband—like some rude peasant because his lifetime as a landowner, as a son and grandson of landowners and scholars, had come to nothing. She looks up, and her face is frail, starred with tears. "I cannot say the truth." She reaches for the old woman and buries her face in her shoulder, mumbling over and over, "I cannot say the truth. I cannot say the truth."

Dwn quiets her with a cosseting hand and a tender, humming tune, all the while feeling the old body thickening as night comes on. The truth suddenly drains the lightness from Dwn's flesh, and she sits heavy with all her years, knowing now there has been no miracle. There has been no visitation of the Grail, no mandate from the Savior of the World. The Servant of Birds has not returned. This is some strange, gentle young woman whom Ailena has somehow bent to her will. The insight brings a soft horror as she realizes the terrible jeopardy of this troubled girl.

When the sobbing young woman is finally still and Dwn knows she can hear her, the crone whispers in her ear, "The truth doesn't matter, Servant of Birds—or whoever you are. Listen to me now, sweet child, listen carefully and always remember this. The truth does not matter at all, only what we *do* with it matters."

David wakes suddenly and sees Falan leaning over him, his lanky-haired silhouette backlit by the glimmery light of an oil lamp. The Muslim knight stands back, and Rachel approaches and dismisses him. "Dawn is near," she says and hooks the lamp on the wall bracket beside the bed. "I will be leaving soon."

"I will dress," David says and sits up groggily. Dizziness spins through him, and the dank draftiness of the castle seems to blow through his bones. "We should be off early."

"No, Grandfather. There is no need. I want you to stay here in the castle."

David bends forward to chase the vertigo from his head, and pretends to rub the sleep from his face. "You will need me on this journey. The abbey is a day's ride away. I can help you."

"My knights will help me."

Rachel's composed voice alerts David to some change, and he observes his granddaughter more closely. The anguish that had harrowed her yesterday, after her talk with Denis Hezetre, has eased, and there is no sign of timidity, no haunted distance in her gaze. Instead, she watches him with gentle concern, her lamp-lit eyes quiescent. *Karm Abu Selim's magic,* he thinks.

"You are still weary from our formidable journey out of Jerusalem," she says quietly. "Stay here and rest, for when I return with the jewels, we must make that laborious journey again."

"I must come with you," David insists. He defies the nausea in his body and rises shakily to his feet. "You will need my counsel and support. The abbey is a nest of fanatics. They will interrogate you thoroughly."

"Have no concern for that, Grandfather. I am the baroness now. I will accept no further challenges of my authority."

"Then your concern about deception, which haunted you yesterday, is well in hand?"

"I have spoken with Dwn," she answers, "about the truth."

Alarm stabs him. "You have told her the truth?"

Rachel smiles and puts a reassuring hand on the fist he has

locked over his heart. "No, Grandfather. Do not be alarmed. I have not told her—though I think she knows."

David presses his fists to his temples and gnashes his teeth. "We are in her hands!"

"No. She loves Ailena enough to guard our secret. She has made no threats. She has not even said that she knows. Nor will she, I think. She is a humble woman. And she has helped me to see that, for now, I am the baroness. That is what Ailena wanted. It is what has come to pass. For now, it is the truth."

"That is surely good," David says nervously. He takes her hands, concern furrowing his brow. "But you are still vulnerable to the doubts in your heart. I had better remain by your side."

"No. You will stay and rest. We will not linger here long after I return." Her countenance has an implacable conviction. "Trust me, Grandfather. Ailena has had her revenge. Her son has tasted humiliation. That is all we owe the baroness, and all her wintry heart wanted. Now let me take our treasure, and Guy Lanfranc can have his barony again, perhaps wiser for his mother's cold-hearted art."

The animals are gathered in the bailey at dawn for the baroness's journey to Trinity Abbey. The camels have been kept behind the stables, as their ill-tempers disturb the horses. At unexpected intervals and without provocation, their heads, deceptively indifferent and sleepy-looking, suddenly snake forward and snap at passersby.

With expert command, Falan drops the camels to their knees and supervises the lading of provisions on one, and the fitting of the special riding saddle and tasseled bridle on the other.

Rachel feels languid and dignified. What Dwn has said to her last night has given her a new strength: *The truth does not matter—only what we do with it.* She lifts her face to the tunnel of fire above the eastern ramparts, testing her resolve. *Yes,* she assures herself, imagining the sun as a giant Grail embracing her in its power: the baroness's truth fits her closely this morning. She is ready to play her role.

Dwn smiles at her, unable to take her eyes from her, fascinated and deeply moved by how precisely this woman mimicks her mistress. But knowing now that this is not Ailena, she cannot help noticing the subtle and vital differences: the slightly wider jaw, the fingers longer and more tapered, the shrewd glint missing from her eyes. Intuitively, Dwn understands that this stranger is here only because Ailena has placed her here, an instrument with which to fulfill her obstinate will. And though she is saddened that there has been no miracle, no Grail, to redeem her mistress, she is, deep within her, strangely exultant that the Servant of Birds has nevertheless found a way to return and undo the grief she had left behind.

David and Maître Pornic emerge from the chapel, where they have been praying together after Gianni Rieti's matin service for the household. At first, David had been uneasy about intoning the names of the One God in a temple rife with idols, with the multiple deities the gentiles called saints. But Maître Pornic was able to move him with his sincerity, and finally David remembered Ezekiel 45:1: *Holy of Holies in all directions*. With Gianni Rieti holding the scroll open for him, he quelled the disquieting nausea that had been with him for several days and read a few passages aloud, then listened patiently to the abbot invoking the blessings of God and His Son and the Holy Spirit.

At their approach, Rachel and Dwn curtsy to the men of God. David, reassured by the confidence of her bearing and the hard clarity in her eyes, promises that he will spend the time of her absence praying for her return.

Harold Almquist will also stay in the castle, in the event of an attack by either the Welsh or Branden Neufmarché in their absence. As Rachel departs, waving to him, her grandfather, and the assorted crowd of family members gathered on the steps, she notices the calf-eyed admiration with which Madelon regards Gianni as he leaves the chapel, spurs jangling, assiduously avoiding her gaze. When Rachel looks to Dwn, the old woman smiles slyly and whispers, "No doubt, the court of love is already in session."

Gianni bids adieu to his dwarf, rubs the small man's curly head for luck, and leads Rachel to the other knights. They stand in a counseling group as the squires finish saddling the horses and yoking the oxen to the carriage that will convey the baroness. Denis alone bows. Only after Rachel has stared pointedly at them do

William Morcar and his sullen Thierry perform the most perfunctory of nods.

"Do we require such a large company for a brief visit to the abbey?" she asks ingenuously.

"The hills are rife with Welsh raiders, my lady," Denis answers. "Our company is actually small for the jeopardy of this journey. But it would be unwise to leave our castle without sufficient men to defend her, especially now that Neufmarché has a chance to vent his hostility."

"Perhaps the baroness would like to reconsider leaving her fortress?" Guy asks twittingly, and tosses a knowing look to Roger Billancourt.

"Your safety cannot be guaranteed in those hills," Roger says gruffly.

"I trust my knights to guard my safety," she replies with bravura; then she demands of Guy, "Show me your payment to Neufmarché."

Guy bridles at her tone, and his eyes narrow before he opens the saddlebag on his horse. Inside are three rolls of fur—miniver from the white marten, black sable, and ermine, the precious pelage of the white weasel from the dim countries called Russia—all gifts of homage he has collected over the years from his harrowing attacks on neighboring baronies. Surrendering these is already a deep humiliation; revealing them to the whole bailey only steepens the shame of his loss. Roger had counseled him to refuse to pay any reparations. But Guy knows that the Pretender would use that as an ample excuse to exile him, and unseating her from outside the castle walls would be far more difficult.

"And the coin?" Rachel asks.

"It is there."

"Show me."

Guy's nostril-wings whiten with withheld rage. He thrusts his hand into the saddlebag and comes out with a plump leather pouch. Rachel signs for Gianni to inspect it, and the priest takes the pouch, opens it, and fingers the coins within. "At least thirty gold pieces, my lady," he figures.

"Thirty-six," Guy says tersely. "All I've left after paying my men."

"We'll consider this a payment in part," Rachel says coolly, "against whatever Branden Neufmarché claims is just and proper." She feels the old baroness stir in her blood with haughty satisfaction as Guy straightens and Roger glowers. The old woman had been very clear about depriving Guy of funds, which could be used against her. She glances about at the stunned knights. "Shouldn't we be on our way? The sun will not stay in his course for us."

Falan's camels rise, and, from atop his mount, he helps Rachel, Dwn, and Maître Pornic climb into the wagon, whose hide coverings have been rolled up. As the carriage lurches into motion, Rachel holds her grandfather's worried stare a lingering moment before signaling the porter to open the gates.

David sits in his prayer shawl at a writing table before his bedchamber's window. He unscrolls a tatter-edged parchment on which he writes his brief prayers, believing the written words spell God's power.

With the sun slanting over his shoulder and illuminating the parchment, he lifts his stylus from the inkstone and writes the word the old woman Dwn spoke to Rachel in her anguish: truth.

Truth: three letters, the first, middle, and last letters of the alphabet, written right to left—aleph, mem, taw—the beginning, the midst, and the end of all things. And as he writes those letters on the parchment, as if out of the sun's glare David pronounces: "Emeth—" and then the gentiles' variant of that Hebrew word, "oh-men—amen."

He puts his stylus aside and, despite a feverish qualm, begins his prayers.

With the castle's swine driven before them in a bristly, snorting herd, the baroness's procession crosses the toll bridge over the rushing Llan and enters the thatch-roofed village. The villagers, alerted two days before to the baroness's intention of gifting them the castle's pigs, are gathered along the rutted avenue, cheering heartily.

The castle's swineherd has himself been given a share of the herd and his own croft near the village, and he happily oversees the equitable apportionment of the animals to the grateful villagers. As the ox-drawn van wobbles down the avenue, wild flowers pelt the baroness and her companions. Guy and Roger shove a way through the crowd with their horses, though even after the village has fallen out of sight behind them, they are lashed by the cries for the baroness: "Valaise! Valaise!"

Midmorning sunlight lifts a violet haze from the pocket valleys and deep ravines of the wilderness. Staring out over the mazy hills and layerings of clouds, Rachel experiences something incomprehensible to her in the listening stillness—the frightful enormity of a secret wish in the green flames of trees and the starflake flowers on the mountains' flanks. For the first time since the horror, she is transported back in her heart to the mystic joy she knew on her hidden knoll in Lunel. A secret dreaming enciphers its own meaning at the eaten heart of eroded rocks and in the frothing water free-falling in silver vertical script. She feels that she and the others with her are suspended in an unutterable thought in the mind of God.

Among the shadows thrown by clouds on the mountain slopes, Rachel glimpses a jumble of huts beside a brown river that wriggles like the biblical Aaron's rod crawling before the Pharaoh. A narrow path leads down the slopes from this high road to the river village. Rachel points and tells the others she wants to go there.

Maître Pornic pulls on the reins to slow the oxen, turns and shakes his head. "That is a Welsh village, baroness. We'll not be welcome there."

"Is it within my domain?"

Denis looks back over his shoulder and nods. "Yes, my lady, we displaced them from the lower meadows last spring."

Rachel, assuming the imperious posture of the baroness, turns to Dwn. "Let us have a taste of the famous Welsh hospitality, shall we?"

"The Servant of Birds was always welcomed in the people's hamlets," Dwn responds humbly in Welsh.

Warily picking their way down the path, Guy and Roger fall back to the flanks, hands on the hilts of their swords, and let Denis take the lead with Gianni. But no danger appears. At the sight of the approaching camels, the people descend from their fields and their mud-and-woven osier huts and gawk openly. And when they are within earshot, Dwn, glad to play her role in her mistress's strategy, cannot resist calling out triumphantly: "Greetings from the Servant of Birds, returned from the Holy Land, made young by the Holy Grail!"

As the ox wagon rumbles to a stop in the packed river mud clearing before the hamlet, Rachel rises and greets the people in Welsh, offering them a humble gift from the land where Jesus lived: baskets of figs and dates, accordingly passed out by the entourage.

The people, garbed in pelts, their hair bowl-cut over their eyes and ears, receive the strange fruits with trembling hands, for they believe this food, grown from sacred land, is holy indeed. Tears glint in the eyes of the women, and the bitter stares of the men soften. The small children hide behind their mothers while the older ones warily circle the camels and the turbaned knight.

Once their astonishment fades to conviviality, several of the villagers step forward timorously to invite the baroness into their homes. The abbot, Dwn, and the Muslim knight elect to accompany her, while the other knights wait uneasily beside their horses, keeping a wary eye on the surrounding hill-forests for signs of warriors. A harp is brought to the meeting ground where the baroness and abbot sit with the hamlet's chieftain, and to its soothing accompaniment, the assembled dine on oat bread, milk drunk out of great ram horns, and root-burl bowls of cheese.

Only after they have eaten does the chieftain, propped on a simple stool, ply the young baroness with questions of her journey and the marvels she has experienced.

Rachel tells her story, and as she speaks, the utter simplicity of the people—with their smells of river mist and tanned hides, their taciturn swaying, intoxicated by awe, their eyes like wounds of soft light perceiving the truth in what she herself cannot believe—enchants her utterly and holds her in kindred thrall.

* * *

The kindness of the Welsh people, the jubilant grace with which they received back the land that Guy and his knights had taken from them over the years, redeems all the fetid feelings of Rachel's deception. When she leaves the hamlet, followed all the way back up to the hill road by singing clanspeople, she feels almost drunkenly free of the guilt that had troubled her the day before with Denis. Even with Guy stony-eyed and Roger Billancourt muttering under his breath, she knows that her role as the baroness has worked some good—at least for the time that she is here.

Shortly past noon, Branden Neufmarché's castle appears among the knolly hills. Trampled fields, an abandoned catapult, and the rubble of a collapsed wall attest to the aborted siege. None of the knights will approach the castle; and on a ridge far out of crossbow range, the Swan banderole is unfurled in the summer breeze.

Branden Neufmarché himself rides out, accompanied by two knights and four sergeants. He looks not at all like the regal-browed, raven-haired Drew Neufmarché of the aquiline nose and heavy jaw whom Ailena had loved without the sanction of marriage for three decades. His son has strawberry hair, oily, pocked skin, and a face as chinless as a toad's. With petulant anxiety, he paces his horse before Guy and Roger, angry and nervous at the same instant. He will not approach close enough to take the saddlebag Guy offers him with a disdainful glare. His sergeant approaches to retrieve it, but Guy withdraws his hand. "Take it yourself, Branden."

With mincing steps and apprehensive looks, Branden snatches the bag and retreats hurriedly.

"Let this token inspire peace between us," Rachel announces loudly.

Branden peers at her incredulously. He remembers the baroness as a knobby, bent hag with a heart of stone. That the rumors about her rejuvenation could possibly be true dents his heart with despair: What God would have mercy on her? Clearly, she is the Devil's scion.

"Your father and I were friends," Rachel adds warmly. "Let there be no hostility between us."

Scorn lifts Branden's lip, revealing thick gums and tiny teeth. "I am not my father," he says and gallops off, stealing one nervous glance backward.

A brooding wind has lured thunderish clouds out of the mountains, and a gray sun crawls down the sky. The ox van, wending on the precarious crossback trails high in the Epynt Hills, is less than an hour's journey from the remote abbey of the Trinity. Yet all that is visible are the ragged cliffs dotted with goats and, far below, rocky gorges where twisted thorn trees gather their wrath among shattered boulders.

Thierry, who with his father, William, brings up the rear, knows that his black moment has come. Yesterday William schooled him in the necessity of toppling the ox van when they reached the high trails. "Power is taken—not given," William had always told him, and that made all the more sense now that the Devil had returned his wicked great-grandmother, the old crone whose curse had doomed her husband, whose evil ways had cruelly haunted his godfather Guy. Now was the moment to win the love of his godfather; his only fear was that the holy man might topple into the abyss with the Devil's daughter. "The abbot will be holding the reins," William had assured him. "And if he lets go, we know at least he's bound for heaven. His soul will bless you for dispatching the Pretender to hell."

William had planned to do the task himself, but realized that the greater danger would be in fending off the saber-armed Falan. To that end, he places his steed behind Falan's camel, and when, at a critical turn along a steep precipice, Thierry lurches forward with a stern shout, as if to control his spooked steed, William advances to keep the Muslim knight from turning on the narrow trail.

Pretending to lose his balance and reeling hard against the ox wagon, Thierry knocks one of its rear wheels over the edge. The wagon lurches and tilts, throwing Rachel from her bench to the side planks overpeering the gorge. A scream jams in her throat as she stares into the vasty depths.

Maître Pornic and Dwn, on the driving trestle at the front of the wagon, clutch at each other and look back to see the baroness kneeling over the brink, staring at the rear wheel on its axle spinning in emptiness. They cry out as one for help.

Falan struggles to turn his camel, but William, feigning alarm for his son and looking away from the Muslim, keeps his horse pressed against the camel's haunch so it cannot turn about. Guy and Roger stand in their saddles to watch, blocking Gianni, who had taken the point.

Mastering his jittery horse, Thierry leans over the back of the van and reaches for the baroness. Before Maître Pornic and Dwn can react, Thierry fakes a stumble and rams the van again with his mount, this time forcing a front wheel over the edge and heaving the whole wagon to its side.

Rachel falls, clutching at the roof pole. It snaps in her hands and, shrieking, she topples out of the wagon. With one arm, she seizes hold of the hide coverings lashed to the outside of the van and hangs there, dangling over the rocky plunge. Her other hand claws for a hand-hold on the hides. Eyes bulging, she sees Dwn above her, on the driver's bench. The old woman slaps away Maître Pornic's hands as they reach to lift her out, and she clambers down into the tilted wagon.

"No!" Rachel yells. *Go back!* she wants to cry, but her breath is used up with the strain of holding on.

Denis, who has maneuvered his steed across the skinny path, manages to pull Maître Pornic from the teetering wagon as the abbot attempts to climb down after Dwn. But the old woman ignores the shouts of the men and the straining bellows of the oxen. She stands resolutely on the overturned sideboard, reaching over to snatch Rachel's arms in her strong root-digging hands. "Servant of Birds!" she yells with all her exertion and provides enough purchase for the younger woman to clamber back into the wagon.

Suddenly—just as they are face to face—the side plank supporting Dwn splinters, and the old Welshwoman hurtles into the abyss. Denis, who has nudged his steed to the crumbling rim, grabs Rachel by the back of her robe as her feet skip out from under her. She dances in the air, watching Dwn's small body smash below, a broken star among the nettle. Denis grunts above her. With his horse wedged between the oxen and the toppled van, its panicked face jerking back from the chasm, he puts all his strength into both arms and pulls the baroness out of the wagon and into his lap.

Falan has driven his camel forward and slid down from its back, and scurries between the oxen. A blow of his saber snaps the traces, and, with a kick, he unhooks the draft pole and sends the empty wagon careening down the gorge side. Rachel watches it boiling smoke and rocks behind it, the long echoes of its crash shattering her heart.

In a downpouring dusk, the pilgrims arrive finally at Trinity Abbey. The baroness, cowled in her mantle and visibly shaken, rides with Falan on his unhappy dromedary. Maître Pornic sits behind Gianni Rieti on his white stallion. The abbot lifts his bony face to the hard rain, grateful to the Maker that they have negotiated the tricky mud trails of the mountains without any further loss of life.

As they approach the wooden gates of the abbey, a bell clangs in the purplish light. The dripping knights, hunched over their exhausted steeds, trail behind the camels and the white stallion. Maître Pornic tries to catch the eye of the baroness, to welcome her to his monastery, but she is as if paralyzed and can only watch with a cold fixed look as the gates open and the monks come running through the pelting rain.

In the middle of the night, Rachel thrashes awake. The room around her is a glowing mass of darkness, and the Devil's voice is intoning: "Never and always, Rachel."

The voice is inside the glisando sound of rain on the roof-tiles, its evil chuckle is the gurgling of water in the gutters. *Not a voice,* she insists to herself. *Just the rain. Just the rain.*

"One and many," the Devil says with a soft laugh. "Like the rain, I am one and many. Dwn is with me now. She is here, finally and truly reunited with her mistress."

Rachel sits up in her bed. Dwn's ghost flimmers in the drafty darkness like incense smoke, her face a fiery vapor without a jaw-bone, her eyes gasps of emptiness.

"No!" Rachel covers her face. The madness thickens her blood like adder venom, forcing her heart to thud harder, filling her head with the arterial seething that has, since the horror, droned into the blind voices of her dead family. They mutter the Aramaic *qaddish*, the holy prayers for the dead she remembers hearing from her childhood but does not understand.

She opens her eyes to make the dead voices go away and sees the wispy husk bones of Ailena's face full of shadowy wickedness. "You killed my Dwn!"

"No! She was murdered. I'm sure of it. That was no accident. She was murdered by your own kin!"

Ailena's fog-face distorts to a goat-visage with eyes of raw darkness, its decayed lips and jagged teeth rooted in a skullbone wormed with holes. "Soon you, too, will be with me, Rachel."

With a cry, she presses her hands to her face. "Never!"

"Always, Rachel. Always."

I am dreaming, she insists. *I am not mad!* She presses her eyes until light flares behind her lids. When the whispering voices dim into the loud beat of her heart, she drops her hands. For a moment, all is dark. When her blindness relents, she sees the hard shapes of the bedposts, the chest, the chair in the corner, and, hanging from a crevice in the stone wall, a crucifix inside a red nebula, pulsing like a heart.

Orange clouds carry off the rain at dawn and leave the sky pink as a healing wound. Rachel dresses slowly, feeling every movement is luckless, a strain against the natural order. The bell chimes for matins. From her window she watches the monks file out of the dormitories and follow a flagstone path across the green turf of the quadrangle to the chapel.

The blackstone buildings and the men in their black cowls seem sinister to her; now more than ever, she is determined to be away from here as quickly as possible. Before she leaves the room, she pauses before the crucifix and studies the precision of the icon—the small madness of the wreathed thorns crowning the head, dripping blood, the beauty of suffering in the woeful face, the flawless submission to torture, pierced hands and feet bleeding darkly, and the side wound like lips grinning at this senseless trial.

By morning light, this gory image is bearable, and there is no hint of the madness that assailed her during the night. How weird it seems to her that gentiles would worship a crucified Jew, one who is not even mentioned in the Jewish chronicles. With gentleness, she touches the tormented face of this dying Jew as though he were one of her brothers—and she wonders what has happened to her brothers and sisters, her parents, Dwn, the baroness, all the dead. *Where do they go?* She knows that the Christians believe that everything that dies someday comes back. That souls would remain separate from their Creator for all time strikes her as sad. She would rather believe, as her grandfather does, that her family are with God now and that death has no dominion at all.

Falan, on his knees, his face pressed to the stone in prayer, sees her and moves to rise. She signs for him to finish his obeisance. She is grateful for the blue shine of morning in the windows and stands by an alcove casement listening to birds chattering in trees that are still hung with pieces of night.

Maître Pornic appears at her side, his face haggard with grief. He has prayed all night long for Dwn's soul.

"Will you join us for matins?" he asks. "We will pray together."

"No, Maître." Rachel is careful to inflect her voice with sufficient ire. The baroness, even after having drunk from the Grail, would be furious at this blatant attempt on her life and the loss of her dear friend. But, after last night's episode of madness, Rachel lacks the strength to act any more than she must. She thinks only of the jewels and returning to her grandfather, where she can be herself. She yearns to be whole. She wants to flee this dangerous country and forget everything about the baroness. "I will say my prayers for Dwn at my husband's crypt," she answers wearily.

"The lauds our monks sing stir the heart. I feel their voices draw God closer to His fallen creation. That is what I miss most during my absence." He cocks a wispy eyebrow. "Of course, now with Canon Rieti to take my place at the castle, I may remain here with my monks."

"You will always be welcome at my castle," Rachel responds

perfunctorily. She sees Falan is standing now and asks, "The gate to the crypt is unlocked?"

The abbot's gray eyes glint shrewdly. "The key is where you left it."

"Good," Rachel responds without hesitation, curtsies to the holy man, and departs.

As she disappears down the passage, Maître Pornic situates himself in the window so that he can see her as she emerges from the chapter house with Falan and walks along the cloisters, past the refectory. When she avoids the lych gate behind the chapel, which is the shortest route to the cemetery, his cocked eyebrow relaxes into place. But as he is about to turn away, he sees her pause and look about at the stone buildings. His gaze hardens. *She does not remember where the library is,* he thinks. *Or she never knew!*

He watches her speak with a passing monk, who points directions. As she detours through the postern to the library, he walks briskly down the passage to the stairs. When he reaches the library, he catches her looking over the shelves of bound volumes.

From the corner of her eye, Rachel notices the abbot, and her mind races, trying to remember exactly where the key is hidden. Not remembering the location of the library may be forgivable but not knowing if the key is hidden in a volume of Plutarch or Plotinus will damn her in the abbot's eyes. She removes the volume of Plutarch's *Noble Lives* and opens it. Her heart constricts to see that there is no key attached to the inside cover. Is she mistaken—or have the monks moved it? *No—the abbot said it is still where the baroness left it.*

With Maître Pornic's steps sounding behind her, Rachel returns the volume and removes the tome marked Plotinus.

"Have you forgotten where you requested us to keep the key?" the abbot asks.

Rachel opens the book and sees a key secured to the inside cover with crossed strips of plaster paper. "Plutarch—Plotinus," she shrugs. "To me, they're just dead Greeks."

Maître Pornic regards her suspiciously. "Plotinus was a Roman."

She closes the volume and hands it to Falan. "But dead enough to keep my key safely," she says and walks off to the quick beat of her heart.

Sunlight slips through the yews and glints on the marble lintel, which is carved with floriate letters: LANFRANC. The austere crypt, a stone box with a dolmen-doorway of marble, sits on a mound in a ring of dark, narrow trees. The monks have kept the ground around it free of weeds, and bees lumber among sprays of white flowers.

Nearby is the more ornate red marble crypt where Bernard, the baroness's father, is interred, but Rachel ignores it. She fumbles with the lock to the smaller crypt, where Ailena promised she would find the payment for her devotion—jewels that the baroness had hidden here in the event she returned from her exile with a mercenary army and needed funds. *But what if she lied? What if there are no jewels?*

Rachel dismisses that fear. The key to the lock was where she had said it would be, in the abbey's library, taped within the cover of a yellow leather-bound volume of Plotinus's *Enneads*. A red ribbon marks a page where one line is underscored, as if to explain the thirteen years of misery she endured with her husband: "Evil was before we came to be."

The key jams in the lock that it has not worked in ten years, and Falan must bend all his strength to it before it clacks open. The gate pulls outward with a mournful whine. Falan lights a rush torch with firestone and flint and sets it in a sconce high on the rime-stained wall.

Fire shadows prance around the small enclosure, illuminating a low ceiling laced with mineral drippings. A life-size marble effigy of Gilbert Lanfranc lies on its back, clutching the hilt of a sword and staring with bald eyes from under a sturdy helmet. While Falan stands watch at the portal, Rachel goes down on her knees at the back of the crypt and feels for the loose tile she was told is there.

But it is not there. She has been duped—and blood rushes into her head with fury and humiliation. The baroness's cackling laughter whirls up in her, before she realizes that the rock weepings have crusted over the tile. She has to get a stone from outside to chip at the crusty salts until the tile comes loose with a grating rasp.

With trembling hands, Rachel reaches into the hole and comes out with a bulky leather pouch. In the cobwebby light of the torch, she sees that it is a thick leather wallet. The moldy flap peels away like flesh, and, inside, gems return the light in greasy red and green starpoints. Her fingers tremble over the jewels, their bright life reminding her of the Devil's mocking voice in her waking nightmare. Has Dwn died for these? *Poor woman:* her life exchanged for something cold to the touch, and hard, the softness of their luminance untouchable.

Falan calls out with hushed urgency, and Rachel quickly closes the wallet and hides it within the loose folds of her bliaut, held snug to her body by a waistband of woven silk cords.

"Grandmère—" a tentative male voice calls.

Rachel goes to the doorway and sees a sandy-haired monk in a white cassock standing under the yew trees. The man has an open countenance of broad jaw, a prowlike nose, and cheeks as angular as a cat's. At the sight of her, he gapes with shock and clutches a yew branch to keep from falling. Falan takes steps to help him, but the monk waves him off and approaches, bent over with astonishment.

"Grandmère? Is that truly you! It is I, Thomas."

Thomas Chalandon, Rachel hurriedly recalls: Clare and Gerald's youngest. This is the young man whom Ailena has sworn Rachel to discourage from living the feckless life of a priest.

Rachel exits from the crypt, offers her hand, afraid to embrace him lest he feel the wallet of gems. "Forgive me, Thomas, for not showing all the joy I feel at seeing you again."

"Grandmère . . ." He kisses her signet ring, then peers into her face with the expression of an astonished child. "Forgive *me.* The abbot told me of the miracle that changed you. Still, I—I—" Tears glisten in his eyes, and he falls to his knees and clutches at her robe.

"Dearest Thomas," she says and strokes his feathery hair. "You were still a boy when I saw you last. You were only eleven, and now look at you." She puts her hands on his shoulders and persuades him to stand. "You were always such a sweet child. I remember you making chaplets of flowers and crying over a dead bird—"

Thomas blinks away tears. "It is you! You've been touched by God! I—I don't know what to say."

"Say a prayer here with me for Dwn," Rachel suggests.

They kneel on the stone step of the crypt, and Thomas intones a prayer of petition to the Blessed Virgin. While he prays, eyes downcast, Rachel studies him, unable to look away, curiously intrigued by his forlorn beauty. When he is done, he helps her rise and offers to pray with her in the crypt for Gilbert.

"No. Walk with me instead. I wish to talk with you. I am concerned about your becoming a monk."

"Concerned?"

"Actually, I am angry, Thomas." Rachel tries to muster the outrage the baroness would want her to feel. "You are not a monk."

"You're right. I am not yet a monk," he sighs and takes her arm. "I might have expected your anger. But I am only an acolyte. I have not yet felt worthy of tonsure. But why are you angry that I choose this life? You, who have seen God's face—"

Rachel signs for Falan to lock the crypt, and leads Thomas away from the lych gate toward the far end of the cemetery, where the round-edged stone crosses end before the chine of a hill. "The priesthood is not your calling, and that is why I am angry. You were always a spirited boy; in fact, I seem to recall you were a little pagan. We were constantly sending the servants to retrieve you from the woods. I cannot think *this* Thomas that I remember so well would wish to sequester himself from the world which gave him so much pleasure. It is not your calling, is it? Tell me the truth."

"I love our Savior, Grandmère—but, I admit, I am no good at ritual. I would rather spend my time tending the garden or just sitting in contemplation on the hillside watching God shepherd the clouds."

For an instant, Rachel feels a sharp nostalgia for her own childhood rise up in her—the summery days when she sat alone among the ruins in her secret place, watching the clouds fit themselves to the wind—and the irremediable longing makes her shiver.

"Are you cold?" Thomas asks.

Rachel pulls her tunic tighter about her. "A little."

"You must still be stunned from losing Dwn. We should get you back to the chapel, where you can rest and mourn properly."

Rachel shakes her head. "I have mourned enough." She releases Thomas's arm and strides quickly to the top of the hill. Mortality wafts through her, Dwn's death not a full day behind her, and the jewels of her future hard against her stomach. So much has been lost to bring her to the gain of this moment, she is afraid to look into the vigilant face of this angel, afraid she will despise herself again.

From the hill crest, she faces the lavender morning, the mists paring among the hills, lifting from the silver threads of streams and rivulets. A heavy, wordless weight rests on her lungs, the dread that Dwn's death was not an accident, that Thierry's shove had not been a riding blunder but murderous intent. With that thought, anger piles up in her and shoves aside the oppressive weight in her breast. Dwn did not have to die. Her family did not have to die. God had not killed them. The evil in men's hearts . . .

"The Grail, Grandmère," Thomas asks humbly, coming up from behind. "You truly drank from the Holy Grail?"

Rachel's body suddenly feels equal to the bluebell slopes and the dark-edged horizon of woods. The same energy rears up in her as in the cloud mass lifting the peach-bright morning into the sky. *Life comes from God,* she tells herself, and she is stronger than the evil in men's hearts.

When she faces Thomas Chalandon, Rachel's dark eyes are large with the deep meaning she has beheld briefly: "Yes. I have surely drunk from the Holy Grail."

As Rachel tells Thomas her wondrous tale of Prester John, he listens with a shining brow of hopeless worship. Watching his boyish adulation, she secretly marvels at his complete lack of guile. How could such a one have survived in the corrosive atmosphere of the baroness and her cruel son?

When she finishes, he sits quite still, pensive and transfigured, his eyes wet with the inner vision of this miracle. "You are right to be angry at me for studying to be a priest," he says finally, his blue eyes searching her face. "I am a lie, an utter lie. Oh, I am happy enough worshiping God in the fields. But field work is deemed inappropriate for gentry. My only other choice was the art of battle with Uncle Guy. I had only one recourse, Grandmère—this abbey. This has been a calling borne out of default, not of truth. Can you forgive me?"

Rachel drops her gaze from his open stare. His innocent yet bold features, which remind her of the Byzantine mosaics she had seen in Tyre decorated with blond, beardless seraphs like him, make her blood stir mysteriously faster in her veins. The feeling shames her. She searches within for the Grail, and when she finds it shimmering there, she recalls the baroness telling her about the knight Parsifal, whose destiny it was to find the Grail, where Lancelot and all the other knights failed. "You are Parsifal," she says softly. "I need not forgive you. To find your way, you must forgive yourself."

Thomas startles. "You think I am a fool, like Parsifal?" His amazement converts to ardor. "Well, perhaps you're right, Grandmère—I am. Here you've just told me the most wondrous account of a true miracle. And instead of wanting to rush to chapel and praise God, I just want to . . . to . . . I can't think what!"

He turns sharply away, his cheeks burning with the perplexity of his feelings for his grandmother. He feels, looking into her face, as if he has suddenly been sucked into an undertow of equal awe and yearning, as well as a deep revulsion at the sudden shocking thought of feeling seduced by his own grandmother. But seduced by what?

Seeing his flustered embarrassment, Rachel's heart knocks loudly, and she stands up from the hummock where she has told her story. Glancing back at the vale of crypts, she watches a swarm of butterflies eddying among the stone houses of the regal dead, Thomas's dead.

"You *are* Parsifal, the naïf," she says, and her voice sounds frail and faraway. *Does he suspect? Is he playing the fool with me?* The gold of the Grail glitters in her mind's eye, and she focuses her full attention on it, needing the assured presence of the baroness to confront this gentle man. When she faces Thomas, her smile is tight. "You can find the Grail, Thomas—but not in an abbey. Come, walk with me. We will begin our quest."

They follow the spine of the hill to where a Roman road sinks into the earth, ferns and black heather like plumes on the helmets of the Legionnaires who have marched upright into the ground. Thomas cannot bring himself to think that this lean woman with mushroom-white skin and ebony hair is his grandmother, the knob-knuckled, liver-spotted old dame with milk haze on her eyes. *Yet she is,* he must remind himself. The abbot said that there had been witnesses to the miracle, and the Holy Father himself agreed she had been made young by quaffing from the Grail.

Despite himself, Thomas cannot resist putting her to the test, reminiscing aloud about his childhood in the castle, purposely getting details wrong. "And in winter, when I'd come back from rolling in the snow, you'd wrap me in a great bearskin and make me drink hyssop tea while you sang about the ice queen."

Rachel, intrigued by the shatter-glass blue of his eyes and the calm strength in his voice, simply nods. Then she sees the harder glint in his stare and realizes, too late, something is amiss.

"There was no bearskin," he accuses, his eyes narrowing slyly. He says in half-mocking accusation: "How can you be my grandmother! Only an impostor would not remember these things!"

Rachel puts a hand to her brow, and her eyes flutter as she searches hurriedly for her cues, feeling them nearby but too jangled to bring them to her aid.

"That was a robe of stitched marten pelts, Thomas," she manages. "And it was comfrey you drank while I teased you with silly stories about Jack Frost. Don't make much of my lapses. It merely distracts me to see you grown into such a striking man."

"I'm sorry, Grandmère—" Thomas casts his hands up, abashed. "I *am* acting the fool. Forgive me. You must realize, the whole time I was growing up, I never thought of you as ever being young. Your youthfulness, and your beauty, disarm me. And all the tomes I've ever read about the sacred science of grace and piety and the glory of the sacraments suddenly seem so empty. Here, right here, is our covenant with God standing before me—and all I can do is test it and make feeble play and allow it to turn me into a stammering—fool!" He laughs.

"I have not come back to be worshiped, Thomas. I am no sign from the Lord. I have been returned to—"

"Undo your errors. I heard you the first time, Grandmère. Still, I can hardly believe the world will simply go on as before after this miracle. How can one just go on like this? You've beheld the Grail! And spoken with the Son of God!"

"And what should I be doing then?"

"Praying—worshiping—preaching."

"If the Savior had wanted that of me, Thomas, I would give it. But the Lord was clear. I am to live in the world as a woman, not a saint or a living covenant."

"And all this while, I have been looking for my faith in books."

"If you had found it there, you would be a priest by now." Looking into that rapt, seraphic face, Rachel's stomach tightens, and, to continue her deception, she must look quickly away. "Leave this abbey, Thomas. Come back to the castle and take your place with the knights."

Thomas rubs the back of his neck, chafing under remembered ridicule. "I was too much the dreamer to ever please Uncle or Roger. And at the abbey I am too much in this world to satisfy Maître Pornic. But now, seeing you made young again—you who saw our Savior with her own eyes, who held His Chalice in her hands—" He makes two fists and presses them against his chest. "I believe now I can give myself entirely to God."

Rachel kicks at a tuft of milk feathers poking through the ancient pavement and sends the bright fluff soaring. "Thomas, listen to me. I drank from the Grail, and it didn't make me a nun. God has enough nuns and priests, women and men who have been called to serve Him from within, not by some miracle outside of them. My vision sent me back here—to embrace life, to live in the world, fulfilling all my humors and appetites. That pleases God, too."

"Grandmère, I want to believe you. You said we would quest for the Grail. You said it was not in the abbey. Is that what you meant?"

"For some, the Grail may be there. But not for you, or you would have found it by now."

"You found the *real* Grail, Grandmère."

Rachel sighs and looks up at the seed sparks drifting among the oak fronds. The baroness had required her to get her grandson away from the abbey. She has done her best, but is afraid to press for more. *Better to leave this matter be.* Still, there is something appealing about this man: his ingenuous blue stare, his strong features composed in a gentle countenance, his self-confessed love of nature so reminiscent of her own childhood passion for Pan's world. How odd and cruel to have found such a man here, where she cannot be herself—here, by this Roman artifact that reminds her of the childhood she cruelly lost—here, at the end of Empire's road, where generations of striving leads back ultimately to shaggy grass and soaring cloud castles, to the whole of the fallen world.

Falan listens to the trees creak and rustle in the wind. Anxiety has splayed his senses out into the world. He tastes the breezes for taints of people, feels the Roman road for the tread of hooves, wary of being caught alone out here on the fringe of wilderness where no one will hear their cries. The knights, he knows from yesterday's tragedy, are determined to kill Rachel. And if she dies, he must die first or break his vow before Allah.

How long can he protect her? He has sworn to install her as baroness of this alien land. That is all. When can he return to the people who have adopted him? *Soon,* he promises himself.

Rachel and Thomas leave the cobbly road and stroll through a cloud of dandelions. He does not understand what they are saying, but he reads their joys perfectly—their furtive sidelong glances and bashful touches. Since the old servant's death, Rachel has been sullen, but this young priest has revived her. Now, for the first time, Falan sees soft excitement in her face—the way young women are supposed to look, he thinks, when happiness is possible.

When they return to the abbey, the monks are already at work in the outlying fields. Many stare openly at Falan as he escorts his charge down a slope of brilliant kingcups past the vegetable garden. He is aware of their hostility. They have given their lives to their icons and saints and trinity of gods, the same deities that his family had been forced to worship at swordpoint on Björkö. He knows these monks resent his presence among them, here in the sanctuary of their faith, and he would just as soon be gone from this place. He thinks coldly, Muhammad fought for freedom but no one had ever been forced into the worship of Islam at the point of a sword.

Wearing his green headcloth, emblem of his pilgrimage to Mecca, and with the *fatihah,* the simple and meaningful profession of faith in Allah, on his lips, Falan marches proudly into the abbey with Rachel and Thomas. With his faith unshaken even here in the temple of the polytheists, he knows he has won the meritorious notice of the angels.

At the inner gate, a monk stops them and gestures at Falan's scimitar. Last night, he and the other knights had been allowed to keep their weapons, but now, if they are to remain on the abbey grounds, they can bear no arms. Reluctantly, and only after he sees Guy and Roger emerging from the refectory unarmed, he surrenders his saber and his knife.

Weaponless, Falan repeats the *fatihah* more loudly, determined not to relinquish the arms of his soul, not even here under the dread gaze of the tortured god.

As Falan escorts the baroness into the refectory for the morning meal, Maître Pornic takes Thomas aside. They walk slowly through the cloisters so as not to be overheard by anyone. "Is she your grandmother?"

Thomas frowns, perplexed. "You doubt her, Maître?"

"Please, Thomas, do not answer my questions with questions. Life is enough of a conundrum. Now tell me, who is this woman with whom you talked at the crypt of your grandfather?"

"Why, she is Ailena Valaise, my grandmother."

"How do you know she is whom she claims to be?"

"She carries her soul in her eyes," Thomas answers, blushing imperceptibly. "I saw her truth there."

"Did you test her?"

Thomas bows his head. "Yes, Maître. Even after you told me of the Grail and how she had drunk from it, I doubted her. I asked her questions of my childhood—and she remembered, even the small details! There is no doubt. And now, by God's miracle, she appears more youthful than even I, her grandson!"

Hidden within the sleeves of his cassock, Maître Pornic's hands wring apprehensively. He still cannot accept that the God who let His son suffer on the cross to redeem the sin in flesh, the God who lets the hawk stoop to kill the dove, the God of the spider's palace and all the sorrows of winter, that He would grace Ailena Valaise with a second life. God has always been so precise in the turning of the stars and the seasons, so unfathomable in His absence that He is present in every sprouting seed and in every sunrise. Why now, with this woman, who loved Him not when she had her health, why with her has He chosen to show His hand?

"Did she speak to you of her plans?"

"Yes. She said that her return had brought death to one who loved her and discord to all around her. She told me that she had fulfilled the vision that bade her come back and make herself known. She intends now to pilgrimage again to the Holy Land and to dwell there the rest of her days. And, Maître—" Thomas stops, says in a troubled voice, "She wants me to leave the abbey and live as a knight at the castle."

Maître Pornic's eyes blaze. "You are a knight of Christ. But she senses your ambivalence, Thomas. You must be strong."

"Maître, her presence has given me the faith to be a priest. I've been here six years, serving and studying, and my faith grew no stronger. I wondered, how can light come from the dark? Have I stolen my purpose from God? Do I, in truth, belong among my family, serving them with love and Christian care? Now she is returned, and I am ready to give myself to God, for I have seen His power. That is not in the books."

"Thomas, Thomas." Maître Pornic places a callused hand against the youth's cheek. "God is the mystery we pay with our hunger. You hunger to know. You have read all the tomes we have. You have discoursed with all our knowledgable brothers. There is nothing more to *know*, my son. You must cast your life upon the water now. You must interpret your own solitude."

"Grandmère's return must be a sign from God, Maître. She is a manifestation of God's power that will draw me closer to Him."

"No, Thomas." Maître Pornic takes Thomas by his arm, and they continue to walk. "It is always a mistake to be led by power, even to God. Let weakness be your guide. Let illness and craving and fear show you where God's love is needed. Then go and be that love."

Thomas blows a long sigh. "I will try, Maître."

"Good. You can begin by returning to Castle Valaise with the baroness."

Thomas balks. "That may not be best. I should wait to return to my homestead until after she leaves again for the Holy Land."

"I need you there with her now, Thomas. Be my eyes and ears. And keep your doubt alive. Miracles are God's unravelings. The world is whole as God created it. Why should He unravel old age and sickness for Ailena when every day, somewhere, babies die of fever and famine?"

"You have often said, God is mystery."

"Indeed, one of the greatest mysteries is that God has created evil. All sin comes from misjudging evil. Remember that, Thomas. The Devil is the master of illusion."

Denis Hezetre sits down on the wooden bench across the table from where Rachel sits with her bowl of berries and cream. The refectory has two long tables with benches on either side. The lancet windows under the rafters admit dusty shafts of sunlight that illuminate bas-relief carvings of mealtimes described in the Gospels: Jesus turning water to wine, multiplying the loaves and fishes, sanctifying the Last Supper, and cursing the fig tree.

"The monks have gone out with Gianni to recover Dwn's body," Denis begins. "She is to be laid to rest in a plot beside the family crypts."

Rachel pokes at her breakfast with her spoon. "I feared Guy and Roger," she says feebly. "I did not think to fear the boy."

"He is not a boy, my lady. He is a knight, who has sworn homage to you. He is cognizant of his actions, and he should be punished."

"He will claim it was a riding accident," Rachel replies, with a sarcastic look.

"Do you believe it was an accident?"

Rachel bites her lower lip, shakes her head.

"Then he must be punished." He gives her a steady look. "I can hardly believe I must tell you this. It would appear that you have lost your edge with your brittleness, my lady."

Rachel's mind focuses sharply at that gibe, and her jaw sets. "I will banish him, of course. Perhaps I will send him to the Levant, and I will not admit him to my castle until he returns with a sheaf of sugar cane to sweeten my grief!"

Alone in her chamber in the chapter house, Rachel unwraps the jewels she recovered from Gilbert's crypt: six rubies and five emeralds, faceted and polished, gleaming with crystal power. These, she thinks to herself, are the sins of the baroness made physical—the land stolen from the Welsh by her father and her husband and herself, tilled by her peasants, cultivated to grains, some sold, some fed to cattle, then butchered to meat and garments and sold, every transaction converted to gold and the gold exchanged for these superb rocks.

She holds up a ruby in one hand, an emerald in the other. Inside them, the light webs, starry horizons carrying the fables of mountains and valleys between her thumb and finger.

Dwn's body is laid on the bier under the lych gate. The monks who retrieved her from the gorge stand beside her, their muddy hands clasped in prayer as Maître Pornic recites from the Psalms. Throughout the ceremony, Rachel keeps her eyes fixed on Thierry, who shifts uncomfortably under her gaze. Guy, Roger, and William return her silent ire, resenting her command to be present, but she ignores them. Her bitter stare locks unwaveringly on the culprit.

Rachel is afraid to budge her stare from Thierry, fearing that if she places her attention on the corpse or too near her grief, then the vacuous silence inside her will explode into voices. She wants only never to hear those voices again. *Thierry should have to hear them*, she believes. *He should have to answer to the Devil.*

Before the ceremony is complete, Thierry slips away. Rachel thinks to protest, but at that moment, Maître Pornic asks if she would like to say anything about her old friend. She shakes her head, studies the blue fabric of her shoes, and feels a pang of remorse. Ailena would have *something* to say; Dwn deserves more than silence. She clutches the gems in her waistband, and their solidity, their promise of a new life for her and David, encourages her to say, "Just this: she was my friend."

She faces the draped body and remembers the old woman climbing down into the tilted carriage to save her—even though she knew the truth. Now tears track down her cheeks, and her lips tremble as she recalls that Dwn's last words were her cry, *Servant of Birds!*

"She was my friend," Rachel repeats in a cracked voice. "She knew the truth of my sins. And yet she loved me. She gave her life for me." Sobs wrack her with sincere grief, and she lets Gianni turn her away from the bier.

Afterward, the villein who serves as the abbey's stablehand reports that the young knight Thierry has galloped off into the hills.

The knights spend the day hunting in the dense forests around the abbey. Rachel fears that they have gone off to join Thierry, perhaps to return to the castle ahead of her and shut her out. She does not care for the castle, only for her grandfather. She is pondering how to arrange for his release when the knights return with a stag and several large birds.

That night, after dinner, Rachel must tell her story yet again of Prester John, his magical kingdom, and how she came to be blessed by the Sangreal. The monks listen rapt, their faces still as wax effigies in the torchlight. At the back of the hall, out of sight of the monks or Maître Pornic, but visible to Rachel, Guy and Roger mime her adventure in broad, comic gestures. Their antics distract her, and when she stops and stares at them, their smiles darken to eagle frowns.

At dawn, before lauds, the monks stop to garland the horse they have given Rachel in exchange for her oxen. They sing a jubilant hymn as she rides the steed majestically out the front gate, flanked by Falan and his camels. Gianni Rieti follows on his white stallion, with Denis Hezetre next and Thomas Chalandon on a cream-colored hackney at his side. Guy, Roger, and William ride ahead, as if alone.

Rachel travels morosely, saddened to leave Dwn behind. Ailena had truly loved her, had once said, "Keep a watch for an old woman with a dark spur of hair on her chin. If she chance to be still alive, she'll be your greatest ally." And indeed she was that. "The truth is less important than what you do with it," Dwn had said. Rachel would not soon forget those words. The doing was all she could make sense of anymore: she had claimed her treasure, the just payment of her years-long devotion to a mean-hearted, and perhaps foolish, old woman. Where was the sense but in eleven bright rocks, eleven big promises for the future, for herself and her grandfather?

Long barrowslike fingers lead down from the mountains, their flanks dense with oak forest. The narrow path back to the castle rides high above those hills on a steep scarp. Directly below are gorges of thorn trees littered with scree. Rachel keeps her gaze on the winding road so as not to look down into the chasm where Dwn had fallen. Suddenly, the knights ahead stop and point among the tall banks and hedges of hazel and holly.

Instantly, Falan and Gianni suspect treachery from the knights, and draw their swords. But Thomas puts out a restraining hand and points to a wall of whinberries, where human figures part the red-tinged leaves—Welshmen armed with spears, swords, and crossbows, who slide down the embankment dragging Thierry after them. The knights brandish their weapons.

"Servant of Birds!" a brindle-bearded warrior calls in Welsh. "Put aside your weapons. I have in my clutches a traitor from your own family."

Apprehensively, Rachel commands her knights to sheathe their weapons. Falan and Gianni comply, but the others do not. "If not for me," she shouts at Guy, "then put your weapons aside for Thierry."

Warily, Denis removes the arrow from his bow, and the other knights reluctantly return their swords to their scabbards.

"Do not come any closer," Rachel calls to the Welsh warriors. "I cannot control my knights. I will come to you."

Ignoring her fear Rachel dismounts, and when Falan realizes what she is doing, he tries to stop her. But she insists; if she can help it, no one else will die saving her. Falan leaps from his camel, and, followed by Gianni and Thomas, Rachel begins to climb up through the bracken.

William shouts to his son, "Are you hurt?"

Thierry, hands bound, held by the scruff of his tunic, shakes his head sullenly.

On a sandstone ledge facing the Welshmen, Rachel sees that there are many more warriors lurking in the stands of ash and rowan on the mountainside. "Is this a trap?" she asks the brindle-bearded man.

"No trap from the Welsh for the Servant of Birds," the large man replies cheerfully. "But this whelk was found digging out a large boulder above this trail. Had it been released as you rode by, well—" He points with his eyes to the chasm. "You'd have been swept into the gorge and straight into the afterlife."

Rachel turns a clenched stare on Thierry. "Is this true? Were you planning to kill us?"

Thierry looks at her sourly. "Whatever I told you, you'd not believe me."

The Welshman shakes him violently, wagging the youth's face to a blur. "Speak the truth, you lout!"

"Stop it!" Rachel demands. She knows that if Thierry is hurt there will be more bloodshed, and the thought appalls her. She knows that she is close to leaving this realm, and she does not want to depart on a trail of blood. "Leave him be. He will answer to his kin."

The Welshman stops shaking Thierry and forces the lad to sit. "'Tis your life you're playing loose with."

Rachel looks over this warrior in his red leather leggings and purple fur-trimmed tunic. "You're a chieftain, to judge by your dress."

"I am that," he answers. "Erec Rhiwlas. My father, Howel, commands these men." He points with his spear to a burly man with a white floss beard and a scarlet cape watching her intently from among the slender trees. The score of men leaning on their lances and gaping at her clearly know of her miracle. "We heard about your gifts. The villagers are talking of nothing else. And then we find this weasel here digging the ground from under a boulder."

"Thank you, Erec Rhiwlas." She looks to the white-bearded giant standing in the crowd, the father himself, and nods deferentially. Ailena had told her about the famous and dangerous Howel Rhiwlas, whose sword is known in these parts as "Bloodghost," for the countless Norman and rival Welsh souls it has freed from flesh. Twice, the old baroness met the chieftain at the lavish summer festivals she sometimes conducted in the meadows, and once he had honored her with a harp song that had much flattered the old woman. Rachel strains to recall the lyric and recites, uncertainly at first, then more strongly:

> "Your beauty is your wisdom,
> that protects you better than sword or lance,
> that wearies the hearts of your enemies with longing
> and assures that they sleep less sound than you."

The slope-shouldered warrior advances and peers at Rachel with slow, lethal eyes.

"I carry your song with me," Rachel says with growing bravado, "still bright in my heart."

By an almost imperceptible tilt of his head, Howel summons two of his men closer. They support an aged man, bald and mottled as an apple, with silvery eyes and a fist of a face. Rachel instantly recognizes him as Howel's bard, the man who had crafted that very song for him. Longsight Meilwr is his name, an acquaintance of the baroness since she was a girl. But now he is blind, and Rachel does not know what to say to him.

Howel takes a lock of Rachel's hair and presses it to the ancient bard's face. The old man smells it, lifts his face to the night air, and abruptly falls back into the arms of the men supporting him. "She is not the Servant of Birds!" he cries out, lifting his spread-fingered hands assertively.

The crowd of Welshmen murmur incredulously. But Howel nods as if he had known this all along. When he speaks, his voice is like summer thunder in a vast blue sky. "No matter. Whoever you are, you act as a friend to us Welsh. We'll not block your way."

With that, he turns and strides away.

Erec shrugs. "My father obeys the old ways. But I prefer to listen to my heart." He eyes her favorably and with evident interest. "I saw you when you first arrived. I brought Dwn to you. And now I hear of her accident from this churl. It is a sadness that she's gone to the saints. But may we all be so blessed as she when we leave this world. Your miracle at least took her out of her dungpile for her last days. Whether that miracle is truth or lie is not for me to judge."

Erec rests his spear against his shoulder and dares to press his thumb to Rachel's dented chin. Though Falan flinches, alert for treachery, the warrior smiles, white-toothed and easy, oblivious to the watchful crowd. "No harm will come to you from me, Servant of Birds," he promises. "My hand is offered you, for whatever need—for I think the bard is right. You are *not* the baroness, the one of old; the Grail has changed you wholly." He removes his thumb. "This face I shall always recognize."

Thomas looks more closely at Rachel as they step down from the sandstone ledge, Thierry skidding ahead of them, his hands still tied. Thomas knows Welsh, and has heard what Longsight Meilwr said. *Is the bard right? Is this some impostor who has stolen all of Grandmère's memories?*

In Welsh, he asks her, "Why did Longsight Meilwr say you are not the Servant of Birds?"

Rachel leans on him to steady her footing on the incline and says nothing until they have reached the road. Then she says casually, "After all that has happened to me, Thomas, how could I be the same grandmother you knew, or the Servant of Birds that the bard praised? And what does it matter? Soon I shall return to the Holy Land." She puts a hand on his arm, and they stop. "I want you to take your place in the castle. Before I leave, I want to announce you as Guy's heir."

Thomas looks stricken. "No! I could never be baron, Grandmère. I am not even a knight."

She casts a disgusted look at Thierry. "Will this snake make a better baron? He murdered Dwn, and he would have murdered me today if the Welsh had not stopped him."

"Grandmère, you don't know that."

"Perhaps you are right to refuse, Thomas," Rachel says thoughtfully. "If you are named heir, you will be Thierry's target."

William dismounts and cuts the thongs binding his son's wrists.

"The Welsh say he was planning to drop a boulder on me," Rachel tells the others.

Thierry sulks and sends an underbrowed appeal to Guy. "That is not true! I had dug a resting place for myself on the hillside as night was coming on. It was under a boulder, where I would be dry from the night rains."

"Why did you flee the abbey?" Denis asks.

"She put the dark look on me," Thierry answers, turning his pinched face to Rachel. "While they buried the old woman, she stared daggers at me, as if *I* had killed her." He looks beseechingly to Guy. "Uncle, I admit I mishandled my horse and struck the ox cart. But it was an accident that killed the crone. And for that I am guilty. The bandits who captured me last night took my horse and my sword. That, I say, is punishment enough."

"And I say not," Rachel asserts. "Dwn is dead. Whether by murderous intent or incompetence, my boon friend is dead. Remember, you have sworn homage to me, Thierry. If you are sincere, you must obey me and make reparation."

Roger groans. "She's found her scapegoat."

Thierry looks again to Guy, then speaks through gnashing teeth, "What reparation?"

"A pilgrimage. To Saint David's at Land's End, to do penance at the shrine there, where you will have Mass said for my lost companion."

Thierry rears back in protest, but William lays a restraining hand on his shoulder. The hand grips him tightly, until he says, "It shall be done." Then the father's hand relents—but the son's heart continues to beat thickly.

* * *

Ummu runs along the rampart walk at the top of the curtain wall to the trefoil archway that admits to the giant tower of the donjon. Following close behind, Ta-Toh flies after the dwarf, and the two bound up the dark stone stairs and emerge into the glaring sunlight on the roof of the great keep. The watch, leaning lazily against the masonry in the shade of the south parapet, startles and shouts "Halt!" But Ummu ignores him and rushes to the edge of the broad roof, where a small round turret lifts the banner of the Swan high above the domain.

With acrobatic ease, Ummu ascends the dizzy ladder to the summit of the banner spire, and there, with his monkey perched on his shoulder, he leans out over the precipice and peers into the wavy horizons of hills. Hand extended to block the twinkling of the Llan, he can see the procession of horses descending from the hill trail to the expansive meadows and elm groves that skirt the high slopes of the river. He had seen their movements from the wall below but was unsure who the riders were. Now he clearly discerns Falan's camels, Gianni's Arabian steed, and even the baroness's argent robes and silken scarves fluttering in the summer breeze.

"The baroness approaches!" Ummu shouts to the watch, who frowns against the river glare and thinks he spies movement on the high road. "Sound the call! The baroness has returned!"

The watch lifts his large horn and trumpets a loud flourish.

In the three days that the baroness has been away, Ummu has entertained the senior couple of the *palais* with his risqué anecdotes of life in the palaces of Jerusalem, his formidable skill at chess and backgammon, and his antics with Ta-Toh. And though, like all others, they had regarded him with a mordant fascination at first, they now openly profess to be happiest when he is at hand to quip with and to challenge them in amusing ways. Compared to the sultans and Latin nobility with whom he and Gianni had cavorted in the Levant, these people are indeed unmannered provincials—yet this is their castle, and Ummu has not forgotten that its comforts are far superior to the rude accommodations of the pilgrims' holy road. Best of all, with fair Madelon endeared to heart-worn Gianni, there is even the possibility of his favorite entertainment: watching from secret hiding places the timeless, classless, and most sacred sport of *amore*.

"Where is Ummu?" Clare frets. She stands before a newly draped tapestry depicting King Arthur surrounded by knights and paladins, among them Sir Gawain and Parsifal—and in the far right corner, half hidden by acanthus fronds, the jewel-studded Holy Chalice. "I must know what he thinks of this."

Gerald Chalandon regards the freshly painted stucco walls, now brilliant red and yellow, hung here and there with other tapestries depicting Charlemagne, Saint Michael, and Roland. The rushes on the floor have been changed for the third time since the baroness's return and strewn again with fresh flowers and mints. "Your mother cannot doubt that you love her, Clare. You have received her like a popess."

Ummu strides into the great hall, takes in the bouquets, posies, and garlands scattered everywhere and pinches his nose. "Even bees will suffocate in this air."

"Ummu!" Clare scolds. "Do not tease. Now, what do you think of this tapestry? It took me all morning to find it. It belonged to Grandpère. But Guy had it taken down years ago."

"That alone commends it, then, fair lady," Ummu says and studies it, hands on hips.

"But do you think the image of the Chalice will offend Mother? Perhaps it is too artful."

"And Mother herself is not?" The dwarf laughs.

Clare glares down at Ummu. "Whatever do you mean by that?"

"God has conformed her to His design, hasn't He?" Ummu shrugs. "We are made in His image, after all. Our only flaw is that we grow old—and we die. Your mother, however, is *so* artful as to defy even this!"

David waits by the outer gate when Rachel returns. The whole time of her absence, he had remained in his chamber, reading from the Torah and praying for her safe return, fasting, accepting only water. He has felt too ill to eat, seared by a fever and torpid with nausea. Rachel dismounts to embrace him and cannot help seeing the misery in his gaunt features.

"You are not well!" she exclaims.

"I am better for seeing you," he manages and must lean against her to remain standing.

By the time Clare and Gerald and various of their children have walked across the bailey to greet her, Rachel is sobbing, trying to explain what has happened.

Drained by the weariness of the trek, Rachel's guilt over Dwn's death is renewed by the sight of her long-suffering grandfather. Unable to understand her broken speech, David grows alarmed at her reaction, afraid that she has blurted the truth to her knights. Then, as Clare flusters over Rachel, cooing and cosseting and shouting orders to the servants, he notices behind her, in the front of the crowd, a strange young man with the solemn beauty of an angel. Clare notices too and cries out, "Thomas!"

As Clare turns her loud affections on her youngest son, Rachel beckons to Gianni. "The rabbi is ill. Please, help me get him to his bed."

"I will be fine," David protests but does not resist as Gianni and Falan lift him between them. "This will pass. It is just an ill humor from the long journey."

On the way across the bailey, he listens with muted concern to Gianni's account of Thierry's treachery and Dwn's death. Warily, he glances past the Italian knight and his granddaughter, and watches Guy and his knights trotting off to the stables.

Alone with David in his chamber, Rachel opens the thick wallet and shows him the jewels. "This is our freedom, Grandfather."

David sits up in his bed and picks up the colorful stones. He studies the radiance imprisoned in the gems and feels the light in his own body brighten, despite his illness. "I was afraid Ailena might have deceived us."

"She kept her word."

"And we have kept ours." He lies back, the gems clutched to his chest. "Now we must leave, at once."

"As soon as you are well."

"No." David is adamant. "At once. I will recuperate on the way."

Rachel does not hide her alarm. "If we leave now, you will certainly die! Sea voyages sickened you enough when you were well. And overland journeys are too dangerous. We must wait until you are recovered."

David closes his eyes. *More waiting.* "I would rather die at sea than leave you in jeopardy here."

"Hush now and sleep." She removes the jewels from his grasp. "I will keep our treasure hidden with your holy books. And that way, at least for now, heaven and earth will be close."

"You were harsh with Thierry," Roger Billancourt says.

"Harsh?" The single slash of Guy's eyebrows is black against his livid forehead. "If his plot had worked—if the Pretender had been killed in a carriage accident or an avalanche—I would be called a murderer."

They are alone behind the stables, where Guy paces between hay ricks, fuming. Roger leans against a post, watching horses' tails swish flies, imagining how furious the baron would be if he surmised this had been his warmaster's strategy.

"We must discredit her first," Guy insists. "The world must know she is an impostor. Then we can impale her head on the flagstaff if we please."

"But the king's men—"

"Let them come!" Guy shouts. "Let the Pretender pay the penalties."

"She won't assume your debts except you pay her homage," Roger reminds him. "The king's men will put you in bond to King Richard."

"I'll flee to the hills first."

"Where Howel will truss you like a capon, as he did your godson."

Guy stabs him with a black look.

"There is another way," Roger says. "Defeat the Pretender in an *assise de bataille,* and exact the penalties from Neufmarché on threat of sacking his castle."

"He won't pay," Guy mutters. "He knows there is too little time for a siege, and we have not the men."

"You saw the castle wall," Roger says. "The tourney is only days away. The wall won't be fixed by then. The *assise de bataille* will give us some shred of legitimacy to assume authority. With the knights who have come to the tourney from across the kingdom, we will have enough force to swarm Neufmarché—or to exact the gold to pay our penalties and keep our castle."

Rachel sits in the warm water of her bath, the aches of her journey melting out of her. She has asked to be alone, and only a young maid remains to comb her hair and sort her clothes. David's illness troubles her deeply; he is old and still wearied by the journey that brought them here. The climate is bad for him, the nights damp and chill. She wants to spend more time in prayer with him, to mitigate her guilty feelings over Dwn and to celebrate the new hope that the jewels have won for herself and her grandfather. But he is too weak. The castle physician has declared that until his fever breaks, he must not even stand to pray.

Several masses must be said for Dwn, and now, with Maître Pornic out of the way, Gianni can conduct the services in a manner closer to Hebraic tradition. *That will please Grandfather.* There will be readings from the Torah and the singing of psalms. The sharing of the consecrated wine and bread will be like the Passover meal. Then, even she can partake without offending God. And the cold inside her that is the heart's fire will trouble her less.

Rachel mulls this over as she soaks her bruises: these people worship a Jewish god. Why not adore the rituals he adored?

Gianni Rieti kneels before the altar of the chapel, trying to pray. Oddly, he misses Maître Pornic, misses the holy man's veteran faith. *How difficult it is to worship the invisible,* he thinks with his eyes closed, seeing only darkness and blood-shadows, feeling no presence but the urgency of his own body. *God—Holy Lord and Master—you have given me a chapel, given me a flock—now give me the strength to be your priest.*

He opens his eyes and sees Ummu curled up asleep on the feet of the Blessed Virgin, Ta-Toh slinking over the statue's shoulders. The statuary of the chapel is exquisite, the crucifix frightfully detailed, the stained glass precise and lit with unearthly fire. *Why do they not move me with half the fervor of my loins? He leans his face in his hands. Is Maître Pornic right? If I hold this burning within me long enough, will it change to something wonderful? Am I that strong? Or is this unnatural? Give me a sign. You blessed the baroness with a miracle. Bless me with a simple but clear sign.*

Listening for thunder or an eagle's scream, Gianni hears only Ummu's raspy snoring and the distant clop of hooves in the bailey. Then Ta-Toh barks, and Ummu yawns: "An apparition."

Gianni twists hard about and sees sun smoke pouring through the arched doorway and a woman's silhouette. Madelon approaches; Ummu clicks his tongue for his monkey and disappears behind the transept.

"I've come to pray for you," the young woman announces, kneeling beside him. "Maître Pornic has been banished to his abbey, and now you must minister to the castle. You must be in great torment."

Gianni stares at her with feverish eyes. "I am."

"How could you not be, Gianni? I know from your life story, you are not a priest. You are only disguised as a priest."

"I have been truly devoted to our Savior since the miracle of the Grail. I saw it with my own eyes—and it has changed me."

Madelon places her perfumed hands at both sides of his face and gazes longingly at him. "Poor Gianni. You are a penitent of love. Why do you deny this? So long as you pretend you are a priest, you belong to the Devil and he burns you with lust. Let love set you free."

"You would love me?"

"If you abandon this pretense of being a priest, if you are simply a knight—then yes, I will love you."

She releases his face and bows her head in prayer. With a childlike shine in his eyes, Gianni watches her cross herself and rise. She nods to him with an elusive smile, then floats away into the darkness and disappears in another gush of sun smoke.

"She is tickling your anus," Ummu says, popping out from behind the altar.

"No," Gianni says with a sad tilt of his head. "I lost my soul a long time ago, Ummu. And that is where she has found it."

Denis Hezetre faces a target at the far end of the lists and fits the nock of an arrow to the string of his bow. He is alone on the field, for the sun has dropped low in the sky and slanting rays fan over the target. This appeals to Denis, for the glare in his eyes corresponds to the blindness in his heart that he has felt since the baroness's return. Only God could have ripped him from Guy's side and turned him into a foe. What a clever and symmetrical irony. But as surely as God makes sport of His creatures and their passions, Denis knows with equal certainty that only God can keep his heart true.

As Denis raises the bow and draws the arrow back on the string, he opens his eyes directly to the sun's shafts. Light winces through him, hurting his eyes, matching the pain at his center. The target is lost in the fiery radiance. But, just as he knows Guy is still there for him, Denis knows the target exists somewhere too.

He fires into the sun, then turns away without looking, knowing his aim is true.

Ginger-haired Hellene sits down on the couch beside the empty fireplace, dizzy with anger. She juts out her lower lip and blows an irate gust of air over her face. Then she fixes a demented, almost cross-eyed look on her husband William, who stands by the window tugging at his thick mustache and staring into the distance.

"Find your sister, Hugues," Hellene says to the glum twelve-year-old in the corner, without looking at him. The husky lad hangs his head and shifts his weight reluctantly, much preferring to stay and listen. "Bring Madelon here now," his mother adds in a sharp tone that sends the youth shuffling out the door.

Once out of sight, Hugues stops, presses his back against the wall and, biting his lower lip, listens.

"Why must Thierry go to Saint David's?" Hellene asks in a voice of hushed violence.

"I have already told you, Hellene. This is a pilgrimage to atone for Dwn's death."

"But that was an accident. You said it was the horse that struck the van."

"Thierry's horse."

"But why can he not atone here at the chapel or at the abbey? Saint David's is four days away. And if Howel's men catch him again—"

"Thierry will take the longer route—down the Usk to Newport. He'll leave after the tourney and have a sturdy escort among the departing knights."

Hellene shakes her head, and her shoulders slump with the weight of remorse. "Why do you never heed me, William? I told you Thierry was to stay here with Harold. The tourney is too near for him to have risked injury on the high road. He's fifteen, William, and a dubbed knight. He's old enough to win his place in a—"

"Fine family, like Marshal or de Braiose," William completes in shrill mockery. He turns from the window with a vexed frown. "Lanfranc is a fine enough family. There's no need to *place* him anywhere. Someday he will be the lord of this dominion."

Hellene fits a perplexed expression to her stern features. "William—even before Grandmère returned, I wanted something better for Thierry than this petty dominion hidden in the hills of nowhere. But now with Grandmère here, fresh as her twenty-first summer, he will never be baron of this castle. He must seek his fortune elsewhere, so why not among the daughters of the great landowners of the south? He's a striking lad of no little skill."

"On that, wife, we are agreed. The best of the maidens will vie for him." William sits beside her, his manner gentled by their shared concern. "But if he marries among the nobles, he will have to serve their fathers—and they serve the king and the Plantagenets, who are contending with Philip Augustus, king of the French, for the countryside northwest of Paris called the Vexin and the frontiers of Normandie. Here, at least, he is free of the royal war games, where they would serve him out on the battle-field as a pawn. Here he will be his own lord, for the king's writ does not run in the March."

"Better lord of a pinkynail domain than cat's-paw for an empire," Hellene agrees. "But Grandmère—"

William lays a restraining hand on her knee. "Is she truly your grandmother?"

"Of course," Hellene responds, taken aback. "The king and the pope—"

"Vellums can be forged." William bends closer. "I must tell you a thing. When Howel appeared in the hill forest, he had Longsight Meilwr with him. The old bard's blind now, but when Howel had him smell your grandmother's hair, the revered fart cried out, 'She's not the Servant of Birds!'"

Hellene purses her lips skeptically. "Your Welsh is weak. For all you could tell, he might have said, 'She's none but the Servant of Birds.'"

William shrugs. She is right, and that is why he did not tell Guy what he thought he had heard. "Even so. Does this woman seem anything like Ailena?"

"Mother believes so."

"Clare is just happy to get out from under her brother's thumb. What do you think?"

Hellene knits her brows. "She behaves very differently. More indrawn, quieter. And yet there is something haunted in her features. She has witnessed wonders."

"Think on it, Hellene. If she presents any sign at all that she is a Pretender, seize on that and tell me—for the sake of our son."

Outside the bedchamber's open door, Hugues pushes off and dashes down the passage to find Madelon and share his amazement.

Gerald Chalandon stands with his son Thomas in an upper apartment of the donjon, the narrow shutters thrown open from the keyhole windows to admit the floral breeze. "This is a miserably hot chamber," Gerald says staring at the dark rafters and drab walls. "Why do you insist on residing here when there are ample suites in the *palais*?"

"You'll need those suites when the nobler guests arrive for the tourney," Thomas answers and heaves open the shutters on one large ogee window. Below is the inner courtyard, the elegant, Gothic arched *palais*, and a rose-trellised corner of the castle garden. "You don't expect the earls of Hereford and Glastonbury to make do with an attic apartment? Besides, here my mother and sisters will leave me alone. Those stairs are too formidable for any of them."

"They see you so rarely, can you blame them for dogging you when you are here?"

"I'd blame them less if they'd stop asking me when I'm going to be tonsured."

"Really, Thomas. You've been an acolyte since you were seventeen. How much more bookwork do you need to be a priest?"

"Grandmère wants me to leave the abbey." He levels an incredulous look at his father. "She wants to name me Uncle's heir."

Gerald rubs his jaw, and grins. "She is right, you know. You are her eldest grandson. And certainly Guy will never spawn heirs. You should be baron."

"Father, I have not the mettle."

"Nonsense. Mettle is for warriors. Wisdom is far more valuable to a ruler than ardor. And you've plenty of wisdom. You should. You've had your face in the books long enough."

Thomas sits on the sill. "I don't want to be baron. I hadn't the heart to tell Grandmère, but—" He smiles luminously. "I'm ready now to be a priest. I'll be taking my vows on Saint Fandulf's Day, the anniversary of Grandmère's departure for the Holy Land."

Gerald's face flinches with his surprise, and he forces himself not to frown as the hope of seeing his son a baron slips away. Then he claps Thomas's shoulder and gives him a broad, crooked-tooth smile. "Your mother will weep with happiness, convinced God's grace has won out. But tell me, what tome raised your heart to heaven?"

"No tome, Father. Grandmère's miracle has convinced me of God's sacred intent in this world."

"Ah, yes. And you doubted that?"

Thomas hangs his head. "You have always taught me the supremacy of the spirit, and I have never doubted you. But for you that supremacy was in song."

"That was my soul's calling," Gerald avers, his eyes fogging over. "Though I am of humble origin, my song was heard by the countess of Ventadour herself, and in her court I learned the art of poetry and courtesy."

"You were touched by the lamentable transiency of things," Thomas coaxes, "and you sang of that."

Gerald nods wistfully, satisfied by his son's indulgence.

"For you, Father, spirit is in the song. But for me, the spirit shines in all of God's creation—in the regal flight of geese or in the morning smoke above the heath. Even the gloomy flags of scum on a pond are precious as silk to me."

"To the great bafflement of your uncle," Gerald says, smiling gently. "He never could understand how you could find beauty in a pond's rinsings."

"But is it not so? What men have crafted is clumsy by comparison to creation's simplest offerings."

Gerald sighs with satisfaction. "You have found your way to bliss, Thomas. Well, then, forget the seductions of power. Ignore your grandmother's pleas to sit in the chair of state and follow your faith."

"It is Grandmère who showed me the way. It's not in books. I'll never be a prelate, Father. I want to be a simple monk and learn from God's first book—as it was in the beginning and ever shall be." He clasps his white cassock nervously. "There is really only one obstacle left."

"Obstacle? Surely not Uncle Guy. He has found his right disciple of the sword in Thierry."

"No, no, that's not it. A shred of doubt remains—the Devil's shadow that falls on every act of grace in this world." Thomas runs a hand through his fine hair. "Maître Pornic questions if there was a miracle and wonders if Grandmère is a Pretender."

Gerald opens his hands, weighing this skepticism. "You must remember that Maître Pornic believes the greatest miracle is the sunrise. He sees God's face in a flower. Of course he would question anything supernatural."

"There is more. On the way from the abbey, Longsight Meilwr came out of the woods and smelled Grandmère's hair. Without hesitation, he claimed she is not the Servant of Birds."

This raises Gerald's tiny eyebrows.

"What if she is a Pretender, Father?"

"Guy will burn the impostor. Your mother will be crushed."

"Worse. It means God no longer touches us except as we touch ourselves."

Gerald grabs the *toe of his chin* and nods slowly. "Poor Clare."

At night, Falan dreams of *al-aswadan*, the two black ones: water and dates. The clatter of sunlight through the fronds of the date palm play over a dazzling dune, beneath which he sits staring into a pool so deep it is black as a crypt. A voice says: "The unknown is not the void. It is the glitter in the void."

When he wakes, he knows it is time to return to the desert.

From her window, Rachel watches the brightly colored tents going up on the wide meadow beyond the tollhouse road and the orchard gardens. Her maid informs her that the first knights for the tourney have begun to arrive.

Rachel sits in the window's broad alcove refusing food, refusing the pleas of Clare to come out, and watches the great pavilions unfurl. She recalls Ailena telling her that the Church long ago denounced tourneys: the prior popes, Innocent II, Eugenius III, Alexander III—and even the current Holy Father, the great and wise Innocent III, Rachel has heard—have all prohibited Christians from participating in staged combat under peril of their souls. "But Richard Coeur de Lion was weaned on jousting," the old baroness fulminated, pounding a tabletop. "So long as he is king, war will be the greater religion."

Ailena Valaise's voice sounds in Rachel's memory as clear as though she had spoken moments ago. The Persian magician, who worked his spells so well, himself no longer has a name or even a face in her mind. But Ailena's face, crumpled-looking as crushed damask, is forever pressed close so that she can whisper her long stories for hours without wearing out her voice.

Rachel wishes the magician were here now, to attend to her grandfather. His fever has abated, but he is seriously enfeebled. Though reluctant to lose hope, she fears that David will probably never be strong enough for the return journey to the Holy Land.

Suddenly there is a knock at the door and Falan enters. Using an argot of sign language, Arabic and Hebrew, he manages to communicate to Rachel that he intends to leave when the tourney is over and wants to know if she will accompany him.

Rachel stares up into his deep blue eyes and sees the colors of the desert in the sandy stubble of his beard, the wind-contoured hollows of his cheeks. "God shall decide," she answers. "If my champions are defeated, I will go with you. But if Allah favors my knights, I will stay and rule as Ailena wanted. Either way—" She touches her throat and indicates the gold band around Falan's neck. "You will be in my bond no longer."

Falan bows and touches the center of his brow, proud to know he has fulfilled his mission so well that Rachel feels secure enough to stay without him.

Falan departs to resume his post outside her door, and Rachel, wistful and lonely, leans deeper into her window to view the bustle of the impending event. Forges ring from the smithies preparing the jousters' gear, horse dealers from Merthyr Tydfil crowd the stables, and troubadours newly arrived with the first knights roam the bailey singing of the *belle saison* of love and war. Carpenters from as far away as Brecon and Strata Florida have been hired to help out the blevy of peasants in preparing the lists and lodges, and the din of their hammers echoes off the herded hills.

No one can say for sure how many champions will arrive. For weeks, long before the baroness returned, servitors had coursed the country for thirty leagues around heralding the event.

To her side, in a sun-laminated pane of the open window, Rachel glimpses her reflection and notices the obsession in her fervid stare. If her knights are defeated, then staying here would be far more dangerous for her grandfather than the perils of travel.

She closes her eyes to pray, though she has not trusted God completely since the horror. She searches for words to petition the Lord, not for her but for David. The words do not come—and she is afraid to reach too deeply for them, afraid she will stir up the prayerful voices of the dead. As always, God is infuriatingly silent.

She opens her eyes, understanding that if she has any destiny at all apart from chance, it is in her hands alone.

"*Baruch ata adonai elohainu melech ha-olam borai pri ha-adamah,*" Gianni Rieti recites and translates as he dips the *karpas,* a sprig of parsley, into a bowl of salt water: "Blessed art Thou, Lord our God, King of the universe who creates the fruit of the earth."

The visiting knights and their families gawk in astonishment at each other, but the baroness, Clare, Gerald, and their children, all sitting in the front pews, receive the parsley with open countenances and nibble it calmly.

David, sitting behind a curtain in the apse, from where he can view the congregation without being seen, smiles. This is not the spring season of Pesach, but the Mass of the gentiles is a reenactment of Jesus' Last Supper, a Passover celebration. So, he figured, why not do it properly? Gianni has learned the ritual well. Arranged on the altar are a boiled egg, a traditional symbol of mourning, and a roasted shankbone, to recall the destruction of the Temple and Israel's redemption with "an outstretched arm." Besides the *karpas,* the parsley that stands for ever-renewed hope in the future dipped in the tears of the people, there is as well a bowl of grated horseradish root, symbol of the bitter herb, and *haroset,* a thick mixture of ground apples and walnuts with wine, spiced with cinnamon, representing the mortar used by the Israelites to build Pharaoh's cities.

Seeing this congregation of gentiles worshiping God much as his own people do, David feels quite exhilarated. The lassitude that has possessed him since he was fevered seems to lift briefly in his joy at seeing the one God honored.

Gianni lifts the large disk of unleavened bread David has prepared at the ovens, and consecrates it as the Body of Christ. The worshipers cross themselves and kneel. While the altar boy fills the wine cups, Gianni briefly recounts the story of the Passover, and the visitors share more puzzled expressions. Questioning murmurs gradually mount to whispers of alarm and outrage. A few exit the chapel scowling and shaking their heads. But most indulge the baroness, believing that the miracle that restored her youth inspired these strange customs; they bow their heads when the Eucharist is raised high again and the priest intones: *"Baruch ata adonai elohainu melech ha-olam hamotzi lehem min ha-aretz.* Blessed art Thou, Lord our God, who brings forth bread from the earth."

After the mass, Thomas Chalandon approaches the altar and finds Gianni Rieti in the apse removing his vestments. "I had heard rumors that my grandmother wanted to include Hebrew in the Mass," he says gravely, "but I did not think this would be a Jewish ceremony. You place your soul in danger, Father."

"The soul is in danger as soon as it comes into this world, young fellow." Gianni kisses the embroidered cross on the bands of his scarf and lays it neatly in the chest with the other canonical garments. "Some wine?" He gestures to a full chalice.

Thomas looks appalled. "That is sanctified wine."

"Yes, an extra cup of it—the Cup of Elijah. I will share it with you."

Thomas peers at the handsomely chiseled face of the knight-priest as if it were a hot ingot of furnaced steel. "Need I tell you, further, these are not the teachings of the Church?"

"But they are the teachings of God," Gianni replies, drinking more than half the chalice's contents. *"Ga-alti,"* he salutes. "'I will redeem you with an outstretched arm and with great judgments.' The Torah. Exodus, chapter six."

"That is the God of the Jews."

"Hm, yes." Gianni finishes the wine and dabs his sharply clipped mustache with an altar napkin. "The God whom Jesus worshiped and died for."

Thomas sits on a cushioned stool and stares at the narrow sword hanging at the priest's side. "You fought for the Sepulcher?"

"I guarded it. I was there the night your grandmother was transfigured."

"You saw the Grail?"

"And the tongues of fire as well. They burned in a celestial cloud charged with the unearthly voices of angels. Yes—I saw it all." Gianni sits on the edge of the chest, his features refulgent as a sunrise with wine and revelation. "I had just recited the prayer of extreme unction over her, had daubed her with the oil and given her viaticum. She was right there, under my hands, shriveled and spent. A dead lizard, really. Then a glory brighter than the desert sun shoved me back and raised her up." Gianni shakes his head. "No words can touch the magnificence of what transpired. To this day, I'm not sure if it was a blessing or a punishment to be there. After a miracle, there is true conflict. Heaven is all at once more real. And then it is far more difficult to stand the earth."

At the gate to the inner ward, Clare and Gerald greet the dignitaries who arrive the morning after Saint Eustace's Day. Six earls appear—first the marcher barons of Builth Wells, Y Pigwyn, Carreg Cennin, and Carmarthen, and then the English lords of Glastonbury and Hereford, all with their squires and families, to be lodged as coevals of the baroness in the *palais*.

Rachel is not required to attend to them, her absence simply explained as a determination to stand aside from her station until her knights have won their *assise de bataille*. She has made it known that, if they should fail, she will readily relinquish her chair of state to her son Guy and return forthwith to her holy devotions in Jerusalem.

This challenge piques the inspiration of the many troubadours who have accompanied their earls and knights, and soon the castle and the outer encampment begin to flourish with songs about the baroness of the Grail and the miracle of her restored youth. The gossips of *palais*, bailey, and village fuel the romances with suspicions of deceit and pacts with the Devil. And glimpses of the baroness in her window inspire intriguing speculations about her relations with the blue-eyed Muslim knight always at her door and the sickly, woeful Jew with whom she and her knights pray and study every day.

When the marquess of Talgarth unexpectedly rides up to the castle with his elaborate retinue of armorers, haberdashers, goliards, and black-armored knights, he has already heard too many alluring tales of the mysterious Ailena Valaise to accept even the possibility of not being attended by her. A herald announces his arrival with the demand that the baroness greet him.

Unable to refuse a noble of higher rank, Rachel dons her finest robes and her gold chaplet. Sweat dampens her with the fear that she will not remember the many fine points of protocol the baroness has taught her.

At the door to the *palais*, the four earls who are her guests have gathered to get their first glimpse of her. She greets each warmly, realizing that they are the witnesses of her fate. If God chooses to defeat her knights, she will never see them again; for now, though, they are her peers, and, summoning her most commodious presence, she lavishes each with a sisterly embrace.

Astride the white palfrey, she canters across the inner ward, accompanied by Falan, Denis, and Gianni. In the bailey, the crowds press close, her sergeants unable to manage the burgeoning throng of awed strangers eager to touch her hem. The marquess's black-armored knights have crossed lances at the front gate to keep the rabble at bay. Rachel dismounts and walks across the drawbridge, her head demurely bowed.

The marquess awaits her, sitting imperiously atop his black stallion. He is tall and imposing, dressed in full ebony armor with a red plumed headpiece, a short battle ax, longsword, and a triangular shield emblazoned with a knotted viper. His steed has a sable foot-cloth embroidered with crimson serpent coils, and on its face is a crimson chamfron, a plaited headpiece with a short spike projecting from the front. Two squires help him dismount—to all outward appearances a dashing figure, but when his visor snaps back, Rachel is surprised to see a toothless old man with a splotchy beard and large, doughy ears.

"I came as soon as I heard you had risked your chair of state," he announces in a thin, piping voice. "That always guarantees a good fight. And how I love a good fight! Let's get on with it then, shall we?"

Clare and Gerald obligingly surrender their bedchamber to the marquess and have their various chests of belongings carried to a smaller cubicle, where they will sleep on a hay-stuffed pallet. Much of the day is spent accommodating the marquess's large retinue, finding rooms in the *palais* for the knights of noble rank and in the donjon for the others.

Hellene and Leora are beside themselves with delight at being able at last to introduce their children to the families of the marquess and the earls, compare lineages, and plot marriages. The *palais* bustles like a marketplace, and the servants and cooks, trying to please so many nobles under one roof, exhaust themselves with unprecedented efforts.

Oddly, the presence of a superior ranking seigneur, the marquess, calms Rachel, and she dotes on him with unyielding generosity and gracious formality. His presence has lifted, temporarily, the caul of leadership from her shoulders and enhanced the fateful complaisance of her life. Without even so much as a breath of perturbation, she acquiesces to his every whim. During meals it is her duty to serve him, and afterward to attend to his amusement. She introduces him to her family, including her son Guy who, eager not to alienate this powerful ally of the king, occasionally affords a smile in the presence of the Pretender. And when the marquess, showing his gums in a mischievous leer, enquires of him: "Are the rumors true that you believe this lovely child is not your mother?" Guy replies with as much civility as he can muster, "This woman is far too gracious to be the mother I remember—and indeed too gracious to rule this wild frontier."

The marquess nods with understanding and slaps Guy's back. "Subversion is good. It keeps power pure. You're absolutely right to challenge her. I wish you luck. But, young fellow"—the sunken-cheeked nobleman narrows his gaze enigmatically— "you're quite wrong about your mother. When one meets grace where it does not belong, how can one doubt that miracles have taken place?"

By the light of numerous candles hung in the pear trees and the rose arbors, Rachel tells her amazing story yet again, this time to the marquess and his retinue. The knights and squires listen with ferocious attentiveness, but midway through the tale, in the midst of the wonders of Prester John's desert kingdom, the marquess begins to snore.

Later, after she has helped the old knight's servitors to put him to sleep, she politely refuses all entreaties to continue her story and instead turns the disappointed gathering out into the bailey to learn the rest—and more—from the troubadours. "Stories are meant to put us to sleep," she says soothingly to her vexed listeners. "In Jerusalem, I once met a monk from India whose master, who was called the Awakened One, claims that the most noble truth, the one truth that wakes us up, is suffering. Think on that as you enlighten each other tomorrow."

Sleep abandons Rachel. She sits by her window all night listening to the festivities in the bailey, on the meadow, and in the village beyond. *Tomorrow I will find out who I am—whom I've become—a baroness or something else. A crazy woman no one will marry? My grandfather's nurse on a hazardous journey? A lonely spinster in the Promised Land and these days in the castle memories as precious as jewels?*

She thinks of her grandfather, who she knows is praying for her defeat, afraid that he has lost her to the gentiles and willing to risk his life on another pilgrimage to get her away from here. If she is defeated tomorrow, she promises herself she will not lament. Let the barbarous task of rule pass from her with the comforts and the dangers, she resolves. Power has never been appealing, except that it provides a place safe from the brutalities of others.

But if her knights are victorious, if she prevails in convincing everyone that she is indeed the baroness, she will have won the time to strengthen David with rest. By the spring, if no more illnesses overtake him, he may be strong enough to survive the journey. Then he will have the satisfaction of dying in the land of their ancestors.

That thought perturbs her with dark memories of her family, of whom he is the last. She must do better by this man who dug graves that she might live. If she perseveres tomorrow, she determines that she will make this domain carry as much promise for him as the Holy Land.

David sits by his window, too weak to stand, his gaze lifted above the noisy festivities to the caste marks of the season, the emerald stars of the summer constellations. His prayer is a deeply silent one, for he dares not impugn the wisdom of the Creator. *Let what will be be—and be best for my Rachel.*

At the first smudges of dawn, half-dressed squires are already running to and fro. The horses, neighing and stamping, are girdled and saddled and led to the meadow. There, the special lists are made ready. Two pairs of strong wooden palisades are erected, the outer line of planks shoulder high, the inner one lower, with many openings for steeds and warriors to pass through. Between the two lines is the space for spare horses, squires, attendants, and heralds as well as privileged spectators who will not mind the frenetic activities of the knights and their helpers. Humbler onlookers stand peering over the outer palisade. To the side, along the length of the meadow, rise the series of lodges, shaded with tentlike canopies, floored with carpets and bright with pennons. In them are stationed the ladies, the nobles' children, and the older, less martial knights.

After a hasty Mass by Gianni Rieti, the knights and ladies hurry to their places. The ladies, riding their white mules, outdo each other with displays of marten, ermine and vair, sendel and samite, gold thread, silk, and pearls. The villagers and the villeins from the neighboring towns and castles crowd against the fenceposts at the far end of the field, gawking and pointing, and applaud loudly when a handsomely clad dame sweeps by. Jongleurs, acrobats, and mimes abound, and the deafening music of drums and pipes stirs the raucous throng and excites the horses.

The camp marshals, the marquess, and the earls, who will judge the contests, advance on foot: each wears brilliant bliauts and helmets crested with the outlandish figures of hawkheads, asps, basilisks, and dragons. Gerald Chalandon, the senior noncombatant knight of the hosting castle, leads them ceremoniously to their places in the stilt-raised lodges overlooking the center of the field between the lists.

Behind the marshals are the lavishly accoutered heralds and pursuivants, who will assist by encouraging the combatants with whistles and jeers. They are followed by the varlets and sergeants assigned to police the crowd as well as to bring new lances, clear away broken weapons, and rescue fallen knights.

The marshals survey the tilt yard from their high vantage and, after they have decreed that everything is ready, Gerald raises a white baton. With a great blare of trumpets, the baroness of the Grail, perched atop a camel, and her family, riding richly caparisoned mounts, enter the field. The crowd surges to the tops of the fenceposts, some toppling over, to view the young baroness. "Valaise! Valaise!" Many of the sergeants turn about to see the living miracle and in the process are nearly trampled underfoot.

Falan guides his camel between the baroness and the stream of people running across the tilt yard. His curved saber flashes in the rising sun, and once out of striking distance, the villeins gape in awe.

Rachel feels feverish, her stomach knotted with repressed anxiety. Looking about for Guy or any of the contending knights, she sees only the melee on the field. Ignoring the shouting mob, ignoring the bilious fear their contorted faces stir in her, she dismounts mechanically and climbs the stairs, her dread mounting with each step. As she takes her place in the central lodge beside the marquess, the aged knight stands with the other marshals, steps forward and bows deeply.

With evident relish, the marquess openly admires Rachel's appearance, her hair twined with gold thread and worn long over her breasts. The saffron-tinted chemise and ermine-trimmed pelisson are his gifts, and he smiles to see how well they complement the elegant bliaut of violet silk that floats thinly above them in many folds and long sleeves. He links her little finger with his, as is the custom of the age, and they sit down together. "If you are destined to exile in the Holy Land," he says ingratiatingly, with toothless sibilance, "I will go with you—and perhaps we will find the Grail again . . . together."

Rachel smiles wanly.

Then the marquess nods to Gerald, who raises his white baton and commands, "Bring in the knights!"

Sergeants on horseback have cleared the field, and, with a loud crash of music and blast of trumpets, the combatants' procession begins. Four scarlet-garbed heralds lead the procession on foot.

Then follows a jongleur on horseback twirling a sword, tossing it high in the air and catching it as it falls back. Next come the contestants, forty knights riding two by two. They parade down the lodge-side of the lists and back past the screaming crowd.

Guy Lanfranc and Roger Billancourt lead them, their faces hard and stern, intent on the grim business of retrieving their domain. Behind them are William Morcar and his son Thierry. This is Thierry's first contest as a knight, and he stares about proudly, ogling the ladies in the lodges. Young and old, the females lean forward and wave in reply, hanging lances, Thierry's included, with colorful streamers, sleeves, and stockings. Gages of love—gloves, sashes, and long bright ribbons attached to locks of braided hair—are thrown to some of the youngest, most handsome and virile knights, but Thierry is not so honored.

Gianni Rieti rides without so much as glancing up into the lodges, though he himself is pelted with gages. Only as he passes before the central lodge and an elf lock of beribboned blond hair falls in his lap does he gaze up. Madelon waves at him. He turns away immediately, finds the baroness nearby and salutes her. Ummu, riding a donkey beside him, blows a kiss to Rachel and winks, while Ta-Toh flies up the banner-draped lodge and presents the baroness with a tuft of monkey fur that Ummu has bound with a daisy. She pats the monkey to the cheers of the crowd, and he scampers back to his master.

The knights promenade around the field in kaleidoscopic array, their scabbards, lance butts, and shields painted with radiant colors, the crests of their helmets set with feathers, and their steeds attired in embroidered cloths. But the marshals are attentive only to the lances, which must be blunted and made of brittle, light wood. Any in question are called to the marshal's stand and examined. Even with these precautions, physicians from every participating castle are in the lists.

Once the knights have completed their circuit, Gerald announces the first contest: "*Assise de bataille*—for the right of rule in the domain of Epynt, the Griffin of Lanfranc challenges the Swan of Valaise. Let the contending knights approach and be recognized."

Falan Askersund crosses the tilt yard on his camel flanked by

Denis Hezetre and Harold Almquist and followed by Gianni Rieti on his white Arabian. The Swede wears a simple white headcloth and a Moorish tunic over a shirt of chain mail, while the others sport breastplates emblazoned with Swan devices, shoulderguards, tassets over their loins, cuisses on their thighs, and lightweight salade helmets. Falan touches his forehead and dips his head, and the others doff their helmets and nod to the marshals. All present their lances for close inspection, then retreat to the lists where the banner of the Swan is raised.

Behind them come Guy, Roger, and William. They wear only breastplates with the Griffin ensign, cuisses, and salade helmets, brightly burnished and otherwise devoid of ornament. When their lances are approved, they take their places in the opposite lists, where their banner flies.

The pursuivants and jongleurs, one from each camp, grotesquely dressed in parti-colored mantles and bliauts, announce the contestants: "Here is the good cavalier, Guy Lanfranc, champion with Guillaume Longsword in his conquest of Ireland. Watch now his mighty deeds and those of his knights as they usurp this heathen warrior and his ingrate companions, who have dared to challenge his right as baron of Castle Valaise, earl of Epynt!"

The other pursuivant executes a cartwheel and a backflip to draw applause away from the Lanfranc camp; then he declares: "Here is Falan Askersund, good knight of Sweden, who journeyed to the Holy Land, found faith in Mahomet and yet put that alien faith aside to escort home the baroness Ailena Valaise blessed again with youth by the Holy Grail! Watch her cavaliers unseat these faithless knights, who spurn the miracle of the Sangreal!"

"Silence all boasts!" Gerald calls. "In the name of God and Saint David, do your battle!"

Thomas Chalandon, seated in the lodges beside Rabbi Tibbon and dressed as a commoner in a brown jerkin, gray leggings, and crushed leather shoes, clutches a small crucifix. Surreptitiously, he watches the old Jew beside him. Is he perhaps a necromancer, as many Jews are purported to be? The old man's lips continue to move in a silent prayer—to Jehovah, or some Eastern demon like Azael or Baal?

The thunder of hooves and a mighty crash turn Thomas's head in time for him to see Harold Almquist fly from his horse at the tip of William Morcar's lance. Harold crashes to the ground, his shield broken. Thomas looks to his sisters. Leora is on her knees, praying for her fallen husband, and Hellene places a consoling arm about her shoulders. When Harold is led off the field limping but alive, they hug each other.

The baroness lowers her face in defeat; but, Thomas notices, her rabbi has raised a grateful visage to heaven.

Denis Hezetre advances from the list, seated tall in his war saddle. He had once told Guy that he would not contend against him or his knights in the tilt yard. How foolish, he thought at the time, for knights to injure themselves in mock battle. So also was this the opinion of the three previous popes, as well as Innocent III, who needed all the knights they could draft to defend Christianity from the Muslims, and who had banned such contests. But as soon as the Lady of the Grail announced that her right to rule would be decided in the tilt yard, he knew he would have to fight. He had sworn to protect her, and even if he has to fight Guy himself, he will not restrain his blows. Guy is beloved of his heart—but the baroness is beloved of God.

William Morcar ignores Denis's salute. The blond archer does not fault him: he knows William is fighting more for his son Thierry than for Guy. And though he and William have saved each other's life more than once while on raids with Guy against the tribes, Denis expects no quarter now.

He nods to Gerald. When William's fresh lance has been approved by the marshals and he has taken his position, Gerald cries out, *"Laissez aller!"* Denis slaps his visor down, dashes his spurs into the flanks of his horse and rushes at a full gallop toward William, who charges at full tilt toward him.

Their lances strike shields, but William's skids off with a shriek and twists his body, exposing him to the full of Denis's thrust. The blow dismounts him, his limbs seem to scatter with the jarring impact, and he flies into a black pit.

Sound returns slowly, echoey. William's helmet is removed,

and a glossy light surrounds the heads of the sergeants peering down at him. *Am I dying?* Their smeared faces congeal to hard smiles, and, with a bitter tang in his throat, he knows he will live.

Roger Billancourt salutes the marquess and gazes with prolonged intent at the Pretender. She stares back at him with such benign contempt that, for an instant, he is convinced she is in truth Ailena Valaise. He slams shut his visor, mumbles a curse, and, at Gerald's command, charges at Denis.

Their collision shatters both of their lances.

"Fairly broken!" shouts the marshal. "A noble course!"

They wheel about and dismount to do foot-battle. Cries of "Remember the Grail!" and "Be worthy of your ancestry!" fill the air as the pursuivants hoot and cry above the bawling of the spectators.

Roger, wearing less armor, is lighter, dismounts and draws his sword more quickly. Denis has barely unsheathed his weapon when Roger drops a double-handed overhead blow on him.

Lifting his sword just in time, Denis deflects the blow from his head, but the force of it wrenches the sword from his grip and heaves him onto his back. With adroit malevolence, Roger places the tip of his sword between Denis's breastplate and helmet. When he looks in triumph to the lodges, the baroness has lowered her face. The warmaster knows then, for sure, she is not Ailena, who never once dropped her gaze, not when her knights fell in combat, not even when her cruel husband, his old lord and master, beat her.

Gianni Rieti prays earnestly before he mounts his Arabian stallion and takes up his lance. His prayer is still on his lips as he rushes forward to meet Roger. Louder than the pounding of the hooves and the bellowing of the crowd, his prayer fills him with a supernal strength and breaks from him with all of his breath as his shield splinters and the lance tip strikes him over his heart.

Gianni floats inside his armor like a vapor. When his helmet is pulled away, he fears he will dissipate into the sky. Oddly the sky does seem to plunge closer—but then he realizes it is because he is being lifted by the sergeants. Every visible observer in the lodges and along the fence is frozen, their jeers tiered to the heavens like a hymn.

Roger lifts his visor and blatantly stares at the Pretender, not even bothering to reach for a new lance until she will look at him. When she does cast him a feeble glance, he shows her his brown teeth in a triumphant grimace. She has one knight left, and he, without breastplate or even helmet, cannot hope to stand against Roger or his lethal protégé. He recognizes the fear in her countenance, and his grin fills his whole body.

Rachel *is* afraid—but not for herself. Her imminent defeat means mortal danger for her grandfather. Already, she is considering how to transport him south without jeopardizing his health. But when she looks to him, he seems pleased, his gray head held high, a beatific smile in his beard. At his age, she knows, death is not his concern but life, *her* life—and if she loses here today, she will leave here with him, even if that means his dying. *At least he will die on the way to the Promised Land,* she comforts herself.

Falan has mounted Gianni's white stallion. His headcloth covers his face except for his blue stare. He salutes Rachel, and out of the hushed crowd, insults hurtle: "Heretic!" "Dung-eating traitor!"

Roger raises his lance to the lodges, and a heroic cheer roars from the gathering. He lowers his visor and trains his weapon on his veiled opponent. As they charge, the warmaster cannot take his eyes off that strange visage. His lance bounces off Falan's shield, and a powerful blow kicks him into the air. When he hits the ground, he is still seeing that blue gaze, which now is as wide as the sky.

Guy Lanfranc's guts burn molten with impacted rage. No one will stand between him and what his father has taken.

"Do not look at his face," Roger groans as the sergeants carry him into the lists.

Guy mounts his destrier and concentrates all his vehemence

into his lance arm. At Gerald's call, he bolts forward, screaming, "Lanfranc!"

Robe billowing, Falan attacks, shouting, "Allah Akbar!"

The two collide with an enormous crash, woods splintering, steeds thrown back upon their haunches, casting up great clods of earth. Each knight flourishes broken lance butts, and across the shield of each is a long jagged mark.

Guy plunges from his mount, drawing his broadsword in midleap. Falan drops off his stallion and unsheathes his scimitar, skipping nimbly to the side as his opponent descends on him. Saber whirling above his head like a stream of light, the Muslim warrior dances about Guy, baffling his every blow without once touching swords.

In fierce frustration, Guy hacks away at the elusive Swede, spending all his strength in futile blows. At last he throws off his helmet, his pug-face blustery red, and charges, swinging his broadsword in a wide arc.

Falan retreats, feints to the left and daringly leaps to the right, sending Guy off-balance. The scimitar whistles, and Guy's topknot flies into the air. The Muslim catches it with his free hand and waves it at the lodges and the shrieking crowd.

The baroness is on her feet. The marquess and the earls, stunned by what they have witnessed, follow a moment later. The contest is over.

But Guy will not relent. He continues to chop and slash at the spry-footed cavalier, until his sword becomes too heavy to lift.

Falan approaches him with casual grace and, with the razor-tip of his saber, pricks the gasping knight's Adam's apple.

A vast shout bursts from the crowd—the Griffin banner is thrown to the ground, and the Swan is raised supreme.

"Unfair weapons!" Guy bawls again and again until the delirious assembly hears him. Hoots and shrill cries of mockery greet his protest.

Rachel looks to David, and he acquiesces in her victory with a smile and palms upturned to heaven. She has won them a place among the gentiles, where he can gather his strength. In the spring, when he is fully recuperated, they will pilgrimage back to their true home.

Abruptly, the crowd noise dims. From out of the lists come uninvited guests who have approached unnoticed during the heat of the contest: a band of wild Welsh in their tatterdemalion armor, brindle-bearded, big-boned Erec Rhiwlas at their head.

Sergeants rally to oust the intruders, but Rachel waves them off and signs the Welsh forward. The spirit of the baroness looms closer, roused by the sight of the people her father had taught her to respect and she had come to love. "The Servant of Birds welcomes you!" Rachel calls out, jubilant with her victory.

"Servant of Birds, Erec Rhiwlas is here to champion you!" Erec announces in Welsh.

"Who is this barbarian knave?" Guy shouts, stepping between the Welsh and the lodges.

"Guy, don't you know Erec the Bold when you see him?" Rachel asks with a laugh in her voice. This is the moment Ailena's ghost has awaited; and Rachel can feel her shining in the dark of her mind, luminous with her son's defeat and humiliation.

The marquess touches Rachel's elbow. "You will admit barbarians to your contest?" He shakes his head. "Bad form."

Rachel wrinkles her nose at the old knight's crabby frown. "In Epynt, under my rule, it is bad form to regard the Welsh as barbarians. With all deference to you, sir, these Welsh warriors are my guests."

The marquess's eyes sparkle at the baroness's feisty reply, and he defers with a smile from one half of his face.

"Let me champion you, Servant of Birds," Erec calls again.

"My day is already won," Rachel answers. "Yet you may join in the many contests to follow."

"Only one contest interests me. I vie for you and you alone." He points to Falan and says, "Your day is won—but by a heathen! Give me the right to win your honor by my own hand. Let a Christian fight for you."

The challenge translates quickly through the crowd. Angry shouts fling out of the gathering from the Normans, offended at the presence of the uncouth barbarians. But most of the crowd are disgruntled that a heretic has carried the day. Shouts for Erec drown out the protesters. The marquess urges the contest with a seigneurial wave of his hand. And when Rachel looks to Falan, the Muslim nods agreement.

Erec hoists his lance unfamiliarly, yet spurs his charger with all his might nonetheless. His lance slides off Falan's shield, and the Swede's lance explodes against Erec's shield. The Welshman's muscles strain like leather straps to keep him in the saddle. As soon as he steadies his jolting steed, he throws down the lance and hops to the ground, longsword in hand.

Having witnessed Guy's frustrated attack, Erec does not waste his strength in a hacking assault. Instead, he charges his opponent with his weapon held low. At the last instant, as the scimitar arcs in, Erec relies on his massive arms to bring around the heavy sword.

Saber and sword clang, and Erec whirls about with surprising agility and kicks Falan's legs out from under him. As Falan collapses, Erec's sword comes down and stops with its edge across the Muslim's throat.

Thomas's blood foams in his ears. The Jew beside him has sunk into himself and hangs on his bones like a man asleep, proving the ineffectuality of his prayers. God has championed the baroness, and Thomas clutches his crucifix so hard it bites into his hand. The excitement of the fighting has stirred him. He has not the strength or skill of these cavaliers, but his faith, he knows, is as strong as anyone's. If God sent the Grail to his grandmother, would He not now send her grandson victory if he but dared to put all his faith where others placed their ferocity?

The crucifix, with its torn and healing figure, seems to beseech him, and he asks it with all sincerity, *How?* He looks to the lists, sees the knights, some leaning on their swords, and he laughs, imagining himself hefting such a weapon. And inside that laugh an idea opens, an erumpent, risible idea that is so unlikely it can only have been sent by God.

Thomas rises. He faces the central lodge, where the baroness has called her Swedish champion to sit beside her. "Grandmère!" he shouts. "Give me leave to stand down this Welshman in hand combat for your honor."

Rachel looks with surprise at the seraphic youth. Mocking cries erupt from the assembly, and his mother Clare howls an objection: "He is an acolyte! He is forbidden to fight."

The marquess smiles with glee and waves the youth down from the lodges. Rachel turns to the old man and frowns. "He is not a cavalier, marquess. I am fain to risk his life."

"Come, come, Ailena. This is a contest, not a battle. Let him taste some humility. It will serve him well when he becomes a priest. And after such serious challenges, the lodges require some levity."

Rachel regards Thomas, who gazes at her with fervid intensity. She acquieses. Clare bawls, the crowd cheers, and Gerald watches agog as his gentle son returns to the list for his weapons.

Raucous laughter swells from the assembly when Thomas emerges with a barrel top instead of a proper shield and, in place of a sword, a bucket.

"I am not to be clowned with," Erec warns, his thick face throbbing. He looks to the baroness. "Do not think to make me a fool because I am Welsh."

"Fight fair!" the marquess shouts. "No foolery here."

"No frivolity is intended," Thomas declares. "These are my weapons."

The marquess shows his gums in an amused grin. "Knock him down, Bold Erec, and the fight is over."

"Knock him down I will!" Erec yells, and lunges at the youth, his sword held high.

Thomas spins about as the sword crashes down. He catches the flying sword-edge with his barrel top, which squeals as the metal bites into it.

Erec's sword lodges firmly in the tough, cross-grained wood, and when he pulls back to free it, it catches. Thomas clings to it with one hand and both legs, lifted off his feet by Erec's great strength. The sword begins to come free, but before it does, Thomas uses his free hand to slam the bucket over his opponent's head.

With one hand, Erec grabs to pull the bucket off, and the weight of Thomas's body pulls the sword free from his grip.

Swiftly, Thomas takes the sword, still embedded in the wooden barrel top, and places the tip at the base of Erec's neck.

The crowd roars. Erec jerks the barrel from his head and stares about, blustering with surprise. His own men roll on the ground, holding their sides, and when he sees them and the ingenuous relief in Thomas's face, his scowl flashes to a broad grin.

"The bards will taunt my ghost with this humiliation," he shouts above the howling of the spectators and knights, "but I'll not begrudge you your victory, Thomas." He slaps the youth on the back, bows to the startled baroness, and faces the gathering, joining in their laughter.

Thomas walks airily across the field toward where the marquess applauds, his parents and sisters cheer, and his grandmother watches him with a peculiar light in her young face. *She knows about miracles,* he thinks as he clutches the crucifix in the pocket of his tunic. The victory is not his but God's. It came down to him in one bright idea, like a drop of sacred blood dripping from the brow of the Savior and splashing across his mind, a tiny miracle from the crucifix in his hand, a small fruit of wisdom that dropped into his hands from the tree of wounds.

SHADOW
OF THE
SUN

*The Grail is the wish for
paradise, the stone of exile, the
quest of spiritual wholeness, the
bridge between higher and lower,
earth and sky, people and God,
the temporal and the infinite.*

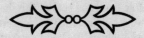

A smoke-blue smell floats from the forest with the night breeze. To Rachel, as she rides from the tilt yard on a camel at the end of the first and only crucial day of the tourney, it is the fragrance of *her* land—a domain won by trial and suffering. The men around her are *her* men—Falan on his camel, Canon Rieti riding tall on his Arabian stallion, Thomas grinning proudly, Denis and Harold on their steeds, even little Ummu astride a donkey.

Overhead, stars gnaw at the darkness. As a child, she believed those stars were angels in the firmament, each angel a particle of God's face. Rachel knows now that this is not true. That is the lesson of the second commandment: *Thou shalt not make any likeness.* Creation does not show God but shows only itself—and God remains exiled from His creation, a stranger, like nothing else—perhaps nothing itself.

Rachel looks down at her grandfather riding on the mule behind her. His face is gaunt and drawn from the fever he survived, yet his eyes are merry. Though he had hoped that her knights would fail, he is content to accept God's will. After the contest, as Rachel descended triumphantly from the lodges, he accepted her victory with a gracious kiss on her hand and a blessing. The marquess, aghast at his impertinence, gummed acerbically to Rachel: "Leave religion to the priests, my dear girl. Send the Jew back to the Holy Land and get on with the unholy business of making this land work for you. You've a domain to rule."

Overhearing the whisper, David retreated. While Rachel received the enthusiastic congratulations of the visiting knights, their ladies and troubadours, he had sat unobtrusively warming his perpetually cold bones in the sun.

Seeing her looking at him now, David offers a proud smile. She has attained; he will not deny her that.

From the pavilions beyond the tilt yard, a destrier approaches at a furious gallop. Falan and Gianni grab their sword hilts when they see that it is Guy. Denis and Thomas, who have been riding in the lead, turn about, and Harold, at the rear, sidles cautiously out of the way.

Guy has removed his breastplate but still wears the tunic with the Griffin device stenciled across it. His hair, now shorn of his topknot, hangs in ragged locks over the tops of his ears, lending his pugnacious features an even ruder appearance. In the glow from the rush torches, his eyes look red and smoky.

"Mother!" he calls in a surly, sarcastic voice. "You've left without accepting my concession."

"There is your concession, Sir Guy," Ummu shouts from his donkey, and points at the topknot Falan has affixed to the tip of his banner pole bearing the Swan ensign.

Rachel hushes the dwarf with a stern glance. "The *assise de bataille* was won in fair contest, Guy. I have answered your challenge."

"And very well, too, Mother." Guy sways in his saddle and tilts forward, clearly drunk, though his gaze is level and cold. "I concede this barony to your rule. The chaplet of presence is yours. The chair of state is yours. The castle is yours." He reels, and his frisky horse turns full about. Jerking fiercely at the reins, he brings the beast around again to face Rachel. "But with all of this come the debts, Mother. They're *your* debts now. The penalty our castle incurred for siding with Prince John when Richard was out of the country—a hundred pounds sterling. Another hundred as fine for escaping personal service overseas. There's also a heavy fee to pay for renewal of the king's seal on your charter. And, of course, there's a widow's fine not to marry—or to marry if your cold blood finds the advantage of that. And don't forget the funds due for this glorious tourney. All told, Mother, you've several hundred pounds to raise—and, my!—only a fortnight till Saint Margaret's when the king's men will be here."

"The bulk are your penalties, Guy," Denis protests.

Guy snorts. "I'm but a vassal here now. A vassal's debts are his lord's. The king's men will want immediate payment—or they'll seize this domain for Richard. And he'll sell it to the highest bidder to help pay off the massive debts of his ill-starred Crusade. There'll be not a day's grace afforded on this obligation, be sure of that."

Rachel turns away from Guy, goading her camel forward. She will not give him the satisfaction of seeing her despair. *Three hundred pounds!* If she sold all the baroness's jewels at their highest value, she might raise half that—and still lose her realm. She fixes her stare on the torch-glimmering silhouette of the castle. Above it, the ticking stars suddenly seem much further away.

Feeling tired and chilled, David sits in a lyre-backed chair in the corner of the council room where Rachel placed him. He lets his attention flit among the pastel frescoes on the stucco walls lit by oil lamps depending from the vaulted ceiling. The images, depicting scenes from the "Song of Roland," are flat and lifeless, with stiff unrealistic figures entirely lacking perspective. To David, they are the color of erosion, the depthless shape of loss, airy as the echoey voices in this room.

"Branden Neufmarché has not appeared at the tourney," Denis says. "By that he makes clear his resentment. He'll be no ally to you, baroness. Therefore, let him pay you for the promise not to assail him."

Seated in the large chair at the head of the council table, Rachel closes her eyes, trying to feel what the old baroness would do. There is no instruction within, only the darkness of her closed lids, yet she knows the baroness would not extort money from her dead lover's son, no matter how insipid Branden is. "No more war," she declares, opening her eyes and regarding each of the serious faces of the men seated around the oval table: Falan— Gianni—Denis—Harold—Thomas—and David, who looks away from the stories on the walls to nod with weary approval. "If I must, I will lose the castle. But no one will die or be terrorized to keep me in power."

"Grandmère is right," Thomas says, rising to her defense. The spiritual certitude he reads in her oblique eyes stirs a pride in him. "This is to be a realm our Savior will bless. We cannot consider violence."

Denis raises his eyebrows at Harold and Gianni. None will say it, but all believe Thomas a fool—as was earlier demonstrated in the tilt yard against Erec.

"Lady," Harold says glumly, "if we lose the castle, our families will be forced to become servants to other barons. All our coin was given to Guy to fund the siege. We've no money. And my children are too young to find advantage through marriage."

"Have heart," Denis says. "Perhaps we will have to forsake privileges but we will not be reduced to vagabonds. Many a castle will be happy for our services."

"As what?" Harold bleats. "A stable groom? Falcon master? I have no other services to offer. And I've a wife and four daughters."

Gianni clears his throat. "I could not help but notice the fond attention our baroness drew from the many nobles in the lodges. Perhaps a marriage of convenience with the proper earl's son would both save the castle and strengthen the domain."

Rachel recoils and from the corner of her eye sees David hide his face in his hands. "No! I will not marry again. Gilbert taught me the folly of that."

Harold rises, annoyed. "Lady, if you will not marry and you will not fight, you lose both the advantage of woman and man. There is no hope then for saving our place here."

Rachel looks hard at Harold. He has the pleated mouth of a sheep, which brings to mind something Ailena had said of him, "He responds best of all the knights to the shepherd's crook." She motions for him to sit. "Harold is right," she declares. "We must abandon hope. If we are to save ourselves, we must rest our faith in God."

Gianni crosses himself, and Denis and Harold follow suit. "God did not restore you to your youth and your domain to thwart you now," the priest-knight says. "He will show a way."

David turns his hands palms-up and rocks his head softly at the gentile's assumption of God's will, afraid for his granddaughter. These are people who see their lives, and God Himself, just as they draw their frescoes, without depth. Everything is flatly apparent to them—even God's will—while, in fact, the world they see is but a sketch of what it truly is. "Perhaps God would prefer us to exhaust all earthly means to save ourselves before He intervenes in His creation," he says.

"What do you suggest, Rabbi?" Gianni asks. "What more can we do?"

"I have learned from the servitors that there is a sizable Jewish community in Caermathon, three days' journey south," he offers. "The barons have traditionally forbade their admission to the guilds and their right to possess and cultivate land. Surely then, they have resorted to moneylending as Jews have in all the inhospitable northern countries. Perhaps they will lend us the funds that we need."

The knights look at one another, then at Rachel, who acquiesces with a shrug of her eyebrows. "If they have such a large sum that they would risk on a frontier estate, that would be an earthly miracle. We have little time to find out. A swift rider must be sent at once."

"Will you draft a letter to them, Rabbi?" Harold requests, his face bright with hope.

David accedes, and Rachel dismisses the council. As the knights depart, the rabbi bows to the baroness and says, "It is best to look for miracles from ourselves before we look to God. We are, after all, God's hands."

Thomas lingers after the others have left. "Grandmère, I know God will intercede—as He did for you with a miracle in the Levant—and as He did for me today with inspiration in the tilt yard."

"What you did today was foolish, Thomas," she says, her voice low, charged with anger. "Why did you take such a terrible risk?"

"You called me Parsifal." His blond face looks like the sun with eyes. "Parsifal would not accept a barbarian for your champion. If God had sent the Grail to you, surely He meant for your family to defend you."

"What do you mean 'if'? Do you doubt that I am myself?"

"No longer."

"But—you did. What has changed?"

Thomas, who has been standing before her, sits on the edge of the table and lowers his gaze. "When Longsight Meilwr did not recognize you by the smell of your hair, when Maître Pornic questioned the very miracle that had changed you—I doubted."

"Perhaps you were right to doubt."

Thomas looks at her, perplexed.

"I've told you before. I am not the same woman who was your grandmother. I am changed utterly."

"But are you my grandmother—or are you not?"

Rachel feels a wind inside her chest and knows she cannot lie to this seraphic man whose features are like a shadow of fire. "I am who God made me," she replies.

They stare at each other in silence.

At length, Thomas says, "The barbarian was defeated by me, Grandmère. God favored *me*. Won't you consider now that the Church is the one true faith?"

So that is why he has lingered, she realizes. "Ah, Thomas—I drank from the Grail, and I can tell you, what I drank is what changed me. The vessel itself is not important. The Qur'an, the Torah, the Church are all vessels that carry the same potent elixir."

"Not the same!" Thomas stands abruptly and takes her hands. "Christ died for our sins. His blood has sanctified the Church."

In the youth's moist eyes there is a reverence that needs her reassurance. He is reaching for something more than he can find in himself. But she knows she must not give that to him. She removes her hands. "I am tired," she says and walks toward the door.

"Grandmère!" He wants to tell her that her miracle has changed him unalterably, made him finally decide: he will become a priest. But she seems unhappy whenever he mentions the Church. *Why?* The Grail and the Savior came to her, not Allah or Moses. "God favored me today. Don't turn from me."

Rachel stops in the doorway and looks back. His pleading face has the hewn clarity of a statue. She wants to embrace him, to sop all the supplicative yearning from that face, to love his needfulness and end her own. But she is the baroness. She is his grandmother. "Thomas," she says in a hard whisper, remembering something a rabbi had once said, "God does. We name. Now get some sleep."

Alone in the dusty attic of the donjon, Thomas's conscience pricks at him and sends a chill creeping up his spine. Leaning in the open window, staring down at the bright windows of the *palais* under the brocaded stars, he shivers.

Despite the miracle of inspiration in the tilt yard this day, despite his love of God and Church, and—most potent of all— despite his blind faith that this woman is indeed his grandmother, he feels strangely unclean, ashamed and mortified by the welter of unholy sensations and emotions he feels when he is near her.

In the forest, blue mist rubs between the skinny trees. Hoar frost hangs from the bare branches. In the crystal silence of the night, the moon has a face, a hazy gaze, the sleepy stare of an opium smoker. It is the face of the Persian magician, Karm Abu Selim, hollow-cheeked as a panther.

"You remembered it wrong," his voice descends from the star-cut darkness. "God names. We do. He has named you Ailena Valaise. Now you must do her life."

"No," she mutters through the haze of her sleep. "I am Rachel."

"Silly child," the magician's voice chides. "You cannot be both. If you try, you will be neither."

"So now it's the Philosophers," Ummu taunts. Upon entering the knight-priest's chamber, he has found Gianni curled up in a window alcove under the glow of an oil lamp, reading the volume of Plotinus that the baroness has brought back to the castle from the abbey. Since his defeat in the lists, he has found that his soul aches more than his bruised ribs. Why has God let a nullifidian skull-smasher defeat him? Has he not witnessed the miracle of the Grail and been changed? Has he not stoppered his lust for the greater glory of God? Is he not worthy of God's favor?

Gianni peers over the top of the book. "Ummu, listen to the Fourth *Ennead,* fourth tractate, verse twenty-three: 'Feeling does not belong to fleshy matter: soul to have perception does not require body . . .'"

Ta-Toh scampers into the room; the dwarf bows to the well-dressed monkey, and the animal bows back. "The opinion of the Pythagoreans is that the Greek vase reflects the proportions of the Pure Mind. On the other hand, the Epicureans believe it mimes the curves of a girl's breasts, thighs, and buttocks."

"Your irreligious prattle will not distract me, stump."

"Irreligious? Dear Canon, I was merely citing the Philosophers. Irreligious?" Ummu thoughtfully twirls a curl about a stubby finger. "Consider then the divorce at Cana where the wine turned to water."

"Stump—begone."

"I am gone and I shall be—here atop the canopy." Adroitly, the dwarf scampers up the serpent-carved bedpost and disappears above the heavy embroidery of the bed's valence. Ta-Toh flits after him.

"What nonsense is this?"

"Oh, sense indeed. The sense of sight and of sound and enticing scent—for the Lady Madelon is paces away. And when she comes, Ta-Toh and I pray you will fare better than you did in the lists. May your lance find its mark, good knight. And a good night may it be. Hie away, beast! She is come."

Clare and Gerald and their daughters have devoted themselves thoroughly to entertaining their noble guests, with a mind to ingratiating themselves. They have taken it upon themselves to appeal to the earls and the marquess for funds to help the baroness with her debt to the king's men. To that end, they have given all their time and attention to lavish amusements: crossdressing costume balls for the adults, and miracle plays and treasure hunts for the children.

During an enchanted night picnic on a river barge, Madelon has stayed ashore, begging off with a feigned *mal-de-tête*. She has already agreed reluctantly with her parents and grandparents that the very real danger of losing their castle requires her to marry well and soon. Suitable candidates among the earls' children are being considered, and before the tourney is over an engagement will be arranged.

Resigned to her inevitable future with some staid viscount but not to her present fortunes, Madelon determines once and for all to experience the adventures of love, the courtly details of which she has been well-versed in since she was a child. Guy's ban on the pastime has only fanned her curiosity. In high spirits, she stops in her chamber only long enough to dismiss her maid to her own earthly pleasures. Then she removes her tight corset and, feeling free and slippery in the clinging folds of her silk robe, skips merrily to Gianni Rieti's bedchamber.

"I am a priest," Gianni protests.

Madelon has closed the door behind her and opened her robe, revealing her erect breasts and the peach fuzz between her legs. "I know the truth of your life, Gianni."

"But your great-grandmother …" he objects, as she approaches and takes the book from his hands and drops it on the sill. "The miracle of the Grail."

"Arrière-grandmère has not become a nun for the Grail." She tugs loose his tunic and reaches down with stealthy fingers for the chimerical ardor that he has been ignoring since that fateful night in the Holy Sepulcher. "God has returned her to her youth to be young. God wants us to be young when we are young. Penance will redeem our old age."

"Maître Pornic—" he whispers feebly as her lips nibble at his face.

"Maître is a holy man," she whispers back, her amazed hands

gripping a tumid strength that feels smooth as rosin and warmer than she had imagined in the restless darkness of other nights. "But you are wholly a man."

Gianni can resist no more. God, in His inexplicable wisdom, had abandoned him in the lists, so how could He expect a mere man, capable of laughing at misfortune and crying with joy, to withstand the amorous necessities of a passionate maiden?

As Madelon wriggles out of her robe, Gianni clutches her hands and stops her.

"Please, Madelon—no more."

She stares at him, befuddled. "Don't you find me desirable?"

His eyes snap open. "Of course! You are driving me mad with your beauty. But there is more—" He pulls her robe tight about her. "There has to be more—or I am damned."

"What are you saying?" Madelon whines. "I am not asking you to do anything you haven't done before many times over. There is no sin if you've never had the spirit of a priest."

"Madelon—" He puts his hands to her cheeks. "I am different now. I have seen a miracle with my own eyes. It has changed me forever."

Madelon frowns. "Then you are spurning me?"

"No!" He smiles radiantly. "What you have said to me in the chapel has worked on my heart, and now I realize you have spoken the truth. I am not a priest. Not in my soul—a soul that was made by God to love woman and be loved."

Her frown deepens. "Are you going to sport with me or not?"

"Is that all you want? Sport?"

"Mother has already found a fusty old earl to be my husband. Is it wrong to want to know some passion before I'm locked away in his castle?" She presses against him. "To want what you've given so many others?"

"I want to give you more." He takes her shoulders and holds her away from him. "I want to love you, Madelon, not just sport with you." He squeezes her shoulders tenderly. "I will renounce my priesthood. I will ask your parents for your hand."

"Marriage?" She shrugs off his grip. "I don't want to marry you. I must marry an earl." With a tweak of his beard, she touches her nose to his. "I want your passion, not your name, Gianni. I want to see what the ribald jests delight in. I want to experience the lover's zeal before I become a matron."

"Marry me and I will give you a lifetime of zeal."

"Marry you!" She backs off with a frustrated huff. "I want to be your lover, not your wife." She strides to the door and looks back irately. "I thought we were going to have fun."

As soon as she is gone, Ummu peers down furiously from the canopy. "She stood naked before you! And you turned her out!"

Gianni starts as if from a dream, and a slow smile widens in his face as he stares at the closed door. "I did!" He faces the scowling dwarf. "You saw it, Ummu. I was sore tested—and yet I was true! I was true to my vows."

"And false to that poor girl." Ummu rests his head petulantly in his hands, and Ta-Toh begins searching for lice in his hair.

"But don't you see, Ummu? I've been true when never before I would have been." Gianni laughs aloud. "Now I am free to do as I please. God knows I am sincere. I can leave the priesthood without shame."

Ummu rolls his eyes to heaven and turns his palms up. "Lord, why do You assail this small man?" From the first, when Gianni, as a libertine adolescent, had seduced the wife of the dwarf's first master, a prominent merchant of Turin, Ummu had felt blessed. Deformity had forced his carnal pleasures to remain vicarious, but with the merchant there had been only rare opportunities for voyeurism, for he had been discreet with his mistresses. Gianni, however, *wanted* him to watch, actually needed him to stand guard during his numerous amours, a chore which Ummu's small size and his prurient fascination made easy. Life had been good for the dwarf with his salacious knight—until the so-called miracle of the Grail tamed his master's lust. *And now marriage!* Seeing the simpering smile on Gianni's face, Ummu determines to thwart these delusions of love however he can.

Guy's head pounds, and with a groan he sits up in his bunk and squints into the dark. Roger, already awake and dressed, looks over from the wooden basin where he is washing his face.

"Is it day?" Guy moans.

Roger opens the shutters, and pearly light slants in. "I'll have the cookhouse bring you some willow bark for a potion."

"No potions." Guy stands and looks down at himself. He is still dressed in the same wine-stained tunic from last night. "The squires put me to bed like this?"

"Your squires are lying besotted in some alley. You dismissed them in a rage."

"I did?"

Roger nods and helps him lift the soiled tunic over his head. From the chest between their bunks, he removes a fresh tunic and gray britches. Seeing the baron bare-chested and sleepy-eyed, he remembers Guy as a boy—and suddenly he feels old and leathery. All his years of plotting war parties and conniving raids with this Lanfranc, and before him his father—all of those battles have come to this: defeated in the lists by a Muslim and the chair of state taken out from under them by a woman. Fatigue drenches him as he ponders all the work that must be done to get their castle back—but a greater weariness rises up at the thought of starting again elsewhere.

Guy snatches the garments and steps clumsily into his unlaced boots. "I'll bathe in the river." He seizes his sword and, wearing only brown trousers, clops past the partition and through the barracks followed by Roger. He ignores the greetings of the visiting knights, who are already awake and dressing, and shuffles past them and out the door in his loose boots.

William Morcar and Thierry fall in behind. As they pass the stables, Harold Almquist and Denis Hezetre look out from where they are chatting with several of the marquess's knights. Guy beckons the two with a wave, and they exchange anxious glances and join him.

"Come with me to the river," Guy says and leads them across the bailey and out the gate. They march morosely across the exercise grounds and down the rocky slopes to where the Llan chatters along the gravel banks, rustling and swirling among the boulders in deep pools.

Guy hands his sword to Roger, steps out of his boots, and dives into the frothing water.

"Why has he called us here?" Denis asks Roger.

The warmaster ignores him and keeps his eyes on the stream.

"Come, Roger," Denis calls out impatiently. "You unseated me in the tilt yard yesterday. I hold no grudge."

"Yes, I unseated you. Yet, your camp won by unfair advantage," Roger grouses.

"Unfair? Your camp was bested in hand combat."

"The heretic used a strange weapon. Who has seen a sword like that in contest?"

"Erec the Bold was not overcome."

Harold shifts uneasily. "Guy has been under too long."

The ire in Roger's face fades to concern as he searches the glinting river for Guy.

Harold climbs atop a boulder and scans from a higher vantage, while Roger paces briskly along the shore, trying to see past the outcrops in midstream. "Perhaps he is gulling us from behind a rock," the warmaster mutters.

"I don't see him," Harold calls.

William and Thierry splash in up to their ankles and, with a curse, Roger drops Guy's sword and begins unbuckling his own. "He's too swacked for the river," he cries. "I should have known."

Denis rushes fully clothed into the stream and dives headlong into the water where Guy vanished. Through the bubbles, he glimpses a body wedged between two rocks. Arms lash out to snatch him. Weighted down by his sword, Denis must pull with all his might for the two to rise.

They break the surface in a tangle, and Guy gasps for breath. With Denis bolstering him, they thrash back to shore, and the other knights drag them out.

Kneeling on the bank, Guy looks at Denis with ironic contempt. "You!" He chokes with sarcastic laughter and river water.

"I should have known," Denis mutters, sitting up. "You did that on purpose."

Guy wipes the tears from his eyes. "I expected Thierry," he says between breaths. "Or old Roger." He wipes the wet hair from his eyes. "But—of course—" He hacks another laugh. "It would be you. Still returning the favor from Eire."

Thierry kneels beside the baron. "Uncle, forgive me. I didn't think you were in jeopardy."

Guy smiles dryly and cuffs the young knight's ear. "Tell me you hoped I'd have drowned, and that would be the Thierry I know. I'd have done the same, lad, were I you. Let the river take the fool and you take the barony. That's the Lanfranc spirit, eh? Well, I don't blame you for it." He pushes Thierry back on his haunches. "But you'd have a hard time of it, wresting the chair of state from that vixen who's got it now."

Denis pushes to his feet with an angry mutter.

Guy grabs his ankle. "Wait, Denis. I must . . . thank you. You have restored some sense to my soul."

Denis shakes his head. "Enough sense to believe my love for you has never wavered? You have your own selfish and stubborn notions of loyalty, Guy."

"It's not the love of any of you I question," Guy protests. "But, after my defeat yesterday, I doubted myself, my worthiness."

"And this is how you must go about proving your worth?" Roger upbraids him. "This feckless gesture of a miffed child? Madness!"

"I think not," Denis says comfortingly and offers a hand to Guy. "You've lost a great deal, Guy, and that must feel like madness. But you've not lost your life. You still belong among us."

"But as what?" He takes Denis's hand and rises. "A knight? This young woman's *son?* What mockery!" He laughs, a cold, hollow laugh, then stares at each of the knights, his arms open, his half-naked body dripping. "Have I not been a good leader? I ask you men. Have I not been the first into battle and the last out? Under my leadership, have we not flourished? All of us together— have we not made of this domain more than it was before?"

The knights nod soberly.

"Then who is this—this woman to take our domain away from us?" Guy asks and looks at Denis and Harold. "Even if she is Ailena herself, blessed by the saints and breast-fed by the angels, has she any right to claim what we have held and fought to hold for ten years? Let her take her place among the women. I will protect her and provide for her—but I will be damned if I will be ruled by her."

"Then we must strike out on our own," Denis says, a new hope rising in him. "Let your mother have this land. It was her father's to begin with. We will fashion our own realm."

Roger groans. "There's a dream the daylight will squander."

"I'll not forsake what my father has taken for his own and what is rightly mine," Guy answers tersely.

Denis nods sadly and turns to go.

"Hold," Guy says, and takes Denis's arm. The baron's gruff visage, beaded with water, softens in the morning light. "Again, I thank you, Denis—for bringing me back."

"You belong among us," Denis replies and puts his hand over Guy's.

"As I am no longer baron, perhaps now we may be friends again."

Roger shoots a chiding glance at William and Thierry, saying with his look, *You should have been the ones to save him.*

Searching Guy's earnest gaze for deception, Denis squeezes his shoulder. "So long as you do not try to sway my allegiance to our mistress, I am your friend."

"As you proved in the river. Today's contests at the tourney include archery. With you in our camp, we will win the boar's head and the wine that goes with it!"

As Guy turns to retrieve his sword and dry clothes, Harold catches Denis's eye and conveys his concern with a fretful look. Denis nods, his expression wary, and slowly meets the stares of the other knights, who regard him with steely looks.

Rachel wakes to dawn's blue shadow in the windows. All she can see before her are the sere hills, the Llan dried up, the riverbed cracked in large hexagonal plates, the fields blowing with gray dust and cinders flaking from the sun-blasted mountain slopes in black whirlwinds, as pestilence and plague devour the land. Nausea seizes her, and she pushes weakly to her elbows.

Never and always, a dry voice crackles from far away. She breathes deeply and imagines the Grail. It appears in her mind shellacked with blood. In growing agitation, she lies back and stares at the rafters hardening in the dawnlight. A nerve flickers between her eyes as she slowly realizes it is only a nightmare—a nightmare of a horrible wasteland.

The realization offers no relief, for the gruesome images refuse to dissipate. She remembers Ailena telling her that the ruler and the land are one. How often the old woman had repeated this: the ruler and the land are one. So it is she herself, her very life that has become a wasteland. And because of David's illness, the wound that will not heal, she is trapped here in a strange wilderness, in a stranger's life. She has lost herself and become someone else.

Panic jolts through her, and she must grip the bedsheets with deliberate vigor to keep from shouting: *I am Rachel Tibbon!*

The strangled cry in her is the clot of her nightmare. Even within her, the scream would mean nothing, she realizes. She does not know who Rachel Tibbon is. She has forgotten Rachel Tibbon long ago and filled in all the empty spaces with Ailena Valaise. Where her own life had been, there is only a lie, a pathetic waste of a life.

She forces her mind desperately to imagine water and greenery and things that bloom. David's face looms before her, gaunt and ruined with suffering. "No!" she shouts and squeezes her eyes shut. Only when she thinks of Thomas does she remember that she had once been in love with trees, hills, and flowers. *Maybe,* she thinks, *he can help me. He is Parsifal. He is the holy fool who can find the Grail.* She sinks back down into the bed and breathes a relieved sigh. There can be no harm, she comforts herself, in telling this holy knight the truth, in having him as a confidant and ally until the spring when David will be strong enough to travel. For do they not share a unity of purpose, did not his grandmother become the Grail for *her,* the cup of her exile that promised to renew her own life someday? A man with a face as sensitive and beatific as his will surely understand that she has been compelled to hide her soul where it would be safe, in the middle of a stranger's fate.

With gathering strength, Rachel gets out of bed. Gently, she wakes the maid sleeping at the foot of her bed and sends her off to summon Thomas.

David's bones creak as he dresses. He feels his age and knows that he hasn't the strength to journey again to Jerusalem. He will die in this alien wilderness, but that thought seems strangely right and good. For the first time in a long while, he lets himself remember his dead children, and his sorrow is a gulf so wide its far side is not in this world.

Ten summers have passed since the horror. The mountains that brooded over his land are still there; the land is still there and maybe even the vineyard and most of the orchard among the citron swaths of grass. Are the people who now own the land pruning the trees properly? Do they ever stop among the trees when the rain mists out of the snow-spangled mountains and wonder who planted the pear and apple garths? That would have been his grandfather, the big-bearded man with the limp and the thundering laugh that used to frighten him as a child.

He remembers his wife, mercifully dead twenty-five summers now. He remembers her as she looked forty years ago when they had gone up into the mountains together, a young husband and wife: her svelte, fierce body naked in the coppery grass by the slow river, her pale breasts and the dark fire fanning from her sex, even the sand grit that stuck to her flanks where they had lain on the dewfall bank learning love's mysteries in each other's arms.

The years have gone. They have taken almost everything from him and left him luckless in a strange land. Yet beneath the stern gaze of Jehovah, even this is right and good. To remember being young, watching the somnolent river flow, thinking the years would last always—that is a blessing, for it helps him believe in his granddaughter, who is all that is left of everything he has ever owned.

David's prayer by the window, under dawn's pearl robes, is not beseechful. *Let what happens to us happen,* he intones.

"Master Thomas has left, my lady," the maid reports. "The porter says he rode off in the middle of the night. Gone back to the abbey, I would think."

Rachel stops brushing her hair. Now that he is gone, and in the cold light of day, her hope of confiding in him seems foolish. He would have loathed her when he learned who she really is, a Jewess sent back as a jape by a hateful and faithless crone. Numb at heart, she feels a bitter relief that she has been spared that indignity.

"The marquess is calling for you," a second maid announces from the doorway. "His lord is hungry and eager to get on with the day's games."

Rachel blows an exasperated sigh and beckons the maids to hurry with her hair. So long as the marquess is in the castle, her duty is to serve him. She regards herself in the mirror. Her face looks proud and remote, with the angular bones of a woman cruel with herself. She sees annoyance in the tightness of her mouth.

How very like Ailena herself, Rachel notices with a chill.

But as she composes herself, she realizes that it is not the demands of the marquess that vex her but her hurt that Thomas has left her without even a farewell. And the hopelessness of that caring, the flicker of wantonness that accompanies it, deepens her chill.

Rachel dutifully attends the marquess at his meals, where she hears from the old man tales of the royal court, of political intrigues among Queen Eleanor and the magnates, of the illicit affairs of the palace's bored wives, and, while they sup on roasted meats and honeyed fruits, of the three years of battles between Kings Richard and Philip of France that have added famine and disease to the miseries of northern Europe.

In the lodges, they watch Thierry fling three knights from the saddle and break lances to a draw against two others. The marquess's black-armored knights fare well in the jousts, emerging victorious more often than not. And they are everywhere, mingling with all the camps, garnering news which they then report to the marquess at table. Orgulous and bullying, they inspire the knights of other camps to arrogant behavior: fields are trampled in private duels, village maids are carried off into the woods for carnal sport, squires ride hacks into mess halls, and brawls seethe in the bailey.

When sunset draws its claws across the sky, heralds timidly summon the bruised, drunken, and exhausted knights to address the accruing complaints of the fairer sex in the court of love.

• • •

Snatches of melody float on the air from musicians wandering in the halls and the court garden. The musical preludes lure the last lingering knights from the gaming rooms to the stone benches that line the vine-scrawled walls. Lanterns strung on twine encircle the terrace, where a dais has been erected. There, the ladies of the castle and of the visiting earldoms sit on cushioned settles with Rachel on the chair of state at their center.

Fragrances waft from the garlands that adorn the dais and from the freshly bathed knights. All odors of the stables have been purged from their bodies by direct command of their lords, the earls having been sternly instructed by their wives and daughters that this event is to transpire without insolence from the men. Under the watchful gaze of the marquess and the earls, who are scattered like commoners among the men, the handsomely attired knights gaup at each other's finery and genteel behavior with amusement.

A young knight rises and requests the attention of the court. He has been solicited by an anonymous knight to put forth the question: "Should marriage to another prohibit lovers?"

One of the countesses replies, *"Causa coniugii ab amore non est excusatio recta."*

Some of the knights frown ignorantly at each other.

"Marriage is no proper obstacle to love," the baroness translates.

"Even," the petitioner continues, "if the anonymous party is married to the Church?"

Gasps pierce the night, and the plucking of lutes from the troubadours stops. While the ladies busily contemplate this point, the knights murmur among themselves about which of their clerics is plucking the rosebuds of desire among the thorns of sin.

After grave deliberation by the full court, the baroness subdues ribald jests from the floor and, in a silence still enough to hear the bassoons of the frogs in the moat, renders the judgment of the ladies: "Though the Church herself will deem us arrant, the court of love rules that mortal love supersedes immortal dogma. If the passion between two lovers is sincere, it is inspired by God. And though it can never be sanctified, it must not be damned. Love, after all, is an inborn suffering."

Amidst the outburst of laughter and offended cries, Gianni Rieti breathes deeper as an iron weight lifts from his heart.

The marquess sits in a dark corner of the terrace, obscured by the knights around him, sucking his gums and coldly watching the irreverent proceedings in the court of love. This new delight in chivalry and romance disgusts him. What a waste of time for a man who has so little time left, each night budging him that bit closer toward forever. He wants his pleasures while he still may— an old face with an old root tired of poking dull-witted peasant girls.

He reviews the available ladies of the court, the daughters, nieces, cousins, all the pert *fideles* of the earls and barons. Young Madelon Morcar draws much attention from the lusty young men, and there is a halo of mad ardor about her, with her reckless mouth and lithe body. Yet there is also a green tinge to her complexion this night, for her great-grandmother, the Lady of the Grail, Ailena Valaise, has the eyes of twice as many suitors in the crowd.

The thought of the baroness stirs the old man's root. Every knight and squire in attendance would spit gall if he took this sloe-eyed, moon-pale maiden for his own, which makes him want her all the more.

At the concluding ceremony of the court of love, the ladies petition for the devotion and protection of the men not only from outside enemies but from the men's own brutality. The castle garrison, on their own initiative, stands.

Master-sergeant Gervais, an ox-shouldered, lump-nosed warrior, his right eye creased closed by a vertical scar, speaks for the others, "We are simple men, we soldiers. We know our horses better than our women. The ways of chivalry are new and strange to us. And thus, we cannot promise always to be courtly in the ways of love. But to a man, we stand ready to give our lives for our baroness, mistress of this castle and land, Ailena Valaise, Lady of the Grail."

The men cheer as one, startling many of the women on the dais. But Rachel sits still, her eyes bright as a panther's, coolly observing the leathern faces, the scar-riven, thick-jawed men who love the idea of her but who would hate her with as much passion if they knew who she really is.

Gervais holds up a blunt-fingered hand to silence the soldiers. "All of us served your son, Sir Guy—many of us served you before your pilgrimage changed you—and a few, like myself, served your husband, Sir Gilbert. To each in turn, we gave our devotion and protection. But to you alone, Lady of the Grail, we would give our vassalage."

Awed murmurs thrill through the assembly and across the dais. Not even the marquess has the vassalage of his garrison, for it is a privilege usually accorded only princes and kings, that these soldiers could offer themselves as personal servants, willing to stand by her their whole lives even if they are not paid.

"With your permission, Lady, your garrison will approach and offer their fealty."

Rachel nods and rises.

Silence holds the court while each of the score of battle-marred men steps onto the dais, kneels, and, with his hands in the Lady of the Grail's, states his name and pledge of troth. When the ritual is complete, a virile cry goes up from the exhila-rated men.

Rachel smiles, but her insides shiver before the ravenous joy of these Christian soldiers.

A splash-black visage bares fangs, and Gianni Rieti shudders awake to see Ta-Toh grimacing down at him. Ummu tugs at his arm to pull him upright. "Good knight, this is a bad night for you."

"What are you talking about, you damnable dwarf. I'm sleeping."

"I am your eyes when you sleep. Up, good knight, and out, I say. For some other bad knight is also up but, sad to say, in *and* out."

Gianni shakes his head groggily. "I don't understand."

"Come with me and you will bless your ignorance."

"Then let me sleep and stop riddling me."

"No. You must end your ignorance or it will hurt all the more later. Come, quickly—for the other may come more quickly."

Gianni crawls into his tunic and slouches out of the room after his excited dwarf. Ummu leads him down the passage and up a curve of stairs to a closed door. "Open it," he says. "Ta-Toh went in through the window earlier and unlatched it."

Small pangs of debauched cries squeak through the closed door, and Gianni's hand hesitates, already knowing with a clotted pain in his heart what he will find. Ummu nudges him, and he cracks the door open sufficiently to see Madelon and a young knight surging nakedly against each other in a turmoil of fornication.

Gianni closes the door quietly, pats Ummu on the head, pads softly down the stairs, and slams his brow so violently against the door to his chamber that he drops to his knees in a supplication of pain and remorse.

The climax of the tourney is the melee. The knights divide into two camps and fight for possession of their opponents' banner. After the pitched battle, the field is strewn with splintered lances, shields hacked and broken, and the debris of shattered armor and dead horses. Shoulders and thighs have been hacked and broken and eyes gouged, but no one is killed. Among the injured, Gianni delights to see the bold knight who romped with Madelon the night before. Thierry, who caught the youth skulking down the stairs from his sister Madelon's quarters, has beaten him half-dead during the melee.

That night, at a final festival in a torch-cirque on the tilt yard itself, Gianni ignores Madelon's alluring glances and drinks himself into a stupor.

Under the stars and gibbous moon, Rachel attends the marquess at the head table. Tonight he leans closer as she pours his wine and touches her hands as she reaches for the trencher they will share. She smiles indulgently at him, disguising her uneasiness with small talk about the contests. And, as soon as her noble guest is sated with food, wine, and jongleurs' music, she begs to retire, claiming fatigue from the long day and the loud company of drunken knights.

The marquess bows, kisses her hands, and waves her off. With puff-cheeked relief, Rachel escapes to the *palais*. But as she is undressing, Falan knocks and announces the presence of the marquess.

Hurriedly robing herself, Rachel admits him, and he kicks the door closed behind him and crosses the room with a jagged gait, drunk and humming a troubadour's air. Rachel feigns exhaustion, but the old man will not be deterred. "I must speak with you alone." He glares at the maid, and she ducks out of the chamber. "With my help, we need not lose this castle," he says, tilting back toward the door and latching it. "Or, if you wish, we can abandon this place and you will have a finer estate in Shropshire."

"My lord, what are you saying?"

"I am without a wife. I have been so these last eighteen years. I had not thought I would ever—" He waves his hand, dismissing his speech. "Be my wife. I have only a handful of years left me. Serve me kindly those few years, and you will be well recompensed."

Rachel bows her head shyly to hide her revulsion. She has spent all the time she can bear seeing that this man's meat is mashed to a consistency he can gum, and she shrivels inside at the thought of sharing a bed with him.

The marquess moves up beside her, and the sour stink of wine wafts off him. "Will you be my bride?"

Rachel forces a smile. "My lord, I am not worthy."

"Nonsense. I am an old man." He studies the stiffness of Rachel's jaw, the downcast of her eyes. "But I am an old and *powerful* man. Your time with me will not be without its rewards."

Rachel permits some warmth in her voice: "I will consider your kind regard for me."

The marquess shows his gums in a broad smile. "Good. You have given me great pleasure. Now let me show you that your time with me will not be entirely fallow." He slips his hands beneath her robe and cups her breasts.

Rachel twists away. "Please. I am not a village girl."

The marquess presses closer and places his hands on her hips. "I would not marry a village girl."

"I did not say I would marry," Rachel confesses and pushes his hands off her. "Your kind regard dims in my eyes."

The marquess steps back and says in a dry voice, "I know your position well, Ailena. Perhaps better than you. On Saint Margaret's, the king's men will not accept charm. If you do not pay them, you *will* be a village girl, and your large and warm family will be no better than villeins."

"There are other castles where we may serve."

"Not if a marquess speaks unkindly of you."

Rachel meets the marquess's glittering stare with cold ire. "Is this how you woo love—with threats?"

The marquess fits himself against her and grabs her buttocks. "This is not your foolish court of love, Ailena. I woo with power."

Rachel vainly strives to pull free. "I am blessed by the Grail. Take your hands off me!"

The marquess laughs explosively. "You said the Grail sent you back into the world. Well then, Ailena, *I* am your lance." He trips her onto the bed and leans over her. "They say your moles and freckles changed when your youth was restored. Is your virginity restored as well?" He pulls up her robe, deftly blocking her kicks and blows. "I have seigneurial privilege to deflower all the maidens in my demesne. You will be no exception."

One of Rachel's blows smites the side of his head, and he rears back, fist raised, face twisted furiously. "Don't force me to strike you!"

"I will fight you!" Rachel cries. "I am not the child I look to be. I am Ailena Valaise. I am! And I will fight you!"

"I think not," the marquess says through a shadowy laugh. He leans his face close to hers and whispers conspiratorially, "You see, Ailena Valaise, my knights are now in all the key positions of your castle—*my* castle. I can do with you exactly as I please."

Shivering with loathing and abject dread, Rachel masters her voice, "You may force me but you will have no pleasure of me."

The marquess leers and jams a hand between her legs. "Pleasure enough!"

"I will be better for you," she grates, squirming away from his groping hand, "if you let me come to you willingly."

"We will talk on that later. Now let me see what you are offering."

"Falan!" Rachel screams.

Falan, who had thought wisely to weaken the door latch, explodes into the chamber, saber skirling the air. Two of the marquess's knights rush in. But before they can unsheathe their swords, Falan whirls about, his scimitar like lightning, striking the knights' cinctures and dropping their swords in their scabbards to the floor.

The marquess stands back from Rachel and straightens his tunic. "I am the king's man!" he bawls. "Slay me and you will bring ruin upon all of you."

Rachel rises, but her legs are too wobbly to hold her, and she sits heavily on the edge of the bed. "Your life is not forfeit. Falan, let him pass."

The marquess stands taller, nods for his men to pick up their swords and leave. "I yet hold this castle," he tells Rachel.

"But if you would hold my heart, you must be more gentle."

"You would be my wife?"

Rachel looks up at him with gloomy eyes. "If I find no other way to pay what I owe." Her stare hardens. "And if you leave here with your knights and do not threaten me. Only then, should God provide no money to save my family, I will be your wife."

The marquess bows graciously and backs out of the chamber with a hard grin on his face, not looking at Falan.

In the front hall of the *palais*, a narrow space with high windows and floor of patterned red and black tile, the marquess faces his sheepish knights. They clutch their unbelted swords to their sides and avoid his irate gaze. Before he can voice his rebuke, one of them holds up a parchment covered with letters shaped like black flames. "The Jews' reply to the baroness's request for a loan. Our men intercepted it on the highway from Caermathon."

The marquess snatches it and holds it to the flame of a tallow lamp in a wall niche. It flares in his hand, and he drops it and watches it curl to a black husk. "Send two men to Caermathon to speak with the moneylenders. The baroness is to receive nothing from them."

Rachel lies on her bed, alone in her chamber, and weeps. Her tears drain the fright from her and leave her relaxed. Her body feels smutched, and she wants to bathe at once but is too weak. Loathing sits like a stone in her stomach. She knows if the money does not come soon, she will fly with her jewels. She will escape into the horizon.

The futility of that plan cankers inside her, for she knows that she will not let her loathing or her fright kill her grandfather. Until David is well enough to travel, she will endure every indignity— even, if she must, marriage to the toothless old debaucher. She will not kill the man who struggled to keep her alive in the wilderness by chopping wood and digging graves.

To calm herself, she remembers the Holy Land, the glassy mountains seen through the heat veils of the desert. Her hot red heart bobs lighter at the memory of the community of stone houses, of Daniel Hezekyah and the simple life she had come so close to having. Simple as growing food out of the dirt. A life of small miracles.

Here, pretending to a large miracle, everything is as barren as the land of her nightmare. *Will there be money? Will there be more murder? More rape?*

Ghostly as an apparition, Thomas Chalandon appears in the lonely deep behind her eyes. Seeing his childlike smile, his large, wondering eyes, her loathing begins to drift away, and she calms down. She can pretend she is not alone. She can pretend they are together, safe and quiet in their distant arbor.

At dawn, after prayers, when the revelers depart, Falan Askersund goes with them. David, ashen and trembly, insists on going along with the farewell party. Rachel knows that he is hoping she will change her mind and agree to return with Falan to the Levant, because he makes sure that she packs the jewels along with the holy scrolls.

Rachel, David, Gianni, Denis, and a handful of sergeants ride with Falan and his camels under hilly horizons burbling with bird songs. Only once does Falan look back, stopping his camel at the crest of the first hill, not to admire the vista of the spired castle rising from the morning mists and the molten-bright Llan, but to see that the marquess has removed his troops entirely from the vicinity. When he sees the caravan of black knights dwindling into the swell of the rising sun, he resets his gaze forward. They might yet return, or other threats could descend out of the forest's gloomy tangle—but those are not his concern anymore.

Falan recalls the thirty-third sura from the Qur'an, and he recites it aloud, "'God suffices the faithful in the fight.'"

David, who learned his Arabic in the marketplaces of Tyre, Acre, and Jerusalem, understands. "We have only our faith to protect us now," he calls up to his granddaughter from astride his mule.

Rachel nods and pulls her steed alongside Falan as they continue. Last night, without Falan, she would have suffered what Ailena had endured with Guy's father, Gilbert. But Rachel Tibbon, she knows, for all her acquired steel would not be strong enough to last this life. Even now, in the gold brightness and leaf-glitter of morning, the darkness of the marquess's brutality clings to her. A voiceless wailing curls through her brain, leaking into the dim madness that has haunted her since the horror: *never and always.* Time has not quelled the terror that found her years ago, when she was only twelve. It only buried it deeper. *Time is no healer.*

Falan has seen this dreamful expression on her face many times in the long months that he has been her guardian. At first, he had thought she was rapt in her illusions and deceptions, that she was remembering the stories that Karm Abu Selim had magically instilled in her. But now, having witnessed these spells overtake her whenever she is assailed by some trouble from without, he knows that he has gotten it backward: the illusion is remembering her.

And who is being remembered? Falan wonders. When he volunteered for this assignment, he was told Rachel Tibbon was a Jewess, the old man's granddaughter, a mere pawn whom the wealthy old baroness had selected to fulfill her vengeful ruse. He had not cared then who that Jewess was or had been before the Persian magician affixed her mask. Only now, knowing he will never see her again, does he truly wonder. *Who is being remembered that such fierce dread should own her?*

"Come with me," he tells her. "Come back to the House of God—Jerusalem."

Rachel shakes her head, aware that David is casting her hopeful looks.

"Much danger here there is," he says in mangled langue d'oc.

"Much danger everywhere." Rachel reaches up, and Falan takes her hand. She smiles tautly, aware.

When they reach the Usk and Falan leads his two camels onto the barge for the journey south to Newport, he is purged of all fear for her. "We are all the cattle of heaven," he declares, then unclasps from his throat the gold band of his servitude. He hands the torque to Rachel. "Go with God."

As the barge is untied and poled out into the current, Falan looks away. Above the river and the broken spine of the land, the sky is a radiant blue. Behind him, his promise is fulfilled, and he does not need to look back to know that his past waves him on, free to be alone in the world again.

"She is gone with her knights," Thierry Morcar says. "Drop the portcullis and keep the witch out."

Guy looks up from lacing his boots with a proud cock of his head. "Noble thought, lad. But this is the Pretender's keep now."

Thierry frowns and looks to Roger Billancourt and William Morcar, who are also fastening their riding boots. They are in the barracks, where they have exiled themselves in a stupor of drunkenness since their defeat in the tilt yard. The oak-raftered structure, with its gray plank walls, wattle partitions, and hay-matted bunks, is empty now that the visiting knights and their squires have departed. "You're not simply giving it over to her?"

"She won the *assise de bataille*, didn't she?" Roger says sourly, not looking up from lashing the cuffs of his boots.

"And that's it? That's all?"

"The garrison have sworn their vassalage," Guy says bitterly.

"They're your men," Thierry presses. "You've been their lord for ten years. Talk with them."

"I want to tell the boy everything," his father insists.

At Guy's nod, William hobbles over to his son, one boot on and one in his hand, and sits on the bunk beside him. "The black knights have had words with your uncle. Seems the marquess has taken a fancy to the Pretender. He's made us foreswear plotting against her—at least till Saint Margaret's, when he claims he'll be taking her for his own. In return for our not molesting her, he promises us the castle."

Thierry's pugnacious face brightens. "Then I need not trouble myself to pilgrimage to Saint David's."

"Oh, you'll pilgrimage, all right," Guy says, standing, kicking his boot tip against a post. With his topknot gone, he has cropped his black hair short over his ears and braided the locks at the back of his head in a tight rat's tail. "You're going to worship at Saint Branden's."

"Saint—what?" Thierry casts a baffled look at his father, who is grimacing too intently to answer as he tugs on his boot.

"Branden Neufmarché's castle," Roger Billancourt says, rising now that he is shod. His faded black trousers are tucked into his boots, but he is still bare-chested, the scars of ancient wars braiding his thick shoulders. "You'll tell everyone that you're making the pilgrimage, but instead, you're to reside with our friend Branden."

"Since when has that toad become our friend?"

"Since we offered him all the land and the fortalice that the Pretender has given to the barbarians," Roger replies, removing his tunic from the bunk post.

"But that's our land," Thierry protests.

"It will be the king's when the penalties are not paid," Guy says, removing his dagger from the hay where he had slept and tucking it into his boot. "The marquess claims he will pay the debt. But we think not. He wants the Grail-Lady to soothe his old age, not a frontier fortress to defend and maintain. The castle is forfeit. We will make our alliance with Branden. We've proven our mettle against him, and he'd rather have us fighting for him than against."

"But, Uncle, you can't be Branden's vassal. That's unnatural—he's a craven, pompous sot!"

"Not his vassal, Thierry, his ally. We will defend the land and fortalice we've given him against the claims of whomever the king bequeaths our castle."

"Whoever it is," Roger adds, "will be no one of consequence to be posted so deep in the wilds as Epynt. In time, knowing the hills and the castle as we do, and with Branden's men in our command, we will have our keep back."

Guy yanks open the door, and sunlight barges in. "Come, Thierry, let's take our falcons to the woods and have our pleasure while we may. There's toil enough to come."

Trees like shaggy oafs crowd the trail, and Rachel and her escort do not see the Welshmen until they are surrounded. The warriors in their pelts and nut-oiled hair lean casually on their tall spears and snicker at the alarm of the Normans. Denis and Gianni swing their horses closer to Rachel, and the sergeants back their steeds against each other, in a futile attempt to guard all sides.

"Tell your men to be at ease," Erec's voice calls in Welsh from the forest. He steps smiling through the ranks of his men. "The Servant of Birds is all the shield they need in these woods." Rachel returns a thin smile, though she feels vulnerable without Falan.

"You show your fear too readily, baroness, now that your master-at-arms is gone," Erec remarks with amusement as he steps between the horses of her knights and takes hold of her bridle. "Are you afraid that I will try to overpower you?"

Rachel glances around at the bearded men, their hardened faces watching her with suspicion and curiosity. "I am scared," she admits.

"Do not be. I have come with news that will gladden you. Step aside with me into the forest. This is for your ears only, as I do not know who among your men understands our language."

As Rachel begins to dismount, Denis and Gianni stop her. "Don't go," David whispers. "He will carry you off and murder us."

Rachel stares at Erec's broad and ruddy visage and says, "For honor's sake, keep me in sight of my men."

"Done." They walk to the edge of the road and stand between the solemnity of two yews, their backs to the uneasy cluster of

Rachel's men. "I know of your plight with your king. You owe him three hundred pounds of silver."

"Yes. I must have it in a fortnight—by Saint Margaret's."

"How will you get it?"

Rachel peers uncertainly at the bear-shouldered man. "Are you offering me the money?"

Erec puffs his cheeks out and lifts his tufted eyebrows. "No *true* Welshman has that much of the king's money." A wolfish grin sharpens his features. "But I know who has. There is a rival tribe to the north in a boar fen above the Bridge of Lost Steps—bandits all, cow-raiders and wife-stealers. They've hoarded twice the silver you need, all of it robbed on the king's highways these last seven years, since Richard has been sending his tax-collectors to squeeze the barons."

"Will they lend me the money?"

Erec squints. "Lend the money? To a baroness of the Invaders? And sworn enemies of the Rhiwlas clan?" He sucks air through clenched teeth. "They'd sooner piss standing on their heads." He leans in closer. "Their chief, Dic Long Knife, has been using those funds to buy damascene steel swords from Irish traders—arming whole clans with them, who before had only staves and arrows. My father Howel fears they'll be coming for his lands soon, but he is too chary in his old age to strike first. His last prayer at night and his first in the morning is that someone might hamper them." He winks. "Give me three of your staunchest men, men whom I can trust, and I will steal Dic Long Knife's money."

Rachel's pulse races. "You can do this?"

"For you." The wolfish grin flashes again. "That is my price. When I bring you the money, you become my wife."

Anxiety rebounds in her. "I cannot marry you."

"Why not? I am a Christian."

Her mind scrambles for some escape. "I am a Norman. Your people despise me."

"You are the Servant of Birds. You speak our language, you know our ways. The people will love you—as I do."

Rachel feels a blush prickle the sides of her neck under Erec's keen gaze. *First the marquess—and now Bold Erec!* Though

there is much about Erec that appeals to her—his brash good
looks, his ready smile, his courage—she does not want to marry
him. She looks back at the men, sees her grandfather watching
after her apprehensively. *Where are the moneylenders of
Caermathon?*

"You must decide soon, Servant of Birds. And even then,
nothing is assured. Dic Long Knife is a man who lives up to his
name."

"Alms! For the sake of Christ, alms!" A group of forty people are
chanting for charity before the drawbridge of Castle Valaise when
Rachel and her men return. They are waifs and vagabonds from
all over the countryside, swept into Epynt with the droves of
tournament-goers and left behind to mingle with the lame and
halt of the village.

The sergeants clear a path for the baroness and her knights.
Once inside the bailey, Rachel orders the porter to bring a bag of
copper obols. Clare and Ummu, who have come from the *palais* at
the herald's trumpet call, scowl with disapproval.

"Mother, there are debts owed in the bailey." She points to the
guildsmen, who have gathered in ranks to petition for payment of
their services rendered during the tourney. "The poor are always
with us, but our guildsmen will leave for more lucrative keeps if
we don't pay them." She says this loud enough for the merchants
to hear, so they will know she has done her best.

"Then we must pay them what we owe them."

"Mother," Clare whispers, "we haven't the money."

"I thought you and Gerald had procured some pounds from
the visiting earls."

"We've ten pounds," Clare says in a proud hush. "But that is
for the king's penalties."

"Is it enough for the guildsmen?"

"Barely. But the penalties—"

"Pay them, Clare. And worry no more about the penalties. I
will fulfill them. The family's home will be secure."

All protest in Clare evaporates at the look of stern confidence and
command in the young woman's resolute face. That is so clearly the

impelling look of her mother's face she remembers from earliest childhood that tears abruptly smart in her eyes. This is, perhaps, the most trying time in Clare's life: having to humiliate herself in front of noblemen by asking for money, all the while pondering for too many days now what kind of life she and Gerald and their family would have if the king should take away the only home they have ever known. Peeping into the abyss of destitution has nearly cost her her mind. Since the tourney, she has pretended to be strong, for she is used to considering herself the eldest. *But no*—She stares gratefully into her mother's beautiful face. She recognizes the authority there, and an internal explosion shatters all pretense in her, reducing her once more to the child she has always been.

"Mother!" Clare embraces Rachel, nearly toppling over the slender woman with her strenuous sobs.

"All shall be well, Clare," Rachel promises, patting those large, heaving shoulders and visualizing the Chalice, gleaming as intensely gold as the sun, to allay her own extreme dread. "All manner of thing shall be well."

Clare moves away and wipes her eyes. "You have always taken good care of us—of Gerald and me and the children. When you left, it was so horrible under Guy." Her voice has softened to the timbre of a young girl's. "But now you're back. And so is the music. Gerald has convinced two of the troubadours to stay with us, two of the best. There is song again, Mother. Just as before."

The porter returns with the bag of obols.

"Pay the guildsmen, Clare, and the troubadours, too. I will attend to the poor."

"Lady," Ummu offers, stepping ahead of her. "If you will permit me. I am not unfamiliar with the deceptions of mountebanks."

With David, Denis, and Gianni following, Rachel and Ummu confront the beggars on the drawbridge. The crowd presses closer to touch the blessed baroness's robes in the hopes of being miraculously cured. From passing through the village on her journey to and from the abbey, Rachel recognizes the blind woman led by a little girl, the lad with the withered arm, the old man with no legs on his wheeled platform, the harmless idiot, and the widow whose husband was slain in a brawl, leaving her with nine children. But there are numerous others she has never seen before. She moves among them, distributing obols, fending off groping hands, and recalling the baroness's counsel that she and the land are one: *then these unfortunates, too, are me.*

While Rachel loudly disclaims her power to heal, the dwarf approaches a crook-backed man disfigured with brown, glossy sores. Ta-Toh reaches out and, to the startled cries of the onlookers, peels away one of the sores.

Ummu takes the scab, sniffs it, and waves it in the air. "Prune skin!" He kicks the man's shin, and the impostor's crooked back straightens with his howl. "A miracle! Ummu works a miracle! Who will next receive my healing touch?"

The dwarf seizes by the back of his neck a young man on his knees foaming at the mouth. "Soap!" he decries and boxes the man's ears. "Another cure! Saint Ummu's miracle hands are reaching out!" He snatches a crutch from a fleecy haired man and drops him to his knees. The man wails piteously, until the dwarf snatches with the crutch at the halt man's groin, then the stranger leaps to his feet; cursing and spitting, he retreats from the gathering, followed by a dozen others.

"Our little saint has driven out the demons," Gianni observes, prying the hands of the devout from the baroness's robes.

"We must do better," Rachel says. *Never and always*, the darkness speaks in her. But she shakes her head; she will not listen to it. "I want you to help these people, Father."

Gianni flinches. "Please, my lady, do not call me that."

"You are a priest."

"I am a knight. I will take Falan's place. I will even sleep on the flagstones outside your door. Let the rabbi be your holy man."

"Something must be done about these people," Rachel sighs, exhausting the last obols in her pouch and offering her empty hands to the disconsolate people. The air rings with something more than the pleas of the poor. The voices of the dead glisten just within hearing: her dead family sings a joyful song in Hebrew. *Why?* She looks to her grandfather to see if he can hear them, and he is muttering a prayer, blessing the people. "Rabbi—and Gianni—I want you both to devise some honest work within the capacities of the blind and the lame, to find some way to give true relief to the widow and the others like her in the village. As for the idlers and lowbrowed rogues, they must be dissuaded from begging and shown the virtues of honest toil. And we must place the idiot where he can be decently cared for. Perhaps the abbey."

"Maître Pornic insists that only the soldiers of Christ may reside and work at his abbey," Denis says. "The poor are to be tended by Christian charity and wandering monks."

"Then we will take care of our own," Rachel decides.

"For so long as they are our own," Denis mutters.

"The money will come."

"From where, lady? The moneylenders have ignored our entreaty. I have sent another sergeant to beg for their help."

"I will get the money."

Denis stares intently at her. "You must not sacrifice yourself. I know about the marquess and his offer. His knights brag how you will be his. But to save us, you must not lose yourself. To marry that lecherous old man would be wrong."

Rachel returns her attention to the thronging beggars and says in a distracted voice, "Love proceeds from wrong to wrong."

Hellene kisses Thierry's cheek, stands back and admires his stocky strength. *He is no fop,* she thinks, *like Father.* She has always been unhappy that her father, Gerald, is a troubadour and not a more manly knight. But her William has been man enough for her, and she passes him a look of shared pride in their son.

The Morcars are standing in the wide court outside the *palais,* bidding adieu. Like a squire, young Hugues holds the reins of his brother's hackney, wishing he could go on the pilgrimage, too. Since Thierry's valiant display of battle prowess during the tourney, the whole family has been plump with respect for him and aching that he must make so hazardous a journey at so uncertain a time. When he returns, the castle, that once might have been his heirdom, may no longer be theirs.

"Keep to the king's highways," Hellene advises. "And when you get to Saint David's, have a Mass said as well for our castle. If God so loves Ailena, he may yet save our keep."

"I shall, Mother." Thierry looks knowingly to his father, but William betrays no sign of complicity. He hugs his son and stands back.

"Do not speak well of yourself," William offers. "Rather, do well."

Thierry nods, turns to his twin sister, who is weeping softly into a handkerchief. "Madelon, stay your tears. I am not off to war. Perhaps on my pilgrimage I will find the Grail and drink from it and come back younger than Effie. Then you can be my nurse."

Madelon sobs a laugh. "Don't you dare."

Thierry punches his brother's arm. "Guard them well," he instructs and then mounts his steed. With a gesture of farewell, he trots across the ward, pauses at the inner gate to look back and wave, and then is gone.

"How could Grandmère do this," Hellene moans, "after he has done so very well in the tourney?"

"She is not Ailena," Hugues announces bitterly. "She is afraid of Thierry, because she is a witch."

Among the clouds a wedge of geese flies north. Rachel, sitting in the castle garden, watches them appear and disappear as they dwindle into the distance. Blythe and Effie are playing dame-and-maid around the sun dial, and under the rose arbor Leora is supervising the petit point of her older daughters, Joyce and Gilberta.

Listening for the dead, Rachel hears only a bright crystal silence mottled with the click of the embroidery needles and the voices of the children. *Why did the dead sing to me when the poor were all around?* she asks herself.

And from the world's edge at the brink of her heart, the question comes back: *What did the dead sing?*

A Jewish song, she answers herself. *A hymn of praise.*

A servitor approaches, whispers to one of the maids, who hurries to Rachel: "The rabbi is calling for you."

Leora looks after Rachel as she leaps to her feet and runs out of the garden. *Like a girl.* One coppery eyebrow arches. *Of course—she is practically a girl!* That is the miracle, the enormous wonder of her return, that has made Leora's and her daughters' prayers so much brighter. Even Harold, who used to nap during morning chapel, follows the new canon's services attentively. She smiles and lifts a grateful countenance to the furry clouds mulling the blue.

Rachel finds David lying in bed, barely conscious. The physician has finished administering a potion of henbane to treat the melancholic humor that is causing the old man's chills and lethargy. "He will sleep now," the physician says. "When he wakes, he may be stronger."

"*May* be?" Rachel whispers. "Why can't you help him?"

The physician's curled eyebrows knit tightly. "He is old and tired in his bones."

Rachel dismisses the physician and the maids and sits at her grandfather's bedside. When she takes his cold hand, his eyes bat open. "We must leave this place," he says in a wispy voice. "The air is cold here even in July! Come back with me to Jerusalem."

Rachel rubs warmth into his hand. "We will, Grandfather. But you must get strong first. Rest now and build your strength, for we *will* return to Jerusalem."

He sinks into sleep, smiling vaguely.

Rachel feels every sense deepen. If she loses him, she will be entirely alone in this strange land. The voices within her thrive on this fear; she senses them turning within her like smoke, needing only her attentiveness to condense into sound. But she focuses instead on her grandfather's slumbering face, and the almost-voices become a music inside her body, the joyful hymn she had heard when she stood before the poor.

She is afraid to listen too closely, afraid of what the music is doing inside her head. Though she believes the dead have an answer for how to help her grandfather, she knows that if she loses herself in their depths, pulled away like a leaf down a whirlpool, David will wish he were dead.

"God is an onion," David Tibbon says to the knights in his Torah study group. The henbane has helped him to sleep off the weariness of his ill humors and given him enough strength to teach his students some Hebrew and to review for them the underlying creed, the Covenant between God and Abraham. He is tired again, but the cold that always stays in his bones feels warmed by this devotional work. Now, for some diversion: "The Hebrew word for onion, which is among the most beautiful of Israel's flowers, is *beh-tsel*—which puns with *Beth-El,* House of God, as well as punning with *bets-al-ale',* in the shadow of God. And Bezaleel, the name of the craftsman who actually made the first *menorah,* the candelabra revealed to Moses in Sinai, means Onion of God—all implying how the humble onion symbolizes the supernal, divine immanence of creation."

They are in David's room, seated on reed mats on the floor—Gerald, Denis, Harold, Gianni, and Ummu. When Rachel enters, only Gerald recalls the convention of the court of love and stands.

"The poor will build a synagogue!" the baroness announces breathlessly. The idea came to her clearly while listening to Clare prattle about how Madelon's wedding preparations kept Hellene's mind off her worries for Thierry. "We will build a meeting place of God—Psalm 74. The construction will employ the beggars of the area in whatever capacity they can serve." *And it will give Grandfather something meaningful to occupy him, to help him regain his strength.*

"But the village has a chapel already," Harold protests.

"A rude building," Gianni replies. Each morning after his sparsely attended service in the castle's chapel, he has celebrated Mass in Hebrew to a full house of worshipers in the village. "A wattle hut, really. Even the crucifix is crudely carved."

"There will be no crucifix in the temple," Rachel says. "No idols of any kind. It will be dedicated to no saint but to God Himself and bear no name other than the House of God."

"As Yeshua himself would recognize," Denis grasps slowly, incapable of surprise anymore.

"Perhaps," Gianni suggests, "after the synagogue is built, Maître Pornic may have his chapel back, to worship as the Church decrees."

"Yes," Rachel agrees. "The synagogue will be for those of Yeshua's faith."

"Then," David says, "it must be built as the Bible prescribes in Daniel, chapters two and six—erected on a high place with numerous windows, for 'light dwells with Him'—and 'He had windows in His upper chamber open.'"

"I know the place for it," Harold offers. "On Merlin's Knoll, south of the village. There is an ancient stone cirque on that hill, a ring of boulders older than the Romans. The Welsh believe Merlin arranged them."

"Merlin will not object if we build a temple to worship as Yeshua did," Denis says. "Arthur was a Christian."

"In Jerusalem," David says, nodding reflectively, the cold in his bones wisping away with the warmth of his excitement, "I once spoke with a monk who claimed that Yeshua's mother, Miriam, had the family surname *Bezalim*—which means onion leaves. And so her name already implied the tears she would shed."

Thunder lobs out of the hills. Gianni does not hear it for Madelon's ribald song of the rooster's love for a cow, a lively *chanson de geste* she learned during the tourney. They sit in a bed of primrose and violets at the wild end of the garden, their laughter hidden from view by dense hedges. With lyrical delirium, she rises to her knees with the rooster's triumphant cry at discovering that his rival in love is a bull who cannot fly.

Their guffawing topples them backward, and they lie among the flowers smiling into the burning edge of the day, where the orange sun breaks into rays among the treetops. Thunder mumbles again from the hills, and Madelon turns her head to see violet storm clouds budging out of the north. "We must go," she whispers, putting a hand on his chest, "or we'll be soaked."

"Come away with me," Gianni says, taking her hand.

Madelon rolls her eyes. "Where?"

"It matters not—"

She sits up, plucks crushed flowers from her hair. "How will we live?"

"I will serve a noble as a knight."

Madelon stands, brushes off petals, leaves, grass blades. "Become a knight to my husband and you can be my lover."

"If you marry me, I will keep you happy with love and you will need no lovers."

Madelon gives him a discouraging look. "Romance is exquisite sport, Gianni—but it is not enough to keep me happy."

"What more?"

"There is nothing *more* than love," she answers. "But position is equal to it. I am descended from earls."

"Position!" He snorts. "This castle and whatever position goes with it are in peril. Come with me, and I will devote myself to protecting you."

"Gianni—" She tweaks his beard and stands up. "I could love you—but you have not favored me with your love. You would rather hear me sing silly songs."

Gianni pushes to his elbows. "I have told you the truth, Madelon. The miracle that changed the baroness changed me. If I am to leave the priesthood it will be for love sanctified by marriage and nothing less."

"Then stay a priest," she pouts. "I will not marry for romance. My parents have found a husband for me who matches my position."

"The lad Thierry trampled in the melee?" Gianni sulks.

Madelon wrinkles her nose. "Mercy, no. *He* was merely someone to sport with because you wouldn't." She wraps a curl about one finger and says with studied indifference, "I am to marry Hubert Macey, the earl of Y Pigwyn's eldest son."

Thunder mutters louder, and a chill breeze rustles the hedges. "But I swear—I am in love with you, Madelon."

"Then show me." She brushes his cheek with her lips. "There is plenty of time left for love," she says nonchalantly. "Marriage need not impede."

Rain dances down from the hills like silver dervishes. Wind tatters the flowers, swatting petals and leaves into the air.

Gianni sits where Madelon left him, alone now that a disappointed Ummu and Ta-Toh have abandoned their places in the hedges to seek shelter in the gardener's tool shack. Like hooves trampling the garden, the torrent arrives.

The clothes that the dwarf has draped over Gianni darken as they soak up the endless, tiny sorrows of the rain.

*   *   *

Maître Pornic lies naked on the stone floor of the sacristy before the statue of the Virgin Mother. Thomas Chalandon, in the white cassock of an acolyte, kneels beside him. His prayers have been repeated to exhaustion, his knees ache, and he believes the abbot has fallen asleep. Just as he is about to touch the prone monk, Maître Pornic lifts his head.

Thomas helps the abbot to his feet and places the black cassock over his head. "You must go back," Maître Pornic says. "The Holy Mother agrees with me. These are your people."

"Father, I don't understand." Thomas had been woken in the middle of the night by one of the brothers and instructed to meet the abbot in the sacristy, where he found him on his face before the Virgin.

"Word has reached me this night from a sojourner," Maître Pornic explains, his graven countenance gaunt in the glow of the votive candles. "The baroness is erecting a Jewish temple—a synagogue! No altar. No saints. No crucifix. And the poor are building it! This is truly the Devil's work, Thomas."

"But the villagers—" Thomas shakes his head in disbelief. "They are devout. They would not tolerate the heretical changes that the gentry have accepted in the castle. Their simple faith is too strong."

"The baroness is more devious than you know," the abbot moans. "Since she has bequeathed them the droves of hogs from the castle, the villagers adore her. Their stomachs are full, their coffers are no longer empty. Their hearts have been won. To them, the baroness is a Grail-saint. But, remember, Jesus drove demons into swine. This woman is a witch who mocks the Bible. You must return to your people and make them see that."

Thomas is alarmed at the prospect of returning to the castle. Impulsively, he wants to blurt out his fear of the baroness, of the unnatural feelings she stirs in him. *Is this because she is not my grandmother, but a witch?* He says instead, "This is a matter for the bishop. We can assume his censure will put an end to this travesty."

Maître Pornic presses a stick finger to his furrowed brow and closes his eyes to calm his intemperate fears. "I have written to the bishop of Talgarth. I have even written to the pope. But Trinity Abbey and Epynt Castle are far-flung outposts in the frontier. Far more pressing matters concern our holy fathers. This is a problem we must solve ourselves."

"Please, Father, send one of the brothers," Thomas pleads, "an ordained priest, who can represent the Church with the authority of Christ."

"No, Thomas, the people are too ignorant to be saved by ecclesiastical reasoning." In the holy man's stare, Thomas reads such divine longing that he sees no use in arguing the point further.

"I will make my grandmother understand," he swears resignedly.

Clare leads the applause as her granddaughter displays the wedding gown designed by the castle's couturière. Madelon strolls gracefully down an aisle of potted quince in the inner ward's garden, curtsying to the ladies watching from the shade of the arbor. She fans the hem of her pelisson and twirls. It is a flouncy garment made of two cloths sewed together, the inner of fine wool, for the wedding will be late in the autumn, and the outer of sheer white bendal. Above this shimmers a nearly transparent bliaut of green silk with billowy sleeves and a long train. Finest of all is the girdle, a mesh of gold set with agates and sardonyx to protect against fever from the heat of the conjugal union.

Hellene steps up behind her daughter and places the mantle on her shoulders, again of silk daedally embroidered with gold thread and dyed royal purple. As she strolls, pointed shoes of vermilion velvet wink from under her gown. Leora approaches her goddaughter and presents her gift, a small saffron-colored veil held in place by a golden circlet studded with emeralds.

Rachel sighs with admiration and joins with the others in feeling the fabric and adjusting the folds. Then one of the maids whispers in her ear and, after complimenting her great-granddaughter, the baroness steps out of the bright garden and into the gloom of the *palais*.

His ash-blond hair luculent in the aquatic light from the tall windows, Denis Hezetre bows. "The sergeant we sent to

Caermathon has returned, lady. The moneylenders have refused our request. They will lend us not a silver penny."

Rachel's heart drops into her stomach. She thanks Denis and turns away before he can question what she will do now. She does not know herself. With David's eloquent request written to the brethren of Caermathon's Jewish community, she had been confident that they would help her, and, though there are only days left, she has not given any serious thought to the marquess or to Erec.

Back in the garden, Clare catches her eye. The matronly woman's joyful expression falters a moment when she sees the dark look in her mother's face. But Rachel pretends she is adjusting to the noon glare, and the next instant she is smiling and fussing over Madelon's elegant attire. Clare beams with appreciation, and all suspicion flies with the thrushes that are flitting like a rumor from shrub to shrub.

Thomas rides down from the hills slowly. Instead of his white cassock, he wears a plain brown riding tunic, gray leggings, and boots. Since dawn, when he began his journey, he has been praying to the Holy Spirit for counsel. How can he convince his grandmother to dissolve this heretical Yeshua cult? And, more to the point, how can he constrain his own stray impulses?

His only recourse is to convince himself, as have Guy and Maître Pornic, that this woman is truly not Ailena Valaise, that the miracle did not happen. Yet, did not God answer his prayer in the tilt yard, when he invoked His help in the name of his grandmother? That assures him that she must be who she claims to be.

As for his unholy attraction to her, that may be a further affirmation: her beauty is of another time, from long before he was born; and his desire for her is but a recognition, a remembrance of the beauty that inspired the carnal love that brought his mother, and then him, into the world.

Thomas's feeble ruminations fall away as he enters the village. A handful of villeins in their fields, who were wont always to ignore him unless directly addressed, wave at him amicably. Where are the usual idlers and beggars who lurk on the outskirts? He stops before the hut of the blind woman, as he habitually does on his way through the village, but she is not home. Legless Owain, who spends his days sitting listlessly under the large oak in the village square, is gone, too. And the village idiot, usually leering from one of the alleys, is nowhere to be seen.

The pen of each cottage is bursting with swine, and each villein seems to be sporting new pig leather garments.

Atop Merlin's Knoll, silhouettes traipse in and out of view. Thomas rides through the switching grass and a haze of midges, following a sparse goat trail past a thorn hedge and a twisted apple tree that has tasted lightning. Outcropped rocks crown the hill, a wreath of mighty stones, each one erect but bent like old women.

At the crest is Aber, the village idiot, lugging away stone debris in a barrow. Behind him, leaning against one of the ancient ritual stones, Siân the blind woman polishes a boulder, working by feel and accompanying her effort with a spritely tune. Legless Owain is beside her, chipping away at the stone. In fact, all the village's idlers are here, hammering at the stray boulders and digging ditches under the supervision of the old rabbi, who sits in a high-backed chair wrapped in a blanket though the summer sun swelters.

Thomas considers for a moment if some spell has been cast, when he notices on the gorse rough below Harold Almquist and Denis Hezetre riding off to the hunt—with the hair of their temples braided like Jews! Stunned, he mutters a hasty prayer under his breath, pulls his steed around, and rides toward the castle.

At the toll bridge, he dismounts and tethers his horse. Across the road, in the expansive garden, he spots his young nieces picking flowers while, farther off, meandering through the maze of herbs, two troubadours sing gaily. A couple sits up from under the ancient elms and waves languidly. With some shock, he sees that they are his parents, lying voluptuously in the shade like lovers.

In a trance, Thomas enters the garden. He has not seen his family use this part of the castle since he was a child—not since Grandmère came here with her troubadours. Ummu is glimpsed among the cherry trees—and is that a woman's chemise fluttering under that hedge? For an instant, he believes he has just spied a woman's bright hair drawing quickly out of sight. But before he can explore further, his mother calls to him.

The troubadours' music swells closer, and Clare and Gerald

greet their son with burbling laughs. They lure him into a giddy dance-of-the-chaplet and enquire what has brought him back from the abbey. Too perplexed by their antic behavior to respond, he asks after Grandmère and is led through the green shade of the elms to a field where the baroness is involved in a spirited game of blindman's buff.

When Rachel sees him, she stops, and the laughter falls away from her face. Tense, conflicting feelings knot in her: hopeless desire twines with the fear of discovery, and thinly overlaying it all, the petulance she felt when Thomas left the castle without saying goodbye to her.

She calls him over, and Hellene and Leora try to get him to play. He demurs. "The abbot sent me. I must talk with Grandmère."

Leora covers her mouth in mock surprise, and Hellene dips in a deep curtsy, feigning awe.

"Mock me, if you must. But this is God's business."

"Oh, do come, Thomas," Rachel pleads impishly. "Play with us. Our Savior said we are to have life and have it more abundantly."

"I do not think he meant in this world, Grandmère."

Rachel laughs jocosely, grabs his hand, tries to pull him into a run. "The good news is God sent His Son to redeem *this* world."

Thomas staggers a few steps and stops. "That we may be reborn into the next."

Rachel pretends to pout, letting go his hand. "There is no mention in the Old Testament that we are to live for an afterlife. And the Old Testament is the Bible Jesus knew. We must do our good here in this world, where God created us."

Hellene and Leora giggle and walk away, deploring their young brother's sullen spirit. Rachel links little fingers with Thomas and guides him away from the distracting troubadours. "I have missed you, Thomas," she confesses, and her stomach tightens. Seeing him again, so unexpectedly and in the midst of her frolic, she is unprepared for the horrific tangle of energy he inspires. Since learning that the moneylenders would not save her, she has given herself entirely to her power. If she is to pay with unhappiness later, she will live as a baroness now and use her authority to bestow on those around her as much pleasure as possible. But she does not know how to please Thomas without betraying her attraction to him.

Thomas's eyebrows are heavy. "Did your vision of the Grail truly instruct you to ignore the Gospels?"

"My vision told me to live as the Savior lived. The Gospels came after Him. I want to return to the original Jesus, the rabbi who lived among the people—who went to the marketplace and to weddings. If we live well now, Thomas, the afterlife will take care of itself."

"You know this verges on heresy, Grandmère. We are to prepare for the Second Coming, to put our store in the glory that awaits us, not in the temporal blandishments of this world."

"Here is where you told me you found the spirit," Rachel breathes. "This is where God lives."

Thomas agrees mutely. Suddenly his mission feels foolish. Here is a woman who has drunk from the Grail, showing him the inexhaustible earth as though it were the true Church. Who is he to disagree? And who is the abbot to say otherwise?

For now—until it is taken away from her—this is her land, Rachel thinks. She *is* the baroness. She knows this will not last long, that each day is more rare than the last. And for that reason she wants this limitless beauty to redeem all her dread, to compensate all the festering fear for herself and her grandfather and the people of this land who believe in her. No urge, no indulgence can be ignored now, and she surrenders to the impulse of fitting herself into the huge glory of this landscape by darting down the slope and hopping across the stones of the slender brook.

Thomas follows reluctantly, but as he jumps the brook, the mossy tang of the earth strikes him almost like a blow—and when he lights on the other side he is remembering flowers and field grass that have been dead for ten years. That was the last time he had run down this slope. Since then, all the books that he has read, that he had expected would lift him higher than the great mountain wall in the west, higher than the ladder of wood smoke rising from an orchard grove where an old cottage is snugly hidden, higher, he had thought, than childhood, have only weighed him down. With the soft turf under his boots exhaling bogland smells, he runs along the clattering brook and into heaven.

Rachel and Thomas lope through the gorse, startling rabbits, skirting sudden shrubs of pink and white wild roses, leaping a bank of honeysuckle and collapsing with surprised shouts into a whole field of foxgloves. Thomas falls on Rachel, and, when he throws himself off her, she holds on and follows, flops atop him. And then their faces are very close, smudged with pollen, noses touching, startled eyes staring into each other's depths, seeing leaf-towers and clouds.

Without thought, Rachel turns her face and kisses Thomas full on the mouth.

Thomas shoves her away and sits up, horrified.

Rachel manages a frightened laugh at the glare of lightning in his face. "It is but play, Thomas."

"Grandmère!" He is on his knees, his arms outstretched to keep her away.

Rachel is too startled to face him; she looks about at the white flames of flowers and the immovability of the grassy hills under the chapel of clouds and is amazed at how savagely young the world is. She wants to live here without illusion of any sort. "Thomas, there is a thing you must know." She strives to bring forth the words that will divulge her secret—but instead she recalls her grandfather and the threat to him if Thomas cannot bear the truth alone. "I am . . . drawn to you."

"Please—" Thomas stands, backs away a step. The touch of her body atop his lingers, and the sight of her staring at him dazed and frail in the hard sunlight swells his heart. "Say no more. I am afraid for us."

"I'm sorry." She looks down at the matted grass where they had lain. "This is my fault."

"No." As the initial shock dims, he steps closer and offers his hand. "Don't you see?" He helps her stand and stares powerless into her baffled eyes. "I am drawn to you, too."

Rachel's heartbeat pauses expectantly, until she turns away. "I'm behaving foolishly—like a young woman."

"You are a young woman," Thomas answers. "But it is I who am the fool. You were right to call me Parsifal. I am on a journey that seems never to end—riding to the abbey and back, trying to discover whom I serve, Maître Pornic and the Church or—something else."

"The truth of yourself," Rachel says, daring to meet his blue stare.

"And what is that truth?"

Rachel smiles plaintively. "Like Parsifal, you must quest till you find out." She releases his hand. "It's taken me a lifetime."

"Was it worth it?" he asks, following her through the flowery field. "What have you learned?"

"That we must get back to the castle and carry on with our lives," she replies, determining to master herself more strictly for the sake of her grandfather.

Thomas strides to her side, both oppressed and elated—contrarily pleased that she carries the same yearning for him that he does for her. As they stroll, he asks, "How will you pay the king's men?"

Rachel frowns, and the wide-open world seems to darken and narrow to the tall horizon of static trees surrounding them like a piked wall. "I don't know."

"Mother has collected some money gifts from the visiting earls," Thomas offers helpfully. "Though I imagine that's hardly enough."

Rachel is not listening. The relief she has stolen for the last few days is gone.

"You *are* a beautiful woman, Grandmère. Surely, you can marry well."

Rachel suppresses a shiver. "When I marry, it will be for love," she says, but her voice sounds hollow. As they cross the brook, she considers that her future wears two faces: the toothless marquess or brawny Erec. She must choose.

Ta-Toh leaps down from a pear tree at the edge of the orchard and bows to the baroness before running with a chittering laugh into the trimmed hedges. Momentarily, Ummu leaps out, says in a loud voice, "Baroness! Master Thomas! Have you seen my knight? The rabbi has directed me to bring him at once to Merlin's Knoll, to discuss where the basins of holy water will be placed."

"There's no holy water in a synagogue," Rachel says. "Oh, you must mean the *mikvah*, the basin for the ritual baths and baptisms. I don't think Gianni would know about that."

"Rabbi has been instructing me," Gianni says, stepping out from behind the hedge, leading Madelon by her small finger. He bows to Rachel, nods to Thomas. "This lady and I were promenading in the sanctuary of the garden's edge. She is seeking my spiritual counsel on her impending betrothal to the good Hubert Macey."

"Well, Sir Gianni," Ummu says, backing away. "If you've imparted your counsel, then perhaps you will come to Merlin's Knoll."

"Forthwith," Gianni says. He kisses Madelon's hand, bows again to Rachel, and scurries off with Ummu, Ta-Toh scampering behind.

Rachel and Thomas share a knowing look and face Madelon.

"Love makes fools of us all." She shrugs. "Did you enjoy your walk?"

Thomas wanders through the garden, trailing behind the others on their way back toward the castle. *Madelon—and Canon Rieti?* He is shocked that a priest would betray his vows. And he is shocked that his grandmother has kissed him—and shocked that he likes her flirting. *This land is bewitched!*

He gazes at her walking far ahead of him, hand in hand with his mother, giggling with his sisters, sharing sly glances with Madelon.

It was just a kiss. Yet that kiss has ripped through his mouth and his throat and locked on his soul. He limps through the languor of the flowers, head bowed beneath the kingdom of the clouds.

That night, a green feather of icy light appears among the stars, a comet, a terrible portent, that alarms everyone in the castle and in the village. Evil burns coldly in heaven; the chapel bell splashes chimes of fear. Gianni Rieti says Mass to a packed worship-house, and though many of the guildsmen grumble that heaven is unhappy with their new liturgy, Gianni sanctifies the wine and the bread in Hebrew, and Rachel, as ever, is first to drink of the cup.

"The ax is laid to the root of the tree," Rachel overhears one of the guildsmen complaining when the Mass is over and the eerie-tailed star is still in the upper air.

Alone in the chapel with David after the others have left, she asks, "What does this omen mean?"

"Shoovaw yisroel kee chawshaltaw banvonechaw," he answers. "'Return O Israel to the ways of holiness, for you have stumbled and failed in your ambition, in your passion for material splendor.' We are done here, Granddaughter. We must leave."

In the dim candlelight, his beard looks silky, pure white, his face weathered dark and sunken under the luminous orbs of his eyes. Tears float in her eyes, but she holds them back. "You are not well, certainly not well enough to return to Jerusalem. The voyage will kill you, Grandfather."

"But I will die knowing you have found your way home."

Later, in her chamber, those words flog her, barbed with the word *home.* She has no home; and when she tries to remember her childhood home, she sees the dead Jews strewn in the woods, many with their hands cut off at the wrist and nailed to tree trunks.

From her window, she can see the streak of the comet, and she knows it is a death star, too ill an omen to risk a voyage with her frail grandfather no matter how much he yearns for their freedom. She must find a way to defy that portent, to use its evil charm for the good of David and the others who need her to act as the baroness.

Rachel opens the chest she has brought from Jerusalem and takes out a curved dagger in a jeweled sheath, the dagger that the old baroness had purchased for her son long ago. She draws the knife and sees her unsteady gaze in its mirroring blade. Ten years before, if she had not gone to her secret place on the knoll, if she had stayed home with her sisters and brothers, Father would have cut her throat, too, bled her like the Paschal lamb, sacrificed her to God to keep her from the atrocities of the mob.

She holds the keen edge of the knife to her throat, tight enough to feel its sting and the rhythm of her pulse. Mother would have laid her out on the bed next to her sisters, and her blood would have pooled with theirs and with Mother's when Father placed her among them. She would be dead ten years now, a twelve-year-old girl forever, never having seen the Holy Land, nor Ailena Valaise, nor this castle, nor yet the death star above it. And the voices that have been ever since an echo in her living blood would never have been heard. *Never.* And yet—*always*—for she would have been among them.

Dark, dark, dark—they have all gone into the dark. Her pulse trips faster against the sharp edge. *Father and Mother and all their children—but one—gone into the dark, into the* btzelem elokim, *into the shadow of Almighty God, where the darkness is the light, and the silence the singing.*

Dizziness makes her stagger and she lowers the blade. Only Father could have killed her righteously, only Father and God— and now only God. But God has many hands in this world, and she chooses finally to bare her throat to them and to take her place among her family.

Rachel puts the knife back in its scabbard. From under neatly folded bliauts and robes, she notices the five vessels of hardened red clay that contain the Saracens' mysterious Greek fire. She lays each of them on the windowsill like icons and places before them the Seljuk dagger. Above them, the comet's tail gleams in the sky like the edge of a sword.

Thomas Chalandon waits all day in the *palais* for his grandmother. Servants and Denis Hezetre come and go from her chamber, but Ailena will not admit anyone else to come near her.

At vespers, she attends Mass, but she is withdrawn and ignores all his entreaties to speak with him. She stares at the crucifix as though seeing the tortured form for the first time, and afterward, she retreats immediately to her room.

Thomas thinks he understands. Just yesterday, she had gamboled with him in the flowery fields—had kissed him on the mouth! She is as tormented by her desire and ashamed of her weakness as he. *God!* he cries from his heart. No woman has ever stirred more than token desire in him—and now: *I lust for my grandmother!* He prays for forgiveness and for relief from the haunted passion he feels for the dark-eyed woman.

Movements in the courtyard catch his eye, and he sees squires leading out four saddled horses. Moments later, Denis, Harold, Gianni, and an unknown, shadow-slim knight emerge from the *palais*, sling saddlebags over their steeds, and mount up. The unknown knight confers with the others, and Thomas leans forward to see who he is. He wears black leggings and boots, a sable tunic, and a cap that does not cover his black, shoulder-length hair.

The stranger's horse turns, and, with a jolt that stands him upright, Thomas sees the moonlight limn the youthful, pallid features of Ailena Valaise. He presses forward to make sure. But too quickly, she turns and gallops across the courtyard with her retinue, and his call is lost in the din of the clattering hooves.

Under the ominous gleam of the comet tail high in the night sky, Rachel and her three knights ride swiftly into the forest. Long wands of moonlight penetrate the boughs of birch and mountain ash and fill the woods with a smoky swirl of shadows.

Each of the knights, who had in turn tried to dissuade Rachel from this adventure, stares about apprehensively. Only Rachel is calm, preternaturally calm. In her mind, the golden light of the Grail assuages all fear, and she feels close to the arrogance that the Persian magician imprinted on her instincts, close to the predatory spirit of the baroness. The troubling voices in her head are gone now, and she hears only the thudding of the horses' hooves, the crackle of the trampled ivy, and the aimless wind blundering through the canopy. The smell of the loam, dank with night airs, soothes her with the knowledge that *there is only one future for all that lives—and that is the earth. Everything comes to rest there.*

Among the moonbeams streaming through small fir trees, three figures rear up, so sudden and sharp that the horses startle. "Hush! You'll frighten the dead." Erec Rhiwlas and two scrawny comrades step out of the bushes, leading their mounts. "Ailena Valaise, I told your knight this afternoon that this adventure is not for a woman."

"If lives are to be risked for my castle," Rachel replies, "mine will be among them."

"I warn you, Dic Long Knife will kill you as readily as any man."

"Only if he catches me. You said we are to steal this money, not fight for it."

"If we're lucky and the guards let their blood drain quietly, we'll not have to fight. Otherwise, our salvation will be our swords. You'll be in the way, woman."

"Nothing you can say will dissuade me," Rachel says, her mouth set tight.

Erec shakes his head, and his eyebrows bend sadly. "I'm doing this for you, Servant of Birds. I don't want to lose you in the fray."

"You do this for me?" Rachel asks imperiously. "As if there's no gain for you in this business? Lead on, Bold Erec, while there's still moonlight to follow you."

Erec sighs and looks helplessly at Rachel's three companions, who shrug their shoulders in collegial dismay. He mounts, and, leading the pack through the thick-boughed forest, they ride silently into the hills. The wind cuts faster, driving the clouds rapidly across the face of the moon.

After riding steadily uphill, they find woodlands spread below them, and away to the south shines the tiny, golden gem of the castle.

The land dips down into Stygian darkness, and the riders must keep close to see each other. Over winding hill trails and whispery moors, among dark summits and the smoldering fringes of the starry night, they creep down into the forest again, into spinneys of large oaks clasping branches, linking roots in thick, muscled coils so that the horses must carefully feel their way. A stream scurries among dense shrubs, and Erec paces the ford until he finds a shoal where they can cross without sinking above the stirrups.

On the far side, they dismount and tether their steeds among the stream saplings. Taking only their saddlebags with them, they walk a long time through near-impenetrable growth before Erec signals to stop. Through a covert of hazel shrub, he points to squat osier huts in a glade of arching oaks, visible by the dull, evil glow of orange embers in a large firepit.

Erec dispatches his two men with large hanks of raw meat brought to bait the dogs.

"We've only a short time to get our treasure and get out before the dogs are done with their meal," Erec whispers. He indicates that Harold and the Welshmen are to stay behind as lookouts.

With Denis, Gianni, and Rachel behind, Erec darts among the bushes, past a cluster of huts, and emerges beside the pulsing embers of the dying campfire. A man sits sleeping beside the hut, lance across his lap. Swiftly, Erec draws his dagger and plunges it into the guard's throat.

Rachel's heart jumps, and she feels her madness stir and strain inside her. But she forces her attention on the Grail within her, and the terror abates. Erec has cut the cord binding the door and is already inside. Denis follows and then Gianni. Rachel looks for other guards and sees only the huddled shadows of the dogs at the far end of the camp. The wet sound of their feeding trickles on the wind with the slack rustling of branches and an occasional rasping snore nearby.

The interior of the hut clinks with money pouches as the knights stuff them hurriedly into their saddlebags. The musty air glitters with the noise of it, and Erec shushes them. Rachel sees mounds in the black stagnation of the hut, dark outlines traced by the amorphous shine from the low campfire. She lifts a pouch and is startled by the dense weight and loud brattle of the coins.

Wincing with every jingle of the loot, she packs one saddlebag so full she can barely lift it. The other bag contains her five Saracen grenades, which she leaves untied.

Denis and Gianni exit the hut hunched over with the weight of their sacks. Erec ushers Rachel out ahead of him. As they cross the threshold a sudden yelling scorches the night. The dogs spin about and charge across the glade. Doors bang open, shadow shapes lurch out with lances and staves. The clang of swords and shouts rips from all sides.

They are surrounded; and Erec motions the others to cut their way through the dogs while he stands off Dic Long Knife's men. But at the first cry of alarm, Rachel has thrown two of her grenades into the sleepy fire. They explode in streaking flames and whirling sparks that hang in the sky, and come down as fiery talons.

With broad strokes of his sword, Erec clears a path through the startled men, and the raiders flee among the huts. Gianni and Denis push Rachel ahead of them and hack at their pursuers.

Rachel pulls out another grenade, but in the rush of their flight, there is no time to ignite it. When they reach the shrubs, she looks back, sees Gianni hurtling past her, grimacing with fear, and Denis standing, swinging his broadsword double-handed.

Hands trembling, Rachel crouches, yanks out her firestone and flint and sparks the fuse on a grenade. It lobs over Denis's head and erupts in the air, showering the violent silhouettes with veils of flame. Denis peels away as Rachel hurls another bomb. Its blast robes men in fire, and she stands momentarily transfixed, watching fighters drop their weapons and dash aflame among the trees, human shapes of screaming radiance.

Erec seizes Rachel and drags her away. At the horses, Gianni and the Welshmen are hauling the heavy sacks onto the backs of the horses. Denis is bent over, and when he straightens, his hands come away from his chest black with blood. Rachel bites back a cry and moves to him, but Erec stops her.

"Have you more of your devil's fire?" He points to the shadows advancing through the glare among the trees.

Numbly, Rachel takes out the last of the grenades. Erec snatches it, strikes a spark to its fuse as he has seen her do, and pitches it into the midst of the attacking tribe. With a throb of thunder and a clout of searing brilliance, a red holocaust flares among Dic Long Knife's men, and they scatter, shrieking with anguish and fear.

Gianni helps Denis onto his white stallion, and the two ride together, using Denis's mount as a pack animal. Erec orders his two men to lead them out, and he follows close behind Rachel. Once across the rushing stream and up the steep bank, they pause and look back at the last serpents of fire writhing and vanishing into true darkness.

The last stars are gasping overhead by the time Castle Valaise comes into view, the stone fortress sulking in its noose of river. Denis is unconscious, but Gianni keeps assuring Rachel he is still alive.

"When the king's men depart," Erec promises, "I will come back for you." He slaps half the saddlebags over his horse. "You were brave, Servant of Birds. You will make a worthy wife for this chieftain."

He offers his hand. She takes it, and it feels resolute as steel.

* * *

"God is laughing," Denis rants.

Rachel has had him placed in her bed, and the castle physician has packed his chest wound with purslane and parsley. "He has lost too much blood," the physician announces. "He is raving. The angels and devils are fighting for what remains."

While the physician retreats to his apothecary to prepare a blood fortifier of toad gall and gold dust, Rachel, Gianni, Ummu, and Harold attend the wounded man.

"God is laughing at you," Denis husks. "Look at you all, standing, staring. You think I'm going to die." His eyeballs roll up white.

Gianni and Ummu, who have attended the dying often enough to know, share a dark look.

"God has all the answers," Denis whispers, eyes fluttering. "He seeks questions. Ask more questions! God craves questions." He laughs, stiffens, then sags.

Thomas enters Rachel's chamber, and Harold gestures for silence. "Denis is sleeping. He has been wounded."

Thomas knows, having spoken with the physician. And he has looked into the saddlebags heaped in the front hall of the *palais* and seen the silver coin. "From where did this money come?" he asks Rachel when she steps from the bedside.

"From a tribesman called Dic Long Knife."

"The bandit?" Thomas regards her smudged, desperate face with broad surprise. "You're mad to risk so much for money. Now Denis lies dying in your bed!"

Rachel takes his hand imploringly. "Pray for him, Thomas." Her face, exhausted with sorrow, is urgent. "He must not die for this! And pray for me, for surely I will go mad." Already the sight of Erec's blade plunged into the guard's throat, the razoring cries of the burning men, the ghastly sight of bodies consumed in flame have begun to ferment in her; and she fears what terrors will come with sleep.

"Grandmère—the Grail—" Thomas cannot help showing his

disappointment. "You have drunk from the Holy Chalice. God has privileged you above all others. And now you steal, you risk your life and forfeit your knights' lives—for money? Why?"

Rachel blinks. The indictment from this countenance, forlorn as any angel's, scalds.

"I have been returned . . . to my domain to rule," she answers weakly. "Pray for me, Thomas."

"I will pray for Denis," he says slowly, "but I leave God to watch over you. You do not need my prayers." He lets her hand drop, turns and walks away.

Ummu calls Rachel aside. In the passage, he leads her to a window alcove where they will not be overheard. Below, she sees Thomas striding across the courtyard, returning to the donjon, and anger invades her sorrow: *He doesn't understand. The castle is saved. His mother and sisters will not lose their home.*

"The king's penalty is paid," the dwarf tells her. Ta-Toh climbs from his shoulder onto the windowsill and licks the pane. "You are duly installed as the baroness of this small realm. Why now do you insist on this ruse?"

Rachel continues to stare out the window. *He is bluffing,* she thinks, too emotionally wrung from the long night to care. *He cannot possibly know.* "The truth or a lie—the world's emptiness must be filled."

Ummu stands back, startled by the depth of this woman's reply. "I am not saying that you must declare your true identity to the world, my lady. That would destroy you, certainly. But those dear to you must know. You must disabuse Thomas and Gianni. These are souls of glass, fragile souls that kindle only with the light that shines into them. Do not impart lies to them."

Rachel looks down vacantly at the little man and hugs herself. "I've never heard you so serious. Where is your wit today, Ummu?"

"It lies bleeding with Denis—who might well be Gianni, the man who carries my soul. If I am to lose my soul, dear lady, I will forsake it only for the truth."

"There is that strange word again," she says, feeling briefly touched by the power of that word, seeing herself as a wastrel wandering the country lanes with her grandfather, their feet wrapped in rags. The memory leaves her shaken, and she must touch the signet ring to remember all that has happened since. "What is the truth, Ummu?"

"Not what you pretend to be."

Rachel drops her arms and looks out the window again, watching sparrows flutter against the wall ivy. "Do you not yourself pretend?"

"I am a dwarf. No pretense will change that."

She looks back at him sadly. "Who do you want me to be?"

"Who you really are. Tell me who that is. No more pretending. No more lies."

"The truth sees me as I see the truth." She sits on the ledge, and Ta-Toh crawls into her lap. "After all that has befallen me, I am not at all sure who I am, or even was."

Ummu frowns. "And you are not what you are. That much I know."

"Are you so sure, Ummu?" she asks, squarely meeting his dark gaze.

"I do not believe in miracles. Look at me! If there were a God of love, would He have shaped me so?" He clicks for Ta-Toh, and the monkey leaps into his arms. "The only miracle is that so many people in this brutal world still believe in miracles."

"She has the silver," Roger Billancourt announces to Guy, Thierry, and Branden Neufmarché as he rides over to them. They are standing on a hill crest with the reins of their horses in their hands. In the distance Castle Valaise lifts her lean towers.

"The villeins know all about it." Roger dismounts, chewing his lower lip. "No attempt at secrecy has been made. She raided Dic Long Knife's camp with Erec the Bold."

"*She* did?" The corners of Branden's long mouth turn downward. "She is a doughty old girl, I'll say that for her."

"The foray was not without cost," Roger adds. "Denis is gravely wounded. He may already be dead."

The shiny-faced Branden smooths a wrinkle in his tunic.

"Denis—Hezetre? The archer. Your old chum, isn't he? I recall your mother telling my père some years ago now that you and Denis were more than just fond of each other—How does that work for the two of you?"

Guy swings around to clout Branden, but Roger seizes his arm and hauls it back.

"Does that offend you?" Branden gloats and casts a glance over his shoulder at the dozen lancers mounted at the spur of the hill. "I'm merely curious. I mean since losing your root in Eire, how do you do it?"

Guy's face clenches, and he says through gritted teeth, "Shut up!"

"Hard luck about him, though," Branden says complaisantly. "Perhaps you had better hie back and see if your mama has truly found the coin for the king's penalty. That will change our plans somewhat, no? I don't think it would be wise for us to siege a tax-paying legate of the king for no more reason than your greed."

Guy stares at Branden through slitted eyes, then turns away abruptly, mounts, and gallops off.

Roger purses his lips, assessing the stout, weak-chinned man before him in his crisp blue tunic with the gold chaplet resting in his vaporous strawberry hair. "Use a little restraint with your tongue, Sir Branden," he advises. "Guy may be under your thumb now, and we do need your protection. But we are your best weapons against Castle Valaise, whoever may occupy it."

Branden glares and says coldly, "Consider this partial payment for the siege of Castle Neufmarché, which you failed to complete. And also consider—now that the baroness has her money, you are weapons I may no longer need."

Roger climbs onto his horse. "You may need us more than you know. Ailena did not enlist Erec the Bold's help for free. It is said she has agreed to marry him. Who will your allies be then—when the barbarians are raiding you from their own castle?"

Branden runs his tongue slowly over his teeth as he ponders this. "I will trust in your vicious grasping, Billancourt. You took the castle from Ailena once before, for Gilbert—now take it again for Guy. Use my men to take the silver from her if you can. And do not forget who has been your ally at this dire time." He turns and signs for his soldiers to follow Guy to Castle Valaise.

Roger bows his head in gratitude. "The lands we promised will be yours in perpetuity."

"And no more sieges, Roger, please."

Roger smiles grimly. "Never."

The gray-whiskered knight rides off, and Branden watches glumly. If he could trust his men to kill Lanfranc and his warmaster, he would, Branden thinks. But his men admire these predatory foes, these soldiers' soldiers who savor the smell of horseflesh and who sleep more soundly on the ground than in a bed. Only fealty to his dead father has kept his soldiers faithful to him, though he is not even a pallid shadow of the gallant warrior his père had been. He would rather entertain earls and flirt with their daughters than hunt or ride or play the gruesome war games his sergeants find so engrossing. His troops would loathe him for murdering Guy and Roger outside the field of combat, and might even defy his orders to do so, and go over to their side. *No,* Branden tells himself. *Far better to keep these devils in our debt.*

Branden turns to Thierry. "You've said practically nothing since you've come here, lad. Tell me, as an erstwhile enemy, what do you say will come to pass between your charming uncle and his blessed mother?"

Thierry watches Guy and Roger riding through the trees and says in a somber voice, "Only blood will answer that question."

Denis winces awake. Guy's angry face bends close. "Dic Long Knife tried to cut your heart out—but there wasn't one there, was there?"

"You took it from me long ago," Denis rasps, his throat parched.

Guy's tar-black eyes glister. "Here's some water, drink." He holds his friend's head up and places a full cup to his lips. "Slowly, now."

Denis falls back, water running down his chin to the blood-sopped bandages across his chest. "I'm thirsty."

"Then you're going to live." Guy feels the flaccidity in Denis's muscles, the utter exhaustion, and he is afraid. "The more miserable you feel, the stronger the hold of your flesh."

"I'm miserable."

"Good." He thrusts his jaw forward. "If you die, I'll kill the bitch who did this to you."

Denis closes his eyes wearily. "Don't harm her, Guy. She is a valiant woman."

"Bosh!"

"She is. Took every risk we did and pulled us out. She pulled us out."

"Be quiet now." With a soft cloth, he dabs sweat from the wounded man's brow.

Denis forces his eyes open to search Guy's face. Only he has ever seen tenderness in Guy, and his look brightens with the hope that he can use his old friend's love to save the Lady of the Grail. "Promise me you won't harm her."

"Would you believe me?"

"Your mother has changed. She is not the viper she once was."

"Be quiet now and rest."

"Promise me."

"My word. Now sleep. I will see you when you wake."

Denis's lids close, his lips move, barely audible, "Ailena has the silver. The twentieth day of July ..."

"Saint Margaret's," Guy says. "I know. She will pay the king's men. You did well to help her. Now rest."

"Your debts are paid," Denis whispers. "Leave her be."

The villagers stand mutely in the street, watching the soldiers under Neufmarché's raven's-head banner toppling drying racks, stabbing thatch roofs, rummaging through grain bins.

"The coin must be here," Guy gripes, kicking over a rain barrel. "Our man saw it taken to Merlin's Knoll, and we know now it's not there."

"All we know is we don't know where to look," Roger mumbles and sits taller in his saddle. "Watch out now. The kitten is crossing the bridge with William at the point."

"Hurry, you men!" Guy shouts. "Search every woodpile, every loft, every scuttle. The coin is here, I know it."

"She's the Devil's whore to hide three hundred pounds where

men who can smell silver can't find them," Roger complains.

A cheer leaps up from the villagers as Rachel and her men gallop into the town. Her sergeants surround her, swords drawn, but Rachel budges her horse through them to face Guy. Her blood roars in her ears so loudly the world seems almost soundless. Within the turmoil in her blood, she can hear the thoughts of the baroness: *To die here in front of all will complete my legend and doom my enemies.*

Guy knows this, and he pulls back from her righteous glare. "You have won by wiles," he hisses. "But winning power and holding it are different contests."

"Dark, dark, dark—" Rachel chants. "Your hands reach for silver and close on the dark."

"She is a witch!" Guy shouts to the villagers. "A witch has possessed you!"

Rachel's sergeants surge forward.

"Halt!" she orders. "He is still my blood." She banishes him with a toss of her head. "Begone and do not return, Guy Lanfranc. You are not worthy of ruling, but only of being feared."

Guy looks away, but Roger holds her gaze, his rheumy brown eyes glinting again with recognition. *The old baroness lives. The canny bitch—she has gotten her revenge by going over to God. But then the Devil can't be far afield. And he has never been one to take defeat lightly. He will find her weakness and reveal it to us. Patience.* He nods acquiescence and gathers the men with a shout.

"William, are you with us?" Guy calls.

William nudges his horse forward, and Guy turns and rides off with his minions.

With Thierry and William gone with Guy, Hellene tries to soften her dismay by spending more time with Madelon, preparing her for her wedding and married life to come. "Perhaps there will be a place with Hubert Macey's people for your brother Hugues," Hellene hopes. "Maybe the earl will want Thierry in his charge, too. He's a valiant knight. We saw that in the tourney, didn't we?"

Madelon wearily agrees with her mother. She tries on her wedding garments yet again so that Hellene can busy herself making adjustments that are not necessary. She listens patiently to her mother's endless assessment of Hubert Macey's fine qualities—his father's bravery at the battle of Drincourt in Normandie where he slew the count of Boulogne, his mother's pedigree of the house of Champagne, his capacious, opulently appointed castle pensioned by the three prosperous villages adjoining it, his burgeoning stables, his many dogs. But there's very little about him, for, as she recalls from the few times she has glimpsed him at festivals and fairs, he has few physical qualities to commend him, being short, pocked, and squeaky-voiced.

When she can get away from her mother's doting attentions and boundless advice on how to comport herself as an earl's wife, she steals time with Gianni. With him, she can be silly or serious, talk about his travels or her love of *chanson*. And there is the perpetual game of glamour, trying to inveigle him in amorous regard; though, by now, she has accustomed herself to the fact that he is too stubborn in his renewed faith to be seduced by her erotic mischief.

From her one experience with the young knight she brought to her bed during the tourney, she considers sporting to be vigorous and pleasurable but not as gratifying as she had expected. The seduction was much more thrilling than the sweaty, athletic act— though she suspects that the experience might be more ravishing with a man of Gianni's expertise.

Of greater value to her than romance—now that she must endure her mother's anxious prattle without the intervention of her twin or her father—is Gianni's friendship. He often seeks her out in the gardens, where they can sit close together without being seen and talk intimately about the important truths of life—the beauty of music and poetry, the expectations of God, and their incessant debate about the preeminence of love or station in marriage.

Even when they sit together without talking, she is happy to be near him. *Is this love?* she wonders, linking little fingers with him and listening to a kind of quiet different than silence.

David sits before a small fire in the shell of the half-built synagogue. On all sides of him the walls stand, mostly just columns of stone with spaces for giant windows. Above, a canopy of stars twists like smoke. Where the grand door of the temple will be, the comet's claw scratches the darkness low in the sky.

Rachel steps through the doorframe, wispy as a wraith in her silken raiment. Her grandfather rises, pulls a workbench against the wall for her to sit. "You come so late to visit."

"I couldn't sleep thinking of you out here." She sits on the bench, and he returns to his place on the ground before the twig fire. "You're too frail to be exposed to the weather like this. Come back to the castle, Grandfather."

David shrugs. "This is my home now. I will not leave here until we leave for the Holy Land."

"Grandfather, don't talk like that."

David juts out his lower lip, stares up at her from under shaggy brows.

"Don't look at me with such sadness," she pleads. "You know I love you."

"If you love me, then you will love your own people, and you will come back to Jerusalem with me." He holds up a thick hand to stay her objection. "I know. You say I am too old to make the journey. But look where this old man chooses to live." He gestures at the mortared stones and the scaffolding. "These hands have hewn wood and dug graves." He presses his fists to his chest. "I am stronger than you know, Rachel. Stronger than you want to know."

"Tomorrow the king's men will come for their money. I will pay them, and our place here will be secure."

"Secure? Ailena's son will cut your heart out, if he can. And the villagers say the wild man from the hills expects to take you for his wife. You are not secure."

Rachel casts her gaze up at the river of stars. "In Jerusalem, the people know I am mad."

"What do they know? That you talked some nonsense when the Paschal lamb was sacrificed? They know the horror you have lived—*we* have lived. Do you think we are the only ones? Many of our people understand. You will find one good man among them, and you will make a life together."

"I have a life here for now, until the spring when you are stronger and the seas are calm."

"You have death here." He spits into the fire. "You are making a glorious death for yourself."

Her jaws clamp together, and her shoulders sag.

David quails before the hurt in her face. "You have done all that the baroness required, Rachel. She would be proud and amazed at how well you have fulfilled her dream. To these people, you are Ailena Valaise. Sometimes I think so myself—and it frightens me. Nothing good can come of that."

"Grandfather, I do feel the baroness in me."

"She is not who you are."

"But she is!" Rachel's face looks childlike in the fire glow. "I have drunk from the Grail."

David stiffens, afraid of what she means.

"The baroness told us the Grail is a vessel to hold the soul." She cups her hands and stares in silence at her grandfather. A long moment passes before she finds the strength to add: "I lost my soul with my family. My soul spilled out with their blood. Yours did, too, Grandfather. Your soul spilled out of you, too—but I became your vessel. I carried your soul for you. You went on living because you had to care for me. I carried your soul. I gave you a reason to live."

David stares dazedly, and whispered words come from him: "*Af bhain hawyoo boso hanais*—woman is not cast aside—she shares."

"I carried your soul, David Tibbon!" she repeats keenly. "I was empty as any cup, empty of everything but your soul—until Ailena gave me a vessel, a name, an identity, a role to play. And slowly my soul began to fill that cup. You had to make way for me. You had to let me become Ailena. And you did, because it is what God wants. He gave me this vessel to hold my soul. He asks only that I drink of it."

David shakes off her spell. "You speak nonsense. God commands us to honor Him by being who we are, who He made us. You are a Jew, not a baroness."

"*God* has made me a baroness, Grandfather." Her features shine with conviction. "Don't you see? I did not seek this. But now that the cup is in my hands, I must drink of it."

"But why, Rachel? Why must you drink of this cup? Come away with me. You have your own life."

"My *own* life?" Her voice quakes. "What is that life, Grandfather? I am the daughter of a man who killed his own wife and children—for God! And who is God to want that? Why did He answer our family's lifelong devotion to Him and His laws with a massacre? Did we transgress? Were we unfaithful? You know in your heart we were not. Then why are your prayers not answered? Why did God let the gentiles kill your children and their children? Why has God permitted us to live and them to die? What is this life God has left me? Am I to go on now and be a good Jew as though I had not witnessed the damnation of my whole family?"

"Stop it!" David hides his face. Her words echo the grief that has resounded in him for the past eleven years, pummeling him with questions neither he nor the wisest rabbis of Jerusalem could answer. The sorrow he has kept silent for the sake of his granddaughter rises to claim him.

Rachel breaks off, kneels beside the old man. With her arm across his back, she feels the sobs breaking in the hollow of his chest. She has never seen him weep. "Grandfather—"

He shakes his head.

"Grandfather—I *do* love you. I would have died long ago, in a dark wood, in a snowy bramble if not for you. You are God's salvation to me. Please, forgive me for having no faith in Rachel Tibbon. This life as a baroness, this is the only life I could say is my own—the only hope. I covet it. But for you, because I love you, Grandfather, I will give it up. Tomorrow, when the king's men are paid, we will leave. And I will try again to find faith in myself and in our God."

David hears her voice as in a buffeting wind. He hears the salty taste of pain that accompanies her words, and a revelation opens to him with bitter clarity. He wants to leave this alien land; he would be happy to die on the way, knowing his Rachel has found her way back, not just to Jerusalem and her people but to her God. But he sees now that this hope is a vain ambition. If she is to find her soul, he must help her search here, where God, in all His shameless mystery, has placed them.

"Grandfather, forgive me, I spoke without thinking."

David shakes his head. "No, Granddaughter." He sits taller,

wipes the tears from his dark cheeks. "It is I who beg your forgiveness. 'Can man hide in the crevices and I, God, shall not see him?'" He frowns ruefully at his own arrogance. "I wanted to hide you away from the atrocities. I wanted to hide you among the people, in sanctity, far away from the abominations and the depth of pain, in a small house of a small community in a small corner of the world. But that is not to be. God sent the baroness to find us. That is His mercy. You recognize it—but I have coveted more. Now I see, I am not worthy of more."

"Do not say that."

"It is true, Rachel. All my life, I have had everything—servants, learning, family. I trusted wholly in God. More. I rested my whole life on God. But now, I see, we must stand alone. That is Adam's curse. We must stand alone among the glories and the atrocities— just as you are doing. You have taught me that. And finally, I see. Yes, it is true. We cannot lean on God, for He leans on nothing."

Hellene sits by her window, sorrow seething in her. Where have her men gone? Thierry to Saint David's—but he should be coming back soon. Or will he return now that William, her stalwart, reticent William, is banished, to where? What of Madelon's betrothal ceremony and wedding? Will Hubert Macey's family break it off now that the bride's father is an exile? And what of Hugues? This is his twelfth summer, when he is nigh on manhood and needs a father. He will also need a patron if he is to be dubbed a knight— but Uncle Guy, who would have sponsored him, is cast out. That pleases Leora and Mother and Grandmother, but Hellene and her family must pay for that happiness—the Morcars must pay.

Outside, trumpets blare, cheers resound, banners snap. The king's men have arrived. The baroness has won another victory. The sounds of joy come to Hellene from a great distance and arrive thin as starlight.

The king's men parade through the outer gate under the flag of the rampant lion. Furred with dust, heavy-shouldered from long weeks of travel on the king's highways collecting taxes, the thirty men who dismount in the bailey are grateful for the squires who rush forward to unbridle their steeds and for the shrewd guildsmen who are suddenly at their elbows with steins of river-cooled wine and redolent loaves of freshly baked bread.

Among the red-robed tax collectors is the marquess of Talgarth accompanied by three knights in black armor. He waves aside squires and wine vendors, and scans the jubilant crowd for the baroness. He spots her with the royal retinue, a head taller than the captain of the king's men, straight-nosed, pale and smiling as an archaic stone carving.

As the marquess approaches, the baroness leads away the captain, who has a wine cup in one hand, a loaf in the other. Vendors jostle, jongleurs leap and juggle, musicians jangle their instruments, but none of these is substitute for silver coin, and the marquess suspects that the young baroness has led the captain aside to whisper a compromise in his ear. That is why he has come himself, to be sure there are no secret deals.

"I have come to collect my bride," the marquess announces jubilantly, offering his gloved hand to the baroness.

Rachel takes his hand and curtsies. "I am honored that you would remember. I'm not worthy of your attentions."

"Don't play coy with me, Ailena. You know you inflame me. Don't bother collecting your things. Come away with me at once. My knights will see that your possessions are conveyed to Talgarth."

Rachel lowers her eyes. "I will not be coming with you, my lord."

"You agreed—"

"I agreed to marry you," she says, removing her hand, "if I could not pay the debt to the king." She signals, and a drooling idiot wheeling a barrow of stone shards through the merry throng stops before her.

The captain picks up a handful of the pebbles, not comprehending.

The marquess frowns. "Only silver can satisfy our agreement, Ailena."

"Only silver," she concurs and nods at Aber.

The idiot leers and tips the barrow. The marquess rears back from the dusty clatter, hand raised to cuff the stupid lout, but is frozen by the loud jangling of coins.

From under the stone shards, a heap of silver money pours forth, its bright music silencing the rowdy crowd. Faces turn and mouths hinge open to behold the spilled treasure.

"Call over your assayers, Captain," the baroness announces loudly. "Castle Valaise offers full payment of our debt to the king!"

The marquess nails Rachel with a stare of irate amazement. And though she bows her head to him, he sees her victorious smirk. With an affronted snort, he strides off and beckons one of his knights. "Find Guy Lanfranc," he orders. "Tell him that the marquess of Talgarth relinquishes all pretensions to Ailena Valaise. He may do as he pleases with her."

A noisy celebration of brass instruments, tambourines, bass drums, and whistles spills from the bailey onto the inner ward as the king's men partake of the castle's joy. The delirium persists into the night, even under the tufted star of doom. The baroness with the king's captain and Clare and Gerald toast the revelers from the *palais* terrace. Denis is there, too, able to stand long enough to salute the king's flag.

Thomas meanders through the festival, staring into all the laughing, drunken, dazzle-eyed faces and seeing only masks, comic visages, clown variants of men and women caroming off each other, dancing in the wide courtyard of the inner ward and slumped giddily in the alleys of the bailey. *Why are they so happy?*

Morosely, Thomas drifts among the celebrants and wanders out of the crowd into the darkness behind the *palais*. The night breeze here dispels the stink of wine and braised meats, and he smells the perfumes of the garden. He knows that if the penalties had not been paid and the king's men had installed a different baron, the bailey would be as loud with drunken revelry.

He does not know why that disturbs him until he notices a disconsolate wraith sitting alone on the step of the *palais*'s side door. The robed figure, shimmery in the thin moonglow, is his sister Hellene. At the sight of her, he understands how everything in the world can be right except one's heart. He goes over and sits down beside her.

"Uncle Guy's star is fallen," Hellene says, looking up at the green splinter of the comet. "And as he falls, he is taking my William and our Thierry with him."

"The baroness will have them back—if they will relent their ambitions."

Even in the dark, Hellene's sneer is scathing. "This is not the abbey, Thomas. Forgiveness has no magic outside the cloisters—not among men of ambition."

Thomas silently accepts the sting of her rebuke. Ambition has always been what he lacked. He is known for it—refusing to be dubbed, spending his childhood days in the wild fields and forests instead of in the lists, avoiding ordination by hiding in the library. *What is this emptiness I have where other men have ambition?*

"William and Uncle are never coming back," Hellene says and pushes to her feet. "I must decide if I will follow them."

Thomas gets up and walks beside her. "The baroness is a surprising woman, Hellene. She may yet find a way to reconcile with Uncle."

"The baroness—why do you keep calling her that? As if she were a stranger."

"But she is. She's not the grandmère we remember."

"That is Uncle's objection, isn't it? Why should this stranger young enough to be his daughter supplant him? It is not natural." She stops, peers at her brother in the dark. "Do you believe her story? Do you believe she is truly Grandmère made young again?"

"Does it matter what I believe?" He looks away, to the garden, where fireflies glitter. "The whole of creation grows old each winter and is made young again in the spring. Why not a woman?"

A monkey wail lashes the night, and a boy's cries screech from the garden. Hugues comes shrieking out of the darkness, Ta-Toh clasping the back of his head, paws over the youth's eyes.

Thomas grabs the boy, and the monkey bares his fangs with a piercing hiss that makes Hellene scream. Ummu darts from the garden, calling to his beast.

Ta-Toh pulls fiercely at Hugues's hair, then leaps off and runs to his master. "The lad surprised my Ta-Toh. Skulking in the dark like that."

"Following Madelon, Mother," Hugues gripes, rubbing his scalp. "She and the priest are in there together now. In the dark alone!"

Hellene gasps, starts forward, and stops when she sees them emerging. The ingratiating grin on Gianni's face, the look of hurry that neither of them can quite conceal, all reveal too much. Hellene snatches her daughter from Gianni's side even as she protests, "Mother, we were just talking."

"I was but counseling your daughter on the duties of her forth-coming marriage," Gianni adds, and Ummu, with his face turned so only his master can see him, rolls his eyeballs.

"That is a mother's task, Canon," Hellene retorts. "And if there is to be any counseling from you at all, it shall be in the chapel or nowhere."

"But the festival around the chapel is so noisy—" Gianni's excuse trails off as Hellene gruffly leads her wayward daughter back to the *palais*.

Thomas turns to Gianni, frowning sternly. "Are you and Madelon lovers?"

Gianni looks aghast. "I have not touched her!"

"I cannot believe that, Canon."

"It is true." He wrings his hands. "All our time together is spent talking."

"Talking?"

"Yes. She is my soul, Thomas. I am convinced of it—but she does not believe me."

Thomas blinks with confusion. "Your soul?"

"Don't you understand? I am in love with Madelon. I want to marry her. But she will not have me."

Thomas's head jerks back. "You are a priest!"

"One word from her and I will be a priest no more."

"That will hardly satisfy Madelon's parents. Besides, she is to marry Hubert Macey."

Gianni sighs sadly. "So she insists. I am just her toy."

Ummu takes his hand consolingly, Ta-Toh grips the dwarf's other hand, and the three wander back toward the boisterous festi-val, leaving Thomas in the dark among the wisping fireflies.

∘ ∘ ∘

Roger Billancourt and William Morcar sit under a hilltop alder in sight of the pavilion tents where Branden Neufmarché has billeted them. Castle Neufmarché squats in the tree-cluttered distance, its repaired wall obvious from the brightness of the new stones. Nearby, on the pebbly bend of a throbbing stream, watched over by a dozen guardsmen in the shade of a spruce grove, Branden, Guy, and Thierry pace like oxen.

"Look at the slump of our host's shoulders," Roger says. "Can you tell by that what he's thinking?" He does not wait for an answer. "'What shall I do with these four knights?' He has tolerated us this long only because we nearly broke him in the spring. Having us working *for* him is a novelty that is yet appealing. But it wears. Look at the reluctant hang of his head as our Guy tries to bend him to a brief local war with the kitten."

"He will refuse," William predicts.

"'How shall I use these four dangerous knights?' he wonders. 'Shall I send them after Dic Long Knife and have them bring *me* silver coin? Or is it better if I dispatch them to the king to serve his exploits on the Continent?' He is not listening to Guy's strategy. He does not want to attack the Lady of the Grail. She is too well beloved of the villeins. The whole countryside worships her."

"But surely Branden must consider Bold Erec's presence a threat," William offers. "When the Pretender weds him, the barbarians will have a stronghold from which to pillage all of Epynt."

Roger sucks air noisily through his teeth. "Branden must see that to believe. For now, he is only concerned with what to do with us." He casts a sidelong glance at his companion. "If Thierry is to regain his rightful place and not wind up muddied or bloodied in France on the king's exploits, we must keep Branden out of this—if we can."

William chews the corner of his mustache. "How do you propose that?"

Roger says flatly: "The baroness must not live."

"She has paid the taxes and the penalties." William shakes his head. "To slay her outright now would be treason against the king."

"Then we shall not be so outright."

A whisper of dread seeps from between William's lips, and he sits taller, facing the warmaster. "I have not forgotten our last attempt to favor her with an accident, Roger. My son was put at great risk."

"No accidents this time." Roger leans his square head back against the tree trunk and thoughtfully scratches the iridescent scar on his temple. "Something far more tried and true. Something more poetic, too. We will use her love of Jesus to dispatch her to her Savior. Drinking from the Grail sent her to us—why not have the Grail carry her away?"

"I do not understand, Roger."

"Poison, you dolt. We will put poison in the wine cup from which she is always the first to drink at the Mass."

"The first after the priest."

"Dispatch him to heaven, too, I say. Hasn't he already broken his priestly vows lusting with your daughter Madelon?"

William's head jerks about as if cuffed. "No!"

"Are you blind, man? Madelon has been well versed in romance by the foppish ways of Gerald's troubadours and Clare's courtly love. Gianni Rieti is just the rake to take advantage of that."

"He must be defrocked!" William stands, lifted upright by a surge of rage. "I will castrate him!"

"For that, we must catch him outright first." Roger shuts one eye and nods. "And we may—once we get past that devilish dwarf who stands guard for them. I have schooled young Hugues in surveillance, and he will find them out eventually. But we need not reveal Madelon's shame at all. There is her marriage to Hubert Macey to think of. Let the priest remain a priest that he may bless our grail and drink of it before passing it to the Pretender." His brown teeth mesh in a heartless smile. "Are you in with me?"

Erec Rhiwlas rides alone out of the forest into the full clout of noon. Ahead is Castle Valaise, reflected proud-spired in the glittery coils of the Llan, her thunder-dark stones tattered with old ivy. This is his fortress now, won by cleverness and daring—though his father doubts he will ever see the inside of it.

When Erec had spilled his share of Dic Long Knife's booty at his father's feet and told of his adventure with the Lady of the

Grail, Howel only shook his bearded head and said, "Be happy with your silver, son, for the woman who lives a lie has no trouble speaking lies."

Dressed in his finest buffed-skin tunic slashed at the sides to cool him on this hot summer's day, Erec rides proudly to the toll bridge. With a silver coin to the amazed bridge-keeper, who has never seen a chieftain's son or any man in red leather leggings and marten-skin tunic, he gains admission to the toll road. Head high and square-shouldered, he crosses above the white crash of the Llan and rides past the color-splashed garden and the dark naves of the orchards. The drovers look out from the byres, and he waves as he goes by and calls down compliments on the beauty of the red heifers. *My heifers,* he smiles to himself.

At the drawbridge, Erec chats with the arabalisters on the rampart while the porter announces his presence to the castle. He learns about Guy's vain attempt to steal the baroness's silver, and the happy reception of the king's men and how, before they departed reeling with drink and bloated with viands, they renewed the castle's charter.

The porter returns and opens the gate. A squire greets Erec, takes his steed's bridle and leads him across the bailey. Guildsmen and their apprentices pop their heads from their shops, villeins stand and gawk, and children point at the burly, bearded Welshman riding by. Awed whispers of "Erec the Bold" flit among the women at the fountain. Erec smiles and nods.

The far gate opens, and Erec rides for the first time over the second moat and into the inner ward of the Invader's keep. The pavements are broader than he had thought, the flags wide and slick, the *palais* ornately pinnacled as a church, and, beyond, a dazzle of blossoms from a garden under the colossal tower of the donjon. But there is no time to take it all in, for the baroness is stepping from the *palais* to greet him.

Rachel looks tremulous and fragile in her flowing sleeves and pale green bliaut, her hair tumbling past her shoulders, black, with its red highlights glinting in the hard sun. She squints up at him and curtsies, and when his shadow covers her and her dark eyes relax, she is regal.

Erec dismounts, bows, takes her long-fingered hand and is surprised by how callus-coarse it is. She reads his expression and smiles soft as a petal of eglantine. "I'm helping the villeins build a synagogue for the rabbi. The stonework has roughened my hands. Did you see the temple on your way in?"

"Those stone columns on Merlin's Knoll?"

"They look crude now, but there was enough coin left after paying the king to hire a mason from Glastonbury. He'll be here in a week. By mid-August, the place will begin to look like a temple. But I may have to sell some jewelry to buy the stained glass for the windows."

"After we are wed, I will use my coin to buy windows."

"No," Rachel says firmly. "We will not be wed until the temple is finished."

"But we agreed—"

"That if you helped me get the money for the king, I would wed you," Rachel finishes for him. "But I did not say when."

Erec stiffens. "Do not pull my beard, Servant of Birds."

Rachel lifts her chin. "And do not think to treat me like chattel. When the temple is complete, I will announce our betrothal. No sooner. I will not be bullied by a man again."

The strength in her unwavering look cannot be broken by words, Erec sees, and he huffs an impatient sigh. *Perhaps the old chief is right, and I am being duped by this night-eyed woman.* But he voices no further objection and, instead, feels a smile widening through him despite himself. "You followed my instructions well on our way to the raid—now I will follow yours to the wedding bower."

Harold Almquist stands beside the inner gate listening to the peevish chatter of the sparrows finding their places in the ivy of the curtain wall as the sun crowns the western mountains. He is tired. Today, as on every last Thursday of the month for the past ten years, he has played the role of chamberlain, making the rounds of the village, the bailey, and the donjon's treasury, his inkstone thinning as his ledger page darkens with all that has been garnered from time—calves born, cows butchered, fields sown, bushels and pecks harvested, garments tailored, rags rendered, coin spent, and coin returned.

He glimpses the children romping in the garden, eager to find the first fireflies. Joyce, his eldest, is nine years old, yet she is still thrilled by the flurry of fireflies and is yet summers away from dreams of a lingering kiss and all it discloses. Nevertheless, that summer will come, and she will flourish into provocative womanhood. In time, so will Gilberta, Blythe, and even little Effie. With inexplicable faithfulness, time will make of his daughters beautiful women and wives, mothers, and eventually crones. He sees himself and Leora aged, watching his grandchildren in the garden, seeing beyond them their children, repetitious mirrors of children, generations in servitude to love.

The strangeness of the baroness's miracle has struck Harold with an unrelenting fright. He had known Ailena only a short time, less than two months, before Guy sent her off on her pilgrimage, yet he well recalls her shriveled, bent body, her flesh like oil-soaked parchment, and her wicked tongue. *The Grail has worked a true miracle,* he acknowledges to the molten sky and crosses himself.

Just as in the Grail legend—when the land is healed along with the king's body—the baroness's youth seems to have rejuvenated the realm. In his decade of bookkeeping, the ledger accounts have never been as profitable as now. Even with the expense of the tourney, the penalties and taxes to the king, and the mason's fees for the synagogue, there will be plenty of funds to manage through the winter—largely because the villeins are working harder and their harvests will surely be the most bountiful ever.

"Sir Harold," the porter at the inner gate calls. "Will you recognize this knight or shall I send for our Mistress?"

Harold tucks his fat ledger more firmly under his arm and accompanies the porter to the closed gate. When the sight-hole slides open, he sees a brutal nose, hawk-bent, freckled, and sun-scarred and, set close together in thick bone sockets, small, dragonish eyes.

"Thierry!" Harold pants with surprise.

"Harold, let me in. I am returned from my penance at Saint David's, and I am shriven."

o   o   o

Erec pulls his steed around on the top of the meadow before the forest. He gazes back at Castle Valaise as the sun meets the mountains and sends golden spokes across the sky's length. Above the bright hull of the fortress, taut cirrus clouds flare crimson.

The afternoon he has spent with the Servant of Birds has left his heart feeling sunburned, blistered with longing. Giddy with envy, he had let the slender woman walk him by the hand through the *palais*'s cathedral chambers, revealing the great hall in the opal light of its lance-long windows, the gaming rooms with their felt-bolstered tables and velvet-armed chairs, apartments appointed with marble-manteled fireplaces and body-length mirrors, counsel rooms watched over by antlered stag heads, even the cookhouse with its enormous oven and gleaming copper caldrons and the donjon's armory replete with disassembled war engines, a catapult big as an oak, wheels taller than a man on a horse.

The Servant of Birds had even shown him her bedchamber with the rosewood sea chest she had lugged back from the Levant. And there was her tall-canopied bed—their bower bed—with valences and coverlets embroidered with hunting scenes. Passion had smarted in him then to imagine this willowy maiden under him on that bed, the sinuous shadow of her hair sprawled under her. And he would have thrown her down then and there but for the jewel of command in her gaze.

After meeting her family and dining with them, he was taken around the bailey and introduced to all the guildsmen in their shops. Then she invited him to stay the night—but that he could not do. He has already sworn to himself that he will sleep in this keep only when it is his own.

Howel will mock him, Erec knows. The old man will say he has been tricked. *And maybe I have,* Erec thinks and smiles tristfully, feeling the burn in his chest, the heat of ardor that has bent the iron of his fate.

Thomas kneels in prayer before the window of his donjon apartment, morning light warming his closed eyes. Since Maître Pornic sent him here from the abbey, since his grandmother lured him out into the countryside and kissed him on the mouth, he has been praying for guidance. But no whispering counsel has descended from the Holy Spirit, no unsuspected wisdom glitters from the dark of his confusion.

A knock sounds softly. Wearily, he rises, brushes the wrinkles from his white cassock and opens the door. Rachel stands in the dark corridor wearing a peach-pale bliaut and a white robe cinched tightly at the waist with gold cords. "May I come in?"

"Grandmère—" he flusters. "No—not here—I mean, this apartment is too rude." He steps onto the dank stairway and stares down the curve of unlighted steps. "You walked up here?"

Rachel smiles. "Despite your Uncle Guy's faith that I am a witch, I cannot fly."

"Come—" Thomas beckons, taking her elbow and immediately suffering a wash of remorse at the soft feel of her. "The roof is just two more flights."

The violet and golden vista of hills under the lofty clouds is so vast that for a while they say nothing, enraptured by the wideness of sky and the plunging hills. The watch before the flagstaff salutes the baroness and fixes his gaze along the clouds' edge.

"I came to apologize," Rachel says at last. "I behaved like a giddy child with you."

"That was days and days ago, Grandmère. I've forgotten."

"No, you haven't," she says with a puckish smile.

He wears a surprised look for a moment, then heaves his head back and relents: "You're right. But why have you come to me now?"

Her large, interested eyes gleam. "Denis is mending well. The king's men have their money. Harold says the villeins' harvest will be their best ever. And the synagogue for the rabbi is to have a master mason. All is well with me for now, Thomas—except for you."

He puts both hands to his chest. "I am well, Grandmère."

"Are you? You do not look at me when we eat in the great hall. When I see you riding into the village to say Mass with Gianni, you pretend not to see me. I fear you are unhappy with me. Is it because I stole silver from Dic Long Knife?"

"I was wrong to reproach you for that," he says. "God returned you here to live as a baroness, not a saint. I'd forgotten."

"Then are you displeased that I kissed you, that I declared my attraction to you?"

He waves that aside and blurts out: "My own feelings are my unhappiness. I have already confessed them to you."

"And I have spoken to you freely of my feelings. We need not be ashamed. They are natural affections for two people in love."

"Grandmère!" He moves to step away, but she takes his arm.

"Can we not love each other?" she asks, clear-eyed. "Look, we are of an age, you and I, Thomas. We are man and woman. And God has put desire in our hearts."

"That desire must never go beyond our hearts."

"Never," she avers with a squeeze of his arm. "But neither should it wither in our hearts. Why can't our affections be open? We have done nothing sinful."

"Grandmère—" He breathes deeper and says in a rush, "I am determined to take my vows. The miracle that has changed you has changed me as well. In September, on Saint Fandulf's Day, I will give myself to the Church."

"Then you have found your Grail, Parsifal." She releases his arm and leans back against the parapet under the weight of a decision. "In many ways I am still questing. In the spring, I will be returning to Jerusalem."

Surprise and relief play across his face. "Guy will be pleased to learn that."

"Perhaps not. I was hoping to name you my heir."

"Me?" he stammers. "I—I'm not even a knight."

"One need not be a knight to rule."

"No—but I will be a priest."

"Prester John, who rules the greatest kingdom in the Orient, is a priest. If you rule in my stead as a priest, the enemies who would unseat you must challenge the Church as well."

He shakes his head, grieved. "No, Grandmère, don't do this to me. The Lord has said we can't serve two masters. The Church is master enough for me."

"As you wish, Thomas. But let there be no more distance between us. Let us love each other."

Her words frighten him, and he puts a hand to his head,

steadying the lightheadedness. "I will love you as a grandson. I feel nothing more."

"Good. Then there is nothing for us to hide." With a grand-motherly hand to his cheek, she smiles complacently. In the brassy sunlight, his eyes appear three times the color of sky; they stir a cryptic longing in her, not for love or passion or belonging but, strangely, for the familiar presence of her grandfather with his dolorous gaze, thick-knuckled hands, and forked beard gray as the ash of which she knows we are made. "I will see myself down, Thomas. Return to your meditations and later, if you wish, come help us at the synagogue."

Walking down the dark stairwell, Rachel is pleased with herself for making peace with Thomas. Now she hopes that the amorous lamentations she feels in herself whenever she sees him will be less distracting—for spring seems a long way off.

With a face as famished as granite, Maître Pornic stares at the temple on Merlin's Knoll. For a long while, no one sees him sitting on his palfrey in the shawl of shadows at the forest's edge, and he has ample time to witness the ardor of the people's efforts. Men and women, even children, come and go from their labors in the fields to chip at the stones and hammer at the pews being assembled in a nearby carpenter's tent. The baroness labors among them, her long hair tied back like a common woman's.

Presently, one of the men atop the scaffolding from whence the rafters are being hoisted spots the abbot and announces him.

Maître Pornic guides his horse up the well-worn path to the summit, generously blessing each of the villeins he meets on the way who kneel before him. At the top, the baroness and the canon greet him courteously, and the rabbi nods from where he sits in his high-backed chair wrapped in his prayer shawl. Gianni offers a hand to help the abbot down, but he refuses to dismount.

"I have come from the abbey because reports continue to reach my ear that a pagan temple is being built here."

"We are building a temple that Jesus himself would recognize," Rachel says.

"Jesus commanded Peter to build him the Church," Maître Pornic states, "not synagogues."

"We will worship God here, padre," Gianni offers, "as our Lord worshiped when He—"

"Say no more," Maître Pornic speaks sharply. "I have heard all this before. I know there will be no saints' statues here, no crucifix to bear testimony to the inconsolable suffering of our Savior—and no altar! No altar upon which to commemorate the sacrifice that redeems our souls of Adam's sin." He shakes his head. "This is not a church. This is an empty building."

"It *will* be empty," Rachel agrees. "It will contain only pews and a cabinet and lectern to store and display the Torah. It will be empty of everything but the Lord and the people He has made."

"That is sacrilege."

"Surely not, padre," Gianni counters. "This is God's house."

"This is a portal to hell for all who forsake the true Church!" Maître Pornic declares loud enough for all to hear. He points to the villeins with mallets and chisels in their hands. "This is the site of a pagan temple—and upon it you are erecting yet another pagan temple. All those who toil here are building for their souls a secure place in hellfire!"

The villeins drop their implements and begin drifting toward the path.

"Come with me, my children," Maître Pornic beckons. "Come away from this place of wickedness and spare yourselves eternal suffering."

The villeins cross themselves and hurry past the baroness.

"Ailena—if you truly are Ailena—remember your faith." Maître Pornic opens a leather vial and scatters holy water over the baroness and the men beside her. "Will you abandon this heathen endeavor?"

"I will not!" Rachel's heart pounds with anger. "Nor can you condemn it—unless you condemn your own Savior, who worshiped as I worship."

Maître Pornic casts a pitying frown over the disbelievers, turns his mount, and rides dolefully after his flock.

∗   ∘   ∗

Rain billows in sheets from the mountains, puddling the hoof-gouged earth to slurry, and drumming atop the pavilion tent where Guy Lanfranc and Roger Billancourt sit. They are playing at draughts, have been since the hard rain woke them at dawn, hours ago. Roger executes a clever slip shot and captures three pieces.

Guy groans, pushes away from the board, and stands by the open flap. The land appears hammered and shiny as metal, and Castle Neufmarché in the distance is a craggy boulder. "Branden gloats that he has us boxed like cattle in the rain while he sits on high."

"This is but a temporary stay." Roger leans back, regards their saddles and rucksacks, all that is left of their worldly possessions. He considers getting wet to visit the two hackneys Branden has lent them. They are tethered under an ash tree behind the tent and should be moved to better provender.

"Temporary, indeed," Guy grumbles. "If we don't convince him of Erec's threat, he won't move against the Pretender. He'll just sit on high while they raid his cattle. And come autumn, we're vagabonds."

"Your father and I wandered the king's roads with no more than we have now," Roger states proudly. "Thinking back, those were Gilbert's and my best years."

"You were lads. You want to grow old living in tents?"

"Fret not. Your keep will be your home again soon enough."

Guy turns his head with slow, reptilelike precision. "You think the poison will work?"

"Bane-root is lethal. It will work."

"Where did you get it?"

"From a witch in the hills—pig-eyed Mavis. Rest assured, Guy, this time we will serve her in kind—deception for deception. And, the beauty is, no blame will affix to us. Thierry reports that when the Jew's temple is complete, a Mass is to be said for all the people. We will be there when she drinks of the cup. With William and Thierry, we will decry such treachery. We will blame religious fanatics seeking vengeance on the Christ-murderers."

Guy is not listening. He is thinking, *So it has come to this— poisoning her as though she were vermin. And is she not?*

Lightning fangs over the mountains, and he remembers how his mother infected him with rage when he was a boy. The very day his father died, and for years afterward, she assailed him with stories of Gilbert's cruelties—how he had loved no one, not even his children, punching her in the belly when she was pregnant, like this— His stomach winces at the memory of her blows, and he presses a fist against his gut. In gruesome detail she had described the slithery red jellies with lidless eyes and pegged fingers that dropped out of her after those beatings. "You would have been one of them," she had stabbed. "He never wanted you."

Roger peels away from his chair, stands beside Guy, watching him gaze into the rain-fog, and pats his shoulder. *Too much musing,* the warmaster thinks. *No edge for cutting through moods. No edge at all.* He strides out into the rain to check the horses, the downpour scattering off his head like a halo of gnats.

Gianni Rieti blesses the last of the parishoners as they leave the chapel after vespers and throw on their cowls to ward off the pattering rain. Though Maître Pornic has supplanted him in the village by resuming services there himself, Gianni is glad that the guildsmen's families and the knights continue to attend his chapel Mass each day before supper. Many have told him that the ceremony has become more meaningful now that it is performed in the very language Jesus spoke and with the very rituals by which he adored God. Even surly-eyed Thierry attends every evening, taking the host and drinking the sanctified wine.

Returning to the chapel, Gianni notices that one attender remains kneeling among the pews. And where is Ummu, who always helps clear the altar? He approaches, then stops—for he recognizes the golden elf locks visible through the diaphanous veil of the blue-robed maiden.

"Madelon—" he means to whisper, but the breath of his adoration and surprise fills the empty chapel. He has not been alone with her for many days, not since Hugues found them out in the night garden during the festival of the king's men.

She rises and turns, revealing pouting lips and eyes glassy with tears. "I cannot stay. Mother will come for me in a moment. But I must tell you. I must tell someone." She gnaws at a knuckle, her pollen-bright face flushed with fever. "Gianni—I am with child."

During the days of rain, little work is done on the temple. The knights continue to chisel stone, instructed by David and the mason, who works for the stone and the baroness who pays him, and not for Maître Pornic. But without the villeins little more can be done.

Rachel makes several trips to the village, her mantle soaked by the torrent, her hair plastered and eyelashes and brows dew-baubled. By now, she has gotten to know most of them. Blind Siân, Aber the Idiot, and Legless Owain need no convincing to defy the abbot, who promises to reward their compliance with a mercy from God they have not known in this life. But the others are sincerely afraid. Only her own miraculous experience with the Grail affords her any validity against the stern authority of the holy man. "Jesus was a Jew," she insists. "He taught us the law of love, so why should we not love His tribe, the tribe God blessed by giving them His son? Why are the rituals that He used to worship God, that He used to sanctify His death for our sins, not good enough for us?"

Maître Pornic sequesters himself in the wattle hut that serves as the village shrine and will not speak with the heretic. Thomas tries to mediate, but the abbot will only repeat Saint Paul's edict from Corinthians: "'You are not your own—you were bought with a price.'"

From that, Rachel remembers Ailena's admonition: "Everything has its price—even the blessing of the pope." And she wraps two of her rubies in a letter of offering to the bishop of Talgarth and begs his blessing for her temple, quoting Exodus: "And they shall build for Me a Sanctuary that I may dwell in their midst." She sends the oblation with a pilgrim returning from Saint David's, and the next day the weather clears, which she accepts as a blessing.

Out of the wet light of the forest, Erec Rhiwlas and fifteen of his men come riding up to Merlin's Knoll. "I've come to build my future," he grins at Rachel. "The sooner this is done, the sooner you will be mine." Boisterously, he sets to work with his comrades.

Rachel turns away from the busy crew, faces the sodden land brilliant with its new-washed colors, feels the urgency to pray to God in gratitude, but is afraid to try.

At the end of the work day, before returning to the castle for vespers and supper, the knights sit on the cut stones, and the rabbi raises the Torah before them.

The Welshmen loiter among the ancient ring rocks, both amused and startled to see Invaders with chin-beards and braided temple locks reciting as one: "*Baruch ata adonai elohainu melech ha-olam asher natan lanu torat emet, v'hayai olam nata b'tohainu. Baruch ata adonai, notain hatorah.*"

"That is the language of Jesus?" Erec asks Rachel.

"Yes. They are thanking God for the first books of the Bible, for 'planting among us life eternal.' It is a prayer that Jesus learned as a child."

"And the beards—" He points to the tufts of hair on the chins of Denis, Harold, and Gerald.

"In Leviticus, men are told: 'You shall not destroy the corners of your beard.'"

Erec tugs at his brindled beard. "When we are wed, that will be one article of faith where the Welsh have not deviated from the Patriarchs." He smiles, elated, glittering with sweat from his day's labor and proud of the envy in the stares of his men as they play over his elegant lady with her bruised hands and smudged nose. Under the broad hat she wears to protect her fair skin from the sun, she is long-throated, hollow-cheeked, a waterbird, a doe.

Dawn purples the thick night. The dreadful tailed star is gone at last. Rachel, who has slept in the temple with her grandfather, Gianni, and Denis, returns from relieving herself in the privy shack the workers built in the soggy willow grove at the base of the knoll, and finds David pacing. He is walking the perimeter of the temple, staring up at it admiringly. All but the glass is in place now.

"Rachel," he says softly to her when she steps into stride beside him, "you have remade yourself in a lonely place—and now I know, where before I only believed, that God is everywhere."

Seventeen days into August, the knights with the help of Erec and his men finish shingling the roof of the synagogue. Even Maître Pornic climbs Merlin's Knoll for the first assembly in the temple, *Beth Yeshua*. Thomas stays close beside him, silently praying that the abbot will not disrupt the proceedings with his displeasure at the Hebrew ceremony. Blessedly, just yesterday a pilgrim passing through conveyed a letter from the bishop of Talgarth, consoling the holy man in his indignation but obliging him to be more tolerant of small variations in the faith so long as the basic tenets of Christ are not disputed.

To see for himself that the Savior is honored properly, Maître Pornic reluctantly concedes to the bishop and leads the villagers to the synagogue. Both he and Thomas are impressed by the large gathering. The entire village and castle have convened on the knoll, and the small temple is so jammed that many worshipers must stand on rock rubble to peer in through the windows.

Rachel and David greet each of the worshipers as they come up the knoll trail. Last to arrive are Guy and Roger. From horseback, Guy calls down, "Will you be truly Christian and welcome your enemies?"

"Are we enemies?" Rachel calls back. "We are only kith who have misplaced our love."

Guy and Roger share a grave look, dismount, and unbuckle their swords.

Gianni, surveying the assembly from the small door at the back of the synagogue, is flustered to see not only Maître Pornic in the front pew but a small commotion as Denis and Harold make room for Guy Lanfranc and his sinister shadow Roger Billancourt. The Welshmen across the room glare hostilely, but Rachel is with them, speaking soothing words.

Unlike the chapel, there is no altar here, only the niche in the wall where the scroll of the Torah is hidden by a veil, a lamp of the Eternal Light hanging above it, and the *bimah*, a small dais set before the pews with a narrow table standing atop it. Consequently, Gianni must prepare for the ceremony in a narrow courtyard flanked by aboriginal worship stones. He relies on Ummu to arrange his vestments and help him with the sacraments while he reviews the Hebrew passages he will recite. William and Thierry are there, too, keeping the crowd back and brushing flies away from the unleavened bread, the *karpas* vegetables, and the wine.

As Gianni carries in the chalice on the silver tray with the other ritual items, Rachel takes her seat between Clare and Denis, and David, with his prayer shawl over his head, mounts the *bimah*. The assembly falls to a hush.

"I am a stranger among you," he begins in his resonant voice. "As a boy, I learned that every stranger is a mystery from God. Yeshua ben Miriam—the Jew we are here to honor today—preached, as the Torah preaches, that we should love others as we love ourselves. In that way, we love the mystery that is God, we love what can be known of God, God's human face, that is Welsh and Norman, Christian and Jewish. Let this house of prayer be the threshold where cruelty ends and love begins."

Before the wine is consecrated to the gentiles' Messiah, David lifts the goblet from the tray on the table, raises the symbol of joy and gladness to the congregation, to the many mysteries of God—and drinks a toast.

The congregation applauds, and with the chalice in his hands, David bows. But suddenly the clapping is coming from far off. When he looks up, the people grow dimmer, flying away down a constricting tunnel. He is falling from them. Falling away into silence and darkness.

Rachel leaps from the front pew and reaches David as he collapses to the platform and rolls to his back. He lies in the sunlight pouring in from a window, his stare bulging wide, the gaping blindness of his eyes reflecting the sky and a radiant star—a whole blue world suspended in the shadow of the sun.

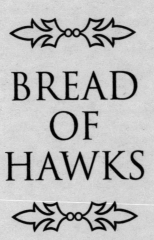

BREAD
OF
HAWKS

The Grail is the symbol of individual destiny.

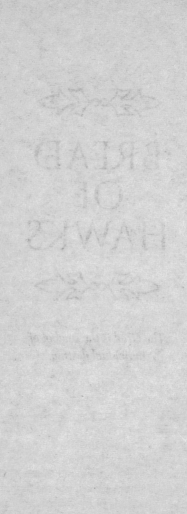

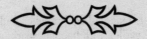

Aber the Idiot squats among the shards of broken stone beside the creek, picking up small, flat pieces and skipping them across the water. A nearly round wafer of rock the size of his palm catches his attention. It is imprinted with the grainy shadow of a face. When he lifts it to the sunlight, he sees that the chiseled scars in the stone reveal with terrifying clarity the dolorous face of Christ.

Shouting the Ave Maria as he runs, Aber carries the visage in both hands, like a priest with the Host. He falls three times to his knees on his way up Merlin's Knoll but takes the punishing pain without dropping the icon. At the synagogue, he bursts in, blithering, "Mary Virgin bless us—Mary Virgin bless us—"

The knights, on their knees before the draped bier, where the rabbi's body has been laid atop the *bimah,* stand. Gianni crosses himself when Aber presents him with the image in the stone. Denis, Harold, and Gerald crowd closer, awed to silence by the gruesome details of the thorny crown and the woeful eyes. Gerald touches the striated exactitude of the rabbinical beard. With careful deference, they pass the stone wafer among themselves before placing it in the wall niche with the Torah.

Aber is dispatched to bring Maître Pornic, and the knights return to their prayers with renewed fervor.

Afternoon sunlight, mangled by branches and leaves, fills the alcove of the castle garden with bobbing sparks and fiery shadows like the cut-gem insides of a turning jewel. Madelon sits on a stone bench at the glittering center, hands folded over her stomach. Tears glint at the corners of her eyes, sharp as diamonds.

Thierry, too, smells the distant rain, watches the sun-shadowed clouds drifting east, and guesses there will be showers by nightfall. He is bored by the intrigues of his father and uncle. The king is fighting the French on the Continent, and he wants to go while there is still time to earn honors on the field before winter sends everyone huddling back to their hearths.

"You're not listening to me," William scolds.

They are sitting atop their steeds at the forest's edge. Having escorted Guy and Roger back to Neufmarché's realm, they have stopped before a swale of willow at the far end of a wide meadow, and William has begun instructing Thierry on how to handle the inevitable questions that will arise from the poisoned wine.

Thierry rocks his head back, annoyed. Denis and Gianni have already interrogated him sternly, but after the death of the rabbi, most of the crowd at the back of the synagogue fled the knoll, and there were many suspects to round up.

"They will question you again," William insists. "Remember what you told them."

"I told them nothing, Father."

"You told them you were too busy keeping gawkers from crowding the canon that you did not see who got close enough to poison the wine."

"Yes, yes."

"You do not seem fully aware of our danger, Thierry."

A perplexed shadow creases the young knight's brow. "It was only a Jew. We would have been in greater danger had we succeeded and killed the Pretender. The villeins and guildsmen would have suspected Uncle at once."

"But that would have been Uncle's danger," William corrects, with a knowing flick of his eyebrows. "If Guy fell to an angry mob, you would become baron, yea, even earl, need I remind you?"

"You'd have abandoned Uncle?"

The sincerity of Thierry's surprise angers William. "Loyalty is for dogs, not men. The poison was his idea. We took our risk with it—let him take his. Though now"—he chews the corner of his mustache—"the risk is all ours. The Jew is dead and Uncle and Roger have fled, leaving us to hazard all enquiries on our own."

"Let us flee too, then," Thierry suggests anxiously. "Let us join with Richard in the Vexin and fight side by side with the king. We will make our own fortune by our swords."

William casts an irate sneer at his foolish son. "That is the dream of a child. War is no tourney, boy. In battle your life may easily be shorn from you or, even worse, your eyes spilled with one sword slash, your legs crushed under a fallen steed. Blind or halt, you will live out your life by the roadside begging alms."

Thierry recoils at being called a child, and his horse sidles under him. "A beggar I might become, but my wounds would be honorable," he sniffs. "What have I to gain here but the dishonor of poison and murder?"

William grimaces testily but masters himself. "You may go to battle and even forfeit your limbs, if that is to be your honorable fate. But not at fifteen. You will stay here this summer, and we will play out this intrigue, monstrous as it is. That is the indignity of our play for power. But the absence of power is far worse than any indignity we might perpetrate. When your place in this castle is secure and you have a home to return to with your wounds, then I say go fight for the king, go with my blessings."

"I will remember that, Father."

"Do. Though for now, bend your mind to the task at hand. We must extricate ourselves from the suspicion of this murder. We alone among the gentry were near enough to the chalice to administer the poison. Our enemies know that—and they have not forgotten your riding accident that took the life of that miserable crone Dwn."

"There is one other who had access and arguable motive." Thierry meets his father's querying stare. "There is the canon's dwarf."

"Ummu?" William ponders this. "That swarthy imp? What motive would apply?"

"A motive many would understand: hatred of the Christ-killer."

William thumbs his chin and chews his mustache. "Have we anymore bane-root?"

Rachel does not hear the knock at her door. She is mesmerized by the molten flow of the Llan.

"Arrière-grandmère?" a meek voice calls. The latch lifts, the door opens, and Madelon pokes her head in. She sees the baroness seated on the sill of the window nave, her knees drawn up to her shoulders, her flaccid face staring blindly into the golden day. "May I come in?"

Rachel hears the question muffled by cottony distance. She turns and sees a young woman with long ringlets of blond hair and a hurt, fervent look. She does not recognize her.

"I am sorry about the rabbi. He seemed a gentle man."

Rachel looks away at the furious tremblings of radiance on the river.

After a while, Madelon clears her throat and stammers, "I need to talk with you—please."

Slowly, Rachel turns and is surprised the woman with the hurt blue eyes is still there. "Who are you?"

Madelon steps closer. "I need your help, Arrière-grandmère," she says and begins to cry.

The sight of the contorted-faced girl shakes Rachel, and she uncurls from the sill. "Madelon—" The name brightens in her. "What is wrong?"

Madelon flings herself at her great-grandmother and presses hard against her, needing her strength. Through her tears, she tries to speak, but only her fear finds a voice in her sobs.

Rachel coos soothingly and hugs the shaken child. She guides Madelon to the edge of the bed, and they sit down together. The tears, the shivering sobs touch Rachel as deeply as her own weeping, which has not yet been able to find its way to her eyes. There is so far for her sorrow to travel—a whole lifetime of learned memories to cross—before she can cry for her grandfather. "Tell me what is wrong, Madelon."

"You—must—" Her voice dissolves, sobs, tries again, "You must—help me."

The girl's need, clasping Rachel so tightly, shuddering against her with released fright, unfurls the strength in her that shriveled hours ago when David died. "I will help you," she says firmly. "What is wrong?"

"I—am—I am with child," Madelon blurts.

The words tumble into Rachel's hearing with a soft crash and a supernatural beauty. The impact of their meaning crashes aside the granite weight on her heart, and a bulge of feeling fills her throat. For an instant, she is frightened by the weird onset of grief and joy intermixed. Then, in a phosphorescent light of understanding, she sees the grief of death and the wonder of birth locked together, like a man and a woman, struggling, copulating, making joy and pain—grandfather dead and a nameless one to be born. The dumb immensity of joined sorrow and rapture grips her, and, without thinking or even feeling, just seeing, she beholds how all of life is the perpetual departure of everything known and loved and the endless arrival of the fearful unknown—on and on—*never and always*—

Rachel laughs, lightheaded and grief-struck, and her tears flow with her laughter.

Madelon pulls away, baffled by Rachel's joyful tears. "Why do you laugh?"

"I am crying with joy for you."

"But what will become of me? Mother will be furious."

"And what will that change?" Rachel's face is slick with tears, and she closes her eyes against the depths of a long sorrow. "What does grief or anger matter now? What does any of it matter?"

"I am afraid. I do not know what to do or where to turn."

Rachel opens her eyes and stares at this girl, remembering that she too had once been this young. Then she shivers as if with blue cold and continues to weep, softly and deeply, not laughing now. "All shall be well," she whispers. "All manner of thing shall be well—even with this child."

Madelon shakes out another sob and hugs her fiercely, and the two lean into each other's pain.

* o o

Thomas stares over Maître Pornic's shoulder at the stone wafer, and his breath tightens in him at the sight of the Savior's image staining the stone. A strange feeling pervades him all at once, as if this is a dream and he has just realized that he is dreaming.

He looks to the others. The knights' faces shine in radiant silence. Tears web Gianni's eyes. Denis, despite his blond beard, looks like a boy thriving on love. Harold is open-mouthed, lips twitching to an inward prayer. Even his father's complexion is luminous with a glare of strength he has never seen before in Gerald's sallow face.

Thomas regards the majestic image again. The sorrowful eyes watch him from their mineral darkness without pretense, knowing what is to come. The cruelty of the thorns in the crown is implacable and vicious, biting into flesh and brains. And the mouth, flawlessly clear, flawlessly beautiful and exhausted, holds its cry inside, deep within the wild stone.

A ghastly shriek jars the temple. Maître Pornic screams—a wounded scream of fearfulness and rage—and now he has released the sacred image. Thomas watches it fall, the wounded visage dwindling away and then shattering like a fired clay dish, its perfection disappearing into muddled pieces.

Cries of grief and gasps of despair leap from the knights, and they are on their knees, snatching at the broken pieces. But Maître Pornic kicks at them and stomps on the largest shards, grinding them underfoot. "There is no semblance!" he screams. "Jesus is not in the stone! He is in heaven, at the right hand of the Father! Be not deceived! That is the face of the Devil!"

Gianni howls, rears up and seizes Maître Pornic by his cassock, and lifts the frail man off his feet. "You greedy monster!" the knight shouts. "You want it all! No miracle but your God! No holiness but you!"

Thomas and Denis pull Gianni away, and he spits at the shaken abbot. Turning Gianni about gruffly so that he is facing the draped body of the rabbi, Denis whispers harshly, "Remember what he taught us. We have seen enough. The second commandment forbids icons. He sent this miracle just for us, just for this one time, from the stone that built this temple, to remind us: the blood of the covenant is invisible."

Rachel, in her implacable grief, slowly, meticulously rips off her clothes, tearing her bliaut, piercing her robe with the grief in her fingers and rending the soft material. The voices inside her sing a dirgeful song in Hebrew, though she understands only some of the words—*Baruch ata adonai elohainu melach ha-olam dayan ha-emet.*

Naked, fingers buzzing with the strength that has reduced her garments to shreds, she stands before a window of her bedchamber, gazing out at the torchlights on the parapets and the celestial torches glinting in the heavens. She remembers when she was feeling strong in Jerusalem, strong enough to ask David, "Why did you burn them? Why did you burn your children and grandchildren—my parents, my brothers and sisters? Does not the Torah say, 'You must surely bury him'?"

That was the one time David had shown anger to her. With a clenched face and an iron voice he declared, "God has taken a lifetime's love in death—everything for His selfishness. And now we are left with nothing, only the Law. But I would not give them to the gentiles' earth. What earth is ours? Where is *our* promised earth? What soil is ours that it can be significant? No. There is no history without land. There is only endings and beginnings. Our land is gone. We belong to the fire that wanders wherever it is fed. Let the fire have us and purge the earth of our memory."

Those words return to Rachel palpably, and her body quakes to hear them again. She will never hear his voice again—and yet she will always hear him. *Never and always.*

She turns and walks across her room and out the door. She knows what the shadowy voices are singing for now. She knows what David wants. As she pads down the passage and the stairs, she mutters to herself, "Liberation from the flesh, which is the past—liberation from the future, which is the grave. Let the fire restore. Let the fire redeem."

Rachel walks through the *palais* without seeing anyone. When she steps into the night courtyard, the stars see her—the distant fires set against the darkness—the tiny *yods* of God's name glinting against His brow of blackness, the sweat of His effort to create the world still shining. "*Yod-hé-vau-hé*—" she chants. "*Yahweh*, who departs when we begin, who rises up when we lie down, who arrives when we are gone."

The porter at the inner gate startles alert to see the ivory nakedness of the young baroness glowing in the dark. And he averts his eyes.

"Open the gate," she commands. "This is where we start, by returning to the dead. This is where God is hidden."

The flustered porter swings wide the gate and watches, astonished, as the naked woman blithely strides into the bailey. Do the others know? Must they be alerted? He looks up at the ramparts, sees the night watch gawking, and hurries to the *palais* to find someone to tell.

In the bailey, an insomniac stablehand, a milkmaid, and a cobbler witness the luminous trespass of the white woman. They hurry to call others. By the time the baroness has reached the outer gate, a gaggle of people scamper behind, muttering in hushed, awed tones punctuated by snickers.

"My lady!" the sergeant at the gate gasps. Several of the guards from the front towers have come down into the courtyard and stand gaping at her. When she commands the gate to be opened, they share troubled looks. "What is wrong, my lady? Why have you come before us undressed?"

"I am come to stand naked before God. Open the gate at once! As you are my vassals, do as I command."

The sergeant looks to the others and nods sternly toward the ogling villeins. The guards rush the small gathering and disperse them back into the bailey. The sergeant opens the gate. "Shall I come with you, my lady?"

"No! This is not your concern. A lifetime is burning. And yours is burning here."

Rachel walks resolutely out the castle and down the toll bridge road. The cows, darker lumps of darkness, pay her no heed. The garden is in deep, black communion with the night. At the toll bridge, the keeper shouts with alarm, "Who are you?"

"I am Rachel Tibbon, come to mourn my grandfather, the last of my family."

"Baroness!" the tollkeeper starts, suddenly recognizing her. He tries to fit words to his astoundment but only succeeds in stammering incoherently as she drifts by and across the bridge.

Through the darkness of the oak grove that fronts the village, Rachel avoids passing the huts and goes directly to the open field that leads to Merlin's Knoll. Only the swine in their pens notice her and jabber among themselves.

Grass-points prick her thighs as she wades across the wild field. Harebells swipe at her and rocks bite her soles. Ahead, the knoll rears against the gritty stars. All around, the hills are floating sleek as cloud banks under the star-struck night.

The knights, sprawled on reed mats before the *bimah*, are sleeping when Rachel arrives at the temple. The *ner tamid*, the Eternal Light, gleams above the *aron kodesh*, the Holy Ark. By that light, she finds her way down the aisle of pews to the bier, climbs the three steps, and stands over the corpse. Gently, she draws back the covering and sees that the knights have treated their rabbi well: David has been washed carefully, his beard and hair combed; he is clothed in *takhrikhim*, white robes, and has been wrapped in his prayer shawl, whose fringes have been torn off, indicating that his earthly responsibilities are over.

Rachel stares into the quiet face of her grandfather and lays a hand against his cold cheek. The hymnal voices in her head hush. They recognize him. They are his children.

"You have found the Promised Land, Grandfather. Its boundaries are evening and morning, its highest mountain is noon, its deepest valley midnight. All this is yours now. Bless the silence, for in it we hear God. Bless the suffering, for in it we find strength. Bless the dead, for they are the treasure paid for our lives."

She kisses the cold stone of his brow and covers his face.

Immediately, the wraith-voices ascend in her: *Hamakom y'nahaim etkhem b'tokh sh'ar availai tziyon vee-yerushalayim.*

"Wake up!" she shouts. "Wake up and bring the fire!"

The knights startle alert and push to their elbows. Shocked silence grips them at the sight of the naked baroness standing above them.

"Bring the fire!" she shouts again.

Denis is first on his feet. "My lady—" He gawps like a simpleton and finally manages to blurt: "You are deeply grieved!" He pulls his tunic over his head and stands naked before her, offering her his garment.

"Put that back on," she orders. "And bring the fire."

"Fire?" Gianni repeats, not comprehending.

"Yes—fire. The rabbi will be given to the fire."

"No, no," Harold says. "Leviticus states, we shall bury the dead."

"Listen to me!" Rachel declares in a voice that rings to the rafters. "David Tibbon will not go into the earth. This earth is not significant soil. Bring those pews close around him. Gather dried grass for kindling. We set the fire with the *ner tamid*. Do as I say!"

The knights look at one another, and Denis shakes his head. He mounts the *bimah* and drapes his tunic about Rachel, trying to lead her away.

But she shrugs him off and holds out his tunic. "Put this on!"

The command in her voice and the strength in her stare overwhelm all protest from him, and he dons the tunic.

"Now bring the pews close. If you are truly my knights, you will do as I say."

"Why do you do this, Baroness?" Gerald asks trepidatiously.

"The light of God is in the earth," she answers. "And from the earth shine forth the grasses and the trees. The darkness of God is in the fire. Let the dark come upon him."

"Lady—" Gianni speaks. "There has been a sign, a most wonderful sign today. A stone bearing the precise likeness of our Savior has been found. We have seen it. It is a sign of the rabbi's holy work—of your holy mission. Do not burn this tabernacle."

Rachel puts her hands to her head. The voices shout mercilessly. She understands little of it, only a phrase from Proverbs: "The spirit of man is the lamp of the Lord." The rest is gibberish, battering her like storm-driven surf. "Obey me—" she cries through the din, "or abandon me!"

Harold begins to drag a pew closer to the dais. Gerald helps him; then Gianni joins. Denis watches Rachel closely, sees the torment in her face and turns away chilled, a cold hand closing around his heart. The countenance of the Savior was shattered in this room today—and before that, the rabbi was murdered. Evil owns this place. The *mal'ah Yahweh* as Satan is here, Denis has no doubt now: perhaps the Dark One has always been here, since the time when the ancient people erected their ring of stones.

Denis descends from the *bimah* and helps to gather the fire-wood that will purge this tragic temple.

Soon the dais is nearly surrounded with pews piled high, and Gerald and Harold strew dried grass over them. Rachel directs Gianni to bring the lamp of the Eternal Light, and she removes the Torah from its niche. She returns to the *bimah* and places the scroll in her grandfather's stiff arms, silencing the protests of the knights with a quick, lightning stare.

The knights throw their reed mats on the stacked pews and gather their boots, trousers, water flasks, and a Bible. In a trance, Rachel walks through the narrow exit among the heaped benches, touching the lamp flame to the dried straw. When she steps out, she throws the lamp onto the pyre and watches the flames swarm over the wood. The sudden heat pushes her backward out the door of the temple. She stands there, arms limp at her side, nakedness burnished orange by the blaze, witnessing the angels moving in the open doorways of the fire, hearing their voices in the crackling conflagration outsinging the ghosts inside her.

As the flames reach the rafters and crimson angels appear on the roof, Rachel takes the Bible from Gianni's arms. She opens to the forty-eighth chapter of Isaiah and, by the pyre light, reads aloud: "'Behold, I have refined thee, but not as silver; I have tested thee in the furnace of affliction. For mine own sake, even for mine own sake, will I do it!'"

Then she closes the Bible, and the haunted singers in her head are gone. The heat of the fire laves her body. From the path comes the drumming of hooves and the shouts of the sergeants. Denis offers her a blanket from his horse, and she wraps it about herself. There is no need to stand naked anymore. God has seen her.

"Mother!" Clare cries as the sergeants escort Rachel into the *palais*. "What has happened? The temple is burning!"

Rachel says nothing. She walks to her room accompanied by Clare and the maids. As they remove the horse blanket from her shoulders and see the mud stains on her legs, Clare, horrified, orders a bath to be drawn at once. But Rachel counters the order with an impatient wave and lies down on her bed.

The odors of grass and dark soil fill her loneliness. And when the lamps are extinguished and the door shuts, the darkness closes on her with its soft fires.

Erec watches the blaze on Merlin's Knoll from the woods where he has camped. He is alone. His men have left, disgusted that the Invaders would poison a holy man in his temple, angry that their chieftain's son would desire one of their women.

After the murder, Erec had tried to reach the baroness, to protect her, but the Norman sergeants had immediately closed ranks around him and his men. They had come within a shout of drawing blood, and had been sent away as intruders. Erec does not blame his men for abandoning him. His love for this woman, he knows, cannot be justified. His men believe him to be ensorcelled by her, and he thinks they may well be right.

For hours now, he has been lying in the darkness, listening to the wind suffering in the trees, staring up through rents in the canopy at the cold fires in the heavens, trying to argue away his love—or is it just lust?—for this audacious, moon-bright woman. Would he have her if there were no castle to go with her? Would he have her without any dowry at all? Quivering with desire, he knows his depraved answer would be yes.

Let Howel curse me. Let my father send me out of his sight. I'll have the woman I love.

On his feet, Erec stares through the trees and clings to his courage. A red cloud squats on the knoll like a wraith of the Apocalypse.

Ummu sleeps soundly in a straw pallet at the foot of Gianni Rieti's bed. Ta-Toh stirs beside him, sits up and chitters. The monkey senses approaching footfalls and lays a paw on the dwarf's nose. Ummu swipes it away and rolls over.

Fists pound on the door. Ta-Toh screeches, and Ummu and Gianni sit up. The next instant, the door swings open and four sergeants barge into the room, followed by Thierry, shouting, "Seize him before he flees!"

With drawn swords, two sergeants stand over the dwarf, and the other two open the chest by the window and rummage through the clothing. Ta-Toh barks and spits furiously, dancing about the men whose swords point at his master.

"What are you doing?" Gianni demands. As he gets out of bed, one of the sergeants pricks his sword point into the canon's chest, and Gianni sits down.

"Search his litter," Thierry orders.

A sergeant grabs the dwarf's arm and heaves him off his pallet, then stirs the straw with his sword. He turns away, shakes his head, and Thierry kneels down and thrusts his hands into the ticking.

"Look here!" the youth shouts and holds up a thumb of black, blistered tuber.

The guard standing over Ummu takes it and sniffs at it. His nose wrinkles and he coughs: "Bane-root!"

Rachel will not talk. She sits in the bay of her window gazing out at the golden scales of morning light on the Llan. Clare and Gianni stand in her room and plead with her to free Ummu. But their frantic voices sound inert to her and do not penetrate the thickness of her mourning. She does not know what they are talking about and is glad when they finally go away, muttering grievously to each other.

At midmorning, Thomas shoves past her maid. "Grandmère, I watched the synagogue burn last night," he says with emotion. "Mother told me it was the pyre for the rabbi. I . . . I am sorry."

Rachel looks blankly at him, standing before her dressed in gray jerkin and brown trousers, his white cassock in hand. Since the fire, the voices have stopped. But Rachel is afraid that if she speaks, the deep choir of voices will return. Her silvered profile does not budge.

Thomas throws his white cassock on the ground before her. "I am done with the abbey," he declares. "Yesterday, while I prayed with the others over the body of the rabbi, Aber the Idiot brought us a stone with the miraculous likeness of our Savior shadowed within it. We all marveled. And Aber called for Maître Pornic. But when he saw it, he smashed it. Called it the Devil's work. But it was not, Grandmère. I saw it. Touched it. It almost lived and breathed in my hand. Yet he destroyed it. He is so afraid of signs, so afraid of the affirmation of your miracle and the rabbi's teachings."

Rachel's gaze follows the young man talking to her. She has not heard what he has said, though the emotion in his voice reaches her. The thick bones under his eyes that make his stare appear so wide, as though his gaze has fallen from heaven, glisten. He has been crying. She looks at the cassock in its thick folds on the floor, and she comprehends that, somehow, he too has lost his world— adrift like herself.

"Father, Harold, and Denis have spent the night in the village," he goes on. "They are preaching about the Sacred Visage and the rabbi's teachings. Maître Pornic will be enraged, but they do not care. He has called this upon himself."

Rachel returns her attention to the sliding light on the river. The silence aches inside her. Where are the dying hymns and the nightmare drift of voices?

"I am done with Maître Pornic and the abbey," Thomas insists. "The miracle of the Grail has not just changed you, Grandmère. Everyone is changed by it." He steps closer and peers into her stony eyes, where the river's sharp reflections cling to the darkness like stars. "You were right when you told me that God wants us to live in this world, not flee from it. I thought that was heresy. But this is the world of the final judgment. How we live here touches eternity."

Thomas lays a hand on Rachel's arm and sits beside her, very close, his heart thudding. Mother has told him that this woman beside him walked naked into the night to set the temple ablaze. Clare is afraid her mother is mad. But the Grail has made Ailena young, and the nakedness displaying her youth is the true testimony of that miracle. Now, at last, he is thoroughly convinced of her sincerity.

"I love you, Grandmère," he says tenderly and kisses her cheek. She smells of smoke, and he lets his face linger in her autumnal scent. "I want to tell you now, I loved you as soon as I saw you standing there at the portal of Grandpère's crypt. I knew it was wrong, and for weeks I could not bear to admit it to myself. But I feel so compelled to tell you—I love you, as a man, not a grandson. There! I've said it! And I'm not ashamed of it. I know I can never have you, but I will always love you. It doesn't matter what becomes of me anymore, where I go or what I do or what God does to me. It only matters to me now that you know I love you and believe in you with all my heart."

Rachel looks at him vacantly and sees his yearning face very close. Her hands come up, and she moves her fingertips over his features, feeling the proud jut of his bones, the velvet down along his clean jaw. The silence shivers in the hollow of her chest with the urgency to tell him something—though she cannot grasp what. Her hands fall away. A swell of fright smothers the tenderness in her.

I am alone, she thinks. *I am all alone—even the voices of my dead are gone. Grandfather took them away with him. It is just me now, with no one else alive or dead. No one else.*

Thomas sees the fear in Rachel's face and believes it is the threat of incest that appalls her. He stands up quickly. "I am sorry," he blurts. "I know this is a love that cannot ever be returned!" Lurching to his feet, he staggers out of the room without looking back.

"Never," Rachel says to his absence, and her heart swells at the echoless ring of her voice. "And always."

Gianni paces outside the council room where Thierry and the sergeants are conferring with the baroness. This morning has been a bitter experience, first following the guardsmen to the donjon and down into the dungeon as they carried off Ummu, with Ta-Toh squawking hysterically the whole way. The leather-faced men were deaf to the dwarf's pleas of innocence, and threatened to lock up Gianni with him if he did not stop demanding the assassin's release. Even Ta-Toh was thrown into the dank darkness. After loud assurances to the weeping dwarf, Gianni had rushed back to the *palais,* seeking the baroness. But her grief for the rabbi was unbreachable. And then she was in her bath, receiving Thierry's report on the arrest through her maids. She will not see Gianni until she has spoken with the sergeants.

Rachel holds up the black tuber that killed her grandfather, presented as evidence by the soldiers. It looks like the charred finger of a corpse.

"Go," she tells the sergeants and Thierry.

The guardsmen bow, and Thierry, stiff-faced to keep from grinning exultantly, leads the way out.

As Rachel turns the bane-root about in her fingers and sniffs its acrid potency, she wonders what it felt like to die by this poison. From far away, the thought arrives that this is another of Thierry's cruel ploys. But then she remembers Ummu cornering her and warning her not to deceive him, not to impart lies to Gianni, for he has a soul of glass. *Would Ummu try to kill me to protect Gianni's soul?* In the new silence of her heart, that possibility rings loudly.

She listens for Ailena. To face Thierry and the sergeants, she has had to imagine the Grail—yet the memories of Ailena seem frail and trivial to her now. And hard as she tries, she cannot hear the old baroness thinking inside her.

"Mother, you must release Ummu at once," Clare demands, bustling into the council room with Gianni in her wake. "He is too dear a man to have worked such evil."

"My lady—" Gianni falls to one knee beside the table where Rachel is seated. "You have known my dwarf since the Holy City. When has he been anything more than a buffoon? There is no murder in his heart."

"Go." Rachel waves the poison root at them.

"Mother, I have come to know Ummu—"

"Go, Clare." Her stare is unyielding. "Gianni, stay."

With a pained expression, Clare departs.

Rachel summons Gianni closer and presses the stub of bane-root against the crimson cross on his black tunic. "I have spoken with Madelon," she says in a slow voice. "Go to her."

Gianni's deep eyes look startled. "I would go to her—but she will not have me."

"Go," Rachel orders.

"But Ummu—" Gianni presses his forehead to her hand, then looks up at her through his anguish. "You will spare my dwarf?"

"Go to Madelon now." She watches him through her emptiness, and he drifts away, disconsolate.

Let the dwarf sit in the dungeon for a while, Rachel imagines the baroness counseling her in her vacuous meditation. But she must strive hard for even this flimsy counsel. *The Grail is make-believe. The baroness is make-believe. Only death is real.*

The piece of death in her hand does not hoard its poison but stings her fingertips, reaching through her flesh for her blood, yet she holds onto it as if it were an amulet.

Madelon returns to the *palais* from a contemplative stroll in the garden to find Gianni at the door to her room. She had chastised herself all morning for getting pregnant. Now Gianni is red-eyed and haggard. "Ummu is in the dungeon," he moans.

"I know," she says with concern. "My brother Hugues says that the dwarf poisoned the rabbi."

"It's not true!" Gianni asserts, wild-eyed. "Ummu is no poisoner."

"I believe you." She places a reassuring hand on his arm. "Have you spoken with the baroness?"

Gianni nods disconsolately. "She is too bereft to see that Ummu is harmless." He runs both hands through his hair. "So much trouble. The rabbi dead. Ummu imprisoned. And you pregnant." Impulsively, he grabs her shoulders and pleads, "Marry me!"

Madelon pulls him into her room and shuts her door. "Be silent! Others will hear you."

"Let them hear me. I want you to be my wife."

"You are a priest! I cannot marry you. Moreover, I am going to marry Hubert Macey."

"You are with child. God has chosen me to be a father. I will forsake my priesthood." Gianni's dark eyes are earnest. "I will speak with your parents today."

"No!" Madelon's mouth is tight, the knuckles of her fists meshed together under her breasts. "This is not your child."

"That does not matter," Gianni persists, taking her fists in his hands. "This is *your* child—and when you marry me it will be ours."

"I want to be rid of this child." She jerks her hands away from him. "I *will* marry Hubert Macey."

Gianni gropes for her, but she steps back. "He can never love you as I do," he pleads.

"You do not know that," she retorts haughtily.

"Even so. I love you." Gianni feels stupid with need. The face of the Savior is burned into his heart. It is a sign that God will forgive him his betrayal of his vows if he can live his love as truly as Jesus lived His. "I will care for this child."

"If you care for me, you will help me."

"How?" His hands open with sincere entreaty. "What more can I do?"

Madelon's face softens. "There is a woman who lives in the hills—a witch. Her name is Pig-eyed Mavis. She will have a potion that will rid me of this child. If you truly love me, take me to her. She is my only way out of this grief."

Denis, Harold, and Gerald stand with a dozen villagers among the ashes in the stone shell of the synagogue, their hands clasped as they pray. Aber the Idiot kicks at the fallen rafters, intrigued by the big flakes of shiny black ash that fall off. Legless Owain crawls through the slag, feeling for bone-chip relics. And Siân listens past the praying voices, deeper into her blindness, to the wind sifting through the clinkers where the corpse has vanished.

"It is my fault," Gianni confesses, face pressed against the iron-barred sight-hole of the dungeon's thick wooden door. He can see Ummu sitting on a rush mat at the far end of the cell in a puddle of amber light from the oil lamp the guards have given him. The dwarf listlessly browses through the volume of Plotinus that the baroness has brought from the abbey. At his feet, Ta-Toh picks at the scraps of the meal Gianni delivered from the cookhouse. "I did not feel worthy of the Sacred Visage. I have decided to forsake my priesthood for love. I was not pure enough to stay with the other knights. If we had stayed, you would not be in such straits. I am to blame."

"Stop bragging, proud knight," Ummu says without looking up from his reading. "You are troubling Plotinus."

"This is God's punishment of me."

"Then God is only a fair shot. His punishment has missed the mark somewhat."

"Stump, I would trade places with you if I could! You are dear to me as my shadow."

"I am honored you hold me in such an esteemed light—though you have gauged my stature rightly." He turns the page. "Instead of glutting me with your praise, you would do better to disclose that vile Thierry's hand in this intrigue. Fair Madelon is his twin. Surely, you have her ear—and, I daresay, more. Speak with her and perhaps you will learn of his scheming."

"I will do that, Ummu. I am already agreed to escort her to a witch in the hills to have the child purged from her. If she knows anything, I will learn it."

"Then after you have freed the child from its dungeon, you will purge me from mine," Ummu sighs wearily.

Gianni thuds his head against the door. "I deceived myself to think I could follow the Lady of the Grail. Ill luck led me to her and placed you in this prison."

"Plotinus thinks otherwise," Ummu says, riffling through the pages. "Consider tractate nine of the sixth *Ennead*, wherein he reminds us that 'those who believe the world is governed by luck or by chance are far removed from the divine.'"

"Sadly true," Gianni mutters, turning and pressing his back against the dungeon door. His hand closes over the crimson cross above his heart and wrenches at it. "I have mocked the divine—I have hidden behind this cross. But now, my only shield will be my heart."

Ummu groans, and Ta-Toh consolingly offers him a grape.

Rachel sits under the shaggy willows in the garden outside the castle. The sun twinkling through the branches creates small, delicate beings of light, who hover in the air about her as she considers the black bane-root in her hand. She has decided to eat it. The silence that has floated inside her since her grandfather's death has become unbearable. Whenever she speaks, she hears herself in its depths. The haunted voices are gone for good now, gone into the soaring sky with Grandfather's smoke.

"*Baruch ata adonai*," she says aloud, but the words sound hollow. Her faith has never been in words or miracles, but always in the trembling trees and laggard hills and the alert wind whispering among them. Now that she is ready to die, she has decided to leave her body here in the soft shadows on the rooty ground, attended by the presences that loved her as a child.

"Grandfather, forgive me," she speaks to the void within her. "I know that what I am about to do you would say is wrong. But I have finished my work in this world. All that the baroness has required of me has been fulfilled. Her cruel son is displaced. The Welsh have had their grazing lands restored. And her grandson Thomas has been saved from the Church. Now that you are gone, why should I stay? To marry some man I do not love? To wait for Guy to murder me?" She presses the blistered root to her lips. "I will not carry this silence any longer."

Gilberta and Joyce bound among the foxgloves and marigolds at the margin of the cherry orchard, and little Effie comes careering after. They see Rachel in the cove of willows and, with laughing screams, dash toward her.

Rachel drops the bane-root into a pocket fold of her robe and gets to her feet in time to meet the charge of the children through the willow curtains. They caper about her, shouting for her to play with them. At first she resists, until she sees that the black silence within her is dimming their laughter. Refusing to have her grief poison the world around her, she lets the children tug her from under the trees into the summer sun. The older two scramble into the tall grass on the far side of the willow swale, and Effie pulls urgently at Rachel's arm to keep up.

Bounding like lambs, the children gambol from the grass field to the meadow, leading Rachel into the slovenly hedges at the remote end of the garden. Hares startle away at their approach. Swifts skid out of the blue, flit over the hedges, and scatter into the distant trees. Effie topples to her back trying to turn herself fast enough to follow their flight, and an unexpected laugh jumps from Rachel. Soon she is drifting through her sorrow, astonished at the lightness of her body, hiding-and-seeking with the young ones in the slum of overgrown hedges.

Suddenly horse hooves clop nearby, but because of the children's giggling and her playful skulking among the shrubs, Rachel does not hear them. She pokes her head into the glittery interior of a sunstruck bush to surprise curled-up Joyce, and hoofbeats drum behind her. She startles and looks up at a hurtling red-maned horse and, astride the majestic beast, Erec Rhiwlas leaning hard to the side, his muscular arm reaching out.

Rachel's cry is lost in the impact of collision as Erec seizes her about the waist and hoists her off her feet. Suddenly she is hugged tight to the brawny Welshman atop the galloping beast, and the children's wide-eyed faces wobble away.

Erec laughs hotly at the baroness's startled expression and tilts his body to see past her streaming black hair. The willows jounce by, and there is Leora with her hands in her red hair, shouting. She blurs past, and they charge into the flowerbeds, cutting the shortest path to the toll bridge road, poppies and daffodils kicking up behind them.

"Put me down!" Rachel shouts, and her cry whips away in the rush of their flight.

Erec's robust laughter streams behind them like a banner. When Crooked Simon, the gardener, rears up from the hyssop patch with hoe in hand, the chieftain's son bears down on him with a war cry, sending him sprawling among the herbs. Then the horse bounds through a verge of acanthus plants and kicks up road dust on its headlong drive toward the toll bridge.

At the sight of the baroness in the embrace of Bold Erec, the gatekeeper rushes to lower the barrier. But the horse has leaped out of the garden too suddenly and too close, and the gatekeeper is alarmed at what would happen to the baroness if the charger—galloping at full tilt toward him—were forced to a stop. He stands aside.

His hooves clanging loudly over the planks, the red-maned horse hurtles across the bridge. The Welshman rides with his brindled head reared back, jubilant, triumphant. Rachel, her eyes smarting in the wind, her body jarred by the desperate run, clings to him, while the gawping gatekeeper glimpses her helpless fright and watches the steed dwindle into silver dust among the tall trees and the shining hills.

At day's end, the knights still roam the forest's murk, searching for the Lady of the Grail. Gerald returns under the brazier of sunset. Harold rides into the castle with the evening star, and Gianni comes back soon after. But Denis continues to search as moonbeams spindle through the woods, the bedraggled trees and tumbling meadows gleaming strangely with lunar sorcery.

✳   ✳   ✳

Branden Neufmarché sends his guardsmen ahead as a shield before he rides over the drawbridge of his castle to meet the two horsemen on the boggy meadow. Though he knows that Guy Lanfranc and Roger Billancourt need him, he fears them nonetheless. He would like to dispatch them to the Continent to serve the king, but he is afraid they will gather a mercenary force and come back for his domain.

"What news, brother baron?" Branden enquires when he is close enough to his enemies to hear their reply yet far enough away to avoid treachery. Since losing Thierry as a guest and potential hostage, he has had to be more careful in his meetings with these desperate and dangerous men.

"Erec the Bold has carried off the Pretender," Guy answers. "As we speak he is rutting with her in the hills."

Branden frowns at his indelicate appraisal. "So the barbarian has held her to her promise of betrothal."

"And now," Roger adds, "is the time to strike. While she is gone—perhaps not to return—a sizable show of your men will make a siege unnecessary."

Branden ponders this. "I think not. The Lady of the Grail has a faithful following."

"But we have our own allies, Branden," Guy says. "I can guarantee that the drawbridge will be down when we arrive. With enough of your men, we can subdue the castle. In the span of one day, the fighting will be done, and you can return my keep to me, the rightful baron. By that act, you will earn not only the lands I've promised you but my lifelong vow of friendship."

"And the king?" Branden stalls for time to think.

"The king will say naught," Roger answers. "The so-called baroness has been spirited away by a barbarian chieftain. Guy Lanfranc is thus the rightful legate even by the king's standards."

Branden nods thoughtfully. "I will submit this strategy to my counselors."

The single dark crease in Guy's forehead darkens. "What more counseling do you need, Branden? The Pretender is gone. The barbarian is wedding her on her back in some leaf bed not far away. Once she realizes she belongs to him, they will return. Do you think she will be content to live in the hills?"

"And when she returns," Roger picks up, leaning forward in his saddle, "Bold Erec will be at her side and with his men. The castle that lies open for us now will become a barbarian fortress, from which he can sack your lands with impunity."

Branden shifts his weight uncomfortably. "The other Marcher barons will not accept this. If the barbarian takes the castle, they will ally with me to overthrow him."

"Certainly," Guy concurs, and narrows his gaze ominously. "But if that happens, I will be the one who rallies the barons to the defense of my ancestral domain. And when the barbarians are routed, the castle will be mine. The lands you would have had will be given to those who fight with me. And we will not be your friends any longer, Branden."

Erec carries Rachel off the king's road and down the deep trails far into the hills. They ride toward blue clouds of mountain rain, higher at each turn in the path, the emerald slopes appearing below patched with dark trees. Alder and ash groves pass, webby with light, the duff so thick that the hoof-falls are utterly silent, and Rachel feels she is floating through this wild land.

The smells of mulchy leaves, dog roses, crushed mint, and honeysuckle drug the air, and Erec, intoxicated with it, sings idly and tries to draw out the Servant of Birds with insouciant charm. But Rachel sits heavily against him, so much baggage. When they stop beside a creek for the steed to drink and rest, Erec pads the saddle with a folded blanket and reminds Rachel of her promise.

She says nothing. Emptiness fills her.

She is merely stunned by this abduction, Erec thinks, assessing her hollow stare. In time she will thaw; he is confident of that. He remounts and offers a thick arm, but she remains motionless. Her buttocks ache from the hard ride into the hills, and all she wants is to sit here in the sun-shot woodland, in a cloud of spices, listening to the purling creek while she searches for the words to tell him she is not the Servant of Birds.

"You're my bride now," Erec insists. He snatches her arm and pulls her close enough to hoick her into the saddle. "I answered my promise. Now, by heaven or hell, you will be mine."

Objections stir in her, but her jaw clacks shut with the jolt of the horse hurrying off. Erec follows the cobbled path of the creek until a fallen tree blocks their way. Then they plod among clustered beeches to open slopes on higher ground. While the sun slides toward the purple-crowned mountains, they ride from hill to hill, down into dark dells of roisterous oaks draped with ivy and back up into hummocks violet with heather.

Finally, on a heath of gorse silvery in the thunderlight of towering rain clouds, Rachel can endure the spanking ride no longer. The stifling emptiness that resists nothing abandons her. She seizes Erec's beard and manages to shout, "Let me down!"

Quizzical surprise softens Erec's hard frown. He has been determined to cross this treeless down and reach the shelter of clumped woods in the blue distance before the rain begins, but Rachel's look is too frantic to ignore, and he stops the horse and lets her slide off.

"Erec Rhiwlas," she says fitfully, rubbing her stunned backside, "I am not the Servant of Birds. I am David Tibbon's granddaughter, Rachel."

Erec brings a leg over the horse's neck and sits side-saddle, smiling confidently. "I know you're not the Servant of Birds. Longsight Meilwr said so. And bards don't lie."

Rachel accepts this with a gruff nod. "Fine. Then leave me here and go back to your people. You don't want me."

"Oh, you're wrong: I want you, for certain." Erec grins cunningly. "Together, we will rule Epynt as the Welsh are meant to. Erec the Bold and the Servant of Birds—chieftain and baroness— we will unite the tribes."

"It will never happen."

Erec is surprised at the vehemence in Rachel's tone. "Why are you outraged? There will be little violence. We will rule by cunning and compassion. I learned something of that from you, Servant of Birds. By deception, you unseated Guy Lanfranc, whom all of Howel's army could not defy. And by generosity, you won the fealty not only of your castle but of the Welsh, who have loathed the Invaders for over four generations. Together, Bold Erec and the Lady of the Grail will earn the respect of kings—Norman and Welsh!"

Rachel backs away. "I am done with deception. I am not the Lady of the Grail. I am not the Servant of Birds. I am not Ailena Valaise. I am no baroness. I am a Jew. A Jew, do you hear! I am

David Tibbon's granddaughter. I am Rachel. Rachel is my name."

Erec juts out his lower lip and lifts his tufted brows. "I like it. Rachel. I will use that name only in private. I will never forget who you are." He puts a broad hand over his heart, and his eyebrows tilt sadly. "I understand now your grief at the rabbi's death. I swear to you, Rachel, I will learn who murdered your grandfather, and I will avenge his death."

Rachel shakes her head so strongly her long hair tosses. "No more killing! There will be no more killing. Leave me. I am done with it all. Go back to your tribe. Let Guy have his castle. Forget me."

Erec slips off his horse. "Rachel—I could never forget you. I want you as my wife. I want you more than I want power over my enemies. We will forsake the castle then. You will come live with me in the hills."

Rachel shudders at the thought and, turning away, strides through the snagging gorse toward a flare of sunlight lifting colors out of the bracken. But her anger is spent; she drifts weightless, a mere ghost. Divulging the truth has unburdened and cleansed her of all pretense. Even the emptiness feels acceptable now. She wisps over the cracked limestone and through the claws of bracken—a sentient vapor, wafting away. Only the pretense of her body is left. She feels hungry and she wants to urinate.

"Come back," Erec calls and laughs. "You belong to me now."

Rachel knows she will never belong to anyone, ever. She will not allow it. Her hand clutches the bane-root folded in her robe. She is more determined than ever to be free of everything, to elude her captor, to slip away from her lies and her grief, to shed her hollow body. An almost blissful warmth pervades her as she removes the black twist of root, and she is grateful to Erec for carrying her out here into the wilderness, where the people who have come to need her will not be appalled by her death.

The stillness quivers. A cool, wet breeze laves over her, and she looks up to see silver auroras of rain ruffling above the remote horizons of hills. Among the mighty clouds, the sky opens, blue and vibrant as a flame. Her gaze falls deeper into the highlands, into the tremendously vast and mysterious terrain with its long valleys, rocky crags, and dark groves. The soul's light, nearly invisible, tints the vista with an opal sheen, summoning her out of this world.

"Rachel," Erec says from behind her. "Come with me before the rain starts." He takes her arm, and she twists away.

When she faces him, rancor clots her stare. "Don't touch me! I don't want you to touch me. I don't want you at all. Get away from me!"

She runs. Her robe snags on the bramble, and it rips as she flees heedlessly, her sandals scruffing a mousy odor from the rock and the dry root weave. Fearful of Erec's brute strength, she jams the bane-root into her mouth as she runs. The bitterness of it burns her mouth and hurts her sinuses. She gags, but clenches her teeth, breaking the blistery husk of the tuber and releasing its acrid poison.

Erec snatches her by the shoulder and whirls her about, ready to heave her over his shoulder. Then he sees the anguish in her eyes and the thread of black saliva drooling from her mouth. He claps his hand to her back; and she spews forth the broken earth nut. He smells it and jerks it away into the brush. "Bane-root!" His glare rages a moment; then it goes flat. "You'd poison yourself before you'd have me?" Seconds pass as his growing hurt couples with his ire. "Go, then!" He gruffly pushes her away, ashamed that he has been fooled by this madwoman. "I don't want any woman who loves death."

A mere fume of a woman, with tangled hair of dried frost, crusty earth-rimmed nostrils, and two black gleams for eyes in a sunken face, Pig-eyed Mavis clings to Gianni's arm with bony hands, her lichenous flesh dull as ash in the afternoon light slanting through the narrow window.

Madelon has already ducked out through the tattered flap of bark that serves as a door, clutching the woven grass satchel with the brown, wrinkled berries that will kill the child inside her. But Gianni cannot extricate himself from the hag's spidery clutch. Sneaking Madelon out of the castle at noon was easier than parting from this witch.

Thinking the witch wants more money, Gianni hands her three more obols and backs out through the bark-flap, glad to be away from the fusty stink of plaited weeds hanging from the knotty poles that support the briar roof. He thanks the hag yet again, but she will not release his arm.

Her pig-small eyes gleam closer, and he feels the sour heat of her breath on his face: "Moons and moons, she sees only the children of the fields, who pay for their herbs with a chicken or a rabbit. And now in this one moon alone, two knights come to Mavis. And of a sudden she's got coppers and a gold coin." Her face widens about a snaggle-toothed grin. "Be kinder than the knight before you and linger with Mavis, tell her tales of the castle and the Lady of the Grail. Come, stay a while."

Gianni pauses in his retreat, and his obsequious smile slips away. "What other knight visited you?"

The corners of Mavis's wrinkled mouth turn down. "How's she to know that? Have you told her *your* name? She'll call you Dashing Blackbeard. Then he would be Sir Battered Head. His skull was dented as an old kettle."

Gianni looks to Madelon, who has been listening from beside the horses. "Roger Billancourt!" she guesses.

"The castle's warmaster." The witch ekes out a whistle. "Mavis has heard of Roughshod Roger—never saw him, 'less that was him. Could have been, now's she thinks on it. He had the scars and the gruffness, all right. Wanted what you'd expect a warmaster wants—power to kill. Gave her a gold coin, too. A copper obol would have done. Was just two wicked twists of bane-root."

Rachel wanders in a daze. The bane-root has set her blood tolling in her ears. Rain sighs in the gorse, glittering about her, touching her with its cold points of light. For a while, she thinks she is dying—all the colors of the world look brilliantly glazed and she verges at the brink of her body, feeling as though she is about to loft free through the rain into the powerful clouds. But her legs insist on working, moving her among the heather toward the clumped trees of the valley, rooting her to the earth.

Glottal whisperings ride the wind from the mountains—distant thunder promising more rain.

Heart treading firmly in her breast, Rachel comprehends that death has not accepted her: she had not consumed enough of the bane-root to die. Lifting her face, she feels the riddling drops beat against her closed lids. A root catches her gait, nearly tumbles her headlong. She curses—then laughs at herself, soaked, alone in the wilds, orphaned by death. Her laugh clutches the deepest breath in her, and amazes her with its loud strength.

The emptiness she has felt since Grandfather's death has filled the whole brimming sky. No voices haunt her now; only the voice of the thunder, monotonously mumbling, and the sizzling of the downpour in the gorse shine in her. Sodden, her hair and garments plastered by the cloudburst, she laughs and cannot stop laughing at the fact that even death has abandoned her. Grandfather would be happy at that, she is sure.

She stops and throws herself to the ground. If death will not have her, she belongs then to life—all of her, the flesh and the lies, the hungers and the fears, all of it carried along swift as the clouds above, full as the emptiness that carries everything.

She rolls over and watches the massive cloud banks hanging over the undulant hills breaking into showers. A strange, holy light slants through the malignant violet of the tumbled cloud masses. Luminous green slopes appear briefly, as if to assure her of her solitude. Then the clouds close and the world silvers.

Rachel traipses downslope, crushing thyme and bog-myrtle underfoot, their spicy scents stinging her nostrils. Her laughter has calmed to a ticklish apprehension: life and death have their own order, apart from any meaning the heart can grasp. From the bottom of her misery, she suddenly cannot help loving whatever fills this emptiness. Let it be lightning streaks and thunder, forest mists and nightfall—and—if she lives to see it again—let it be the castle and all its lives. Seized by the bane-root's intoxication, she lets her life slowly reclaim her. For she is convinced she cannot throw it away again, or even lose it here among the endless gateways of the rain.

Moonlight brightens the clouds to a magical boiling mixture, and the stars glisten among them like dark bubbles. There are too many rabbit holes to continue on horseback, and Madelon is adamant about not spending the night in the forest. So Gianni and she walk together through the silver woods, leading their mounts, and bickering.

"You don't even know Hubert Macey," Gianni argues. "Have you even met him?"

"I've seen him at the festivals in Talgarth and Y Pigwyn," Madelon answers defensively.

"Then you know the pox has disfigured him. His nose looks like nibbled cheese."

Madelon glances sharply at Gianni. "How do you know that?"

"Your grandmother, Clare, has told my dwarf all about the old man."

"He's but thirty years old."

"Twice your age!"

"You're not much younger."

"Five whole years. And I've no children from a prior marriage."

"Who knows how many bastards you've strewn behind?"

"But . . . but none will seek me out. Whereas the Macey children will be all about you. And the oldest is merely three years your junior. Think how she'll feel, her mother in the ground a year and you in bed with her father."

Madelon stops and squints angrily. "The castle is over that rise. May we please go the rest of the way in silence? I don't want to talk about this anymore."

"Why not? Are you afraid to dwell on it? Afraid that you will see there is no love in your heart for this man?"

"Of course I have no love for him. Marriage is not about love, you fool. Hubert Macey is an earl."

"Am I the fool, Madelon?" His chiseled face holds the moonlight like marble. "Whether you are the wife of an earl or a simple knight in the service of a baroness, we grow old and we die. At least with me, you will know love and passion."

She huffs a laugh. "I will know humiliation. You are a priest."

"I am a knight-priest. And I will renounce my priesthood for you and be a knight. There is no humiliation in that."

Madelon continues walking. Feelings swirl and pulsate like the moonshadows flaring around her. Does she dare hope for what Gianni promises? Her head dizzies as she tries to disengage from her fear and think this through. She is gripped by the intimacy of the life growing inside her. All her fibers want to weep—but with caring or rage? She stares up stupidly at the radiant clouds, wanting some clarity from heaven. But all she can bring to mind is the image of Arrière-grandmère weeping with joy at the news of the frailty inside her and promising all would be well.

Abruptly, she pitches forward, her foot sunk in a rabbit hole. A tearing sensation has immobilized her ankle, and pain cuts to the bone. Gianni is over her even as she cries out, steadying her, gently extricating her caught leg. He lays her on the ground, and she clutches at his shoulder as he examines her ankle.

"No bones are broken," he reassures her. "It hurts, I know. The muscle is torn." He forestalls her fright with a quick smile. "Ripped like the fabric of my heart. Only yours will heal."

The hot wash of pain subsides as he unlaces her shoe. She watches him burst the shoulder seam on the sleeve of his blouse and expertly wrap the cloth over the arch of her foot and around her ankle. Clouds slide over the moon, yet even in the tense darkness his presence is vividly familiar. The slant of his shoulders, the handsome cut of his profile, and the assured and tender strength in his hands disperse her gloomy lamentations. *Could* she give herself to pox-scarred Hubert? Now that her own castle is secure, perhaps, indeed, there is no necessity to marry simply to have a home . . . ?

When Gianni lifts her and she puts her arms about his neck, she senses that heaven has answered her, intuiting that answer more than comprehending it. She feels, unthinkably deeper, the terror of her baby relax. Perhaps there will be no need for the purging herbs now? Mountains of silver spirit shine again as the moon peeks over the clouds; she feels affirmed in her decision. *Arrière-grandmère is right,* she thinks with relief. *All manner of thing shall be well!*

"Gianni," she says quietly as he sets her atop her steed. "I admit I have been wrong. I have been much too stubborn to see. I do love you."

Gianni steps back, then presses closer in the grip of a precarious feeling. "You will be my wife?"

"When you have put off the Church's cloth and done your penance—yes, I will marry you."

Gianni closes his eyes, offering a silent prayer, his whole body fringing with joy. He kisses her hand and looks up at her with radiant satisfaction. "I will earn your love anew each day, I promise."

On the way over the rise and across the moony field under Merlin's Knoll, the two fervently discuss the many possibilities of their future and all the small obstacles to their love. At the toll bridge, they pause. Madelon throws the grass pouch from Pig-eyed Mavis into the Llan, and Gianni draws his dagger, cuts the crimson cross from his tunic, and tosses it after.

They enter the castle and traverse the bailey laughing conspiratorially, and do not notice one of the sergeants running ahead along the rampart of the outer wall. Riding atop her steed, Madelon is barely troubled by the hot pain in her ankle. This very night, Gianni will write the bishop at Talgarth and, at dawn, he will seek out Maître Pornic and beg penance of the holy man.

The inner gate opens at Gianni's call, and William and Thierry stand before them, their torchlit faces tight, dark, and savage.

From behind a thorn hedge, Erec watches Rachel climb a ferny hummock and scan the maze of forests, hills, and turbulent streams. All the previous day and throughout the night, he has followed her unseen, waiting for her to need him. But she did not try to kill herself again—nor did she seem troubled traversing the somnolent woods far from her castle. She knew where to find edible mushrooms and berries in the dense coverts, and seemed at ease drinking brook water from her hands. When the rain beat her, she opened her arms to the wind, and Erec thought his heart would burst at glimpses of her nakedness shining through her robes.

Between bouts of storm, she found wind-blown briar wedged among boulders, dry inside, and she concocted little fires by twisting a stick in a burl packed with dusty leaves. Sweet smells of burnt myrtlewood and cedar weave around her, and drift downwind to where Erec crouches, aching with desire. He has had time to consider how much she has dared and suffered to be the Servant of Birds, and he loves her all the more for that audacity.

Several times he has been tempted to approach her and declare his love again, but each time he stops himself. *Love is not enough for a woman like this,* he finally believes. *Fate alone can join us— or not.* A chill blows through him. For the first time since his childhood, he longs for supernatural power, for the rhymes his grandmother whispered to the singers behind the sunset.

A rider appears among the cloud-shadows on the meadow, and

Erec backs away, tarrying only long enough to see that the horseman is a Swan knight. Once he is sure that the knight has spotted the Lady of the Grail, Erec turns and disappears into the dark mouth of the forest.

Rachel sits under a yew tree, weary and hungry, watching sunlight glisten on the wind-brushed fur of a grassy field, when a man on horseback approaches.

Yesterday she wandered through the country in the rain, the wide vista of rain-lit forested hills and misty valleys a shining, gray-banded agate. By twilight the storm had passed, and the fiery tumult of the sky cleaved heaven from earth. All the dreaminess of her brush with death dimmed with those drastic vapors. Watching the claw of the moon riding through the night clouds, she felt despair all over again. Grandfather's murder, Dwn's death, and the life she had shaped from the baroness's deceptions—all seemed futile. When she finally fell asleep curled up in a root cove, she wished she would not wake again.

She woke famished and weak. For a terrible, disoriented moment she believed she was back in the woods with her grandfather, a child again, and all that had happened since was a dream. Despair clutched her—and then, eyeing the splendor of her muddy and tattered robe, with its fine lace and delicate fabric, she realized what terrors lay behind her. Nothing was worse than those cruel, numb years of aimless wandering had been. Even Grandfather's death was mercifully swift and good compared to the degradation he had endured as a vagabond, to sustain her.

All shall be well, she greeted the new day and foraged for berries.

Emptiness deepened about her again, but she remembered enough of yesterday's intoxication to understand that this was the stillness of heaven that embraced everything—it was God's high silence in which the world, with all its people and things, flowed like clouds. She wandered across the morning and deep into the afternoon enraptured by the strange beauty of fate that had brought her through such sorrow to these strong hills with their nettles and cow-parsley and flowering grass jangling their colors.

At last, her strength drained, she sat down under a yew, where a few shaggy trees staggered out of a forest into a wide, tussocked field. She dozed for a while. When she woke, she saw a rider approaching across the field. Now he is close enough for her to recognize the sugar-white hair of Denis Hezetre. She stands and waves, and his horse trots over, Denis with an easy smile in his boyish face.

"Where's Bold Erec? Is he nearby—or were your Angevin charms too hot for his Welsh blood?"

Denis dismounts and removes a flask, a wedge of cheese, and a heel of black bread from his saddlebag. As they eat, she tells of her abduction and attempt at suicide.

"After Gilbert," Denis says soberly, "you would never marry by duress again. If Erec knew you at all, he would never have forced your hand." He presses his brow to her knee. "I am so grateful God has spared you. We need you, Ailena." He lifts a careworn face. "I need you."

Rachel's spine tightens, and she sits taller. *He does not need Ailena Valaise as she was before,* she tells herself. *He needs the Ailena Valaise before him now.* He has abandoned his staunchest friend for *her*—not for an Ailena whom he had helped to exile, but for *her,* whatever name he calls her. And that is so for the others as well: Clare, Madelon, the villagers—all would be impoverished without *her.* The helplessness she had experienced yesterday, that had inspired her to want to die, was a delusion. She had lost faith in the lie that Ailena Valaise had lived her last years to make true. But that lie *is* truth. She is the baroness so long as she believes in herself. *That,* she sees, *is my Grail—all of Ailena's memories and training wanting to be remade into a destiny—my destiny.*

She places her hands to the sides of Denis's face and says sincerely, "God has favored me."

Clare drops the vellum to the floor and stamps on it. "To damnation fire with all of Guy's demands!"

Gerald bends to retrieve the letter, but Clare seizes his shoulder. He looks apologetically at the other knights sitting at the table in the council chamber; Harold runs an anxious hand over his bald pate, and William and Thierry glower. "Until the baroness returns," he says indulgently, "Clare *is* the eldest authority."

"Ailena's been gone two days," William complains. "She may never return. And if she does, she will not be alone. She will occupy our keep with an army of barbarians."

"I will not have Guy commanding us!" Clare shouts. "He acts as though he were our lord. How dare he write a letter of demands?"

"Grandmère," Thierry intercedes firmly, "Uncle is the domain's rightful heir."

"Ailena has been gone only two days," Clare answers. "If she does not return by week's end, I will accede to his authority. But not until then."

"That is not one of your options, Clare," William says. "Guy states, if we do not accept him back at once, he will come with Branden's men."

"Then let him come!" Clare grinds her foot over the letter defiantly. "Mother's soldiers are sworn vassals. They will fight."

"Clare!" Gerald puts his arm about his wife and coaxes her to sit. "We dare not squander the lives of good men."

"They have sworn their allegiance," Clare insists. "I will not be squandering their lives. They do not obey me. If they did, they would immediately release Ummu and Canon Rieti."

"Ummu poisoned the rabbi," William states loudly, half-rising from his seat. "And the canon has been fornicating with my daughter!"

"I cannot believe dear Ummu would murder anyone," Clare says. "As for Madelon, she is old enough to know what she is about. You were too rough with the canon—blackening both his eyes."

"Not rough enough," William rasps. "He should be castrated! He's a priest who has slandered God!"

"We may yet hear from the baroness," Harold interjects, wanting to deflect the hostility in the room. "The heralds that have been sent to the Welsh camps may return with word of her."

"Regardless, we must still respond to Guy," Gerald says. "We must think of a way to borrow time."

"Let the castle decide," Clare says, lifting her head haughtily. "If the castle will fight, then we will stand off Guy. Let the sergeants and the guildsmen and the villagers decide. Their lives are the castle's strength."

"Men have no authority to supersede their lords," William laughs darkly. "That is like asking the limbs and organs of the body to supersede the head! That is madness!"

"No greater madness than turning ourselves over to my iron-hearted brother." Clare rises. "Call an assembly. The castle will decide its own fate."

"She loves me, stump!" Gianni says from the dark corner, where he lies on his back in a heap of straw.

"So you have reminded me since your grand entrance," Ummu responds. "My heart craves pause to your addle-pated talk of love. Madelon's love has hardly spared us any grief. Your bruised eyes must hurt less to say it, though—you say it so often."

"She was sincere, Ummu. She cast the purging herbs into the river. She has chosen to trust in me."

Ummu walks his legs up the stone wall so that he is standing on his head. "Madelon has been as sincere with at least one other knight."

"Am I to begrudge her the same playfulness that once was my life?"

Ummu sighs. "Would that our jailers had as fine a sense of justice. Ta-Toh and I begrudge their comfort." At the sound of his name, Ta-Toh stirs from his nest and makes a disconsolate noise. "Listen—even this animal can find no home in our dark hole. Stay this prattle of love and tell us again what you learned from the witch."

Gianni expels a weary breath. "You've heard it twice before. There's no more to tell. Roger Billancourt purchased bane-root from Pig-eyed Mavis. Madelon heard. But to whom will she testify?"

"You forget—I am not unloved by Clare. If she knew—"

"That her son-in-law and grandson are poisoners, stump? If she challenges that heartless pair, she may well be joining us."

Ummu slumps into the straw. "What will become of us?"

"Far better to dwell on love, little man."

Maître Pornic squeals like a pig. He stands on the main avenue of the village, hands to mouth, oinking loudly. Among the huts scurry guildsmen in leather caps with earflaps tied under their chins and vests embroidered with the devices of their trades: armorers' anvils, cobblers' shoes, chandlers' lamps, butchers' cleavers, drapers' spools, saddle-makers' horseheads. Every guildsman has several apprentices, and all bear quarter-staves.

Thomas Chalandon, coming over the toll bridge, is stopped by Blind Siân, who hears the castle's chapel bell tolling and has come down from her prayers on Merlin's Knoll to learn the news. "Good sir, stop a moment and share your eyes with a blind woman."

"Gladly, Siân—though you'll not like what you hear."

"Master Thomas!" Siân gusts with surprise, feeling his leather jerkin and the airy texture of his tunic. "Why are you not wearing your cassock?"

"I've thrown it off, Siân. When our Maître broke the Sacred Visage, he broke my faith in the Church. I saw then that it is God who holds my love—and He is not confined to chapels or creeds."

"If the Maître did that, he blessed you."

"So I think, Siân—though the villagers will hardly think he is blessing them today."

"Is that Maître Pornic I hear yoicking like a pig?"

"Yes, it is. He has come from the castle with the guildsmen. The sergeants and my family have chosen to defy my uncle's demand to return the castle to him."

"The baroness has been away only two days! Your Uncle Guy is an impetuous one."

"That is indeed one of his traits. And belligerence is another. With Branden Neufmarché's men, he will strive to take our castle. The guildsmen do not favor war, for it eats their profits, so they have sided with Maître Pornic and the Morcars, who have no love for our baroness. They have come to the village to collect the swine the baroness drove from the castle two months ago. They argue that they will need the meat in the event of a siege. But, in truth, they have always resented the villeins receiving this bounty."

"But the villagers will not stand for it," Siân declares.

"They had better. The guildsmen crave an opportunity to crack villein skulls. And if there is a row, William Morcar and his son Thierry wait in the lists with enough sergeants to enforce the edict. They would like nothing better than to command the vassals loyal to the baroness and perhaps win that allegiance to themselves."

Siân swats imaginary flies from her face. "The Devil's pestering minions are in the air, Thomas. And why is our holy man Pornic in the midst of them?"

Thomas takes Siân's arm and guides her back several paces to make way for the first drove of pigs running onto the toll bridge ahead of the jeering guildsmen. "Maître Pornic has no faith in miracles, only in the Church. So you can understand his joy that Ailena Valaise is gone. Now he can restore the world to its former order."

The squealing of the driven pigs and the shouts of the guildsmen drown out Thomas's voice. Siân tugs at his arm, pulling him away from the cacophony, back toward Merlin's Knoll, where prayers might lift them above this precarious world.

Afternoon shadows darken the bailey when Denis Hezetre enters the castle with the baroness seated before him. The herald's trumpet announced her when she was spotted on the toll bridge, and the rest of the *palais* have hurried into the bailey to greet her.

Clare wails at the sight of her bedraggled mother, and takes the horse's bridle to guide it to the inner ward. But Rachel, seeing pigs rooting in the alleys, pulls on the reins.

"Why are there swine in the castle?" she demands.

"Guy threatens us, Mother. We brought in the pigs for food against a siege."

Rachel looks about at the numerous faces watching her expectantly. Several hundred people—the whole castle—throng about her, yet even in their midst she still feels the reverberations of embracing emptiness. "There will be no siege," she declares.

"Mother, we have told Guy early today we would fight him before surrendering your castle."

"And our scouts tell us," Gerald adds, "Neufmarché's men are marching here even now."

"Then send a herald to declare my return," Rachel says. "Tell him that his mother would like to come and go as she pleases without his trying to steal what is hers."

Laughter courses through the crowd.

"What of Bold Erec?" someone shouts.

"He found only my face young," she retorts. "My heart is too old and gristly for his taste."

She nods to Denis, and he nudges the horse through the crowd. On the way, Rachel sees William nervously chewing the corner of his mustache. Beside him is Madelon, head hung forlornly.

Rachel scans the gathering. "Where is Canon Rieti?"

"I will tell you later," Clare says discreetly.

Thierry shoulders closer. "The false-faced priest has dishonored my sister. I demand high justice."

"Where is he?" Rachel asks.

"In the dungeon," Gerald replies.

"Release him at once," Rachel orders.

Clare clutches her mother's leg and asks hopefully, "Ummu, too?"

"Yes. I will meet with them in the *palais*. I want Madelon there as well—with her family."

Rachel rides on, and the crowd parts. Only Thierry stands his ground as she passes, watching her with eyes hooded as a falcon's.

Branden Neufmarché stirs uncomfortably in his saddle as the herald from Castle Valaise rides off. Behind him, on the vast meadow fronting his fortress, his army mills, readying a caravan of wagons laded with supplies and horses caparisoned for battle. Roger Billancourt paces on horseback among them, shouting orders, while Guy Lanfranc budges against Branden's personal mounted guard, trying to get through to see what message the herald has conveyed.

For a moment Branden entertains the idea of asserting his command and ordering the army to stand down. But then Guy blusters through the helmeted horsemen and approaches Branden. "What news from the herald?" he demands, annoyed to have been held back.

"Bad news," Branden admits. "The baroness is returned to her keep."

"And Bold Erec?"

"Somehow she has removed herself from him." Branden's chin

folds glint with sweat, and he casts a disparaging look at the glowering sun. "Now, at least, we shall be spared a sweltering campaign."

"Bloody hell!" Guy glares. "Who knows what secret arrangement with the barbarians the bitch has won by her loins? Why else would they have set her free? We strike *now*—hard and swift—and be done with her before she opens her castle's gates to the Welsh as wide as she spread her legs."

Branden plucks at his lower lip. "It seems a great risk to take with so little known."

"What more do you need to know?" Guy sweeps his arm at the meadow of mailed soldiers. "*They* know enough to fight. They know they'll win and they'll have crofts of their own, each of them a little baron with their own peasants. There's land to be had—or to be lost. Will you take or lose it?"

"Then it is war." Rachel sits in the chair of state, muscle-sore from her wandering but refreshed by a lilac-petaled bath and clean robes. The chaplet of presence glints among upswept hair that has been brushed free of nettles and washed in fragrant soapberry water. "War," she repeats, fear of disaster churning in her. She wants the fear to expand into the emptiness of all she has lost, but it just twists inside her. "Is that what you want?" She looks around the table at Gerald, Denis, Harold, Thomas, and the several sergeants invited into the council chamber by the knights.

"None of us wants it," Gerald says. "But Branden Neufmarché has assembled armored forces outside his fortress, and Guy *is* among them with his warmaster. Our scouts report they are bivouacked by the oak glade in the disputed pastureland between our realm and Branden's."

"How long will it take them to reach us?" Rachel asks.

Gerald looks to one of the sergeants, and the soldier answers, "If they decamp at dawn, they will be at the Llan by noon, my lady."

Rachel presses her fingertips together, stares into the emptiness they hold, and pretends she is holding the Grail. *What to do?* she asks the sacred chalice—but no answer budges past her fear. She looks up and asks, "What should we do?"

The knights exchange perplexed glances. "Before Denis

returned you to us," Gerald replies, "your knights and sergeants asked themselves that very question. We decided to defy your son. But now, my lady, the decision is entirely yours."

Rachel shakes her head. "No. I have no heart for war. What objection is there to submitting to Guy?"

Gerald and Harold lower their eyes. Denis looks at them and then at Rachel. "Baroness, if we submit, you will be deposed."

Rachel smiles weakly. "I will return to the Holy Land. Those of you that wish may accompany me." She looks pointedly at Thomas.

"Grandmère," Thomas says, "what of your edict from heaven? The Lord has returned you to the world."

"But to kill?" Rachel frowns. "There was no anticipation of war in my vision."

From the back, a sergeant speaks. "Mistress, the villeins will suffer if you submit to Guy. Already they have lost their swine. They are angry about that. And their anger will provoke the baron."

"And what of the rabbi?" Denis queries. "Canon Rieti claims that the bane-root which killed our rabbi was purchased from Pig-eyed Mavis by Roger Billancourt. That is murder! Will we submit to murderers?"

"Rabbi would not want vengeance," Rachel murmurs quietly and sits deeper in her chair, feeling suddenly heavy.

"Not vengeance," Denis proclaims, "but justice. Vengeance belongs to God!" The white-haired knight speaks with uncontainable emotion, his lifelong love for Guy now warped into hatred. The knowledge that his old friend has defied God with a holy man's murder enrages him. For without God, there is only the arrogance of men, he thinks, and his lifelong denial of sexual desire, the ache of his effort to match Guy's impotence with continence, serves not love but only Guy's pernicious ambition. The waste of his devotion has sickened him. "Let us face Guy on the field—and let God arbitrate."

"God is not a weapon," Rachel replies.

Despondently, Denis pushes back from the table. "Lady, you have already decided. There is to be no battle."

"No." Rachel stares with half-opened eyes at the men before her. No voices or distant hymns stir in her. Only silence answers the dread in her, as if the whole world where she sits is empty, waiting for her to fill it. And if she refuses, it belongs to Guy. *No,* she decides and says aloud again, "No. David Tibbon was murdered. If we submit, then his death serves his murderers. We will not submit."

The men, who had sat locked in the stillness of her indecision, are suddenly animated, turning to each other, muttering encouragement.

Rachel breathes deeply, confirming her strength to flee no more before those who have killed her family. She rises, and as the men stand, declares in a strong voice, "It is war."

Madelon gasps when she sees Gianni Rieti enter the council chamber, the flesh around his eyes mollusc-black. She pulls away from her mother's grasp and runs to him, throwing her arms about him.

Rachel silences Hellene's protest with a gesture begging patience. She summons the couple closer. "Where are your father and twin brother?" she asks Madelon.

"They would not be present," the young woman answers.

"Father is ashamed," Hugues pipes up, "and Thierry is too angry." His mother shushes him, and he scowls at her.

"Then they have no faith in love," Rachel says and looks to the pair before her. "Are you both prepared to swear your love for each other before God and all others?"

Embracing, Madelon and Gianni smile at each other and nod. Hugues wrinkles his nose, and Hellene puts a hand over her open mouth.

"Gianni Rieti, you will forsake your vows to the Church?"

"In my heart, lady, I already have."

"Then I will write to the bishop at Talgarth myself and recommend that your penance be light, for you have been called by God to serve Him in a way more difficult than solitude and prayer. Now you will meet God in the harshest discipline of all, fulfilling the demands of love."

The banked colors of sunset fill the tall, tapered windows of the *palais* room where Clare and Gerald sit with Ummu at a banquet table. Servants hover nearby, ready to refill the crystal decanter with apricot wine and replenish the silver trays with mint-jellied meats and salad trimmings of cucumber and wormwood. Ummu, curly hair coiffed, attired in the silken finery that Clare made for him during the tourney, eats with gusto. Ta-Toh, dressed in a fresh green tunic, sits beside him on the table and helps himself to cherries and grapes.

Gerald, too, eats, but Clare is too distraught. "Do you think Guy will actually attack us?" she asks the dwarf.

Ummu defers to Gerald for a reply, and the old troubadour casts him a look of fatalistic certitude.

"War," Ummu says around a mouthful, "is the cage where men are happiest." He hastily swallows. "I saw enough of it in the Levant. But I'm only half a man and so had twice my fill. I think your brother still finds it savory."

"But to attack his own castle!" Clare wails. "His own mother!"

"She is not your mother," Gerald says, delicately placing a sliver of meat on a pastry with his knife-tip.

"Gerald!" The whites show atop Clare's eyes. "Are you with Guy?"

"Certainly not. But we have all observed that this woman is not the piss-and-vinegar baroness we loved in fear."

"The Grail has changed her." Clare turns to the dwarf. "Isn't that so, Ummu? You saw the transformation yourself."

"I did, indeed. And it did baffle me." He stuffs a pastry in his mouth to keep from saying more.

"I do not doubt the miracle," Gerald adds. "But I do think she has been changed utterly."

"Uh-er-ly," Ummu concurs with a packed mouth.

"She is not your or Guy's mother anymore," Gerald says. "She has been made into another woman, a woman with a different soul. Guy is not unjustified in challenging her right to rule."

Clare tilts her head back, her eyes wide. "Gerald, are you saying you will not defend her?"

"Yes, Clare," he answers gently. "I will not defend her. I am saying that when I take the field tomorrow I will be going to battle to defend you and our children—not the baroness."

Clare's umbrage lifts, her eyes bat with surprise, and her plump face wobbles toward tears. "Oh, Gerald—I'm so frightened."

Gerald leans toward his wife and puts his arm around her. "We are all frightened this night, my dear. But it will go better tomorrow for those of us who know what is worth the cost of our lives. As for me, that could only be you."

Ummu shakes his head ruefully, and Ta-Toh pats his cheek consolingly and feeds him a cherry.

An owl cry announces the night. Rachel kneels on a reed mat among the ashes inside the burned husk of the synagogue. Denis Hezetre and Harold Almquist kneel beside her, and, behind, sergeants and villeins, kneel or sit on the toppled masonry. Gianni Rieti, in a blue tunic like Denis's and Harold's, with the emblem of the Swan emblazoned on it, reads aloud from the Bible. At first he had demurred when the others asked him to read, claiming not to be worthy. But the knights, the sergeants, and the villeins, who have all become accustomed to the dignity of his Continental accent, insisted. And now as he reads the Psalms asking for their souls to be delivered from the battle, his own soul speaks clearly.

Afterward, the worshipers depart while the evening star still gleams above the ragged forest. They return to castle and village to rest and to make peace in their own hearts. Rachel lingers in the dark, watching the light of the quarter moon slant through the empty windows of the temple and gloss the black slag, where David's ashes are buried.

Tomorrow, she speaks to the spirit in the fallen rafters, *your ashes will still be here. But where will here be? Will it still be mine? Or was it ever mine?* Rachel looks overhead at the solitary stars, paying special heed to the void between them, holding them in their places. That same emptiness, she learned in the wilderness, holds everything in its place, even death.

Grandfather—you are right. This is not my place. It was my madness brought us here. If I had accepted the dying of my family as much as their dead bodies, if I could have believed as you do— as I do now—that everything is perfected in death, then I would have taken from my family's defeat what they left me—the emptiness only my own life can fill. That sacred emptiness. The empti-

ness of the Cup. If I had understood then how it holds everything, how it purifies every death, no matter how horrible, if I could have seen how it is the reply to all our imploring, I would have been myself. There would have been no need to be someone else. Daniel Hezekyah would have had me, and our lives would have completed themselves in their proper place—in the Promised Land.

Rachel bows her head to the silence that carries the owl's cry, the rustling wind, and her sorrow.

Denis waits until the evening star sets before approaching Rachel. "Come away now," he advises.

She shakes her bowed head. "Go, Denis. I will be all right here."

"And if Bold Erec returns?" Denis sits on a rock beside the mat where she kneels. "No. I will wait here with you."

She looks up from her prayer and sits back on her haunches. "For so many years you have loved Guy Lanfranc. How can you possibly face him tomorrow on the field of battle?"

Denis's jaw pulses. "It is true I loved him, my lady. But I think now it was not him I loved, it was his strength. His strength has been my weakness, my blindness. Only now, as I've gotten older, I've found the greater strength lies not in the muscles of men, but in their spirit." He sighs remorsefully. "All these years I loved what I thought was noble in Guy. He had saved my life and paid dearly for it, and I called that strength noble. But his is a hideous strength after all, which is noble only in battle and which battles even God."

For an instant, Rachel thinks she hears the baroness's spiteful cackle, and a chill finger touches her between the shoulder blades. *What hatred that old woman bequeathed her son.*

"Then are we right and just in this, Denis? Are we right to meet Guy in battle?"

Denis peers at her in the dark and remembers when she had stood naked here before him and the other knights. "How unlike you you have become, Ailena! In earlier days, you would have been so outraged, you'd have sent your men to attack Neufmarché's camp at night. If nothing else, your miracle has shown us God's power to heal and transform."

"You've not answered my question, Denis."

"Is there an answer?" Denis's pale hair shines with moonfire like a nimbus. "Remember what you said before we built this temple, when we were wondering what to do with our poor? You said love proceeds from wrong to wrong. *That* is my answer. Tomorrow Guy will take the field out of hatred of you. Branden will be there out of greed. But we—we will fight for love."

Thomas Chalandon loiters among the ritual stones on Merlin's Knoll until Denis Hezetre steps out of the ruins of the synagogue. The bearded knight takes up his post atop one of the moonstruck rocks, searching for scouts or signals from the castle. Thomas waves to him as he enters the temple, and Denis nods back.

For a while, Thomas stands in the doorway, watching his grandmother in the silvery darkness. He knows she is sitting on the far side of a decision that he had thought was impossibly beyond her. He had not believed she had the old strength, the will, to choose for war. *God lives in each heart,* he had reminded her at the council meeting. *God bleeds on every battlefield,* she had replied resolutely.

"Grandmère," he says softly. When she looks over her shoulder, moonlight glints off the tracks of her tears, and he wishes he could snatch his voice back and slip away. She beckons him closer and wipes her cheeks and eyes. "Do you weep for tomorrow?" he asks, sitting on the mat beside her.

Rachel has let her tears flow for her grandfather and the rest of her family, killed not by God but by men. Even so, she nods.

"Have you forgotten, it was you who said we can find God in all of His creation," Thomas says. "Then we will find Him tomorrow as well, won't we?"

"God—" Her mouth bends in a numb smile.

"I believe He will be there, Grandmère. Since throwing off my cassock, everything has opened around me. He has jumped out of the holy writings and the sacraments; He is truly everywhere, as you say." Thomas takes her hand and feels a flicker of attraction as he gazes into her young face. "Grandmère, when I told you of my desire for you—it is true—There is . . . the most strange and remarkable familiarity I feel in your presence that I can't explain. Nor can I express it—well, certainly, I've expressed it wrongly. But the desire is so strong to be with you, to share your presence, to hear your thoughts. Surely, there is no sin in that. No sin in desire, only in wrongful actions."

Rachel removes her hand. Her mouth opens to speak, but nothing comes out. The deception is too cruel. She manages to mutter, "Poor Thomas—God is a sickness." Then she turns away, unable to look him in the eye.

Bewilderment plays across Thomas's face.

"We are the cure," Rachel says finally, in torment. "Is it not ironic? God is an ailment people must heal."

"I don't understand."

"But you do understand!" Rachel replies. "God is a mystery. We can never understand why things work out the way they do. We have only to trust in our own meanings."

She looks back at Thomas and sees, even in the darkness, the childlike sincerity of his gaze and the angelic grace of his gentle features. The moonglow intensifies his enigmatic beauty, and in the face of this grace, in the face of this Parsifal whose heart was meant only to be pure, she knows with certainty that she must tell him who she is. "I desire you, too, Thomas. And if that desire is from God, then I must tell you, out of love, out of caring for you, that I am not your grandmother. I am not Ailena Valaise. My name is Rachel Tibbon. The granddaughter of these ashes."

Thomas stands before he even realizes he has moved.

Hurriedly, Rachel tells him her story, leaving out nothing, not even her madness. She does not know if it is rage or disgust that widens his eyes and pulls back his upper lip.

Thomas listens immobilized, then sags under the weight of her words. He sits on the masonry beside her, stunned, feeling the implications prickling at the numb edge of his soul. "Your vision—the Grail—all of it a lie?"

"Not a lie, Thomas—a story."

"A lie!"

"No! There is a difference. The Grail is real! But not as you think. Look, it has healed me. It has washed the blood of madness from me. It has made me a baroness."

"But you're not—" Thomas shakes his head, dumbstruck. "You're a Jew. A cruel joke played by Grandmère from her grave."

"Thomas—" She reaches for him.

"No!" He recoils and is on his feet again. "Say no more!"

"Thomas—I love you. I told you because I love you."

With a cry, Thomas reels away and runs horrified from the ruins.

Rachel walks out of the synagogue a husk, lighter than when she entered. The weight of her history—all of it—lies behind in the ashes. But the burden of her lie has run off into the night. When Denis takes her hand to help steady her step on the dark trail, he is surprised at how light her gait is. Whatever is going to happen tomorrow, she walks toward it with the freedom of knowing she can lose no more of herself.

Thomas runs away blindly from Merlin's Knoll. The villagers have always said the place is haunted. No wonder the Sacred Visage could not remain whole there. No wonder the rabbi died there. *Rabbi! He was no rabbi.* The thought flogs him faster, and he trips over a rock, shoves himself back to his feet, and bursts into a field of tall, tasseled grass.

Thomas runs to the verge of exhaustion, then drops to his knees. *What is left to worship?* he asks himself, in the one chapel where for him God has always dwelled. The wind soughs through the hay; the moonlight ripples across it.

Hurtful thoughts assail him: *If there is no Grail, if the old man was no rabbi, maybe the Sacred Visage was not real, either—just an odd rock in whose surface people wanted to see Christ just as they foolishly want to see Ailena Valaise in Rachel Tibbon. So Maître Pornic is right. This fodder grass is a miracle. The stars are miracles. But the Sacred Visage was only a distraction from the real miracle of God's creation and our redemption in Christ. All else is deception, the Devil's work. Maître Pornic is right. He knew about Grandmère! He knew from the start.*

Thomas rises and staggers through the hay field, astonished at his true grandmother's vindictive cunning and the stupidities of people hungry for miracles. Anger lances him, anger at Rachel for deceiving him and at his grandmother for mocking his faith from her grave.

Now what? He is more alone than he has ever been. Wading through tracts of barley, the night breeze garlanding him with fragrances of pollen, river mist, and cow droppings, he is afraid. *Who is God to allow such illusions? Who is the Devil with the strength to defy this God?*

The village rises from the fields. To the left is the stand of alders that blocks the mountain winds, and there the village dung-pile where Dwn had been exiled. *Did she know? Did she die believing her mistress had been lovingly singled out by God?*

The glittery fields of the Milky Way soar above the perishable world, silhouetting the thatched huts. He clambers the stile of a low, crumbly rock wall and passes under a walnut tree, where a dog barks awake, recognizes him, and drowsily lowers its head to its paws. He thinks to pass through the village, cross the toll bridge, and return to the castle, to his garret in the donjon where he hopes sleep will ease his distressed soul. But then he sees the village's shanty chapel with its walls of woven branches.

Inside, he kneels on the packed earth before the bark-covered rail and peers into the dark at the crude crucifix. Head resting in his hands, he prays for the Comforter, the Holy Spirit, to come to him. The silence is quilted with the scents of wild mint and rosemary seeping through the walls with the draft from the fields. On the split log that serves as an altar, someone has left an offering of blackberry brambles wreathed into a thorny crown. The humble gift brings tears to his eyes, and he weeps at the sincerity of people's love for God— the very sincerity that serves so gullibly in the Devil's work.

"Shed no tears at the altar," a hushed voice says from the entry, and Thomas turns to see Maître Pornic on his knees in the doorway, crossing himself. The holy man rises and advances between the pews of splintery benches. "Jesus wept tears of blood for us all. His sorrow redeemed our souls. Now we should approach God with joy."

Thomas wipes the tears from his face. "There can be no joy in my heart tonight."

"Yes, I feel the same pain, Thomas." Maître Pornic kneels beside him. "Tomorrow, men will die."

"Men die every day," Thomas says and lifts his face toward the crucifix shrouded in darkness. "I would think you would be happy. They are departing this sinful world for heaven, aren't they, Maître?"

"Those who die in grace, yes." Maître Pornic lays a bony hand on Thomas's shoulder. "My son, are you distressed at something deeper? Are you still angry at me for shattering the icon in the Jew's temple? The rabbi would have been pleased."

"I cannot say what troubles me, Maître. Please, leave me to my solitude."

"You are a soul I thought marked for service to God. You threw off your cassock when I destroyed the icon. I have been deeply troubled since that my zeal has deprived God of your love."

"I understand why you broke the Sacred Visage," Thomas mutters, his clasped hands pressed against his face. "Now, please, go away."

"Only an absence of faith requires miracles," the holy man says and squeezes Thomas's shoulder. "Your faith has always been strong. What you have always questioned is not God but your own worthiness to serve as God's priest. Am I wrong?"

Thomas turns so that Maître Pornic must remove his hand. "I do not wish to speak now. My soul *is* troubled, and only God can help me bear this. Please, leave me to speak with Him."

Maître Pornic lowers his chin to his chest, and, in the dark, the ring of his silver hair gleams like a halo. "After you departed the abbey, an encyclical arrived from our Holy Father Innocent the Third. In it he describes a new way of purging the soul that he encourages all of his flock to practice. It is a general confession of the soul's disturbances and sins. When heard by a priest, this confession is received directly by God."

"God hears us in our hearts," Thomas says and turns back to the rail.

"Yes. But let Him hear you also in your voice that you may be forgiven not only in your heart but in your body, which carries the heart's burdens."

Thomas shakes his head. "What troubles me is secret. It is a confidence I cannot break without betraying myself."

"What you tell me, Thomas, belongs to God. Speak, my son.

Unburden yourself, find favor with God—and quiet my earthly concerns that I may know I have not driven you from the Church."

"I threw off my cassock because I cannot become a priest," Thomas says to the darkness on the altar. "I cannot abide the strictures of faith. God is in all things, and I do not need to reside in the Church to find Him. I am sorry that I have taken so many years to see so obvious a truth."

"Then I am reassured that I did not estrange you." Maître Pornic pats his shoulder, crosses himself, and stands. "I will pray for you, Thomas. Whatever path you choose from here will lead you to God."

Maître Pornic pads away, and Thomas's gaze falls again on the wreath of blackberry brambles. The expectation that shaped this offering and placed it here awakes in him a kindred feeling, a tender trust in what cannot be seen, yet what is nonetheless craved for, a love that death cannot gain on, a love that saves us from the frights of living. Sadness overwhelms him that such a supernal love would be sought in a crown of blackberry thorns, in the stain of a rock shard, or in the deception of an embittered old woman.

"Maître—" Thomas calls. "Come back. I need to confess."

The men sleep restlessly in the barracks. A nightmare yodel from a sergeant fighting tomorrow's battle wakes the man beside him, and he sits up and blinks into the yellow shine of oil lamps. Sergeants stripped to their loincloths sit at the edges of their bunks muttering angrily. *Is it a raid?*

The sleepy-eyed man hears no alarm, looks about to see if anyone else is girding for battle; then he sees Maître Pornic among the whispering men. *Someone has died,* he thinks and rises from his bunk.

"You," one of the master sergeants points to the groggy man. "Wake the others. Maître Pornic has important news."

Madelon lies awake in her bed, hands crossed over her belly, imagining the child growing within her. This soul has found refuge in her— and in her Gianni. Their love will defeat the doubts of others. For now only the baroness believes in them, but in time her love for her baby and for Gianni will matter far more than the anguish of her parents, the ire of Thierry, or the mockery of Hugues.

She prays for the baby, for this soul so fresh from God that He must be all the closer for this new life in her: *Protect my Gianni on the field of battle tomorrow. Spare him mortal wounds and the misery of defeat and return him to me so that he may accomplish his penance to You and be this child's father and*— How had the baroness said it? *Please, Father in heaven, let my Gianni live that he may fulfill the demands of love.*

While Gianni sleeps in the sacristy, clutching a ribbon twined about an elf lock of Madelon's hair, Ummu paces before the altar. Ta-Toh watches drowsily from his resting place in the crook of the Virgin Mary's arm.

"How can he sleep this night?" Ummu mutters, half-hoping his displeasure will rouse the slumbering knight so he can berate him again for agreeing to marry that wanton gamine. "Tomorrow he cannot beg off fighting as a priest. Tomorrow he risks his life for the privilege to marry! How grotesque!"

Blue stars and the half moon dangle above the vineyard, and the cherry orchard is full of nightingales. Thomas wanders slowly along the toll bridge road feeling bright within. All the darkness of his grandmother's deception passed out of him with his confession to Maître Pornic. Now, as he wanders through the night, he contemplates all the good that Rachel Tibbon has done for the village and the castle in the short time she has been among them.

She is a good woman, he realizes, recalling how she risked her life to steal from Dic Long Knife so that the castle would not be lost. There is no anger in his heart for her anymore; she had not sought out this fate, but had been selected for it by his wily grandmother. He laughs aloud with evil joy to think he had actually believed that the bitter and cruel old woman who was Ailena Valaise could have become the playful, selfless lady with the dark eyes.

But sadness still taints him with the thought that Rachel's story of the Grail is just a story. He sees again the blackberry wreath on the altar in the village chapel, and a pang of remorse troubles him. The greatest good Rachel has accomplished—greater than enriching the peasants or saving the castle—is strengthening her people's faith in the divine. Aber the Idiot, Blind Siân, Legless Owain, and all the village's other unfortunates have been renewed by her miracle. Even the knights and sergeants, so cynical under Guy's command, have become suddenly Bible scholars, great contemplators on the life of Yeshua ben Miriam. Another laugh rises in him at the thought of his father worshiping as a Jew and businesslike Harold Almquist and prosaic Denis Hezetre growing rabbinical beards.

Then another wave of concern sweeps through him and the smile fades. He stops walking before the road that leads to the castle and wonders if he must tell the others. Should the men ride against Guy tomorrow believing they are fighting—and dying—for the Lady of the Grail?

He walks onto the field toward a byre, where the cowherd has left a stool, and sits down. He looks up at the castle, the torchlit fastness a massive chesspiece of heaven held in place by the darkness. The watchmen on the ramparts ignore him, not realizing that such an insignificant figure in the dark among the lowing cows could carry a secret that might decide their fate.

Above the castle spires, the distant torches of heaven flicker. *There is a God,* Thomas believes, the mystical beauty of the night touching his soul. *And this whole world is His chapel.* With those words spoken silently to himself, he has his answer: the lives in this castle and in the abbey where he dwelled for so long—for that matter, the lives in all the castles and abbeys, in all the synagogues and mosques, in all the cities and villages of the world—all exist together in God's house. Though they go off in different directions, following their destinies like startled birds, they are yet in God's house.

Thomas stands. He will tell no one other than God what Rachel has told him. Tomorrow these men will fight and die for the Lady of the Grail—because she is real. As his uncle is real. If Guy Lanfranc prevails, all will be as before. The villeins will lose their pigs and the chapel they might yet build from the ruins atop Merlin's Knoll. His mother and sisters will lose their troubadours and courts of love. But they will all lose much more as well. They will lose the Lady of the Grail and the sustaining hope of the divine that Rachel Tibbon has made out of an old woman's curse.

Rachel cannot sleep. She has lit every oil lamp in her bedchamber and has had three more brought in. She wants light, enough of it to keep out the night. Out in the darkness a murderous mob lurks, waiting for dawn to attack. They have different faces than she remembers from her childhood, yet they are the same mob that destroyed her family estate, slaughtered her uncles and cousins, and forced her parents to slay their children and themselves. And now they are coming for her.

Each flame perches at the lip of each lamp, delicate and alert. Sitting on her bed, she stares at them, wanting to take them in through her eyes to illuminate the darkness inside her. She knows she would see the emptiness holding all her memories, and her fright would shrink into place instead of swelling all around her. If she could let in enough light, her memories would be just memories, not forebodings. She reminds herself, this is a war that the people want to fight to stop Guy Lanfranc. This is not her war. Her memories of her family's massacre are just memories, she tells herself again and again. With enough light inside her, she would see that. Tomorrow has its own freedom to be what it will be.

Her ruminations are interrupted by a knock at her door. She has told her maids to leave her alone, and she opens the door expecting a herald with news from the scouts. Instead, Thomas is standing there, his countenance soft and contrite. Rachel hides her surprise and dismisses the maids hovering anxiously behind the young man, and invites him to enter.

"Rachel," he says once the door is closed. "I shouldn't have run away."

Rachel feels the sides of her neck and her cheeks warm with relief. "I shouldn't have lied to you—to everyone."

Thomas smiles gently. "Not a lie. A story. There is a difference."

"Is there?" she asks, trying hard to perceive if he is mocking her.

"Yes. One deceives. The other conceives. The good you've conceived during your short time here—that is truly a miracle."

"I fear it is more a curse than a miracle to have brought this castle to the brink of war."

Thomas's eyebrows go up. "But you haven't! That is my uncle's doing. I am surprised he has not struck at you sooner."

Pain flinches in Rachel's stare. "Grandfather—and Dwn—they were both killed by him, I am sure of it. I am so afraid for the many more who will die tomorrow."

"Here in the March, there has always been war, Rachel. If you had not come, the very men arrayed against us tomorrow would have fallen at Uncle's siege of Neufmarché's castle."

"I would submit to Guy if that is what is best for the others. My grandfather's soul does not want vengeance."

Thomas takes Rachel's shoulders in his hands. "When our castle fights tomorrow, it will not be for vengeance, but for the good that we have known from the Lady of the Grail."

"Then in your heart my story is true?"

He looks at Rachel's pale face, her eyes round as night. "Let tonight be the one night that your story is not true, the one night when you are not my grandmother but the woman you really are, Rachel Tibbon." Impetuously, he kisses her mouth.

For a supreme moment, he feels her resist, then relent and press hard against him.

He sits her down and kneels before her. "Do you doubt my sincerity?" he asks.

"I believe my love for you is sincere," she answers. "I've not felt as I do now with anyone else."

Cautiously, solemnly, Thomas begins to undress her, and she does the same to him. They regard each other's nakedness, open-mouthed at first, feeling and caressing, astonished. Then they kiss again, touching as they have never touched before.

As Thomas draws the curtains around the bed and encloses them in the amber shadows of an amorous solitude, a sobering thought of battle claims Rachel again—where will they be at this hour tomorrow?

"Do not be afraid," he whispers and strokes her sable hair. "There is only tonight—and for as long as it lasts, we will be together."

Rachel closes her eyes and pulls him to her. She will not let fear rob her of this moment, the one, perhaps only, moment she will know of love. She lets the emptiness of her grief carry away her fright, and imagines herself floating, airborne with Thomas.

She opens her eyes and sees him rearing above her. A stab of pain joins them; a cry widens in her throat to a gasp and then a sharp sigh. Molded by a slick heat, they join, their fused bodies burning in a hot commotion of limbs. At first awkward and clumsy and then in a perpetual delirium, they find the rhythm of their slippery pleasure and glide in each other's arms, astute and flexible as old lovers.

Later, they lie as if stuck together, exhausted by their relentless hunger for each other. Then, joy dims to tomorrow's hopelessness. And from this brightest moment, the future darkens.

The chapel bell clangs furiously against the incandescent dawn. Rachel pokes her head out the door to receive the news that everyone is being summoned to the chapel. She refuses her maids' offers to help her dress.

By the time she and Thomas arrive at the chapel, everyone is gathered there. The guildsmen and their families jammed in the doorway part to let her enter. At the altar, Maître Pornic stands among a cluster of her sergeants. With his sunken cheeks and dark eye sockets, he looks like a cadaver.

Rachel stands at the rail before the altar. "Who rang the alarm?"

"I have," answers a thick-shouldered man with a fiercely ugly face—Gervais, the master of her sergeants. "Maître Pornic claims that you're not the baroness Ailena Valaise. He claims you are, in sooth, one Rachel Tibbon, the rabbi's granddaughter."

Rachel's face goes pale. She glares at Maître Pornic. "Why do you foment this lie on the very day our castle's fate is to be decided?"

"It is no lie," the holy man says vibrantly. "I swear on Christ's blood, it is the truth."

The assembly gasp as one, and their excited murmurs echo through the vaulted chapel.

Rachel tries to master her panic and says in a tremulous voice that the others mistake for anger, "Since my return, you have tried to usurp me, Pornic."

"You have usurped yourself. I have been privileged to learn the truth from one among us in whom you confided."

Rachel holds her gaze steadily on the abbot, knowing if she even glances at Thomas she will betray herself. Her throat is too tight to speak. *Can it be true?*

"Thomas Chalandon has confessed what you have told him, Rachel Tibbon." Maître Pornic points a gnarled finger at Thomas. "I have betrayed your confidence, Thomas. And for that God will punish me. But I cannot allow good men to die defending a lie."

For a near-eternity, Thomas stands stunned. He feels the eyes of those assembled upon him and realizes with despair that his simpleminded faith has condemned to death the woman he loves. "No!" he shouts, surging to the altar rail, his face dark with fury. "I have said no such thing!"

Maître Pornic gapes, appalled. "Thomas! Do not deny the truth before me. Your very soul is in peril. If even one life is lost by this deception, you will be condemned to eternal damnation!"

"I never said what you claim!" Thomas insists with all his breath. He turns about and faces the shocked crowd. "He lies! He is jealous of my grandmother's miracle."

"Thomas is in love with Rachel Tibbon," Maître Pornic announces. "He would foster this lie for his own selfish lust."

"It is not so! This woman is my grandmother."

Maître Pornic beckons to the crowd for two of Rachel's maids to come forward. "Was Thomas Chalandon in your mistress's bedchamber last night?"

"What does that demonstrate?" Thomas shouts. "Can I not converse with my own grandmother?"

"At what hour did he depart her bedchamber?" the abbot enquires.

"At dawn," one of the maids says, and the other nods. "At the ringing of the chapel bell."

Cries of outrage erupt from the assembly. "Deceiver!"—"Witch!"—"Devil!"

"Arrest her!" a sergeant calls from the throng.

Rachel stands impassively, her eyes cold, staring at Maître Pornic, who watches her with a pitying gaze.

"I spent the night taking war council with my grandmother!"

Thomas calls out—but his voice is lost in the uproar of shocked cries and loud jabbering. He looks to Rachel to speak up for herself. Only she can silence the outcry now. But he sees her pasty face, and he knows she is lost.

Clare is on her feet with her hands to her mouth, staring with frightened eyes at her son. Beside her, his father's head is bent and his sisters are arguing with each other. Harold and Gianni stand dumbstruck. Only Denis is shouting into the crowd, trying to win some silence. But he is ignored. Maître Pornic has swayed enough of the sergeants with the fear of hellfire that there is no chance of calming them. And now the guildsmen, recognizing a chance to protect their profits from the ravages of war, are shouting, "Lanfranc! Lanfranc!"

As William and Thierry take Rachel's arms to lead her away, she manages to hold her head up and even to dilate her nostrils as though she were angry—desperately remembering her training—though her insides cramp with fear.

Rachel stares from her window at the inner ward and the curtain wall surrounding it. The few sergeants still faithful to her have posted themselves in the towers guarding the inner gate. Without them covering the drawbridge with their crossbows, the guildsmen would have swarmed into the *palais* and made a spectacle of Rachel's execution. She can hear their distant shouts of "Burn the heretic—burn the Jew deceiver!"

The voices of the crowd sound small and far away, like the voices of the dead that had once haunted her blood until Grandfather died. Now that there is no one to see her, she lets her fear loose. Her hands at her pallid face tremble, and she wants to cry, afraid of what the mob is going to do to her—but her fear of fear will not let her.

Below, she sees Thierry running across the ward, the banner of the Swan he has taken down from the flag turret dragging behind limp like a shroud.

"Did you confess to the abbot?" Denis asks Thomas as they hurry across the bailey. Most of the guildsmen and their families are crowded along the inner gate, and the stunned people milling around the shops muttering with grave consternation are villeins and servants sympathetic to the baroness.

A milkmaid seizes Thomas's arm. "Master Thomas, tell us the truth. Who is the baroness?"

"She is my grandmother, the Lady of the Grail," Thomas answers earnestly. His anger at Pornic for betraying his trust and threatening his love offers a ready defense: "The abbot lies, thinking to counter a greater evil with a smaller one. He hopes to avert war with a lie."

The milkmaid smiles gratefully and scurries off shouting, "Valaise!"

"The villeins have faith in Ailena," Denis says. "They have not forgotten that Maître Pornic shattered the Sacred Visage and cursed their temple. Nor have they forgotten how the guildsmen took away the pigs the baroness gave them. If we can muster the villagers and bring them into the castle, we can rout the sergeants whom William commands."

Thomas casts a worried look to the front gate where a knot of sergeants stands before the lowered portcullis. "The men loyal to Grandmère are holding the inner gate to protect her. But these men here are the abbot's. They won't let us through."

Denis claps a hand on Thomas's shoulder. "You must open that gate—and you must keep it open until I return with the villagers."

"I—" Thomas's mouth works without speaking.

"Remember who you are. With your grandmother under arrest and your uncle absent, you are by birthright the legitimate master of this castle." He unbuckles his sword and hands it to Thomas. "Take this and use it if you must. Now go. I will get my horse."

Denis runs toward the stables, and Thomas looks at the gate. Before it the burly men talk gruffly among themselves. He tightens the sword's cincture about his waist and shifts it about as he walks, trying to make the weapon hang more comfortably. But it simply dangles at his side, an unnatural appendage. As he approaches the gate, he hears his uncle's name bandied about in tones of cold respect.

"There'll be moaning in Howel's camp when they learn Lanfranc is back," one of them says.

"And they'll be moaning no less in Neufmarché's keep if Branden even tries to cut firewood in the disputed lands."

"Guy will have Neufmarché shitting green in a week."

Thomas stands before the men, and they pay him no heed until he says, "Open the gate and lift the portcullis."

The sergeants stop their chatting and look at the young man with a mixture of bemusement and annoyance. "Go back to the *palais*, boy. Your mother may need you."

The men laugh. "She's lost *her* mother! Go and console her."

"Open this gate at once!" Thomas shouts.

The sergeants' laughter flares louder.

Thomas draws his sword, amazed at how swiftly the tapered steel slides from its sheath. The weapon hovers in his grip, so perfectly is it balanced. The laughter stops, and the granite-faced men watch him with level, flinty stares.

"Put that away, boy. Don't draw your sword lest you're ready to use it."

"I'll use it if you don't open that gate."

The nearest sergeant unsheathes his sword. Thomas turns to meet him. With one upward stroke, the sergeant's powerful blow knocks the sword from Thomas's grip, and it clatters to the pavement.

"Go back to your mama right now," the sergeant rasps, laying the edge of his sword against Thomas's cheek, "or I'll leave my mark in your pretty face."

Anger sears through Thomas's shock. "Cut me, sergeant, and I'll watch you dance on the gallows! Don't you know who I am?"

"They call you Tom the Dreamer," the sergeant answers with a grin. "Your face should be stuck in a book, Tom—not at the point of my sword."

"I am Guy Lanfranc's nephew," Thomas says coldly. "You'll be spilling his sister's blood from my veins. That will not please Uncle Guy." With one finger, Thomas pushes the blade away from his cheek. "Put your sword away and open the gate. Or I'll see that you spend the rest of your days as master of the latrines."

The sergeant's face tightens, and his sword rises menacingly. "You son of a cur—"

The other sergeants grab him and pull him away. "Get Gervais," one calls to the porter.

Thomas retrieves and sheaths his sword. A moment later, the master-sergeant steps out of the turret. The soldiers step aside for the bull-shouldered man.

"Master-sergeant, open this gate," Thomas orders.

"On whose command, Master Thomas?"

"On whose command is it shut?" Thomas counters.

"Sir William so ordered it."

"I speak for the baroness," Thomas says. "Open the gate and raise the portcullis."

Gervais shakes his large head. "You know I can't do that, Master Thomas."

"Why not? Are you not the sworn vassal of the baroness? Are your word and your honor worthless, master-sergeant?"

The scar creasing Gervais's right eye twitches. "I've proven my honor with my blood. I am no longer bound to my vassalage. Maître Pornic has said this woman is not the baroness. She is a Jew."

"Ailena Valaise a Jew?" Thomas laughs. "You are a turniphead, Gervais, to believe that. Have you ever seen a Jew? Maître Pornic has gulled you, for he knows that is the only way to break your devotion to the baroness. I never confessed to him anything of the kind."

"You did not?" Gervais queries, his good eye squinting with disbelief. "You expect us to believe that the holy man has lied?"

"Maître Pornic is devoted to the Church, not to our barony. He loathes Grandmère for worshiping as Jesus did, rather than as the apostles that followed him. That is heresy to the holy man, and to combat that he would do more than lie. If he had to, he would fornicate."

Several of the sergeants guffaw, and Gervais nods, comprehending. "We are sworn to honor and serve the baroness Ailena Valaise—not the Church," Gervais announces. "Open the gate! Raise the portcullis!"

Seeing the portcullis go up, Denis mounts his steed and rides across the bailey. At the gate, he pauses to nod at Thomas, then gallops across the drawbridge and down the toll bridge road.

"Who opened that gate?" a grim voice bellows from across the bailey. William Morcar strides angrily from the barracks. "Drop that portcullis! No one is to be admitted without my recognition."

The sergeants flinch, but Gervais stays them with a raised

hand. "Sir William, Master Thomas speaks for the baroness."

"You fool!" William barks. "Didn't you hear the Maître? She is a deceiver! A Jew!"

"The abbot lied," Thomas says flatly. "Ailena Valaise is the mistress of this keep, William. Go and release her at once or you will be charged with treason."

William stalks up to Thomas, seizes his tunic, and jerks him to his toe tips. "Listen to me, you lovesick dolt. That Jew will never rule here again. The true legate of this domain is on his way here now. If you dare challenge him, you and your Jew lover will be burned as heretics."

"Gervais—" Thomas croaks.

The master-sergeant puts a heavy hand on William's arm. "I am the baroness's vassal, Sir William," Gervais says apologetically but firmly. "My men will follow me."

William stares at him, confounded. "You believe this—this troubadour's son, who is not even a knight, who has thrown off his cassock? You believe him over the word of Maître Pornic, God's true servant?"

Gervais pulls William's hands away from Thomas. "I am not a cleric, Sir William. I am a soldier and a sworn vassal. My allegiance cannot be swayed by hearsay. Give me proof that my mistress is a deceiver, and I will myself bind her to the stake and set her afire."

A roar of crowd noise erupts from the gate. Denis rides proudly over the drawbridge leading the villagers. They had gathered at the toll bridge when they saw the Swan banner atop the turret struck; now they stream through the gate shouting, "Valaise! Free the baroness Valaise!"

William gnashes his teeth, and wheels about to get out of the way of the rushing villeins. Thomas runs ahead of the villagers, keeping pace with Denis astride his mount. When the guildsmen see them coming, their cries dim away, and they pull their wives and children behind them and back against the moat.

Denis stops the charging villagers by sidling his horse in front of them. "This is the keep of the baroness Ailena Valaise!" he shouts. "We will not dishonor her by murdering each other!" He pulls his steed around and addresses the guildsmen: "Those among you who will not stand with the baroness and defend her will leave now and make your fortunes elsewhere."

Several of the guildsmen gather their families and advance. Denis and Thomas clear a way for them through the crowd, and they retreat under loud jeers and catcalls. As the gate to the inner ward opens, Thierry steps out, accompanied by five sergeants; Hellene and Hugues follow, imploring the young knight, "Take us with you!"

William grabs his wife and stops her on the drawbridge. "Take Hugues back to the *palais*," he commands.

Hellene is bleary-eyed with panic. "No! Don't leave us behind!"

William's thick-set face looks blighted. "We shall be back for you," he promises with concern. "You are safer here than in the field." He nods to Hugues. "Keep your mother out of danger."

"I want to go with you, Da," Hugues insists. "I'm old enough to fight."

William claps a hand on his shoulder and hooks a half-smile. "There will be other battles, son, be assured of that. But for now I must rely on you to protect your mother and Madelon. Where is your sister?"

"I saw her with the canon," Hugues says. "The Pretender says they are to marry!"

William's face flushes crimson with his restrained shout, and he moves toward the inner ward.

Thierry snags his elbow. "Da, not now. We'll meet Rieti on the field."

William lets his son pull him back and mutters, "I should have gelded him when I had the chance."

"Then the Pretender would have us in the dungeon," Thierry consoles. With a jerk of his head he signals Hugues to take Hellene back into the ward. "We shall have our proper revenge soon."

Father and son march purposefully across the drawbridge and through the throng of villeins, glancing neither at Denis nor Thomas.

At the chapel, Maître Pornic and Gianni Rieti watch as William and his comrades lead their horses out of the stables and load their weapons.

"You have lost the protection of the Church, my son," the abbot says to Gianni. He glances into the chapel, where Madelon stands in the dark, out of sight of her father and brother. "Do not lose your soul as well. Forget this woman who tempts you with the weakness of your flesh. I implore you, come with us and use your sword to avenge the deception that has robbed you of God's grace."

Gianni shakes his head. "I cannot, padre. Whatever grace God has shown me has come through a woman. Whether she be a baroness or a Jew, I will stand or fall by her. And Madelon. I have spent my life running after desire and from its consequences. With Madelon, my desire has found a home, and with it, the very idea of desire is changed and made holy."

The abbot crosses himself. "Woman is the Devil's instrument."

"No, padre." Gianni smiles tolerantly. "Your ignorance abuses you. Woman is a miracle you have yet to understand."

The holy man frowns skeptically. "Nothing I can say will change your mind?"

Gianni shakes his head.

"Then God protect you," Maître Pornic mumbles and clambers down the steps to the mule that will carry him away.

Gianni looks on dolorously as a good number of the sergeants mount up and take ranks behind the abbot, William, and Thierry. When the portcullis creaks closed behind them, he murmurs, "God protect us all."

In the council chamber, grim faces watch as Rachel takes her place in the chair of state. No escape offers itself in the solemn stares that fix her in her role. Only Thomas, who watches with proud attentiveness, sees her as other than the baroness. His parents, Clare and Gerald, sit opposite her at the long council table, anxiously holding hands, eager for her to speak. Denis sits to her right, beside Rieti, his worshipful regard shared by Harold and Gianni to her left. They all know what must happen. Ummu alone, sitting in a window nave with his monkey, looks at her with an amused pugnacity, challenging her to say something meaningful before the destruction to come.

The dwarf's glittering stare inspires doubt in Rachel. She lowers her head as if in prayer, and searches within for the Grail. It is there—flashing gold but spilling blood so vividly her head jerks up with a startled expression. Since her wanderings in the wilderness, her madness has retreated. But now she shivers with the dumb-founded nearness of insanity. The chalice of her destiny brims with the blood that will be spilled today! And she sees with sad clairvoyance that the killing to come is already inside her!

She looks about in a fright, sees her fear reflected in the con-fused looks of the knights and Clare. *Only a full confession can avert disaster,* she thinks, and says aloud, "I have been too selfish. No one must die for me."

Thomas leans forward to catch her eye and shakes his head, his face urgent.

"My lady," Denis speaks. "We know you are tormented by the imminence of bloodshed. How could you deny the grace of God that has changed you and feel otherwise? But, be assured, we are not fighting so much for you as for your kingdom—the kingdom of Yeshua—the kingdom of the Grail."

Rachel looks stricken. A cold draft blows out of her heart, and she strives to recall the peace she had won for herself in the woods. It is gone; the clear emptiness she thought she had glimpsed is mere illusion now. Everything crowds rapidly around her—the plangent faces of these men who are willing to die because they believe her story—and, there, even the dwarf's small, cold eyes daring her to be other than herself.

"I cannot do this!" She stands and must touch her fingertips to the tabletop to steady herself. "I cannot."

"Grandmère!" Thomas calls out sharply and rises. "You and the land are one."

Rachel holds his spirited gaze, and her bounding heart beats even louder.

"Whatever the outcome," Thomas continues, "we *must* fight Guy. For the land itself. For the villeins that work it."

"They all go into the dark," Rachel mumbles. The cold wind from her fluttering heart sends horrid memories racing through her, jagged images of slashed throats and corpses stacked like cords of firewood. What is to come has already happened, and will happen again. "Everything goes into the dark."

The knights send alarmed glances at each other. Clare moves to rise, to go to her mother and comfort her, but Gerald stops her;

he wants to hear his fate in the words of the baroness. Gianni crosses himself and begins a silent prayer.

Thomas props his hands on the table, leans forward, and says fiercely, "You've come too far to stop!" His fervency softens to yearning, and he mouths voicelessly, "Remember!"

In that woeful look, Rachel sees past her helpless fear to the calm she accepted last night with this man—to the ease she found in his arms after their passions had hammered them free of yearning. The cold wind in her veins slips away. The gory images that wring her brain vanish. She blows a heavy sigh, and a fugitive smile touches her anguished face. "I *have* come too far." She nods, directs her balanced gaze to Clare and each of her knights in turn, and finally, addressing Ummu, says, "I pray you to forgive both bad and good. All shall not be well—unless we make it so."

Thomas sits, slips his hand in his jerkin to clutch his crucifix, and thanks God. Today there will be war. But without it, there would have been tyranny, which in the guise of rightful rule and the Church, there has been too much of already. He thanks God for inspiring his grandmother to send Rachel, to free them all from the stultifying tyranny of themselves. Whatever the outcome of today's battle, they are no longer hidden in their fates. Grandmère has flushed them out to fight, bleed, and die for what they want to be.

"Clare," Rachel says in a new voice of authority. "I want you to prepare the great hall to receive the wounded. Go now, and on your way, send in the sergeants who are not on watch."

Clare, pallid and fluttery, hurries from the chamber.

"How long before Guy arrives?" Rachel asks.

"If we wait till then," Denis answers, "it will be too late. Once Guy seizes the fields and the village, we will be forced to shut ourselves in. But we haven't the resources for a siege. We must meet him in the open before he traps us here."

"Then we must advance at once," Rachel says.

"If it is already not too late."

Gervais enters with a dozen sergeants, who line up against the frescoed wall, frightening Ta-Toh into hiding behind Ummu.

"How many men have gone over to Guy?" she asks the master-sergeant.

"More than a third, my lady," Gervais replies. "But the men we have—we are ready to lay down our lives to stop Sir Guy and Sir Branden."

"*Can* we stop the forces arrayed against us, Gervais?"

"Sure to say, we are outnumbered," Gervais answers. "But not too greatly. For the Lady of the Grail, we will fight valiantly."

"Gerald," Rachel says, "you will stay and command the castle."

"Lady—" Gerald rises. "It is true I am not a dubbed knight, only a simple troubadour. But I can ride and am not too clumsy with a sword. I will take the field."

Rachel feels a pang of dread but ignores it and nods. "Denis, I have no skill for battle strategy. I rely on you to be my warmaster."

"I will lead the men with my best cunning."

"No," Rachel counters. "You will guide the men—but I will lead the way to this battle."

Protests crowd the chamber, until Rachel holds up both her hands.

"I will bear the standard of the Swan into battle," she announces with steady resolve. At last, it has come clear to her— she has grasped the significance of the blood in the Grail. It is the blood of the sacrifice, the sacrifice she refused to accept when her father slew his family and himself. With the certainty of the eleven years she has spent looking away, she must never look away again. "I will not hide behind these walls while my men fight for me. When my fate is decided, I will be there to see it for myself."

"Lady," Gianni objects. "A battle is not a tourney. It is savage chaos! If you are there, you will have to be protected, and that will only distract the soldiers from fighting."

"I disagree," Gervais says. "Is she not the Lady of the Grail? With her on the field, the men will fight harder."

"But the enemy will have a prominent target to attack," Harold retorts.

Rachel interrupts the ensuing debate: "We've no time to argue. Denis, you are in command. Take us into battle. If the rabbi is right and we are God's hands, then there is much work to be done."

Rachel seeks Thomas outside the armory of the donjon, where the knights and sergeants are girding themselves and their steeds for battle. He wears a chain-mail vest and cowl like the others, and is busy checking his horse's saddlestraps when she summons him.

"Beloved, you were my strength in the council room." She thanks him after he steps away from his squire. "I had forgotten the peace I'd found with you—until you reminded me. There is no going back now."

For a moment, Thomas stares unbelieving at her black riding pants and armor. Over her red gambeson, a vest thickly padded with felted cotton, she wears a tunic of chain mail. Her hair has been tied back and piled atop her head so it will not tangle in the mail. "The battle will be too dangerous," he warns. "You should stay."

"It was you who made this risk necessary, Thomas," she says with cold simplicity, "when you kept me from telling the truth."

"The truth?" Thomas shakes his head and takes her chin in his hand to focus deep into her eyes. "What is the truth, Rachel? That you are a Jew? Then Christ is a Jew—and hundreds of martyrs and Crusaders have died for a Jew—then all of Christendom worships a Jew. No. Christ is not a Jew. Jesus was—but not Christ. He wept blood that the Cup would pass from him. But the Cup did not pass. And so you are not a Jew, either. You have drunk from the same Cup—you have drunk from the Grail. You are not my grandmother—but you *are* the baroness. The truth is what we make of it."

Rachel's gaze deepens, and she feels angry. There *is* a truth—one truth, neither concealed nor separate. She knows this from long years of attentive watchfulness. The truth gives her no choice: she *must* act, fulfilling the destiny that began when she looked away from her dead family eleven years ago. But she will not look away again. She will face the truth today on the battlefield. No matter how bitter it is, she will, at last, be herself.

She takes Thomas's hand. "Remember, you were my strength last night—and in the council room—and even now." Her maids step through the bustle of varlets distributing weapons and announce that her horse is ready. She holds them off with a nod. "But you are wrong about me, Thomas. You are my strength—because you are wrong."

She walks off surrounded by her anxious maids, and he watches her disappear in the crowd of dazzling iron.

❖   ❖   ❖

Clare and Ummu stand at the barbican as the Lady of the Grail leads her army out of the castle. Ta-Toh perches atop the wall of sharpened poles, waving and squawking in imitation of the crowd of villeins who line the toll bridge road. Clutching Ummu's hand for comfort, Clare watches her Gerald ride to war. "It is for the best, isn't it, Ummu?" she asks, wiping tears away.

"The best often requires the worst," he answers, his gaze on Madelon, who stands opposite him across the road. Her mother Hellene and brother Hugues are conspicuously absent among the castle well-wishers; the dwarf knows she is there only to wave farewell to Gianni.

When the Italian knight rides by on his Arabian stallion, Ummu lifts his hand in a gesture of bravura. Gianni winks a bruised eye at him, but he turns a fixed, lingering gaze on Madelon. The dwarf waves emptily and shrugs. "Worst of all is to be bested."

"This will be a rout." Guy is convinced. He rides between Roger Billancourt and Branden Neufmarché, dressed in a chain-mail bodysuit with breastplate and greaves and his helmet on his pommel so that his view of the terrain can remain unhindered.

"How can you be so damned sure?" Branden asks sourly. In full armor, he is exhausted from the chafing, sweltering ride. "What I've been hearing from our men since we camped last night is how remarkable this Lady of the Grail is. They say she can cast befuddling spells—as she did on her grandson Thomas. And confounding Erec the Bold at the tourney. They also say the Devil's fire leaps up from hell at her command, and that's how she burned Dic Long Knife's men."

"All rot!" Guy casts him a baleful frown. "And you believe such fairy tales, Branden?"

Branden disavows it with a humorless laugh. "Not I. But Maître Pornic says she is a Jew, and everyone knows they practice necromancy, learned from the Egyptians. All the men have heard of the temple she built on Merlin's Knoll and how she burned the old rabbi there. With witchcraft like that, how can you be so sure we'll rout her forces?"

"Then we shouldn't have left Maître Pornic back at your castle,

Branden," Guy chaffs. "His blessings could have countered her spells."

"We'll win because we've more men and horses," Roger answers sternly. He has already donned his bascinet helmet, body-mail and breastplate, and with a mace dangling from one arm and a battle ax hung from his saddle, he is prepared for an ambush. Apprehensive about the Pretender's reputation as a miracle work-er, he suspects there may be an ensnaring attack by a cadre of fanatics. To her own people, she is blessed by the Grail and to her enemies, she is a witch. He is grateful there will be no siege, for that would have left too much time for her renown to work on the troops. He is determined to commit all his forces. Their first engagement must be decisive to break her mystique. "Our scouts report that the Pretender awaits us in the meadow beyond Devil's Foot ridge. Clearly she expects we will post defenders atop the ridge and surge through the cleft in that mound."

"That would be to our advantage," Branden states. "With the hillocks on either side topped with our own men, our flanks will be protected. And with our archers atop the ridge, we can keep her forces far enough back to bring through our full corps."

"So she reasons," Roger says. "Or rather, so thinks Denis Hezetre."

"It smells of Denis," Guy agrees. "He is thinking like an archer, hoping to pelt us with arrows as we come through the cleft, weak-ening our numbers."

"But we will divide into three," Roger decides. "Branden, you and I will lead first strikes from either side of the Devil's Foot. That will soften their flanks and draw off their center. Then, Guy will charge through the cleft and shatter them."

"*I* will take the central charge," Branden corrects and gestures to the column of horsemen, sumpter mules, and wagons behind them. "These are *my* men. I will lead them. The two of you will conduct the forays."

Guy bridles at Neufmarché's imperious tone, but a sharp glance from Roger stays his retort.

"So be it," Roger concurs. "But your timing is vital. You must not strike until the center is weakened—and then you must not hesitate."

"Send William on the foray," Guy suggests. "I will stay with Branden."

"Pish!" Neufmarché stiffens. "I'll not have you directing me in front of my men, Lanfranc. Do as the warmaster says."

"If you blunder, toad, I'll come for your head," Guy rasps.

Branden reins his horse to a stop and narrows a threatening gaze at Guy. "At my command, these men will turn. 'Less you apologize, you and your handful of knights and sergeants can carry the battle on your own."

Guy rears up in his saddle, but before he can speak, Roger cuts his horse between them. "Come away, the two of you," he commands and waves them off the main body of soldiers. He grabs the bridle of Guy's horse, turns him around, and leads the reluctant barons to an alder copse out of earshot of the men. "Stop this bickering at once!" He scowls at Neufmarché. "Do you think your men will gladly turn back now, with victory so near? You will find yourself with a very unhappy army, Branden."

He turns his dudgeon on Guy: "And you— Where do you find the gall to threaten our one ally?" His head bobs angrily. "Apologize at once and let's get on with this battle. By midafternoon you'll have your castle back and Branden and his men will have their lands. Let's fix on that!"

Guy mumbles an apology, and trots off through the copse and back to the trail, far enough ahead of the column to be alone. He is perplexed by his feelings. His anger at Neufmarché masks something like fear. Yet he knows he is not afraid. He has been carried on the rushing current of battles before, where everything slides toward the brink of death and no prowess or courage is sufficient to guarantee anything—where a stray missile, a false step and flesh becomes carrion.

A hard sigh passes through him. He is not afraid to die. Still, a foreboding wilts the usual eagerness he feels before combat. Doubts crowd him. What if Neufmarché balks? What if he meets Denis on the field? Will he want victory enough to strike his friend?

These thoughts leave a sour taste in his mouth, and he spits. *The truth is, I am alone. Since my father died, I have always been alone.* The broadening clarity of this fact encompasses the cruel wound he received in Eire that sheared all future lineage from him. A detached, lonely feeling pervades him with the conviction that he has been cut to the warrior's most lethal shape—a man with nothing more to lose. Yes, he will kill anyone who gets in his way.

"Da, perhaps we should speak with him," Thierry says, leaning forward in his saddle to see past Neufmarché and Roger to where Guy rides alone.

William Morcar vetoes that suggestion with a chop of his hand. "He's cut himself away from the warmaster. He wants to be alone."

"Is that his usual way before battle?"

William looks askance at his son, and sees for the first time since they left the castle how callow he is. *This will be his first taste of war,* he reminds himself, and admits the concern that rises in him, determining to keep a close watch on his boy even if that should jeopardize his own life. Such a thought brings to the fore all the love he has fostered for his first-born—a love that has moved his hand to deceit and murder. *All redeemed by love,* he swears to himself.

"Each must prepare for what is to come in his own way," William answers. "Each battle is different and yet the same. I regret that your first real combat must be against those whom you know."

"That will not stay my hand, Da."

William nods grimly. "Nor should it. When you've seen enough warfare, you will understand—we are all the same, all on one battlefield, and whom you are fighting does not matter. Strangers or friends, death makes us equals."

From horseback, Rachel plants the pole of her banner firmly in the hummock, and the Swan ensign flutters in the cool wind out of the mountains.

Denis canters to her side from his brief lope into the meadow. "This is the best place for you to stand, my lady. The rise gives you a commanding view of the field. And when the enemy see your banner and you beside it, they will come right for you. That will focus their attack and enable us to deploy our archers and lancers with some anticipation. Also, the low outcrops ahead will afford you some small protection."

Rachel surveys the landscape, once again struck by the beauty of the quilted hills embroidered with thickets and groves, and the vales between them dark green with wildwoods. Ahead, at the far end of the meadow is the Devil's Foot, a thistly mound between the forested hills that looks as though cleaved in half by a giant's ax. A gush of colors mottles the field with flowers—bluebells, daffodils, pansies, and fireweed.

"One last time, won't you reconsider returning to the keep?" Denis asks.

Rachel shakes her head and looks to the mob of villeins gathered at the skirt of the woods behind her hummock. They have followed her from the village armed with staves, sickles, and scythes, chanting "Valaise! Valaise! Lady of the Grail!"

"They are no real good to us," Denis says, following her gaze. "They expect a miracle from you. But the real miracle will come from those men." He points to the sergeants in their dented helmets and chain mail at the meadow's edge, some astride battle-ready horses, others on foot, leaning on their lances. "They will carry the day—if our knights lead them well."

Gerald, Gianni, Harold, and Thomas parade before the ranks, stopping here and there to address the troops. Rachel notices that Thomas is a favorite among them; his clever victory over Bold Erec in the tourney has won him a reputation among the sergeants, and though he has never wielded a weapon, no one questions his leadership. Eliciting quiet laughter and confidence from them, he moves along the file, checking weapons, answering questions, offering encouragement.

But in fact, he is terrified and is glad for something to do while waiting for the carnage to begin. The crucifix in his pocket offers little solace. His victory over Erec had been no more a miracle than his grandmother's return from the Holy Land. God is remote in His heaven, and men are at the mercy of chance and their wits. Luck and daring spared him then in the lists, and he feels little of either now. Denis has already promised to stand by him in battle, to help address his lack of experience. But he knows that when the fighting begins, it will be every man for himself.

He looks to the hummock where Rachel sits atop her red palfrey, and when he sees that she is watching him, he nods. Last night's erotic union comes back on him in a shiver of power. She has given him her strength, and he clearly feels his courage multiplying as he stares at her. She has told him everything about herself. Knowing all she has suffered to be here—all the instruction she has so flawlessly absorbed from his irascible grandmother and the deadly horror that orphaned her, the vast loneliness of losing her grandfather and the loneliness that pressed her to confide in him—knowing all that, he marvels at her clear stance, marvels that she can hold any regard for him at all. Her last words to him wring his heart: "You are my strength, because you are wrong."

Am I totally a fool? he wonders. *Am I wrong to have pressed her to this?*

He is caught up in the rush of events, and the answer he seeks is impossibly beyond him. All he knows is that he loves this brave, lonely woman, and if he had let her speak the truth, Maître Pornic would have destroyed her as surely as he had smashed the Sacred Visage in the stone.

So, he has lied—and his lie has opened the way to war. But war is nothing new, only his presence in it is. The terrible moment approaches. The wound that will leak his life flies closer. And though he is humming with fright inside, his secret sharing with the Lady of the Grail surrounds him with a magical calm.

Atop the Devil's Foot, men appear, and a shout goes up from the soldiers grouped around the Swan banner.

"The moment has come, my lady," Denis says, quietly. "It is time for you to bless the troops, and I will deploy them."

Rachel feels light-headed and incompetent as she glances down at the crowd of men watching her—knights, sergeants, squires, varlets and villeins, rough-faced men and ruddy-cheeked youths, all looking at her with mixed expressions of adoration and curiosity, waiting for her to speak, to justify the misery they are about to inflict and endure. As in some unfathomable dream, she drifts above them astride her horse.

Thomas's face sharpens out of the cloud of faces, and his caring look stills her doubts. She has everything to tell this man and his people, everything she has won from the grief their kind have inflicted on her. But she knows she must choose her words carefully; there is no time, yet this is all the time there is, the last minutes of many of their lives, and they deserve to hear something of the truth of this world.

"I have been to Jerusalem," she begins slowly, her voice quavery. "I have stood by the dragon's well, by the dung gate, by the king's pool under the tower of flies. Everything there has been built by the sword. Though the Savior trod those very streets, I tell you, everything there has been built by the sword."

Her voice rises: "People—it is no different there than here! Every valley is the valley of tears. Every river the river of time. And we are all the children of Eve—and must live with the curse God laid on her and all her children. Everything that is built is built with the sword! There is no peace in this world. That is God's curse on Eve and her man. So long as we live in the light, in the light of the sun and the moon and the stars, we live in the darkness of God's curse, where everything must be built with the sword."

She looks closely into their faces and sees the anguish she herself feels. "But the light is not always in the world. Is that not the grief of all our lives? In Jerusalem, on the hill of skulls, the light went out of the world—and the Son of Man was glad when his day was finished. There as here, night follows day. And there as here, when the day is done, the people are glad for the night. And when *our* day is done in this world, after much striving and many obstacles, we shall go gladly into the darkness. Do not be fooled by your fears and your doubts, men. When we die, we leave behind God's curse, we leave behind the river of time and the valley of tears, and we enter the darkness to find the light."

Her arms open to embrace all of her soldiers, who are watching her raptly. "And we *will* find that light. I promise you, there is a light too bright for mortal vision that appears to us in this world as darkness—and in that light within the darkness we are in God.

"But here in this world, in the shadow of Jerusalem, bearing the curse laid on Adam and his mate, if we want anything of our own, we must build it with the sword. And it shall stand until the darkness comes upon us, which shall be the darkness of God."

Her shoulders sag, and she sits back heavily, head lowered. The sun touches the back of her neck, and she thanks her Creator. For the first time since the horror, she prays thankfully, grateful that He has sent her words worthy of the suffering to come.

Silence swells across the meadow laced with bird songs and the chuffing of the horses. Then, as she raises her face, the men lift their weapons and bellow: "Valaise!"

Rachel's knuckles glow white where she clutches the pommel of her horse. Diffidently, she watches the soldiers atop the Devil's Foot position themselves close to the edge, and she sees the tiny shapes of their bows. The appearance of Neufmarché's archers on the ridge is just as Denis has predicted, and she looks now for the first signs of the expected charge through the cleft of the cloven mound.

A swell of wind flurries the banner beside her and carries the chirrups of scolding birds, the honey-balm fragrance of the blossoming meadow, and the distant squabble of the river. In the religious hush, she surveys her troops from atop her grazing horse. A dozen bowmen kneel in midfield, butterflies lazing among them. Footmen back them up with their lances, a human wall for the archers to fall behind. Chittering swallows dip and glide among the horsemen, whom Denis has positioned at either end of the wall of foot soldiers—and, behind them, waiting for the expected charge to crash into the bowmen's arrows and slow down to hand combat against the foe's lancers are the squires and varlets, armed with swords and axes. At the van of the deployment, the villeins mill anxiously, some muttering prayers, a few joking among themselves as they gaze hard at the Devil's Foot, eager to see the enemy.

The knights are preoccupied with their own fears and expectations and sit unmoving on their steeds. Inside their helmets and chain mail, they seem nearly indistinguishable to Rachel: Denis alone carries a bow and wears a bascinet, a helmet without a face-guard, the better to train his arrows. Gianni sits astride his white Arabian. Harold has hung a long tress of his wife Leora's red hair from the crest of his helmet. Gerald's head is too large for any available helmet, and he has no armor of his own, so he wears simply a cowl of mail. And Thomas, unfamiliar with his weapons, hefts a sword in one hand and a mace in the other. Over their breastplates, all wear blue tunics patterned with the white emblem of the spread-winged Swan.

Rachel glances over her shoulder to where the castle physician has drafted several villeins to build small fires and set kettles of water boiling. Into the kettles, the physician drops tufts of herbs and felicitous animal parts: dogteeth, catpaws, toad livers. In the flames themselves, the tips of iron rods glow dull red, ready to sear closed severed blood vessels. And downwind a pot of tar bubbles and fumes acridly, waiting for the wounds to come, the hacked and gouged gaps of flesh that it will fill with its black mercy.

A plume of dust rises from the cleft in the Devil's Foot, and a shout goes up among the men. Lances rattle and arrows nock into place. Several startled ponies, dragging cane rakes behind them to stir up dust, appear in the throat of the defile, and the soldiers stare at them confusedly before war cries from their right and left split their attention.

Rounding the flanks of the Devil's Foot, two groups of charging horsemen explode into view carrying green banners stained black with the Griffin. Startled shouts from the defenders mix with loud curses as they scramble to re-form, and Denis's yelled orders are lost. Before the archers can split their line and position themselves to form fronts along their sides, the enemy are upon them, gouging with lances and slashing with whirling battle axes. The bowmen scatter and fire wildly into the pincering attack.

Rachel's horse stamps skittishly at the uproar of whooping assailants and screaming wounded. With trembling hands, she steadies the animal and fights the overwhelming impulse to look away, forcing herself to behold the devastating assault. Her men scatter into small fighting groups set upon by horsemen fiercely hacking at them with axes and swords. Neufmarché's footmen charge into the meadow, yelling and waving dagger-tipped pikes.

"Valaise!" the villeins shout and rush forward. In moments,

they are swallowed in the din and confusion.

Despite the shock of the unexpected flank attacks, the defenders do not relent. They scatter but continue to fight. Rachel's whole body clenches to see spears thrust through the bodies of horsemen, skulls smashed and brains scattered like clods of earth under the swipes of battle axes, horses' throats hacked open, their great bodies collapsing and spilling their riders into the knives of the foot soldiers.

Clamping her jaw so tightly her neck muscles ache, Rachel makes herself watch the gruesome melee. Ogreish cries of men and horses pummel her, yet she sits firm, staring hard at sword strokes spilling entrails in shrieks of horror and men plastered with blood hacking pathways of lopped limbs in a wallow of thrashing bodies. The noise is all the noise her head can hold, becoming a cacophonous deafness of screams.

Guy presses the attack toward the hummock where he sees the Pretender on her horse beside the Swan ensign. He wants to reach her, to see the look on her face as he strikes a death blow to her mount and sends her sprawling to the ground in defeat. But first, there are these benighted fanatics to cut away, like so much gangrenous flesh around the cancer. His battle ax jars against metal and bone, and a blow from his mace frees it so he can swing it in another deadly arc.

An arrow slams into his chest and lodges firmly in his breastplate. With the mace he knocks it off, and rears his horse back on its hind legs to fend off a rush of varlets with swords. Across the bristling crowd of lances, pikes, and flourishing blades, he sees Roger. The warmaster twirls his steed rapidly in a tight circle flailing a morning star, a mace with a spiked ball on a chain, cracking skulls in a crowd of villeins.

Muscles already aching from the strenuous wielding of ax, Guy lets his mace dangle by its wrist-strap, seizes his reins, and charges to the outside of the meshed warriors. He hopes to dash swiftly around the muddle and attain the hummock where the Pretender waits. But as he breaks free, a knight in blue tunic and Swan insignia charges at him, sword raised high.

Guy has a moment to see that his opponent is his brother-in-law Gerald. He bolts forward and cuts sharply away, swinging mightily behind him with the flat of his battle ax.

Gerald's sword gashes through the empty space where Guy should have been. The hard blow that strikes his back flings him face forward and topples him to the ground. He manages to roll to his back in time to see soldiers scurrying toward him with daggers bared, and strives to get up, but is too stunned to move.

Horse hooves stamp the earth beside his head, and he looks up into Guy's furious leer. "You're the key that will make my sister open the castle gate!" Guy shouts. "Don't kill him," he orders the soldiers.

As they drag Gerald away, Guy wheels about, dodges a thrusting spear, and bolts forward to cleave the skull of the pikeman. The battle surges around him again, driven onward by raging howls and anguished cries.

Harold is exhausted with fury and wants to ride clear of the battle. He chops with his sword at the angry faces cursing him and pulls hard on the reins to steer his beast away from the crush and clamor of the fighting. But the animal, spooked by the death-struggles on all sides, carries him deeper into the fray.

The horse shudders violently beneath him, and he sees a soldier stabbing at the destrier's throat. The steed drops to his knees, and suddenly Harold is facing the crimson blade of the horse-killer. He strikes at the enraged face behind the blade, and the man's nose vanishes, and the gaping hole where it was gushes blood.

Harold lurches off his fallen mount, trips, and sits down. Wailing and grunting surround him, but through his visor he sees too little—the noseless soldier clutching his face, blood seeping between his fingers, chain-mailed legs jerking in and out of view, his horse lying before him, watching him with its large, gentle eye wide with fright.

Using his sword as a prop, Harold lifts himself and glimpses another horse rearing down on him. Roger Billancourt's blood-speckled face looms closer, grimacing, showing brown teeth and an insane stare. He holds a club with a blur at the end of it. The club swings close, and, with a searing flash, pain knocks him blind.

Denis chooses his targets carefully. The wound he received from Dic Long Knife's men aches with each shot. Retreating to the fringe of the meshing armies, he directs his arrows at the most aggressive of the enemy. Neufmarché's horsemen charge for him, and he manages to elude them by prancing his steed in and out of the conflict.

Time and again, he sights a warrior of maniac strength and lets fly his shaft, sometimes missing as his horse jolts under him but more often dropping his target. Poised in his concentration, he sights a raging horseman plunging among the foot soldiers with a scything battle ax, and he trains an arrow on him before realizing that this is Guy.

The arrow whistles toward the knight and hurtles over his shoulder. Relief fills Denis even as he wonders if he has missed on purpose. Then, out of the corner of his eye, he spots two lancemen on horseback bearing down on him, and he spurs his steed into the thick of the battle. From there, surrounded by his own warriors, he pulls around, swiftly aims, and fires.

One of the lancers flies backward off his horse, clutching at the arrow wedged between his helmet and breastplate. The other peels off.

A shrill cry turns Denis around to see the men behind him lying broken on the ground and Guy trampling over them, his battle ax brilliant with blood. Denis slings his bow over his pommel and draws his sword.

"Stand down," Guy commands, lifting his visor and grinning darkly at his old friend. "I'll take you prisoner."

"You stand down!" Denis shouts. "Before God and the right ruler of this land!"

Guy's grin brittles. "Fie on you, the bitch you serve, *and* God!" Slamming his visor down, he charges.

Denis veers but too late. The battle ax smites him in the chest, rending the metal plate, snapping the mail, and cutting into his flesh with a raucous pain. The sword flies from his hand, and he falls from his horse into an engulfing darkness.

o   o   o

Gianni and Thomas fight back to back, their horses jostling the fallen bodies. At the start of the fighting, Thomas became separated from Denis, and panic had gripped him. But now, as he hacks at the enemy, he is amazed at how easy killing is—bones snapping under the blow of his heavy sword like so much wood, blood sloshing like water, screams breaking against other screams like the squeals of packed animals.

Gianni cries out. A crossbow bolt has slammed under his upraised sword arm, and he sags forward and slowly slides from his stallion. Soldiers grab for him and thrust daggers under his breastplate, trying to snap the chain mail and pierce him vitally.

With a brutal cry, Thomas hurls his horse about and beats at the soldiers with his sword. They fall back, and he grabs Gianni and tries to haul him upright. But he is far too heavy.

The enemy surge closer, spears lowered. Thomas slides his horse behind the white stallion, and the Arabian rears up and takes the blows of the spears. Quickly, Thomas charges around the wounded animal and hews at the spearmen, dropping three and driving the others off.

Gervais appears out of the tumult on horseback with four mounted sergeants, and they surround Gianni. A squire removes the canon's helmet, and as soon as the sergeants see that he is alive, they hurtle back into the riot.

Thomas searches about for imminent danger, and his blood thickens at the sight of horsemen galloping toward them from the cleft in the Devil's Foot. The red banners flapping from the grips of the lead knights bear the Raven's head insignia of Neufmarché. At the sight of them, cheers resound from the enemy and groans from the defenders. Abruptly, Thomas's trial of courage and strength has become senseless. The fight is lost.

Rachel feels her teeth ringing, her bones aching, her blood shivering in her veins. Her eyes seem like tiny holes gouged into her deadened flesh by the terrible force of what she has witnessed. The flowery meadow has been churned to mud, and the bodies of men and horses lie in a monstrous sprawl. The wounded weep and yowl, while overhead clouds drift airily by in the ordinary blue.

She is vastly relieved to see Neufmarché spearing toward the battle. Most of the fighting abates at the sight of these reinforcements, and she sees that only one of her five knights remains on horseback. She has not looked away. She has seen it all. And though her body feels beaten, there is silence inside her. No wicked voices haunt her. What she has seen has happened, and the depth of its happening has absorbed all the screams and voices. Now there is only the thunder of the approaching horsemen and the weeping of the survivors.

Enough have died.

She puts her hand on the stave of her banner, yanks it out of the earth, and drops it to the ground.

As if that were a signal, an enormous shout bounds from the forested hills. She looks left and right, and her eyes wince, not believing what they see—the spectacle of horsemen dashing out of the woods on all sides, swords raised high, battle cries their only banners.

And even though her brain is battered and her bones ache from the slaughter that gaped around her moments ago, her blood still brightens to recognize the pelt-garbed, bearded warriors of Erec the Bold.

Thierry rides headlong at the front of Neufmarché's column. At the sight of the Welsh charging straight downhill ahead and to the sides, he jams his heels hard into his steed's sides. This is his first battle, and he is determined to win the respect of his godfather and the men to prove he is worthy of his knighthood.

The standard bearers flanking him and William fall away, flaring out to the sides to protect the Raven's head banners from the screaming barbarians. William, too, balks at the sight of the tribesmen swarming out of the woods, and he shouts at his son: "Pull up! Defend the standard!"

But Thierry has his heart set on fighting alongside Guy and the legendary Roger Billancourt, and he aims at full pelt for the thick of the battle. His mount leaps the fallen bodies of men and horses and strikes aside a varlet with an upraised ax. The impact swerves the warhorse and sends it plunging into the struggling crowd.

A pikeman thrusts a lance at Thierry, but he deftly strikes the sharpened pole aside with his sword and tramples his attacker. Clutching the reins with one hand, sword whistling through the air and crunching against metal and bone, he bounds among the enemy. The air shakes with howls and threats; arrows blur past his head, and one thuds into the saddle beside his thigh. The horse shrieks, lunges furiously, and, for an instant, Thierry overbalances and nearly topples into the cursing mob. But his flailing sword arm rights him, and he slashes at the blades snicking at his chain mail.

Another leap, another vicious chop of his sword, and he is within sight of Guy and Roger. He rears up proudly, weapon lifted high— and then the whooping Welshmen are all around him. A wrenching pain cracks his shoulder as an ax slams against his sword arm. He sways backward, and is seized from behind. Snarling, bearded faces thrust close, and he tries to strike at them with his free hand. But his arm snags, and his helmet and breastplate clang as swords batter him, striving to pierce beneath the armor.

One blade wedges under his helmet, and he bucks and kicks, desperate to squirm free. A wild scream hurtles through him; and then the blade slides over the collar of his mail and stoppers his throat with steel.

Guy bellows "No!" at the sight of his godson heaved to the ground, the gap under his helmet spurting bright arterial blood. Yelling his rage and anguish, he swings his battle ax blindly and heaves his destrier toward the exultant barbarians.

They are everywhere, darting into the brawl without armor or even helmets, heaving themselves fearlessly at his hacking battle ax. Cursing maniacally, he flails at them, and they bark laughter and swipe with their swords. Two go down under his chopping blade. He whirls to face their comrades on the other side of him, and a stab of agony pierces the back of his neck.

Reflexively, his left hand shoots up and feels the arrow jammed deep into his shoulder at the base of his neck. All his strength curdles into pain, and as he slides from his horse, he glimpses the barbarian who has shot him. The Welshman is raising his crossbow over his head triumphantly, his face ghastly with gloating.

* * *

When Branden Neufmarché sees Guy fall, he signals for retreat, and trumpets sound the wailful note that sends the Norman attackers flying back into the cleft of the Devil's Foot.

Roger Billancourt yells at them: "Fight, you cowards! Fight!"

The hoof-chewed meadow is swiftly empty but for the dead, the wounded, a few straggling defenders, and the boisterous Welsh, who crisscross the field swaggering their weapons and hooting jubilantly: William Morcar kneels over his dead son, and Guy Lanfranc lies inertly beside his champing destrier.

One lone horseman remains of the defenders, and Roger trains his fury on him. Throwing down his morning-star, he unsheathes his sword, kicks his heels to the flanks of his mount, and hurtles forward with a demented battle cry.

Thomas has removed his helmet, and when he hears the horrible war shout, he heaves a frightened look over his shoulder. There is time only to cast the helmet aside and draw his sword before Roger is upon him. Thomas's sword swings wildly, and Roger's blade cuts across his face.

Spraying blood, Thomas reels back stunned, then lurches forward and clasps the neck of his horse as pain jerks through him. Blood films over his eyes, stinging him blind, and he gasps and chokes on the hot fluid, thinking he is dying. But sight blinks back into his smarting eyes, air wheezes into his lungs, and the hurt of his face sears hotter. Fear sharpens his wits, and he realizes that his cheek has been flayed open—he can feel the flap of it against his neck—but he is alive; he is still astride his horse, and his sword is in his grip.

He spits blood, and looks up to see Roger pulling around, curving back toward him, sword shining. With an angry kick to his horse, he leaps forward, and the pain jags brighter with the jolting gallop, inspiring a hateful defiance in him. The swords clash as the horses charge past each other. Both riders stagger and pull their steeds around.

Roger is faster, and his experience anticipates Thomas's arcing blow, so that he pulls to the side just enough to miss the blow, yet near enough to slash upward. Thomas twists and takes the hit against his back; the metal plate clanks, and the force drives him forward. With expert precision, Roger slides his sword into the gap between the wounded man's arm and breastplate. Chain mail blunts the stabbing blow, yet its force jars enough to knock the sword from Thomas's hand.

Expecting Thomas to pull away, Roger presses closer to block his escape. But Thomas, ignorant of fighting strategy, sits upright, dizzy with hurt, cringing in anticipation of another blow. As Roger slides by, Thomas reacts with irate swiftness and grabs him by the back of his helmet. The warmaster, taken off guard, keels backward, and the two collapse to the ground.

Thomas lands on top. Roger stares up into the gashed open cheek, sees the skull's gritted teeth, and punches with his sword hilt. The blow throws Thomas to the side but splats blood into Roger's eyes. Momentarily blinded, he wipes at his eyes and swings aimlessly, lurching to his knees. Head reeling, Thomas seizes his fallen sword, pulls himself upright, and aims a double-handed blow that strikes the warmaster squarely across the top of his helmet.

Roger collapses, and the Welsh warriors, who have been watching, cheer. One rushes over to the fallen knight, and sticks a dagger under the helmet.

Surprised, Thomas finds himself standing. His hands welded to the sword hilt, he stares in mute awe at the carnage around him. The pain is gone, and his face feels like a mask of wood. His limbs, too, feel empty as wood, as though his soul has been torn from his body.

A Welsh warrior claps a firm hand to his metal shoulder and declares, "Your courage has won your life!"

With a dim cry, Thomas falls to his knees and begins to weep before the altar of death.

Erec Rhiwlas spurs his horse to the top of the hummock where Rachel sits on her red palfrey staring with regnant calm at the slaughter. "Your knights fought valiantly," he says.

She nods. A tear tracks down her cheek. All words are voided in her; only fearfulness matches her astonishment at what she has beheld.

Erec dips from his saddle and retrieves the fallen banner. He sets it upright in the earth. "Yet flies the Swan—"

"The Swan flies," she whispers as if to herself, and nods again as understanding comes clear. She heaves a sigh, staring at the palpable price of victory: squires, varlets, and the intact survivors are hurrying the wounded off the field to the physician's tar pot and potions. She looks wearily at Erec. "I thank you. All was lost before you came."

"I could not let you suffer defeat," he says, his look soft and caring. "Though I cannot have you as my wife, I should rather have you as a friend than Guy as a foe. Howel and the tribe agreed." He smiles disconsolately. "Actually my father is glad you put me aside—and this is his thanks to you."

Rachel puts a hand on Erec's. "Would that I could have pleased you. I truly like you, Erec. But the difficulties of my fate are not finished."

Erec squeezes her hand with understanding. "What will you do now? Your enemies are dead and vanquished—and you are the Servant of Birds."

"No." She lowers her head and closes her eyes. In the violet light, the Grail appears, lying on its side, drained. She faces Erec exhausted but clear-headed. "The Servant of Birds died on this field today. Her destiny completed itself here. Now I must find Rachel Tibbon where I left her eleven years ago. And this is no place for a Jew on her own. I will return to the land God has given my people."

"But who will rule in your stead?" Erec asks with some alarm. "No, you must stay."

Rachel turns away, sees Harold limping past, a hand to his head, his eyes staring dazedly. "Come, there are wounded I must attend."

"My lady—" Harold croaks, his gaze sharpening at the sight of her. "Guy is asking for you."

"He is alive?" Erec starts.

"He is dying," Harold answers. "But he is calling for his mother."

Guy lies on his back, his helmet off, his head propped on a torn saddle. The bolt that has pierced his shoulder still juts from under his neck, and his tunic is soaked with the blood that has leaked from the wound. The physician, who bows over him, shakes his head when Rachel approaches, and backs away.

Rachel kneels in the mud beside Guy, startled to see her strong and fervid enemy glassy-eyed and pale. A shiver of fear pricks her, and she checks to be certain that he has no weapon in his hands.

"Mother—" he gasps. The dark lids of his eyes narrow. "You have won."

A pang of sorrow tightens her chest, and she must remember that this is the same man who willed David's and Dwn's murders. "I did not want to fight you, Guy. You have defeated yourself."

"It is true," he whispers. Though he can see sunlight blazing on the hillsides, a shadow lies over everything, and the air is chill as autumn. He remembers feeling this way in Eire after being trousered in his own blood, when war gelded him. He is proud that he has been faithful to war since then, not scared into passivity by a loss that would have broken lesser men. He is glad that death has found him in his armor with his enemies dead around him. Only one mystery remains to be acknowledged—one unfinished sorrow to be completed—"Mother—" His eyes snap open and stare wildly at Rachel as acceptance gels in him. "You *are* my mother." He coughs, and blood speckles his face. "Only one woman could have defeated me. You are she. I accept it now."

He reaches out for her, and she takes his hand. It is heavy and cold. His eyes play over her face, still wild, seeing her for the first time. "The Grail—it is true. All along I have refused to see. It is true."

"Yes."

"There is a God."

"Oh yes, Guy—there is a God, and He will not judge you unkindly."

Guy's hand flinches, and his desperate stare locks on her eyes. "But I have sinned!"

She shakes her head. "Life is its own sin," she tells him tenderly. "By living true to yourself, you have redeemed the sin. Fear not. You have served God well."

His grasp relents. His last breath gargles blood as darkness widens in his fixed vision.

· · ·

The caskets of Guy Lanfranc, Roger Billancourt, and Thierry Morcar ride out of the castle on one carriage bound for Trinity Abbey. Behind follow William, Hellene, Hugues, and Madelon on horseback. Maître Pornic, dispatched by Neufmarché, leads the funeral procession on his white mule over the drawbridge and through the barbican. Slowly they proceed toward the village where the abbot will bless the sergeants and villeins who fell in battle.

Harold Almquist stands with Leora and their daughters at the gate to the inner ward, watching solemnly. The baroness has forbidden all but the immediate family to attend the rites of these fallen gentry who have been responsible for the deaths of so many of their own people. The guildsmen and their families stand before their shops, heads bowed in prayer.

In the garden of the inner ward, the baroness meets with her knights. Denis Hezetre and Gianni Rieti have been borne into the sunlight on litters, giddy with relief that they are still alive. Denis's breastbone has been cracked; the hurt feels to him like the physical anguish of a broken heart—Guy is dead, and his undoing is a paradox of relief and sorrow that their love failed at the limits of faith. Still, he is glad that the tyranny of anger is finished, the fierce raids and battles done with, the impossible love between them canceled by death and, with it, his vow of continence.

For Gianni, the arrow that struck him serves as a lasting sign that God will allow him in good faith to leave the priesthood: a fraction either way and it would have punctured his lung and drowned him in blood. "It is a miracle that none of the knights who serve the Lady of the Grail are mortally wounded," Gianni marvels.

Gerald nods from where he sits on a stone bench, arm in arm with Clare. "That miracle's name is Erec the Bold. He and his men should be here among us to celebrate this victory."

"We will have that privilege," Denis says, "after Erec buries his dead."

"Would that Erec had lived up to his name and been bold enough to come sooner," Ummu complains. "Then my master would not be as we find him."

"We have him alive," Clare admonishes the dwarf. "And sufficiently well to draft a letter this morning to the bishop at Talgarth surrendering his rights and duties as a canon."

"Forsaking one master for another," Ummu grumbles.

Clare frowns benignly at him and wags her finger. "That is not certain yet. Rumors sour the truth, Ummu. You should know better."

Ta-Toh, who has been squatting in Ummu's lap beside Gianni, sees Clare's extended hand and waving finger and leaps onto her arm. She shrieks with surprise as the monkey climbs onto her shoulder and busses her cheek, and she reaches up and pats its head. "Has Ta-Toh finally grown to like me?"

"Nonsense," Ummu says. "He merely wants to hear the rumor for himself."

"I am to be married," Gianni says.

"Madelon," Denis surmises and slaps Gianni's good arm. "Welcome to the family!"

"What of William?" Gerald enquires. "Will he consent?"

"Madelon has consented," Clare says. "That is all that matters in these modern times. Isn't that so, Mother?"

Rachel lifts herself from her reverie. From afar, she has been watching Thomas sitting under the rose trellis and wondering if this is what the baroness had wanted for her grandson. His angelic countenance is marred now along the left side of his face by a wound from the top of his ear to the corner of his mouth. Its purpled, swollen flesh is laced with black stitches, which distort his appearance so malevolently that he appears dangerous. *Perhaps,* she thinks, *his menacing look has appeared now that Ailena's wish has been fulfilled and he has abandoned the study of God for the lessons of men.*

"Forgive me," she says, finally rising from her chair beside the potted quince trees. "I am still unsettled from yesterday." She blesses her knights for their bravery and their sacrifices and announces that she would like to speak privately with her grandson.

Thomas stands, and the pain in his face throbs deeper. Since the physician cleaned and sewed his wound, he has been inflamed with the pulsing hurt of his cut flesh, and has tried to mute his suffering with wine. Yesterday he quaffed so much he passed out before dark.

Rachel links little fingers with him in a show of grandmotherly affection, and they stroll to the far end of the garden, where bushes of rhododendron and an arbor of morning glory seclude them. Once out of sight, she kisses him gently and closely examines his slashed face. "Oh, my Thomas—you suffer."

"Mine is only the suffering of flesh," he mutters, each word barbing him with fresh pain. He touches the pale line of her jaw, and an upwelling of love gives him the strength to say: "But yours, Rachel, your suffering is of the soul."

She shakes her head. "No more. The horror I witnessed as a child completed itself yesterday—and I did not look away. I saw it all, Thomas, all the suffering we can inflict. Christians killing Christians! These men did what was hard. How much easier for them to kill Jews and Saracens." She suppresses a chill. "The hatred of it—the terror of it—that wound has healed in me now."

He braces himself against the trellis and asks, "Are you numbed to it?"

"No. I feel it still, as the scar remembers. That is the wonder of the horror, that one can feel such despair without being destroyed. All these years, the horror of such violence has been inside me. I have been alone with it, yet afraid to face it. In that solitude, the dreamer is no more real than her dreams. If Ailena had not come, I would have lived out my life locked in my madness. But she gave me someone else to be. And then I was no longer alone. I was with her, and she was with me, always. I didn't have to face the horror alone anymore. Until yesterday. Her destiny—the destiny I had made my own—led me to the horror, and I saw it again, outside of myself."

Rachel takes Thomas's hand and searches beneath his wounded face for his understanding. "No, I am not numb to it, Thomas. But it is not inside me anymore. It is out there in a world of lunacy, violence, and greed. I see that clearly now. We are all alone in this shameful world, each of us so terribly alone. What I have learned from my suffering is that we *must* strive for communion. We must reach out of our solitude in compassion, or else we are doomed, like Guy, or as I was, to live in a desolation of solitude in a world of phantoms that feed on our memories and desires."

"You have won back your soul," Thomas says, but it comes out in an incoherent murmur. Instead, he squeezes her hand and touches his forehead to hers. *What will become of us?* he wonders. *How long can we hide our love before the others see?*

As though she can hear his thoughts, Rachel answers, "We must reach beyond our solitudes, Thomas—but with other people. It can be no other way."

Frost bites into Thomas's heart, and he pulls back to confront her with his baffled hurt.

"Keep that grief in your heart," she responds and puts a finger to his brow to relax his frown. "Show me only your happiness." She kisses his lips. "Remember I told you that you are my strength because you are wrong? You said I am not a Jew, that I am the baroness. That gave me the courage to go on. But now that destiny is fulfilled. The Grail that Ailena gave me has been drained. I am not the baroness anymore. I am a Jew again—and it is time for me to quest for my own Grail." She lets his hand go and steps back. "I will return to the Holy Land, Thomas."

"I will come too!" he groans.

"No. Please. Your Grail is here, Parsifal. Have you forgotten? The ruler and the land are one. When I leave, you must be the castle's baron, the earl of Epynt."

"No!" He seizes her hand. "I will come!"

She clasps her free hand over his. "Have you heard nothing of what I've said?"

"I love you!"

"Then you must let me go. My place is with my people."

"Together—" His eyes wince with the effort of speech. "We will go together."

"Thomas, listen to me." Her grip tightens in his clasp. "If you leave, you will abandon these people who need you. Your solitude belongs here, in your people and your land. If you forsake that, you forsake your true destiny."

"We make destiny."

"Do we?" Her head tilts skeptically. "I think not, Thomas. Have I chosen to be a woman, a Jew, an orphan? Have you chosen to be a man, a Christian, the heir to this kingdom? We can accept or forsake our destinies, but we cannot make them."

"For you, I will forsake mine."

She frowns. "Thomas, will you abandon these people who have fought and died for the vision of the Grail? If you leave, who will rule? Clare? Hugues backed by his grieved father William? Or will some other lord of the March fill your absence with his tyranny? No, Thomas. Too many lives need you. Don't you see? You are blessed. Your Grail is here—and that Cup will not pass from you."

Thomas hangs his head. What she says he hears with his heart and knows it is true. "Stay," he says without looking up.

"This is not my place. I belong . . . " She trails off, not really knowing in her heart where she belongs.

"But—" He grimaces, looks up and says through his teeth: "The Jews think you are wrong—here." He taps his brow. "Mad."

"Love proceeds from wrong to wrong," she answers with a soft smile. "I will earn a place for myself as Rachel Tibbon."

You have every answer, he thinks, looking sadly at her, imprinting each small detail of her face in his memory. *But you have won those answers through hardship—and that has made them unbreakable.* He knows he must bend before their truth, and he collects himself and kisses her fingers in his grasp. "When?"

"Now," she answers, "after we leave the garden. My maids have already packed for me."

Panic shakes him like a puppet. "So soon!"

"Please, don't be afraid," she comforts. "It is better this way. The longer we are together, the greater our suffering when we part." She removes the baroness's signet ring and presses it into his hand. "Ailena would want you to have this."

He feels Rachel's body heat in the ring, holds it tightly, and to keep from weeping asks, "How will you go?"

"I have arranged with Erec and his men for an escort to Newport. The jewels your grandmother bequeathed me will pay for my passage and for my place in the Levant." She takes his hand and adds, "I will leave now, Thomas, and you will stay and rule. And if you remember what I have told you—if you can learn from my suffering—you cannot fail. We must reach out of our solitude in communion, or else we are doomed." She squeezes his hand and looks deeper into his eyes. "Reach out to Denis. He will be your warmaster. Harold will steward the domain's monies. And William will lend you his wrath to fend off the greed of the other baronies, if only for the sake of the one son left him. With Erec as your ally, the Kingdom of the Grail will outlive you and your grandchildren." She smooths the crease between his eyes with her thumb and smiles softly at him. "Do not fear for me, Thomas. I have grown wise on the cruelties of this world. And I have learned to trust in the mercies of love."

The news that the Lady of the Grail is departing again for the Holy Land spreads through the village by midmorning. At noon there is a crowd from the castle and the village lining the toll bridge road. All mourning for the dead stops, and flowers are tossed with jubilant cheers.

Clare weeps uncontrollably and must be restrained by Gerald, Ummu, and her maids from accompanying her mother. And Ta-Toh scurries onto her shoulder and, to appease her, offers her a fat beetle he has caught.

The knights weep, too—quietly. Harold kneels to kiss the hem of her bliaut. Gianni blesses her in his last act as a priest. And Denis insists on standing as she passes, though his wound hammers like a spike through his chest. "We will keep our faith in Yeshua ben Miriam," he promises. *"Baruch ata adonai!"*

Thomas, as the heir and appointed ruler, rides beside her as her palfrey exits the castle with its gawking crowds and trots past the kneeling villeins. One of them leaps up and hands her a crucifix so expertly woven from Welsh osier the figure of Christ wears a bristly crown. When she holds it aloft, the people shout, "Valaise! Chalandon!"

At the forest's edge, Erec and a dozen of his warriors greet Rachel and Thomas. Rachel removes a velvet roll from her saddlebag and opens it on her lap, revealing two things: the Seljuk dagger with the ivory hilt, and the golden torque from Falan Askersund inscribed in Arabic.

"You two must rule Epynt together," she says to the Welshman and the Norman. "And these shall be the tokens of your union."

She hands the curved dagger to Erec. "I give you this dagger, forged by a far-off hand, by which to cut away foreign influence and remain pure.

"And to you, Thomas, I give the torque, to hold you in thrall to this foreign land. I trust you to serve it with honor and love."

She takes each of their hands. "You both know who I am in truth. So I can speak to you in truth. I am a Jew, Rachel Tibbon. I know what it is to live in foreign lands—and what it is to struggle against foreigners. You are both Christians. If you forget what love was won by your messiah's suffering, who will remember?"

During the ride through the woods, both Erec and Thomas try to convince Rachel to stay. But her heart is determined, and the more they talk, the more her preoccupation deepens. No further explanation is possible. She does not know what will become of her in the Holy Land. She simply knows she must go there. Only stillness is dreadful to her now. It is as though the land itself is finished with her in this place—the hazy mountains above the forest peer through their shawls of rain watching her pass. She knows she must find the landscape where she belongs, the granite-browed mountains from where the rains wander into the desert, rare and true as faith.

At the river Usk, a ferry receives her and the Welshmen, and she parts from Thomas. Tears silver his cheeks and glisten the raw length of his scar, but he lets her go. *Every river is the river of time,* he recalls her saying as the barge drifts into the current and she shrinks to a mote on the watery horizon. For a long time afterward, he stands on the shore listening to the fruity burble of the river, his tenacious animal patience fed by the nostalgia of an impossible love.

On the ferry, Rachel leans at the stern, apart from her escort, alone with herself at last, no longer a baroness, just a woman listening inward and hearing nothing but her own silence. *I came here haunted,* she thinks, staring at the dazzle of trees on the shore and the deer watching her from the tussocky grass. *But I leave whole. Now it is the world that is haunted. That is as it always was.*

Beneath her, the river moves like a slow, strong heart; reassured by the distances it promises to carry her, she tries to think through what has happened, to make some sense of all she has endured in this strange land.

Her grandfather's sacrifices and labors had saved her life but could not heal her. All his prayers in the temples, all the rabbi's prayers, all the blood of the sacrificed doves did not move the dark, mysterious heart of God enough to lift His madness from her brain. Until now, she had never understood why such sincerity had failed. As the river bears her away from the place of her transformation, she only comprehends this much: *God is not only good. God is All. God is both good and evil.*

So the rage and the predatory deceit of the baroness have worked a miracle, after all. Ailena's implacable fury and cunning exploited very effectively her people's faith in God—a faith simple and strong enough to believe that miracles happen, that mere bread could be a Savior's flesh—

That humble faith had joined with the ferocious rapacity of the baroness's wicked heart, and that merger of good and evil had created a role for her to play that had actually healed her.

An ironic laugh swells out of her silence and vanishes into the absence of her grandfather and her family—good people whose ancestors had sacrificed countless unmarked birds to their wrathful God begging for peace. But it was not the blood of doves that God had wanted from her. All along it had been the bread of hawks.